MY CONE AND ONLY

ALSO BY SUSANNAH NIX

Chemistry Lessons Series

Remedial Rocket Science

Intermediate Thermodynamics

Advanced Physical Chemistry

Applied Electromagnetism

Experimental Marine Biology

Elementary Romantic Calculus

King Family Series

My Cone and Only

Cream and Punishment

Starstruck Series

Fallen Star

Rising Star

Penny Reid's Smartypants Romance

Mad About Ewe

MY CONE AND ONLY

SUSANNAH NIX

Haver Street Press

MY CONE AND ONLY. Copyright © 2021 by Susannah Nix

FIRST EDITION: July 2021

ISBN: 978-1-950087-09-9

Haver Street Press | 448 W. 19th St., Suite 407 | Houston, TX 77008

Edited by Julia Ganis, www.juliaedits.com

Ebook & Print Cover Design by Cover Ever After

For everyone who's always wanted to have a book dedicated to them. Now you have.

1

ANDIE

I sensed it the moment Wyatt walked into the room. Like an electrical charge or a change in barometric pressure, I could always feel when he was near. I didn't even have to turn and look.

It was Saturday night, and I'd come out with some friends to go dancing at King's Palace, the local country-western dance hall here in Crowder, Texas. There was a bar to one side of the stage at the back where live music played every Friday and Saturday night, and an open space for dancing in front of the stage. People came from all over the state to two-step in the historic dance hall, but for us it was just one of our regular local hangouts.

"Wyatt just got here," my friend Kaylee said, because I wasn't the only one who noticed Wyatt King. Every head at our table snapped toward the door at the opposite end of the hall.

Except mine.

I didn't need to see Wyatt with my own eyes to know he'd be looking fine as hell, and I was in no hurry to inflict the sight on myself. Besides, I knew he'd find his way over to me eventually. He always came to pay his courtesies.

I also knew he'd be stopping to say hello to every pretty woman he passed on his way through the dance hall. Wherever he went, he had to work the room like some sort of celebrity. Wyatt was addicted to attention, and most of the people in this town were only too happy to give it to him. Like the three women I'd come out dancing with tonight.

We were standing around one of the high-top tables by the bar. The band didn't take the stage until eight, so a George Strait song was being piped over the sound system. The Palace was one of the oldest buildings in town, five thousand square feet of weathered wooden floor beneath a pitched beam ceiling, the rough-hewn walls decorated with vintage music posters and old tin signs. There were a couple of pool tables on the other side of the stage, and rows of long wooden tables up at the front where Wyatt was currently mingling his way through the room.

Kaylee sighed and rested her chin in her hand. "I'd let Wyatt King ruin my life."

I didn't bother to suppress my eye roll. The irony was, I more or less *had* let Wyatt King ruin my life, just not in the way Kaylee meant.

"I'd let any of the King brothers ruin my life." Megan smiled as her eyes tracked Wyatt's slow progress toward the bar. "Even the stuffy suit and tie one."

"Nate?" Kaylee's pierced nose wrinkled. "Isn't he like forty?"

"Thirty-eight," I corrected without thinking. Kaylee gave me a sidelong look and I shrugged. "Nate's eight years older than Wyatt, who's the same age as my brother. It's not like it's hard to remember."

"Whatever," Megan said. "I'd still hit that."

"Same," said Rain, who was standing across from me, twirling one of her box braids. Rain and I had been in the same high school graduating class, while Megan and Kaylee were a couple of years younger—young enough not to have known

Wyatt in high school as well as we had. "Although..." Rain's brown lips tilted. "I'd rather break me off a piece of Brady King."

"Who wouldn't?" Megan's gray eyes lit up as she nodded. "And he's even older than Nate, right?"

Brady was the oldest of Wyatt's siblings and the town's only homegrown celebrity. He'd left Crowder when he was twenty-one and wound up the lead guitarist for Ghost Ships, who'd been topping the alt rock charts for more than a decade. Brady also hadn't been back home or spoken to his family for almost twenty years, so there was pretty much zero chance of Rain getting her wish.

"Quite frankly, it's rude of all the King boys to be so good-looking," Rain said.

"Right?" Megan set her beer bottle down a little too hard, sending droplets of foam flying. "Like it's not enough that the Kings are made of money and own half the town. They all have to look like the sons of Aphrodite to boot." Megan had been a classics major but was currently waiting tables at the new craft brewery that had opened in town.

"Mmm hmmm," Rain hummed in agreement. "And don't forget all the free ice cream they can eat. Total bonus."

I smiled, probably the only one at the table who knew how much Wyatt King hated ice cream.

His family owned King's Creamery, the second-best-selling ice cream brand in the country, which had been founded by Wyatt's great-grandfather here in Crowder. Between the corporate headquarters, the ice cream plant, and the accompanying amusement park that brought hundreds of tourists into the town every day—not to mention all the other businesses that fell under the King corporate aegis—the whole town had basically been built on a foundation of ice cream and King money. Even the dance hall we were in right now, King's Palace, was owned by Wyatt's uncle Randy.

"I'd sure like to lick Wyatt King's ice cream cone." Megan waggled her eyebrows as the others snickered.

"I'd let him eat my ice cream sandwich any day," Kaylee added with a dramatic nod, and even I snorted in amusement.

Megan slapped a hand over her mouth, her eyes widening as her attention caught on something behind me. "Holy shit, I think Brianna Thorne just stuck her tongue in Wyatt's ear."

Everyone turned to look, including me this time. Sure enough, Brianna had her lips stuck to Wyatt's ear like some kind of suckermouth catfish. He was laughing as he sipped a beer someone must have given him, seemingly in no hurry to shake her off.

Of course he was enjoying himself. It was Saturday night, and if he was here, it was probably because he was looking to get laid. All the single women of a certain age would be vying to keep Wyatt King company for a night.

He looked just as good as I'd known he would, with his longish golden brown hair hanging down in his face and the sleeves of his midnight blue shirt rolled up to expose the tattoos on both his forearms. The sight of him with Brianna plastered to his side made my whole body clench.

I turned back to my beer, knocking back a mouthful to hide my grimace. It shouldn't still bother me after all these years. This was exactly who Wyatt had always been, after all.

And yet, here I was, totally freaking bothered.

"Shameless." Rain shook her head as she tipped back her own beer bottle.

Megan shrugged. "Whatever works, I guess."

"It won't work," Kaylee said, pursing her glossy pink lips. "He likes it better when they play harder to get."

"How would you know?" Megan's eyes went to slits.

Kaylee shrugged. "It's obvious if you watch him. Wyatt gets off on the chase."

"Don't all men?" Megan muttered.

"Is that your big plan to seduce him?" Rain asked in amusement. "Hang back and watch him obsessively until he's so captivated by your cool disregard that he drops to his knees at your feet?"

Kaylee smiled and stuck out her tongue. "Something like that."

As she shook her head, Rain's eyes fell on me and narrowed. "I feel like Andie's been awfully quiet on the subject of Wyatt King."

"That's because I don't have anything to say about him." I wiped my sweaty hands on my jeans and rested the toe of one boot on the floor, trying to look casual.

"Come on, Andie." Megan gave me a gentle shove. "You've spent more time with him than any of us. Tell me you've never lusted after that bod."

"Yeah," Kaylee said. "You have to admit he's tasty as hell."

"No me gusta." I wrinkled my nose and repeated the lie I'd been telling for years—the lie I could tell in my sleep at this point. "I don't think about him like that. He's my brother's best friend and was over at our house so much when we were growing up, he might as well be my brother too."

"You're crazy," Megan said, brushing her copper brown hair off her shoulder.

Not crazy, just realistic. I'd learned a long time ago not to think about Wyatt like that, because he'd never shown the slightest inclination to think about me that way. Wyatt treated me like another little sister, and he'd made it very clear over the years that I'd never be anything else to him. I was practically the only woman in town he'd never hit on, even jokingly. If that didn't send a clear message...

Kaylee stood up straighter. "Oh shit, he's heading over here." She smoothed her shiny blonde hair, arranging the long locks over her shoulders while Megan scrambled to give her lipstick a quick check in her phone's camera.

As I watched my friends primp, I wondered—not for the first time—if they'd invited me out tonight for my company or for my connection with Wyatt. Even Rain was swiping her fingers under her eyes to clear away any stray flecks of mascara.

I'd never understood why people bothered with makeup. If I was going to go out dancing and get all sweaty, I'd rather not have to worry about shit dripping down my face. How did that look any better than your actual, natural skin? Since my job at the state park involved a lot of tramping around outdoors in the woods, makeup seemed like a colossal waste of time and money.

The subtle scent of Wyatt's cologne greeted me a second before he did, and I felt my stomach tighten.

"Hey you." He gave my ponytail a tug before draping one of his tattooed arms around my shoulders.

"Hey you," I said back, smiling as I looked into his familiar blue eyes.

As an avid collector of trivia, I knew that blue eyes weren't actually blue. They had no pigment at all, and their blue appearance was merely a trick of physics—a result of scattering light similar to the effect that made the sky and water look blue. That meant Wyatt's eyes had no set color, and their appearance depended entirely on the available light wherever you happened to be looking at them. Tonight, for instance, against his midnight blue shirt, under the lights of the dance hall, his eyes were a brilliant azure, like the ocean on a painfully clear day.

He pulled me into a crushing hug, his arms encircling my rib cage and squeezing hard enough to drive the air from my lungs. I closed my eyes as I pressed my face into his chest, savoring the sensation while it lasted. Which was never long enough.

Letting go of me, he turned to greet the other women at the

table. "Evening, ladies." His azure eyes twinkled, and his mouth tilted in a sultry smirk as his gaze traveled over all three of my friends. "How's everybody doing?"

"Great!" Kaylee chirped, blinking rapidly. I couldn't tell if she was trying to bat her eyelashes or if it was more of a deer-in-the-headlights situation.

"Better now." Megan smiled brightly as she sidled closer to Wyatt, close enough that their shoulders brushed. "Where's my hug?"

"Right here." Wyatt grinned as he leaned in to embrace her. It wasn't as vigorous a hug as he'd given me. Instead, he stroked his hands up Megan's back in an almost sensual caress as he turned his head to nuzzle into her hair. I heard him whisper something I couldn't make out over the music playing over the speakers, and Megan let out a peal of laughter.

Wyatt went around the whole table like that, passing out hugs and flirtatious comments calculated to make every recipient feel special. That was his gift—his ability to turn his charm on you and make you believe for one magical moment that you were the most important girl in the room. Even when you'd just watched him turn the exact same charm on every other woman in the room before you.

They all ought to know better than to fall for it. Wyatt had the attention span of a gnat when it came to women. Actually, scratch that. Gnats were persistent as hell—unlike Wyatt. No woman had ever managed to hold on to him for longer than a few weeks, and most didn't even rate more than one night.

Yet here we all were, putty in his hands anyway.

As I watched Wyatt brush Kaylee's carefully placed hair off her shoulder, I scowled and downed another mouthful of beer to chase away the bitterness in my throat. My friends were so busy envying my friendship with Wyatt that they'd probably never considered I might envy *them*.

At least they had a fighting chance. I would never be anything to him but his best friend's tomboy little sister. Fun enough to hang out with, but forever beneath his romantic notice. I didn't get sensual back caresses, hair nuzzles, or sweet nothings whispered in my ear. I got the same hearty hugs Wyatt gave my mom, who'd practically helped raise him, and my aunt Birdie, who'd been his preschool teacher. I probably ought to be honored by that, but it was hard when I'd been yearning to feel Wyatt's lips on mine since I was old enough to understand what kissing was.

Wyatt continued to chat up our table as we waited for the band to take the stage. He had his arms around Rain and Kaylee, casually holding them both against his sides, but his eyes kept jumping to Megan with a heated sparkle I'd seen too often to count. If I was a betting woman, I'd lay odds on Megan taking home the prize tonight.

Once the band started playing, however, Wyatt peeled himself off his two sidekicks and came around the table to claim my hand. "Your first dance is mine," he declared and pulled me toward the quickly filling dance floor.

My body went into autopilot mode as I fit myself into Wyatt's arms, my right hand in his, and my left hand resting on his shoulder. We inserted ourselves into the growing whirl of dancers as we'd done so many times before, his thigh brushing against mine as he glided me around the floor with an offhand grace.

My parents used to bring me and my brother here almost every weekend of our adolescent years, and Wyatt was always around in those days. He and I had learned to two-step, waltz, and swing dance in each other's arms.

My stomach squeezed at the memory. Back then I'd still had dreams of turning Wyatt's head, and every dance had left me flying high with hope.

I knew better now. A dance was just a dance. A chance for Wyatt to show off his moves without committing himself in any particular direction. I had accepted that I'd never turn his head, because he was too busy trying to turn every other head in the room. The only reason he wanted me in his arms was to help him do it.

We moved in unison as he spun me, just starting to get warmed up. "I didn't expect to see you here tonight," I said once we were face-to-face again. "I was starting to think you'd found something better to do with your Saturday nights."

His gaze remained fixed somewhere over my shoulder as he grinned. "Never."

"It feels like I haven't seen much of you in a while." Almost three weeks, by my reckoning, which was unusual. If we weren't bumping into each other at our usual haunts, he was turning up at my aunt Birdie's house for a home-cooked dinner, or showing up at my place with my brother. Wyatt was always around, a permanent fixture in my life. It was odd that I hadn't laid eyes on him in weeks. "It's almost like something's been keeping you busy."

For a second, I swore his smile slipped a little. But before I could be sure, he spun me into the sweetheart position, backing me up against his chest with my arms crossed in front of me. He followed up with a series of complicated spins and a behind-the-back pass before he pulled me into a standard dancing frame again.

"I love dancing with you," he said as we settled back into a simpler two-step rhythm. "It's like you know what I'm gonna do before I do it."

I laughed, lightheaded from the spins, or maybe from the two beers I'd had before the dancing started. "That's because I do, usually. We've been doing this since I was twelve. I know all your moves."

"Are you saying I can't surprise you anymore?" His face pulled into an expression of mock offense.

I let my gaze meet his, knowing he'd take it as a dare. "Maybe."

Eyes glinting almost violet in the pink and yellow lights above the dance floor, he lifted his arm and spun me into the center of the floor for a series of complex western swing combos, starting off with a princess dip to test my trust in him. My pulse jumped when he leaned me back, his strong arms taking all my weight as I lifted my feet off the floor and extended one leg toward the ceiling. After that we did a move called a sausage roll, and my stomach tightened as he slid me between his muscular thighs, my face passing just inches below the crotch of his jeans.

Wyatt was the only one I trusted enough to do any of the advanced swing steps with. I loved the athletic thrill of executing the moves, but more than that, I loved the opportunity to feel Wyatt's hands all over me—not to mention all the tantalizing, exhilarating ways our bodies came into contact.

My heart pounded as he lifted me into his arms. I had a split second to enjoy the sensation of being cradled against his chest before he bounced me, and I scissored my legs around his neck. He bounced me again with my thigh resting on his shoulder as he flipped me over in his arms, cradling me to his chest once more before setting me down.

There was no other man I'd be willing to do this with. It wasn't just the intimacy of the positions, it was the act of placing myself entirely in his trust, relying on him to hold me up and keep me safe—like Wyatt always had.

He spun me out, and when I spun back to him he lifted my left leg, his right arm under my back as he swung me up and into the air. I draped my thigh over his biceps as we whirled, then he dipped me down low to the floor again, my head still spinning when those piercing blue eyes focused on me before he swung me upright again and my boots hit the floor.

I nearly stumbled, but Wyatt held me steady until I'd found my balance, knowing instinctively when to let me go. As soon as I'd recovered, he spun me again, but this time his right arm wrapped around my hips, pulling my arm behind my back. He stepped back and bent down, scooping me up and flipping me upside down and over his shoulder.

While I was flying through the air, my perception narrowed to the feel of Wyatt's hand sliding up my thigh and the way my breasts were pressed against his arm. Then my feet hit the floor with a thump, and his hand grabbed onto mine, his strong grip grounding me as I found my footing.

His eyes met mine again, flashing with mischief, and I saw his mouth twitch. I readied myself for something even more challenging, but instead he clasped both my hands and rotated me toward him. Lifting his left arm over my head, he curled it around my neck before lowering me back into a simple kissing dip.

Except it had never been a simple move for me. Not with Wyatt, with his face so close to mine, our lips nearly touching and his arm tucked around my neck in a dangerously intimate position. Every time we did it, I couldn't help wondering if he was actually going to kiss me—or if I'd finally crack and kiss him this time.

His eyes bored into mine as he lowered me toward the floor, his breath hot on my lips as his hair fell forward, curtaining his face and narrowing the world to just the two of us. I was surrounded by him. Enveloped by his heat and the scent of sweat mingling with his cologne. We were so close, I swore I could hear his heart beating in his chest.

I sucked in an unsteady breath as my eyes involuntarily

dropped to his mouth. His lips parted, and something clenched deep in the pit of my stomach.

Both his hands squeezed mine, and he lifted me back up into a standing position. Letting go of my left hand, he spun me away from him like a top. With our arms extended and his hand grasping mine, his gaze once again homed in on me.

Slowly, I became aware of people clapping and whistling around us. Not for the first time, we'd made quite a spectacle.

Wyatt spun me back into a basic dancing frame and led us into the flow of couples circling the floor again. "That was fun."

"Yeah." My heart was still trying to beat its way out of my chest. Why did I do this to myself? *Every. Damn. Time.*

His smile softened, shedding some of its usual cockiness. "You're my favorite partner, you know that, Andie?"

I looked away, my stomach twisting painfully. He didn't mean what I wanted him to mean. He only meant for dancing. That was as close as he'd ever allow me to get to him. The rest of him was reserved for all the other women who managed to catch his eye.

It reminded me what we'd been talking about before, and how eager he'd been to change the subject. My gaze returned to his face, narrowing. "*Has* something been keeping you busy?"

It was as close as I would ever come to asking straight out if he'd been seeing someone. We didn't talk about his love life much, which I was grateful for. It was bad enough that in a town this size I couldn't avoid noticing the parade through his bedroom. Hearing about it directly from his lips would have been too much.

"Me?" He gave an innocent shrug. "I'm always busy."

He was about the least busy person I knew. Instead of living off his family's money, he took handyman jobs to support himself—but only as much as he needed to pay for his weed, beer, and shithole apartment. On top of that, he played occasional gigs at a few bars around town with the band he'd formed with some of his high school buddies. I highly doubted that both of Wyatt's "jobs" put together came close to a forty-hour workweek.

Which meant he just didn't want to tell me what he'd been up to. Fair enough. If he'd been spending more time than usual with someone, I didn't actually want to hear about it. I already had a sick feeling in my stomach just imagining the possibility.

When the day finally came that someone managed to make Wyatt fall in love, my heart was going to break into pieces.

The song ended and Wyatt let go of me to clap for the band. "Thanks for the dance. I'll let you get back to your friends now." Then he started to walk away.

"Wyatt," I said, and he stopped, just like I knew he would, spinning on the smooth floor to face me again.

His eyebrows tilted, his forehead creasing slightly, and he lifted a hand to push his hair back from his face. I took a second to drink in the sight of him. The layer of stubble that covered his jaw. The languid cant to his hips. The way his jeans hugged his thighs.

When I'd looked my fill I said, "You're my favorite partner too."

For a second, his smile seemed to freeze in place, and he blinked at me the way Kaylee had blinked at him earlier. Then he seemed to come back to himself, and his lips twitched at the corners. Without another word, he sauntered away.

Straight to another woman, no doubt.

I didn't know what I'd expected him to say. It wasn't like he was going to suddenly profess his undying love for me because we danced well together.

If anything was ever going to happen between us, it would have happened long before now. Maybe there'd been a window once and I'd missed it. More likely, he'd never seen me as anything other than a surrogate sister.

I turned my back so I wouldn't have to see which direction Wyatt headed and which girl he went to after me. There was a simple enough solution to my problem, at least temporarily.

I needed to find my own company.

Someone who could make me forget Wyatt King, at least for one night.

2

WYATT

It took all my effort to walk away from Andie Lockhart.

I always had to force myself to walk away from her, and each time I did, it got a little harder. You'd think it would get easier after all these years. You'd think I'd have so much practice it would be a fucking piece of cake. Except it was the opposite of that. I was like that Sisyphus guy pushing the rock up the hill. Instead of me getting stronger, my rock kept getting heavier each time.

So I distracted myself the only way I knew how. I headed straight to the bar and ordered two shots of whiskey, downing them both in quick succession. Once I was good and drunk, I'd find myself a woman to take my mind off my best friend's little sister.

The bartender gave me a knowing smile when I ordered another shot with a beer chaser. Her name was Mariana and I'd taken her home once, a few years back. Or maybe she'd taken me home. My memories of that night were fuzzy.

I considered the possibility of a repeat engagement, but she probably wouldn't get off work until three. I wasn't in the mood to wait that long tonight.

My dilemma solved itself when Brianna Thorne sidled up to the bar next to me and ordered herself a beer. She'd made her interest pretty clear earlier when she'd stuck her tongue in my ear. It wouldn't take much effort to close the deal, which was exactly what I needed tonight.

I leaned over, letting my hand skim the small of Brianna's back, and told Mariana to put her beer on my tab. We took our drinks over to one of the nearby two-tops, and I pretended to listen as Brianna chattered about her cosmetology classes.

While she talked about barbering and beard trimming techniques, my gaze wandered away in search of Andie. I found her almost immediately, my eyes seeming to know exactly which direction to look, like she'd been implanted with a tracking device wired directly into my brain. She was talking to two dudes I didn't recognize. City boys down from Austin, by the look of them. Tourists checking out the local wildlife. Andie laughed, her dimpled cheeks pinking beneath her freckles, and one of them touched her arm.

I grabbed Brianna's hand. "Let's dance."

She wasn't as good a dancer as Andie, but then no one was. Brianna didn't have Andie's athletic physique or self-assurance. She was slimmer and more delicate, despite being taller, and too busy playing coy to match Andie's quickness.

Brianna wasn't as funny as Andie either. Or as smart. Andie was way too fucking smart for me. Smart enough to skip a year of elementary school when I'd almost been held back a year. After graduating close to the top of her class, she'd gone off to college in Huntsville and come back an ecosystems biologist. Then she'd earned herself a master's degree while working at the state park nearby, and now she taught a class at Bowman— the same local college I'd dropped out of.

Brianna was much more my speed than Andie. She kept up with me fine on the dance floor, but I didn't try any fancy moves with her. I moved on autopilot, my gaze locking onto Andie and her new city friends with every revolution around the floor.

She wasn't wrong that I hadn't been around much. I'd been avoiding her intentionally, and I hated that she'd noticed. But then she always noticed everything. That girl saw through me like no one else alive ever had. She saw me so well, I had to be careful around her, or she'd figure out my secret. And I definitely couldn't have that.

I couldn't let her know that I'd been half in love with her since I was seventeen years old.

Me and Andie's brother Josh, we'd been best friends since first grade, when we were assigned seats next to each other in homeroom. King and Lockhart—lucky for me, K and L came next to each other in the alphabet, or my life might have taken a whole different path.

Josh and I were inseparable growing up. I'd spent almost as much time at his parents' goat farm as I did at my own house. More, after my mom died. Josh's family accepted me as one of their own and made me feel more wanted than my own father ever had. Josh's little sister Andie had been tagging along with us for as long as I could remember, but Andie was cool, so I'd never minded. Even as a kid she was tough as nails and game for anything, with a nose for mischief almost as finely honed as mine. As far as I'd been concerned, she was just one of the guys.

Until I hit puberty and discovered girls—or more accurately, girls started to discover me. I guess I went a little girl crazy after that. What could I say? I loved the attention.

I loved the way their eyes followed me when I walked through a room. I loved the way they couldn't keep their hands off me. I loved how smooth their skin was and how sweet they smelled. I loved kissing them and discovering they tasted even sweeter. I loved their soft parts and their hard parts and all their parts in between.

I just really loved girls, okay?

I was so busy loving girls, I might have been a little slow to notice Andie was one too. She was two years younger, so the girls in my class had a head start on her. But *damn*, when she caught up, she caught up with a vengeance.

I don't even remember when I first started to notice. It must have happened gradually. But at some point, my awareness of her changed. The way I thought about her changed. The things I wanted to do with her changed.

Fortunately, as much of a dumbass as I was back then, I was smart enough to keep my hands off her. I knew instinctively it wouldn't be cool. You didn't hit on your best friend's baby sister.

Josh had always been hella protective of Andie. Because she'd skipped first grade, she was only a year behind us in school and younger than all her classmates. In fifth grade, Josh got in trouble for getting in a fight with some dickhead fourth-grade boy who'd pushed Andie down on the playground. In eighth grade I helped him fill Caroline Tingle's locker with dead cockroaches after she shit-talked Andie to a bunch of her seventh-grade friends. Then there was that time, senior year of high school, when Bradley Squires ditched Andie at the home-coming dance to stick his tongue down Sienna McElwee's throat. It was the closest I'd ever seen Andie come to crying, and the first time I'd ever seen murder in Josh's eyes. The two of us cornered Bradley before school the next Monday, and without even laying a finger on him, Josh scared him so bad he nearly pissed himself.

By that point, I'd been deputized as Josh's second when it came to looking out for Andie. That was what you were supposed to do for family. You stuck up for them and watched their backs. You made sure everyone else knew there'd be hell to pay if anyone came for your people. And the Lockharts were as much my people as anyone.

Nobody was allowed to fuck with Andie. *Nobody.*

I knew exactly how fast Josh's temper would turn on me if I ever defied that inviolable commandment. Every time I'd made an only sort of joking comment about asking Andie out—or so much as hinted that my interest might lie in that direction—Josh's eyes had gone hard and cold, reminding me I'd find no forgiveness if I ever crossed the line.

Which I never planned to do.

Josh and Andie were the two best friends I had. They meant more to me than some of my blood family did. If I ever acted on my baser urges with Andie, I'd lose Josh's friendship and probably Andie's too.

Josh didn't think I was good enough for her, and he was right. If I'd been her brother, I wouldn't have wanted a guy like me dating her either. I didn't trust myself not to hurt her, and if I ever hurt either of them, I'd never forgive myself.

That was why she remained my one unbroken rule. The one line I'd never dared to cross and never would.

But I couldn't stop torturing myself. I couldn't stay away from her. Couldn't stop thinking about her and craving her attention. Couldn't resist imagining how it'd feel to tangle my fingers in her sleek, brown ponytail and tug her head back for a kiss. Couldn't help the ache I felt every time I laid eyes on her.

Dancing was the closest I ever got to be to her. The one way I could enjoy touching her without ruining everything. I loved it, even though it nearly killed me every time. The feel of her hand in mine. The warmth of her body, so goddamn close. Her strong thighs and generous hips brushing against me. The smell of her skin when it started to heat up—which wasn't a smell I should have known by heart, but thanks to years of dancing together, I did.

But the thing I loved most about it was the way she followed my lead, not just unquestioningly, but so reflexively it was like we were one person instead of two. Like she was an extension of my body, and I was an extension of hers.

It wasn't anything I'd experienced with anyone else. And let me tell you how badly I wanted to find out if that connection between us extended to the bedroom.

But that wasn't something I'd ever get to do, so I danced with her instead.

Dancing was also the only time that girl ever did what I wanted without giving me shit or mouthing off. She was the kind of woman who could start an argument in an empty house. Not that I didn't love bantering with her, because I fucking did. I got off on it big time when she smarted off at me, which probably said something twisted as hell about my psychological profile. But I didn't care, as long as she kept looking at me with that fire in her chestnut eyes.

I was a glutton for punishment. I always had been. Always doing shit I knew would get me in trouble. Maybe sometimes doing it *because* it would get me in trouble.

Yeah, there was definitely more than one kink in that psych profile of mine.

So I couldn't just leave Andie alone altogether. I had to see her. I had to keep her in my life. I had to *dance* with her.

I had to push myself to the very edge of my self-control again and again.

And then I had to walk away, every time.

After one dance, I led Brianna back to the bar for more shots and more beers. I needed to be a lot drunker than I was. Fast.

By that point, Andie and the arm-toucher had moved to a table not too far away, and the arm-toucher's wingman had peeled off. I positioned myself so Andie was in my line of sight, just over Brianna's shoulder.

That whole glutton-for-punishment thing was a powerful compulsion.

Brianna was talking about hair again, and she reached up with both hands to comb her fingers through mine as she described how she'd cut it if I let her. My eyes flicked involuntarily to Andie, and I caught her watching as Brianna fondled my head. Our gazes locked for a second, and she wrinkled her nose at me before turning back to her tourist friend.

"How about another round of shots?" I said to Brianna. Untangling her fingers from my hair, I headed to the bar again.

"You might want to pace yourself," Mariana said, raising an eyebrow when I ordered another round of shots and chasers for me and Brianna, plus an extra shot for me to drink on the spot.

"This is me pacing myself," I replied with a wink, and she laughed, shaking her head as she set out three shot glasses.

By the time I got back to Brianna, Andie's city boy was leaning in close, his hand on her shoulder as he spoke into her ear. I shoved Brianna's shot at her as I downed mine, trying to quench the burn in the back of my throat.

The alcohol was finally starting to do its work. Some of the hard edges in my brain were getting softer. My limbs felt looser, and the spiked band around my chest—the one that always tightened when Andie was near—had eased up some.

My stomach only churned a little when I saw the guy with Andie press his mouth to her neck, right in the exact spot below her ear that I'd always wanted to taste.

"Did you hear me?" Brianna said, and my attention snapped back to the woman I was allegedly trying to seduce.

I reached up to twirl a lock of her hair around my finger. "Sorry, I got distracted for a second thinking about how pretty you are."

Brianna blushed and repeated her question about whether I'd ever seen some reality TV show she was obsessed with. While she was telling me about this dude on the show who apparently had sex with his Volkswagen Beetle, I caught a glimpse of Andie in my peripheral vision, pulling away from the guy she was with. She wasn't smiling anymore, and the stiffness of her posture set off all my protective instincts.

I stayed where I was, keeping my eye on the situation. Andie was more than capable of standing up for herself, as I was certain this fool was about to find out.

He made an appeasing gesture as he said something to her. Whatever he'd said *really* pissed her off, because her face flushed bright red and her eyes got that same cold, hard look she and her brother both got when they were about to lose their temper.

I clenched my hand around my beer bottle as I watched, not even pretending to listen to Brianna anymore.

Andie said something back to the dude, her jaw tight and her lips drawn in a scowl. He threw his head back and laughed as he replied, which only pissed her off even more.

"Call me kiddo one more time, shitbird." Her voice was loud enough to carry. Loud enough that Brianna turned her head to see what was going on.

Instead of backing the hell off like he should have, the asshole grabbed Andie's arm.

"Oh *fuck* no," I breathed as he yanked her toward him, trying to pull her into his arms. It was one thing to let Andie fight her own battles, and another to stand idly by when a man laid hands on her like that.

Blood roared in my ears as I closed the distance between us. By the time I got there, Andie had already stomped the shit out of the dude's instep and shoved him off her. I put myself between the two of them, holding up my hands in a warning gesture. "You're gonna want to back the fuck off, buddy."

The smug asshole actually had the balls to look annoyed. "I'm trying to have a conversation with the girl, if you don't mind. It doesn't concern you, *friend*."

Great. He was one of those dumbasses with something to prove, instead of someone with enough sense to cut his losses and walk away.

I stood my ground, my eyes boring into his. "Seems pretty clear she doesn't want to talk to you."

Andie grasped my arm, her fingernails biting into my biceps. "Forget about it, Wyatt." She tugged on me, trying to pull me back. "Just leave it."

"Yeah, Wyatt," the city boy sneered. "Why don't you just walk away?"

Shaking Andie off, I cocked back my fist and aimed for that smug fucking mouth of his.

City boy dodged, leaving me off-balance as my arm swung through empty air. He came back at me lightning fast and his fist connected with my face. All that drinking had slowed my reflexes, but on the bright side it also numbed me to the pain. I recovered quickly, aiming for his stomach this time and landing a solid enough blow to double him over. He shoved me while I was getting ready for my next punch, and I shoved him back, hard enough to send him stumbling a few steps.

He came at me again and tackled me to the floor. The breath rushed out of my lungs as he landed on top of me. He reared back and landed another punch on my face before he was dragged off me by some benevolent bystanders.

"Goddammit!" My uncle Randy's voice roared through the ringing in my head. "This is a family establishment."

Groaning, I rolled onto my side and squinted up out of my uninjured eye. Andie's face appeared in my somewhat blurry field of vision, looking like an angel.

"You're such a dumbass," she said, kneeling beside me, and I couldn't help laughing, even though it made my head ring even more. She touched her fingertips to my cheek, and I flinched at the sudden pulse of pain. "Are you okay?"

"I'm great," I mumbled, draping an arm across her legs as I pillowed my head on her lap. My head was hurting so fucking bad, all I wanted to do was curl myself around her until it stopped.

She laid her hand on my hair and I nuzzled against it, dimly aware of my uncle shouting at the guy who'd manhandled Andie, telling him he was banned for life and ordering someone to throw him off the premises.

A shadow loomed over me, and I blinked up at Uncle Randy's angry mustache. "Get up off my goddamn floor."

I tried to push myself upright, wavered, and felt Andie insert herself under my arm.

"Can you walk?" Randy asked. "Or do I need to have you dragged to my office?"

Andie pressed herself against me, her arm wrapping around my back to lend support, and I managed to get to my feet. "I can walk," I told Randy. With Andie's body up next to me like this, I could probably fly.

"Then get your ass in there and wait for me." Randy's eyes flicked to Andie and softened. "Are you all right?"

She nodded, and he gave her a nod back before tilting his head in the direction of his office. The crowd that had gathered began to disperse as Andie guided me toward the hallway next to the bar. When we passed Mariana, she handed Andie a plastic bag full of ice.

My head was throbbing even more by the time we made it into Randy's office. Andie dumped me on the long leather couch beneath a mounted set of steer horns, and I laid my head back, closing my eyes.

"Here." She sat down beside me, and I flinched when she held the ice to my face. I tried to push it away, but she captured my hand to stop me. "Don't be such a baby."

"But it hurts," I whined, knowing I was an asshole for enjoying this more than I should.

"Good," she shot back, but her hand kept hold of mine, her soft fingertips pressing into my palm.

Just that simple, quiet connection between us was enough to ease the ringing in my head and make my dick inconveniently jerk to life.

Until Randy strode into the room, slamming the door behind him, and my dick tried to crawl inside my body. I sat up straight, taking the ice bag from Andie, and prepared to get a dressing down from my favorite uncle.

Randy sat down behind his old wooden desk and crossed his arms, glaring at me. "What did I tell you about fighting?"

"Never start a fight I can't finish."

A muscle twitched in Randy's jaw. "What did I tell you about fighting *in my place of business*?"

I attempted to look contrite. "Never do it at all."

"Under any circumstances," Randy added for emphasis.

I jutted out my chin stubbornly. "Okay, but if you'd seen the way that prick grabbed Andie—"

"Then I would have alerted my security staff and let them throw him out like they're paid to. Which is what you should have done.

"Sorry," I mumbled.

"I'm sorry too," Andie said.

Randy shook his head. "You don't have a thing to apologize for, Andie. I'm sorry for the way you were treated in my establishment. That kid's picture has been added to the wall of shame, and I promise you he won't ever be allowed in the door again." Randy's gaze swung back to me with an expression like a raptor that had just sighted a mouse. "Exactly how drunk are you?"

"Not that drunk," I lied, trying to keep Mariana from getting in trouble.

"You know I can check your bar tab, right?"

"I was buying drinks for other people," I said with a shrug.

Randy sighed and gritted his teeth. "I guess we better find someone to drive you home."

"I can do it," Andie said.

I swiveled my head to look at her, feeling guilty and elated at the same time. Then even more guilty for being elated.

"You sure?" Randy asked her, arching an eyebrow.

"I don't mind." Andie turned to look at me with a smile that shot straight to the center of my shriveled husk of a heart. "I'll take Wyatt home."

3

ANDIE

Wyatt fell asleep five minutes after he climbed into my car. I had to shake him awake and pry him out of the passenger seat when we got to his apartment.

He seemed a lot drunker now that the adrenaline from the fight had worn off. I should probably count myself lucky he hadn't thrown up in my Jeep. He leaned against me heavily with one arm slung around my shoulders, stumbling slightly as we trudged up the walk to his duplex.

When we got to his door, I propped him against the wall and held out my hand. "Keys."

His eyes had fallen closed again as soon as we stopped walking, and he had a hand pressed to his face like it was hurting him. He plunged his other hand into the front pocket of his jeans and promptly dropped his keys on the ground. "Shit," he muttered, wincing, and tumbled forward to retrieve them.

"Whoa." I grabbed him, shoving my shoulder against his chest to force him upright again. "Let me get those. If you hit the floor, that's gonna be it. I'll never be able to move you, and you'll have to spend the night outside with the possums."

Wyatt had a fear of opossums—also known as didel-phiphobia—that dated back to an encounter on our farm when he was a kid. They were harmless—beneficial creatures that ate pests, helped clean up messes, and were nearly immune to rabies—but he'd never gotten over the sight of one hissing at him and showing off its impressive mouthful of teeth.

"I don't like possums," he mumbled as I held him in place with one hand while I stooped to snatch up the keys with the other. "They're like giant rats, but with even more teeth. They have more teeth than any other mammal, you know."

"I'm the one who told you that," I said as I flipped through his key ring looking for his apartment key.

"That's how come I know it."

I found the right key and jammed it in the lock. "They also have a bifurcated penis."

He frowned at me. "What's bifurcated mean?"

"It means it's forked." The lock was sticky and I had to wiggle it a few times before it opened. "It's got two heads."

Wyatt shuddered as I draped his arm around me and guided him inside. "How do the lady possums feel about that?"

"Since they've got two vaginas, I imagine they find it convenient."

Wyatt's shithole apartment was in real shithole top form. Beer bottles and weed paraphernalia littered the coffee table. Discarded clothes lay on the floor and most of the furniture. The kitchen was full of dirty dishes, and I couldn't even bear to imagine what the bathroom looked like.

Speaking of, Wyatt made it all of three steps inside before he groaned, muttered, "Oh, Jesus," and launched himself at the bathroom, slamming the door behind him.

I heard retching sounds and went to stand outside the door. "You okay?" I asked him during a pause. "You need help?"

"I'm fine. Don't come in here."

The retching started up again and I left him to it. It wouldn't be the first time one of us had held the other's hair back while we barfed, but I wasn't going to push my way in if he didn't want help.

While he was otherwise occupied, I surveyed his apartment with disgust and concern. Wyatt hadn't ever been much of a homemaker, but I'd never seen his place this bad before. I wondered again what he'd been doing with himself the last few weeks. Based on the state of his apartment, nothing good.

I loaded his dishwasher and started it running, then picked up the dirty clothes scattered around the living room and dumped them just inside the door of his bedroom. There were more discarded clothes lying all over the room, including a sock hanging from the swing-arm floor lamp, but what caught my eye was an open spiral notebook lying out on the unmade bed next to his guitar.

My curiosity got the better of me, and I ventured into the bedroom, which smelled like dirty laundry but also unmistakably of Wyatt, a scent that grew stronger as I got nearer to the bed where he slept most nights. The open pages of the notebook were covered with scribbled writing that on closer examination looked an awful lot like song lyrics and chord progressions.

Wyatt had always told me he wasn't interested in writing or playing original music. And yet this notebook contained evidence to the contrary. I riffled the pages with my thumb and saw almost every one was filled with verses. There had to be dozens of songs here.

As I drew my hand back, my eyes skimmed the lyrics on the page facing open.

> *Laughter in her eyes and a smile bright as the sun*
> *I can't be sure but I think she was the one*
> *Maybe she could have saved me if I'd let her*

She might have made me a better man
But our love story ended before it began

I stopped reading and backed away, a flush of shame burning my cheeks for intruding on Wyatt's privacy. I didn't know what I'd expected, but it certainly wasn't anything that romantic and emotional.

It was a song about a girl he'd really cared about, from the sound of it. I didn't have any idea who it could have been, but it wasn't any of my business. None of this was my business. He hadn't offered to share this piece of himself with me. In fact, he'd purposely kept it hidden from me. Lied to keep it a secret, even. That was how much he hadn't wanted me to know about it.

Still feeling ashamed for snooping, I hurried out of the bedroom and busied myself collecting all the empty cans and bottles from the living room. As I carried them to the recycling bin, I thought about how vehemently Wyatt had always insisted he was happy playing in a cover band and performing other people's music. How he'd brushed off any suggestion that he should try writing his own songs.

It hurt that he hadn't trusted me with the truth. I'd always thought I knew Wyatt inside and out, but he'd kept his song-writing aspirations to himself. Just like he'd kept this girl who'd inspired the song a secret. Maybe I didn't know him so well after all.

By the time Wyatt emerged from the bathroom, I'd nearly finished straightening up. "You didn't have to clean up my shit," he mumbled, blinking at the apartment around him.

"Someone does." It came out more snappish than I intended, and I softened my tone. "You didn't give yourself another concussion, did you?" I walked over to him and took his chin in my hand, tilting his head down so I could look into his eyes.

He smelled like toothpaste and soap, which meant he'd been

lucid enough to clean himself up, at least. His eyes were clear as aquamarines as they reluctantly met mine. Both pupils appeared normal, but he was going to have one hell of a shiner.

"I'm fine." He pulled out of my grasp and sank down in the middle of the couch. Leaning his head back, he pressed the heels of his hands against his eyes.

I felt bad for him, although only half of his predicament was my fault. The drinking he'd done to himself. I filled a glass of water in the kitchen and got two ibuprofen out of my purse.

"Here." I nudged his knee with my leg. "Take these."

He accepted them and popped the pills in his mouth. "Thanks."

I went back into the kitchen and opened his freezer. It was empty except for a glacier of ice buildup and a few frost-covered pints of King's ice cream. Wyatt couldn't stand ice cream, but he'd told me he kept a supply for when he invited girls to his place, because they always expected him to have it because of his name. I supposed free ice cream was a powerful aphrodisiac.

I walked back to the couch with a spoon and a pint of Thar She Blows! bubblegum ice cream. "Here, this is for your face."

Wyatt had closed his eyes again, but he opened his good one to squint at me, and his lip curled when he saw the ice cream I was holding out. "What the hell?"

"You don't have any ice cubes or frozen peas, so this is what you get." I sat next to him and set the ice cream on his knee.

He took it reluctantly and pressed it to his cheekbone with a wince before his head swiveled toward me. "You don't have to stay or anything. I'll be okay."

"I don't mind staying." I leaned back on his ugly thrift store couch, thumping the spoon against my leg. "If you did give your-self a concussion and you die of a brain bleed in your sleep, I'll never forgive myself."

His lips twitched. "Are you saying you'd actually miss me if I died?"

I knew he was kidding, but it wasn't funny to me. Not when he gave me so many reasons to worry about him. "You know I'd be devastated, right?"

The smile slid off his face and his hand fumbled for mine, tangling our fingers together. "I'm not going anywhere. You don't have to worry about me."

I did worry about him, pretty much constantly. I worried that he drank too much and smoked too much weed. I worried about his penchant for making reckless decisions and getting into fights. I worried that he never seemed to take anything seriously. I worried that his carefree slacker attitude was just an act to hide the fact that he was aimless and miserable. And I hated that he slept around so much, not just because I was jealous—although there was definitely that—but because it felt like he was intentionally denying himself a chance to be loved.

I didn't say any of that though. He wouldn't listen, and anyway he was probably too drunk right now to remember. Instead, I squeezed his hand and hoped that would be enough.

"I'm sorry I puked," he said.

"It's okay," I told him. "Just let me know if you're gonna do it again so I can get out of the way."

He smiled, his eyes soft and slightly unfocused. "Remember that time you decided to drink all those B-52s a few years ago?"

"Not very well, no." That had been one of my more epic bad decisions. Some friends—including Wyatt—had taken me out to celebrate my twenty-third birthday, and I'd gotten a little carried away with the shots.

"I drove you home and had to help you into the bathroom." His thumb stroked over my wrist absently.

"I'm still sorry about that." And still plenty embarrassed. Part of the reason I'd downed so many shots that night was to work up enough liquid courage to finally make my move with Wyatt. But I'd misjudged my tolerance and shot myself in the foot by getting sloppy drunk, thereby killing any chance of a romantic end to the evening.

"Your head kept falling forward, and I had to hold it up for you so it didn't fall into the toilet."

I grimaced in embarrassment. "Lovely."

He leaned forward to set the ice cream on the laminate coffee table. When he leaned back, his head lolled toward me again. "You got vomit on your shirt, and I had to change you into a clean one before I put you to bed."

"I never knew you did that." *Jesus.* No wonder he'd never found me sexy. I didn't know what was worse, the fact that Wyatt had undressed me under such revolting circumstances, or that I couldn't even remember it. I suspected he'd withheld that part of the story to save me further embarrassment. He probably wouldn't have told me now if he hadn't been so drunk himself.

He looked down at our clasped hands, and his eyes narrowed as they focused on my wrist. Frowning, he pulled my arm into his lap and ran his callused fingers over the red mark that was turning into a bruise. "That fucking asshole. I wish to god I hadn't been drunk so I could've made him eat all his teeth."

Wyatt was a tactile, affectionate person, and he'd touched me casually a million times before. But something about the way his fingers were stroking my arm felt too intimate. *Dangerous.* Too close to the way I wanted him to touch me, which wasn't casual at all.

I pulled my hand away, despite the voice in my head whispering *more*, and tried to make my voice sound stern. "I wish you hadn't been so drunk *and* I wish you hadn't gotten into a fight at all."

"Don't be pissed at me, Andie." His lower lip jutted out in a play for sympathy. "My head hurts."

Fond irritation prickled in my chest. Impulsively, I reached up and brushed his hair back from his face. His eyelids fell closed, and he purred like a contented cat.

"I can take care of myself," I told him. "I don't need you barrel-rolling in and throwing fists." I kept stroking his hair, because he seemed to like it. Maybe it was wrong, considering he was drunk and his defenses were down, but I was weak and it seemed harmless enough. I remembered Brianna running her hands through his hair earlier, and how the sight had made me seethe with jealousy. And now here I was, the one in Wyatt's apartment with my fingers in his hair.

Too bad he probably wouldn't remember it tomorrow.

"I know you can take care of yourself." He opened one eye and peered at me.

My hand stilled with my fingers threaded in his hair.

"But you shouldn't have to." His eye shut again, and he pressed his head into my hand the way the goats on our farm did when they were begging for affection.

I stroked his hair some more, brushing back the silky soft strands and running my fingernails lightly over his scalp.

"Besides," he mumbled with a satisfied smile, "Josh made me promise."

My hand stilled again as I frowned. "Promise what?"

"That I'd always look out for you when he wasn't around."

I retracted my hand from Wyatt's hair. "When?" Leave it to my overprotective brother to enlist his best friend as a part-time bodyguard.

Wyatt yawned, stretching his arms over his head. "Tenth grade."

That would have been right around the time I started dating, which tracked. I could totally see Josh bullying his horndog best friend into some stupid oath to protect my honor.

"I think you can let it go now," I said. "I'm not a kid anymore."

Wyatt's eyes met mine, heavy-lidded and somber. "A promise is a promise."

The way he was looking at me unnerved me. Like he saw a lot more than I'd ever given him credit for—things I'd never found the courage to say. The possibility made me uncomfortable, so I leaned forward and grabbed the ice cream off the table, ripping the lid off and spooning a bite into my mouth. It was soft from sitting out and so sweet it made my teeth ache.

Wyatt laid a hand on his stomach, looking a little nauseous as he watched me. "How can you stand to eat that garbage?"

"Because it's delicious," I said around a mouthful of ice cream.

"It's horrible. That's the worst flavor we make."

"I like the sour bits." I shrugged and shoveled another spoonful into my mouth before leaning forward and setting it on the table.

He shook his head, smiling faintly. "I remember when you were little, you used to lick the powder off Sour Patch Kids and leave the gummies."

I cocked an eyebrow at him. "I remember you used to eat the gummies after I'd licked them."

"The gummies are the good part."

"Did you know if you took all the gummy bears manufactured just in one year and lined them up head to toe, they'd encircle the earth four times?"

"How do you remember so much random shit?" He yawned and laid down, resting his head in my lap.

A tingling ache erupted in the pit of my stomach, and I forgot how to move for a second.

"Is this okay?" Wyatt asked sleepily.

I managed a nod. "Sure."

His eyes fell closed. "Remember that night we watched the meteor shower?"

"Yes." I think I'd been about fifteen. Wyatt had slept over at our house, and he and Josh had set an alarm for three in the morning, when it was supposed to be the best time for viewing the meteors. They came and got me out of bed, and we all piled into the back of my dad's pickup with a bunch of blankets to keep warm while we watched the night sky.

He stretched out his legs, letting his socked feet hang over the armrest. When he spoke again, his words came out softly slurred. "Did any of your wishes come true?"

We'd taken turns making wishes on the shooting stars. Jokey ones mostly, trying to make each other laugh. But I'd also made a few silent wishes that night. Ones I hadn't wanted to say out loud in front of my brother. Or Wyatt.

"Well, I never got to meet Taylor Lautner," I said. "But technically I guess there's still time for that."

Wyatt's face had grown slack, his lips parting, and I could hear a faint rush of air in his throat with every rise and fall of his chest. The night we'd watched the meteor shower, we'd all fallen asleep in the bed of my dad's pickup. Me in the middle with Josh and Wyatt on either side of me. It'd been cold, and my brother had been hogging the blankets, so I'd burrowed against Wyatt in my sleep for warmth. I remembered waking up with my face in his chest and lying there counting his heartbeats until my parents came out to get us. It was one of my most treasured memories from those years.

"Wyatt?" I said quietly, wondering if he'd dropped off to sleep.

"Hmmm?" he murmured.

"Did any of your wishes come true?"

A single furrow appeared between his brows. "Not the one that mattered."

I was tempted to ask him what it was. I desperately wanted to know what actually mattered to Wyatt King. What heart's desire still eluded him after all these years. But it felt like an invasion of privacy, and I'd done enough of that already by looking at that notebook. Alcohol had loosened his lips, and if I pressed he might tell me something he'd rather keep secret. I was here to take care of him, not take advantage of him. Just like he'd do for me if the roles were reversed—like he *had* done for me.

The top few buttons of his midnight blue shirt were undone, exposing the top of his chest and the small gold St. Christopher medallion he never took off. His mother had given it to him a few months before she died. I'd never seen him without it in all the years since.

I laid my hand over it, the tiny gold disk warm from his body heat. The furrow in his brow smoothed away, and he shifted to lay his hand over mine, trapping it above his heart.

I stayed with him, counting his heartbeats, until I was sure he'd fallen asleep.

WYATT

When my phone started vibrating under my ass, I tried to roll over and fell off the couch.

Fuck.

I lay on the floor, cursing my poor decision-making skills as my ass continued to vibrate. My head felt like it had been run over by a tractor, my throat burned like I'd gargled acid, and my mouth was as parched as the Rio Grande Valley on the tail end of a hundred-year drought.

A montage of scenes from the night before played behind my puffy, closed eyelids. Dancing with Andie. Drinking. That Austin dickhead laying hands on Andie. Getting my ass whupped by the Austin dickhead and then chewed out by my uncle. Andie driving me home and taking care of me.

I paused at that point in the replay, trying to piece together exactly what we'd talked about. I remembered telling her how I'd changed her shirt and put her to bed the night she had too many birthday B-52s, which—*fuck*—I'd never meant to tell her about that. I also remembered something about sour gummies, and something about the night we'd fallen asleep watching the meteor shower.

Jesus, what else had I confessed to her? I had a tendency to run my mouth when I was drunk—which was a pretty good reason not to get drunk, but that whole poor decision-making thing always managed to bite me in the ass.

I hoped to hell I hadn't told her how on the night we watched the meteor shower, when she'd fallen asleep next to me, I'd realized that of all the girls I knew, she was the only one I really liked. And how I'd stupidly wished that we'd get married one day, so she'd fall asleep next to me like that every night. Or how I'd woken up a few hours later with her face burrowed against my chest and a raging case of morning wood I wasn't sure I'd managed to hide.

I'd better not have fucking told her any of that, or I'd need to start making arrangements to leave town under the cloak of darkness and change my name so I never had to face her again.

At least my ass had finally stopped vibrating. Experimentally, I tried opening my eyes. Both seemed to work, although the light shining in the windows ramped my headache up a few notches.

My ass started vibrating again. Goddammit.

What if it's Andie?

I didn't know if I was ready to talk to her yet, but curiosity drove me to dig my phone out of the back pocket of the jeans I'd fallen asleep in last night.

Fortunately, it was only my older brother, Tanner, one of the members of my family I least minded talking to. My dad had offspring by three different wives, so our family tree was a messy hodgepodge of half and step relations. All told, I had five half-brothers, two half-sisters, one adopted brother, and Tanner—the only littermate I shared both a mother and father with.

"Tell me you're out of bed," Tanner said when I answered the phone.

"I'm out of bed." Technically, that was true. Lying on the floor in front of my couch counted as being out of bed.

"Good. I'll be there in five minutes."

I frowned. "Why?"

"Very funny."

"Ha ha yeah. But seriously..."

"The thing with the photographer? The family photo at the shop followed by brunch at Dad's? Don't tell me you forgot."

I pushed myself upright, wincing as my head throbbed in response to the change of altitude. "Forgetting would require knowing about it in the first place."

"We talked about it last week."

"Did we?" I rubbed my forehead, unable to dredge up any recollection of such a conversation. But then I had a habit of tuning out when Tanner started talking about family business. Especially if it involved me being expected to do something.

"You said I'd better come pick you up or you'd forget. There was also an email."

Groaning like an eighty-year-old man, I pushed myself to my feet. The room tilted a little—or maybe I did—but I managed to stay upright. "I don't check my email."

"And a group text."

"I have the family group text muted."

"Jesus Christ, Wyatt."

Moving carefully, I shuffled toward the bathroom. "I get enough texts without being bombarded by Nate's boring company updates and Heather's attempts to guilt us into volunteering for one of her whackadoo charities."

"Well, we're having a family photo taken this morning for some big PR thing Josie's putting together, and I'll be at your place in exactly three minutes to pick you up, so you better make yourself presentable."

"Cool." I stared at my black-and-blue face in the bathroom mirror. "Awesome."

———

"OH, GREAT," Tanner said when I let him into my apartment and he got a look at my face. "This is fucking perfect."

True to his word, he'd showed up exactly three minutes later. I'd had just enough time to piss and brush my teeth before he'd knocked on my door.

"I'm fine, thanks for asking." I left him standing in the doorway and went into the kitchen, hoping I still had a Monster Energy in the back of my fridge.

Shutting the front door behind him, he trailed after me. "What happened?"

Tragically, the only thing in my fridge was some leftover coleslaw of indeterminate age and a mostly empty bottle of orange juice. I grabbed the juice and elbowed the fridge shut. "Some tourist at the Palace made a grab for Andie Lockhart."

Tanner whistled. "Did you kick his ass?"

I chugged the last of the OJ and wiped my mouth, grimacing at the way it interacted with the taste of toothpaste. "Not as much as he deserved, unfortunately."

"You got your ass kicked, didn't you?"

"Little bit, yeah." Looking around the kitchen, I realized Andie had cleaned up my place. The counters were clear, the dishwasher had been run, and the recycling bin was full of empties. *Shit.* I'd let the place get into a real state recently, and I hadn't intended for her to see it like that. She'd probably give me an earful about it later—on top of the earful I had coming about the drinking and the fighting.

"I guess I don't need to ask if you were drunk." Tanner's lip curled. "You smell like a distillery."

People said the two of us looked a lot alike, only he was the respectable, clean-cut version of me. We were like a before-and-after makeover. Which one of us was the "before" and which was the "after" depended on whether you liked good boys or bad boys.

"I need to take a shower." I shouldered past him and headed for the bathroom. "Gimme five minutes."

"That's all you get," Tanner shouted as I slammed the bathroom door on him. "I'm walking out that door in exactly five minutes, with or without you. I can't afford to be late. Dad's already pissed at me."

"Why's Dad pissed at you?" I called through the door while I waited for the water in the shower to get hot.

"Work stuff. You don't want to hear about it."

He was right about that. Tanner had foolishly let himself get suckered into working for the family business. Unlike me, he'd always followed the straight and narrow path, trying to please everyone and do what was expected of him.

You know what it had gotten him? A shitty mid-management sales job at the creamery and both Dad and our asswipe older brother Nate hounding him constantly about work. Tanner was living proof that my personal strategy of giving all that company bullshit the finger was the superior one.

I jumped in the shower and stood there for a minute letting the hot water soak away some of the aches in my bones. By the time I'd washed and shampooed, I felt a lot more human. I dried myself off, applied a liberal coating of deodorant, and ran my hands through my hair before yanking open the bathroom door.

Tanner threw his arm across his eyes as I strode through the apartment on my way to the bedroom. "Aww, dammit, Wyatt! Cover yourself up. I didn't need to see that before breakfast."

I ignored him as I dug around for a pair of clean underpants.

"After we get all this shit over with, can you drop me off at the Palace? I left my truck there."

"How'd you get home?"

"Andie drove me."

My last decent clean shirt was the one I'd slept in last night, so I rummaged around until I found an old T-shirt that had been shoved into the back of one of my dresser drawers.

"Did she now?" Even from the next room, I could hear the implication in Tanner's tone.

"Don't start," I warned as I dragged on a pair of jeans.

Tanner was the only other person who knew about my long-standing crush on Andie, and he'd been pushing me to declare myself to her for years. He'd always been one of those romantic saps who wore his heart on his sleeve, and he had this idea that if I confessed my undying love to Andie, everything would somehow magically work itself out and we'd live happily ever after. Like I said, Tanner was a sap.

"I'm ready," I said, coming out of the bedroom and shoving my feet into a pair of tennis shoes.

Tanner stared at me. "That's not what you're wearing."

He was wearing a dress shirt and blazer. I reckoned I might be underdressed.

"It's all I've got that's clean." I grabbed my keys on my way out the door, twirling them around my index finger as I waited for Tanner to catch up. "Let's roll."

———

"THE SHOP" was the site of the original creamery and retail ice cream shop our great-grandfather had opened on Main Street in 1921. Even though we had the big plant now, with a cafeteria and ice cream tasting room that was open to the public, we kept the shop in town open—with a nice subsidy from the taxpayers of

Crowder—to help attract tourists into the downtown commercial district. The original ice cream making facilities had been restored and converted into an ice cream museum attached to the shop, which had an old-timey soda fountain vibe.

I hadn't actually been inside the place in years. I hated ice cream, and I especially hated my family's ice cream. Growing up, we'd had ice cream for dessert every single night. Which probably sounded great to most people and made me seem like an entitled little shit for complaining about it, but it had pretty much ruined ice cream for me. There had never been any other kind of sweets allowed in the house. No cookies, no candy, not a single goddamn Ding Dong. It was ice cream or nothing. On our birthdays we got an ice cream cake—which was also what we had at Thanksgiving and Christmas instead of eating pie like regular people.

My headache, which had begun to recede, roared to life again as soon as I walked in the back door of the shop and heard the clamor of my family's voices. My dad was at one end of the room looking ticked off, growling at everyone in earshot, and generally sucking all the oxygen out of the room like he always did.

I hung back as Tanner slunk in and tried to put himself in Dad's eyeline so his presence would be noted without actually attracting too much of the old man's attention. Surveying the assemblage, I spotted my brother Ryan's red hair in the crowd and headed in that direction.

Before I'd made it halfway there, I was attacked by a three-foot-high tornado that nearly racked me as it attached itself to my leg. Peeling it off, I tossed it up into the air before peering into the giggling face of my niece, Isabella.

"Again," she commanded, and I obliged her because I was a sucker for the little munchkin.

"Don't get her too keyed up," her father Manny said, looking tired as he trailed after her. "We're trying to keep her from melting down until we get this picture taken."

Isabella bounced in my arms. "More! More!" She shared Manny's jet-black hair and light brown complexion, but her curls and her huge round eyes were one hundred percent her mother's.

"Can't right now." I switched her to my left side and balanced her on my hip, trying not to wrinkle her pretty yellow dress. "My arms are too tired because you're getting so big."

Manny's mouth twisted into a sardonic grin as his gaze settled on my chest. "Nice shirt."

Manny's father, Manuel Sr., had been my dad's best friend and right-hand man at the creamery. When Manny was ten years old, both his parents had died in a boating accident and my parents had adopted him. Although Manny had kept the Reyes family name, he was as much a part of the King family as any of my other siblings.

Isabella's tiny fingers touched my sore cheekbone. "Why's your face look like that?"

"It's bruised 'cause I ran into something."

"Boo-boo." She smacked a wet kiss on my cheek. "Make it all better."

"Thanks, it feels better already." I returned her kiss with a loud sucking sound that made her giggle and try to squirm away.

"Whose fist was it?" Manny asked.

"No one important." While Isabella played with my hair, I glanced across the room at Manny's wife, who was sitting with her bare feet propped up on a chair. "When's Adriana's due date again?"

"Eight more weeks." Manny rubbed his forehead. "I might need your help painting the nursery. I'm starting to get a little underwater." Manny had followed in his father's footsteps and gone to work for my dad, who'd recently put him in charge of all our plant operations.

"No problem," I told him. "Just let me know when."

"What the fuck are you wearing?" my asswipe older brother Nate demanded, stalking up to us.

I covered one of Isabella's ears with my hand and pressed her other ear against my chest. "Dang, Nate, even I know not to curse around a three-year-old."

"Fuck!" Isabella shouted, squirming free. "Fuck! Fuck! Fuck!"

Nate winced and offered Manny a muttered, "Sorry."

Pressing his lips together to stifle a laugh, Manny relieved me of his daughter and left me to face Nate alone.

The two of them worked together at the creamery, but Manny was a thousand percent less of a prick than Nate, who I tried to avoid as much as possible. Which mostly wasn't too hard, because he felt the exact same way about me.

I looked down at my *Adios Bitchachos* T-shirt proudly and tugged on the hem. "Like it? I got it in South Padre a few years back, but you can probably find yourself one on the internet."

"Did you not read the part of the email that said 'church dress'?" Nate was wearing a suit, but that wasn't a surprise because he always wore suits nowadays—ever since he'd been promoted to executive vice president of sales.

"You don't think I should wear this to church?" I asked him, flashing a shit-eating grin.

Nate finally noticed my shiner and his face got even redder. "Jesus Christ, Wyatt!" The muscles in his jaw tightened as he ground his teeth together. At this point the man's molars had to be smooth as glass from all the angry tooth grinding he did. "You just had to go and mess up your face right before we're supposed to do this photo."

"Yes, Nate, that's what I did. I intentionally threw my face in front of someone's fist with no other thought than to ruin your precious little picture. Because you and your priorities are always at the forefront of my mind."

While Nate continued to bitch at me, my gaze flicked over his shoulder and I saw Dad eyeing us, his attention caught by the sound of Nate's raised voice. As soon as Dad noticed me looking at him, he turned his back.

Typical.

"What happened to your face?" My sister Josie appeared beside Nate and grabbed my chin. I winced as she jerked my head to the side, examining my injuries. "My god, Wyatt."

"And just look at what he's wearing," Nate growled. "Can we do the picture without him?"

That would have been fine and dandy by me, but Josie shook her head. "Of course not."

Nate and Josie were the progeny of my dad's marriage to Trish Buchanan, his first wife. They both looked just like their mother: same hazel eyes, same shade of straight brown hair, same long noses and angular jaws. They were like two peas in a pod, except Nate was the arrogant, hostile pea, and Josie was the calm, decisive pea who got shit done while the other pea was having a rage stroke.

"I'll take care of this," she said as she appraised me coolly. Nate started to open his mouth—to bitch some more probably —but Josie quelled him with a look. Despite being two years his junior, she was the only person besides Dad and Manny who Nate ever seemed to defer to.

Taking me by the arm, she signaled to some well-dressed, uptight-looking dude as she dragged me off to an empty café table in a quiet corner of the shop. When the guy reached us, she ordered him to trade shirts with me.

"Seriously?" I said while the other dude, who I assumed worked for her, started undoing his buttons.

Josie nodded. "Seriously." Apparently being executive vice

president of marketing meant she was hot shit enough to make her employees surrender the shirts off their backs on command.

I pulled my T-shirt over my head and regretfully handed it over to the poor guy. After I'd shrugged into my new dress shirt, Josie helped me with the buttons and straightened my collar before stepping back to appraise the effect.

"Tuck it in," she told me before addressing the dude now stuck wearing my *Adios Bitchachos* shirt. "Can you go start getting everyone into position? Tell the photographer we'll be there in a minute." When he'd scuttled off to do her bidding, she turned back to me and pointed to a chair. "Sit."

I did as I was told, keeping my mouth shut as she took a makeup bag out of her purse and began applying a creamy, beige concoction around my bruised eye.

"Does it hurt?" she asked, frowning in concentration.

"Not too bad."

"You always have to be a pain in the ass, don't you?" She didn't actually sound all that angry. Josie never lost her temper, but when she was pissed at you she could get real cold and scary.

I tried to charm a smile out of her. "Yeah, but you love me anyway."

All I got was a twitch at the corner of her mouth, but she didn't try to deny it.

Josie was okay, although we'd never been especially close. All my dad's kids with Trish had lived with their mother when I was growing up, and as a teenager Josie hadn't had much interest in me. She'd gone off to college when I was twelve and mostly stayed away after that, working in Dallas for a while and then New York, before moving back to Crowder a few years ago to take over marketing and advertising for the creamery.

"That'll have to do." She tilted my head to examine her handiwork. "The rest can be fixed with retouching." Her gaze shifted to my hair with a frown, and she reached into her purse for some styling wax. I let her comb my shaggy hair back with her fingers, knowing it'd just fall right back into my face again. "Forget it," she said, finally giving up on me. "Let's just get this done."

I followed her over to the others, who were standing in front of the soda fountain counter with the original antique King's Creamery sign behind them. Dad was in the middle, of course, with his bushy gray beard and his balding hair pulled back in the hippie ponytail he'd stubbornly worn all his life. Other than me, he was the least formally dressed, in a sport jacket and T-shirt bearing the company logo over jeans and his signature cowboy boots.

Josie pointed me to an empty spot in the back row next to Tanner before taking her place beside Dad. We all tried to smile and pretend we were happy to be there while the photographer snapped a million photos.

Until finally Isabella lost her shit and started wailing in protest at being forced to stay still for so long. We were all right there with her by that point, and there was a collective sigh of relief when we were finally released.

"Thanks, everyone!" Josie shouted above the din of voices as everyone started milling around. "I know it was a pain, but it'll look great in our new public relations campaign."

"Time for brunch!" trilled my stepmother, Heather. "We'll see y'all at the house in fifteen. Don't be late."

After I got my shirt back from Josie's flunky, I rode over to the family homestead with Tanner, who seemed like he was in an even worse mood than when he'd picked me up earlier.

"Everything okay?" I asked, eyeballing him. "You're gripping that steering wheel like you want to rip it out of the dash."

He loosened his fingers, shaking his hands out one at a time. "I got an earful from Nate is all."

"Work stuff?"

Tanner worked for Nate, managing one of the regional sales divisions. Dad liked to start his kids at the bottom and make them work their way up from merchandiser—stocking product in grocery store freezers—before letting them advance through the company ranks. It was how both Nate and Manny had started, and Tanner was supposed to be following the same career path. Only he hadn't taken to it the way they had. Ever since he'd moved into sales management he'd been seriously fucking miserable.

He nodded as he rolled his shoulders. "I've gotta go to Oklahoma next week."

"How long?"

His frown got deeper. "I don't know. Hopefully only a few days. As long as it takes to figure out why our numbers are down."

"You should just quit," I told him even though I knew he'd never do it. Quitting was more my style than Tanner's. I'd quit that merchandiser job after three days. I'd quit college after a semester. I'd quit on every woman I'd ever tried to be in a relationship with, and then I'd quit trying to be in relationships altogether.

Tanner was Mr. Dependable. The guy who was in for the long haul. The one who kept showing up, no matter how hard it got.

"And do what?" he shot back with a snort.

"I don't know. How about literally anything else? Maybe try writing that book you've been talking about forever."

When we were kids, Tanner's nose had always been stuck in a book. He'd go off on his own and do nothing but read for hours. He'd even majored in English in college, which seemed like a waste now that he was stuck working in sales.

He snorted. "Sure, like it's that easy."

"I didn't say it was easy, I said you should do it."

"I don't want to talk about this." He shot me a sidelong look. "No offense, but you're the last person I'm interested in taking career advice from."

"Fine," I said. "Keep martyring yourself, then."

"Once I fix this mess, things will get better." His knuckles were turning white on the steering wheel again. "At least it's only Nate's wrath I've got to deal with for now. Dad's been too distracted by this new real estate thing to breathe down my neck like usual."

"What real estate thing?" I was pretty far out of the loop these days when it came to Dad's business dealings.

Tanner shrugged. "One of his buddies from the Chamber of Commerce talked him into partnering on some real estate startup. They're buying up properties around town on the cheap so they can squeeze a bunch of condos onto each lot and flip them all for a tidy profit."

"Great." I shook my head as I stared out the window at the bluebonnets that sprang up all over the place every spring and would be gone again in just a few weeks. "Just what this town needs. A bunch of overpriced, shoddily built eyesores."

My dad had cultivated a public image as this benevolent, earth-loving peacenik to align with the company's socially conscious branding. But behind closed doors he'd always been all about the money. It was his barracuda-like business instincts and not his affinity for progressive causes that had grown the family business from a dinky regional ice cream company to one of the top brands in the country.

The only thing Dad loved more than making money was using his money to make everyone else do whatever he wanted.

"Anyway," Tanner said as he turned onto the tree-lined drive leading to the house we'd grown up in, "I'm just going to spend the next two hours trying to avoid Nate and Dad."

The King family villa was a mammoth ranch-style house Dad had custom built in the late eighties after the business had started to take off. It squatted on forty acres of land on the outskirts of town that featured a pond, fishing pier, horse barn, greenhouse, gazebo, and swimming pool.

Tanner parked behind our brother Ryan's big silver truck on the circular drive out front, and we both trudged inside. Neither of us were overflowing with good memories from those days, so it wasn't our favorite place to spend time.

Our stepmother Heather had a mimosa bar set up in the kitchen, but I bypassed it and headed straight to the fridge for a beer. Winking at my little sister, Riley, who was helping her mom set up the buffet, I wandered out to the patio and collapsed into a lounge chair next to Ryan. We were having a rare bout of perfect spring weather, but I wasn't in any mood to appreciate it.

"You look like shit," he told me, arching a ginger eyebrow. Ryan was nine years older than me, the same age as Manny, and my half-brother by my mother—the stepson my dad had inherited when he married my mom.

I held up my middle finger as I chugged half my beer, and Ryan laughed.

"I sure as hell hope the other guy looks worse than you."

"Probably not," I admitted. "I was kind of drunk."

"I know I taught you better than that."

Ryan was a burly, mountain of a dude with a thick beard and our mom's red hair. He'd been the one who first taught me how to make a fist, how to throw a punch, and—most importantly— how to evade one. I hadn't exactly done him proud last night.

"Too bad you weren't at the Palace last night," I said. "It would have been nice to watch you wipe the floor with him."

"I'm too old to go around getting into fights. Besides, I was working last night. A drunk flipped his car on 71 and caused a three-car pileup." Ryan was a fireman, but he spent more time using the jaws of life to cut people out of crumpled cars on the highway than he did putting out fires.

"Did everybody make it?"

"Everybody but the drunk." His eyebrow arched again as he directed a pointed look at the beer in my hand.

I might be an irresponsible, hard-partying slacker, but I didn't fuck around with drunk driving. "I didn't drive here," I told him. "And I didn't drive last night either."

"Good." Ryan lifted a meaty paw to give my head a rough swipe. "I really don't ever want to have to scrape you off the asphalt."

"Chow's on!" Heather called out, ringing the loud-ass fucking dinner bell Dad had mounted next to the patio doors. It went with the nouveau-riche dude ranch aesthetic of the house, and it made my head throb.

I pushed myself to my feet and followed Ryan to the buffet, where I piled my plate high with migas, bacon, sausage, and tortillas. Heather's housekeeper was a damn good cook, and I managed to snag a seat at the opposite end of the table from Nate and Dad, which made the meal itself pretty enjoyable. I stuffed my face while Cody, my youngest brother, told me about the college courses he was taking this semester at Bowman, the local university where he was a freshman. Riley was directly across from me, doing that bored, sullen teenager thing, and I amused myself by making dumb faces until I got a laugh out of her.

Sometimes hanging out with my family wasn't half bad. I should have known it couldn't last though. After the meal, when we were all milling around again, Dad came and found me.

"Let's you and me talk," he said, jerking his head toward his office.

A sense of impending doom obliterated all the pleasant feelings I'd managed to build over the last hour. I followed Dad into his office, and he nodded at me to shut the door.

"Nice shiner," he said, not bothering to sit down. Apparently this wasn't going to be a long conversation. "The shirt's a cute touch too."

"Laundry day." I offered a casual shrug to show I wasn't intimidated by his disapproval. "You know how it is."

As usual, Dad wasn't amused by my quip. His expression hardened as he advanced a step toward me. "I know you don't give a shit about anyone but yourself, but a lot of people worked their asses off to make today happen. Especially your sister Josie. Showing up today looking like a frat boy on the wrong side of a spring break bender is the equivalent of dropping a big, steaming turd in the middle of her desk. I think you owe her an apology, don't you?"

Well, fuck. Now he'd succeeded in making me feel guilty.

Without waiting for me to answer, he barreled on with the lecture. "I'm sure it seems like pointless posturing to you, but this family is the face of this company. The image we present to the world is part of what people see when they're looking at all the ice cream in their grocery store freezer case and trying to decide which one to buy. This isn't just for my own glorification. People's livelihoods depend on this company's success—on *our* hard work and good decision-making skills. Not just the people out there—" He jerked his thumb in the direction of the door. "—your *family*. But the people who work for this company and the people who live in this town and rely on the tourism and money we bring into it."

He was really working up a head of steam now. This part of the speech was a familiar refrain. The duty I owed to the family and to the company. The number of people who needed us to continue being filthy fucking rich so we'd keep injecting our money into this town. I could practically recite it in my sleep.

"But since you don't seem to feel any sense of pride or responsibility, maybe I need to remind you of the financial stake you have in this company like the rest of us. This is your inheritance the rest of us are breaking our backs to preserve. The guarantee of your future security."

"You think I care about your money?" I shot back. "I support myself. I haven't asked you for a damn thing since the day I moved out." I'd been nineteen, and he'd given me an ultimatum. Either I stayed in college, or I'd have to move out of his house and support myself. I'd chosen the latter, and I'd been earning my own keep ever since.

"Sure, you're doing just fine right now taking odd jobs to pay your rent. But what happens the first time you get yourself into trouble? When you have an accident or get sick and can't work? Or when you get a little older and realize life's passing you by and you've got nothing to show for it? When you finally wake up and realize how pathetic it is to live your life like a disaffected stoner who's too cool to give a crap?"

"I'll do what I've always done. I'll take care of myself."

"You? You've never known a moment of real hardship in your entire pampered life. At the first sign of difficulty, I promise you'll come crawling to me for help."

I snorted at the thought that I'd ever been pampered. When I was little, maybe, and my mom was still alive, but definitely not since. Sure, I'd grown up in the lap of luxury, but I would have traded this big fancy house and everything in it for a living mother or a father who'd actually wanted to spend time with me.

There was no use arguing the point with him, however. His opinion of me wasn't ever liable to change, and I'd long since given up trying.

When I didn't say anything else he shook his head like I was the one who'd let him down. "You know, Wyatt, I keep waiting for you to show me a sign that you give a single god damn about anything at all. But you continue to disappoint me."

"Is that all you wanted to say? Are we done?"

"I guess we are."

I hightailed it out of there as fast as my feet would take me and spotted Tanner lurking in the foyer.

"You ready to get out of here?" he asked, pushing off from the wall.

I stalked past him on my way to the door. "Fuck, yes."

5

ANDIE

"I have *never* seen a vagina do that before!"

My friend Mia was giving me a play-by-play of the goat birth she'd witnessed last night—and I wished she would stop because it was interfering with my ability to enjoy my burrito.

I couldn't blame her for being excited. Growing up on our family's goat farm, I'd seen plenty of kiddings myself. Gross as the freshening process was, there was something about the sight of a newborn kid that could melt even the hardest of hearts.

Mia was new to farm life, having recently moved in with my brother on the farm he'd taken over from our parents, so this spring was her very first kidding season. "And then Josh just reached his arm in, all the way to his elbow and—"

I held up my hand. "I'm trying to eat here so I'm going to stop you right there." Next she'd be talking about the placenta, and I'd dealt with enough goat placentas to know it wasn't a good topic for mealtime conversation.

We'd come to Groovy's Tacos, one of our favorite lunch places, during Mia's break between classes today. Despite the name, no one came to Groovy's for the tacos. If you wanted those you went to Rita's Taqueria down the street. The giant burritos were the star attraction at Groovy's, made to order with your choice of ingredients, and wrapped in a fluffy flour tortilla still warm from the griddle.

"Oh, right." Mia looked down at her own burrito, which she'd barely touched because she'd been so caught up in her goat birthing story. "Sorry."

We both taught at Bowman, the local university—Mia as a full-time soon-to-be assistant professor in the math department, and me as a part-time lecturer in the college of forestry and agriculture. I only taught one class—on forest insects and diseases—as a side gig to go with my full-time job as a resources specialist with the state parks and wildlife department. As part of the deal, my students got to do their field work at Gettinger State Park, the thousand-acre forest just north of town, and I got to use the university's lab space to do my research for parks and wildlife.

"But I'm glad you're excited about it," I added, so she wouldn't think I was annoyed. "It is pretty cool seeing a new kid come into the world."

After a bit of a bumpy start, Mia and my brother seemed really happy, which was a huge load off my mind. I'd been rooting for them to get together almost since the moment I'd first met her, after she'd moved to Crowder last fall.

My brother had been through some stuff back in college that had left him sort of closed off afterward. After our parents had retired to Maine and Josh had taken over the farm, he'd withdrawn from the world a little too much for my liking. For the last several years, he'd mostly kept to himself except for a small, trusted circle of people that included me, our aunt Birdie, and his best friend Wyatt.

Shit, now I was thinking about Wyatt, which I'd been trying not to do.

I hadn't heard a peep from him since I'd slipped out of his apartment Sunday in the early morning hours after staying up half the night watching him sleep. He hadn't really needed me to stay, but I'd enjoyed being close to him too much to leave. Wyatt didn't often let his guard down that much, and it was hard to walk away when he was like that.

I could never fully walk away from Wyatt, even when he was being an ass. The two of us were tethered by years of friendship, not to mention our loyalty to my brother. Watching Josh retreat his way into a case of agoraphobia had drawn me and Wyatt even closer together the last few years as we'd confided our worries to each other and teamed up to help my brother as best we could.

But now Josh was doing a lot better—seeing a therapist and willingly venturing out into public again—thanks in large part to Mia. He didn't need us as much, which meant Wyatt and I didn't need to see each other as much to commiserate and strategize ways to save Josh from himself. Maybe it would be better if we just kept on that way. Maybe with a little more distance between us, I could finally move on and let go. Stop hoping for something that was never going to happen.

Yeah, right.

I realized Mia had started talking again and snapped myself back to the present, trying to look like I'd been listening.

"Josh let me name her. She's the first generation of kids who'll be named after female scientists. So I chose a mathematician, of course."

"Well?" I asked, when she didn't elaborate. "What's the name?" My brother had a long-standing tradition of naming all his does after novelists, but he'd run through so many names by now that he'd needed to pick a new theme.

"Emmy, after Emmy Noether, the most creative abstract algebraist of modern times. I've got a whole list ready to go for this year's kidding season. Ada Lovelace, Sofya Kovalevskaya, Katherine Johnson, Hypatia—"

"Cool," I said before she could finish reciting the entire list for me. I had something else on my mind that I wanted Mia's take on before we had to get back to campus. "Speaking of my brother, Wyatt told me something the other night that kind of pissed me off."

Mia's attention perked up. "You saw Wyatt the other night?"

She always got real interested whenever the subject of Wyatt came up. Specifically, the subject of me and Wyatt. She'd asked a lot of pointed questions about the two of us early on in our friendship, and although I'd vehemently denied any romantic inclinations in that direction, I had a feeling she might have seen through my lies.

"Just at King's Palace," I said casually. "I went there on Saturday with some friends."

"So what pissed you off?" She frowned. "Something he told you about Josh?"

I nodded as I reached for my drink. "I guess Wyatt was pretty drunk, and when some dude got handsy with me, he took it upon himself to defend my honor."

Mia's frown deepened. "Are you okay?"

I waved my hand. "Yeah, it was nothing." The mark on my arm had already disappeared, leaving only a lingering sense of embarrassment for having such bad taste in men.

"Wyatt's going to get himself hurt one of these days."

"He kind of got his ass handed to him this time." I winced at the memory of him lying on the floor, curled up in pain. For a second there on Saturday I'd been scared he was going to land himself in the emergency room.

"What happened?" she asked, sitting up straighter. "Is *he* okay?"

"He's fine, just a little bruised—both his face and his ego. But when I told him I didn't need him starting fights on my behalf, he said that Josh had made him swear some stupid oath that he'd always look out for me. Like some kind of dumbass knight protector. This was way back when they were in tenth grade, mind you, and apparently Wyatt took it so seriously that he still thinks he has to play bodyguard around me. Can you believe that shit?"

"Well...actually..." Mia's brow furrowed as she chewed on her straw.

"What?"

"I asked Josh once if he thought Wyatt might have a crush on you—"

"He definitely does not. Believe me." I tried not to sound bitter, because I wasn't supposed to care that Wyatt didn't see me like that.

"Says you. I'm not so convinced." Mia gave me a defiant look before she went on. "Anyway, Josh said there was no way, because—get this—Wyatt knows Josh would kill him if he ever caught him 'sniffing around' you." She made air quotes with her fingers so I'd know that choice phrasing had come straight from my brother's mouth.

"Jesus," I muttered, getting even more pissed.

"The thing is, he wasn't kidding around. It sort of freaked me out how serious he sounded about it—not that I think he'd literally murder Wyatt, obviously. But I have a feeling it might end their friendship."

"That's ridiculous." I couldn't believe my brother was acting like such a Neanderthal. No, actually, on second thought, I could. At least where I was concerned, he'd always been a bit of a caveman. "Since when does he get a say in who I date?"

Mia pointed at me, nodding vigorously. "That's exactly what I asked him!"

"He can fuck off into the sun with that patriarchal bullshit." I crumpled the aluminum foil my burrito had been wrapped in, wishing it was my brother's face. I'd been planning to make a dragon out of it, but now I was way too mad.

It was a tradition at Groovy's—every time you finished one of their gargantuan burritos, you made a sculpture out of the leftover foil. Every available surface around the restaurant showed off the foil shapes people had created—animals, flowers, monsters, vehicles, and anything else you could imagine. Everywhere you looked, they decorated the windowsills, counters, tops of the cabinets, and even dangled from the ceiling.

"I agree," Mia said. "But he told me it wasn't about that. He said..." She paused, like she was trying to remember Josh's exact words. "He said he trusted Wyatt with his life, which meant he also trusted him never to hurt anyone he loved. So if Wyatt ever treated you the way he treats the other women he messes around with...all bets were off."

"What if I want to be treated like that?"

Mia's eyes widened. "Do you?"

"Of course not. But that's my decision, not anyone else's. Definitely not my stupid brother's."

"You'll have to take that up with Josh," Mia said with a shrug.

I damn well would.

But there was a more important question on my mind now.

Should I take it up with Wyatt?

———

AFTER LUNCH, I dropped Mia back on campus and drove up to the state park. Spring ended early in Central Texas, giving way to the crushing heat and humidity of summer by May. But we had a few weeks of temperate weather left yet, and the fields along the highway were covered with swaths of bluebonnets and scarlet paintbrush.

I spent the rest of the afternoon deep in the park's northeastern woodland area collecting red oak samples to test for *Bretziella fagacearum*—the fungus responsible for oak wilt—but as I trudged through the forest undergrowth, I kept thinking about what Mia had told me.

Had Josh threatened Wyatt to keep him away from me? Was that part of the promise my brother had extracted from him? I kept coming back to that somber, knowing look in Wyatt's eyes when he'd told me about the promise he'd made Josh.

A promise is a promise.

He'd looked almost...regretful when he'd said it. Like he knew I wanted more—like maybe he'd always known.

But more than that, he'd looked like he might have wanted it too.

It could be that was just my imagination doing some wishful thinking. But what if it wasn't?

I was so distracted thinking about Wyatt that I let a low-hanging tree branch catch me across the face and gave myself a nice, angry scratch. Muttering a curse at my carelessness, I forced my mind off my nonexistent love life and back onto my work.

That kind of inattention could be hazardous in the field. Traversing uneven terrain came with a high potential for accidents, even on seemingly flat ground. The layers of decomposing litterfall that made up the forest floor could conceal all manner of dangers. It was too easy to miss a hidden obstacle until you'd stepped in a hole and broken your ankle or tripped on a hidden rock or vine.

There was wildlife you needed to be wary of out here as well, like bobcats and javelina and the odd cougar. Even deer could be dangerous when cornered or provoked, especially during rutting season or when they were protecting fawns. It was always best to give Bambi a wide berth.

Additionally, the park was home to its share of venomous species, such as copperheads, coral snakes, cottonmouths, rattlers, black widows, brown recluses, asp caterpillars, velvet ants, and my favorite—*Scolopendra heros*, the giant Texas redheaded centipedes that could get up to eight inches long. The biggest one I'd ever spotted was five inches, but I'd love to find a full-size one of those babies.

I wasn't afraid of the park's wildlife—but I did have a healthy respect for it and the dangers it could pose to a person. It was my job to help protect the native species and their habitats. Blundering around carelessly out here could put both myself and the wildlife at risk.

All of which meant I needed to keep my mind on the task at hand and off Wyatt King. The task at hand being oak wilt—one of the most destructive tree diseases in the United States. It had been killing off our Central Texas oaks in epidemic numbers, and the only way to control it was early identification and removal of diseased trees to prevent fungal spread. It was easy to spot in the more common live oaks by the obvious veinal necrosis on the leaves. But other types of oaks often didn't exhibit distinct symptoms, and required laboratory culture to confirm the presence of *B. fagacearum* fungus.

I spent the rest of the afternoon collecting my samples without further incident. It was only after I'd dropped them off at my office and headed home for the day that I allowed thoughts of Wyatt to preoccupy me once more.

Was Josh the reason why Wyatt never flirted with me? Never touched me in a way that could be mistaken for anything other than platonic, brotherly affection? Never directed any of his innuendos at me, or made the sort of suggestive, leading remarks he enjoyed making with everyone else—even my brother's girlfriend?

When Mia had first moved here, before Wyatt knew Josh liked her, he'd unleashed his full charm attack on her. But as soon as he realized my brother was interested in her, Wyatt had backed way the fuck off, fast. After that, Wyatt had treated her a lot like he treated me. Friendly, but from a reserved distance, and without any suggestion behind it.

Until Josh and Mia got together. Once they were safely coupled up and disgustingly, madly in love with each other, Wyatt went back to flirting with her in that harmless, playful way he flirted with women he wanted to flatter without actually trying to lure them into his bed. The way he flirted with older or happily married women or with his lesbian friends Alexis and Xuan. Women he considered "safe" because they posed no temptation and were likewise in no danger of taking him seriously.

The kind of flirting he never did with me. Maybe because he knew I wasn't "safe." There was a chance I might take him seriously. But did I pose a temptation to him? That was what I didn't know. Did he have impulses where I was concerned that he was afraid of acting on?

Or was he just afraid of giving my brother that impression? Maybe Wyatt was being extra cautious to avoid invoking my brother's wrath over nothing. He could also be sending me a message—trying to keep me from getting the wrong idea. Showing me there was a line in the sand, and I was on the other side of it.

But would I be on the other side of that line if it wasn't for my brother? Or did the line reflect Wyatt's real feelings about me? I had no idea.

Ugh. I was going to make myself nuts obsessing over this. But I couldn't stop. Not until I knew the truth. And the only way I'd ever know for sure what Wyatt was thinking was to confront him about it directly. Even then, I wasn't certain he'd tell me the truth.

I couldn't decide whether I should try to raise the subject with Wyatt or let it lie. On the one hand, ignoring it wasn't likely to bring me peace of mind anytime soon. But on the other, I wasn't sure I had the nerve to ask Wyatt outright how he felt about me—or fess up to how I felt about him.

Most people who knew me would probably be shocked to hear that. I'd earned a reputation as a feisty, tough-talking, assertive-as-hell chick who didn't shy away from anything.

Except when it came to my heart.

Admitting I cared about someone was my Achilles' heel. It was so much easier to pretend I was too tough to care than to let myself be seen as vulnerable. I'd messed up a couple of relationships because of it and been accused of being detached and withholding.

So baring my soul to the man I'd quietly been in love with for half my life? Not exactly something that was easy for me to do.

I was feeling good and maudlin when I parked in the driveway of the house I'd inherited from my grandmother. I had to park my car in the driveway, because the garage door had fallen partially off its tracks and wouldn't open anymore. The front steps I walked up were similarly sagging in places, the wood grown soft and starting to rot. Peeling paint flaked off the porch railings, and patches of mildew grew on the siding, which boasted more than a few rotten boards and holes in need of repair.

It was a 1925 two-story Victorian that had originally belonged to my great-grandparents and was the house my grandmother had grown up in. She'd held on to it after her parents died, renting it out to supplement the income she and my grandfather had earned from the shop they used to have on Main Street. But after my grandfather passed, the house maintenance got to be too much for Meemaw to keep up with, especially once her own health began declining. So it had been sitting here empty for a lot of years, slowly falling into disrepair.

I wasn't really sure why she'd left it to me instead of to her daughters—my mom and my aunt Birdie. Maybe because she'd decided to leave her other house—the one she'd lived in with my grandfather—to Birdie, who'd moved back in to take care of her. And because my parents had started talking about retiring to Maine, where my dad had already inherited property from his family. And because everyone knew Josh wanted to take over the goat farm—and I didn't.

Maybe Meemaw just wanted me to have something for myself. I liked to think she knew how much I'd always loved this house, and she'd wanted it to go to someone who would take care of it the way it deserved.

I loved the pink siding, and the Victorian scrollwork on the gables, and the beaded trim all along the front porch. I loved the double-door front entry, and the wavy antique glass windows, and all the old tile in the bathrooms.

The only thing I didn't love was how much it was going to cost to fix it all up. I'd been fresh out of college when Meemaw died, and I'd had to borrow money from my parents just to cover the taxes on the house the first few years. Aunt Birdie had let me live in her garage apartment rent-free so I could save my money to fix up the house. It had taken three years just to get the place inhabitable enough that I could move in, and I still had a lot of work to do on it.

I'd get there though. Slowly but surely.

On my way in the front door, I fetched the mail out of the

mailbox. I headed into the kitchen and grabbed a beer out of the fridge as I flipped through it. Most of the mail was junk, as per usual. The only thing I didn't throw straight into the recycling bin was a letter from the homeowners' association. I opened my beer and took a long drink before I tore open the envelope to see what they wanted.

A black, oily tendril of anxiety wrapped around my stomach as I read the letter. By the time I'd gotten to the end, that tendril had been joined by a dozen others that had twisted into a giant knot of panic in my gut.

The letter claimed I'd been delinquent in paying a number of previously assessed fines for violations of HOA rules. Except I'd never received a notice of any fines or violations. I definitely would have remembered something like that.

Owing to this alleged delinquency, the attorneys for my homeowners' association were writing to inform me they'd be filing a lien on my house on the HOA's behalf unless all fines, fees, and late charges were paid within thirty days.

They'd included a list of the violations, all of which had to do with exterior property maintenance, and all of which I fully admitted I was guilty of. But it wasn't like the condition of the house was anything new. Most of the cited issues had existed for years—long before I'd even inherited the place. Why had they suddenly decided to enforce the HOA rules now? And why was this the first I was hearing about it?

The worst part was that I'd been assessed late fees on each and every fine on an ongoing monthly basis going back three years. *Three years!* Without a single word to me, they'd been quietly ratcheting up my debt until the number was so unimaginably large I'd never be able to pay it.

I could barely even stand to look at the total, it was so big.

I felt myself start to hyperventilate and sank down on the

floor, pulling my knees to my chest. Pressing my cold beer bottle against my forehead, I tried to calm myself down.

This had to be a mistake. It was fixable. There was a way through this, and I'd figure it out.

I didn't understand how they could spring this on me out of nowhere. It wasn't fair.

Not that fairness mattered. People got away with shitty stuff all the time that wasn't fair. They intimidated and threatened and bullied their way through other people's lives, banking on the fact that most folks wouldn't have the resources to fight them.

Just like I didn't have the resources to fight this. I didn't have a lawyer to protect me or the money to hire one. My family would be willing to help me as much as they could, but none of them were exactly swimming in extra cash. My parents needed their retirement savings to live on. Birdie worked three part-time jobs to pay her modest living expenses. All of Josh's money went right back into the farm.

As I stared at the letter, the question that kept running through my head was *why now?* When I'd owned this place for years, and it had sat here empty and ignored for a good long while before that. I hadn't heard a peep from the HOA before today. I'd honestly forgotten there even was one. So why had they suddenly come at me, guns a-blazing?

There had to be a reason.

I went into the living room and grabbed my laptop. Plopping down on the couch, I flipped it open and started doing some research. I looked up my HOA and found a list of the current officers. None of the names were familiar to me, so I started looking into them online.

It never ceased to amaze me how much stuff you could find out about people on the internet. Their employment history, their friends and family, their hobbies and interests. People should really be more careful about what they put out into the world.

It didn't take long before something clicked. I remembered something, and when I put the pieces together, I thought I might have a guess as to what was behind this—or who.

I knew what I needed to do next.

I needed to call Wyatt.

6

WYATT

"Thanks for doing this, man. I really appreciate it."

I shrugged as I crouched beside Josh's bathroom toilet to connect the water supply hose to the new valve. "It's nothing. You know I don't mind."

Josh finished tightening the mounting plate bolts on his side of the toilet and straightened, wiping his hands on his jeans. "I thought I'd be able to install it myself, but then I started doing some research. Once I realized I'd need to put in an electrical outlet, I figured I better call in an expert."

I shot him a grin over my shoulder. "And then you found out all the experts were busy, and that's why you called me, right?"

He prodded my leg with the toe of his work boot. "You shouldn't run yourself down like that."

"It's just a joke," I muttered under my breath as I tightened the connector on the hose.

"You might think you're just joking, but a habit of negative self-talk can affect your sense of your own worth over time and invite other people to view you negatively too."

I glanced up again, raising my eyebrows at the surprising collection of words that had just come out of my taciturn best friend's mouth—the same guy who thought yoga was "touchy-feely nonsense."

He ducked his head in embarrassment and rubbed the back of his neck. "That's what my therapist says, anyway."

The comeback I'd been on the verge of offering—that the ship had already sailed on everyone's negative opinion of me—died on my tongue. It was a big deal that Josh had finally started therapy after too many years of trying to ignore his issues and cope on his own. So while I wasn't exactly hankering to put my own emotional well-being under a microscope, I was too proud of him for overcoming his reluctance to seek help to undermine the progress he'd made by belittling his therapist's advice.

"You're right," I said, dropping the bullshit for once. "It's a bad habit. I should try to cut it out."

He nodded, and I turned back to the valve I was tightening.

Once I'd finished connecting the water supply, I turned the water to the toilet back on and plugged in the brand-new bidet attachment we'd just installed for Josh's girlfriend.

"Let's see if it works," I said as I hauled myself to my feet.

Josh pressed a button on the control panel and a small chrome wand extended from the seat and shot out a jet of water. "Have you ever used one of these things before?" he asked, giving it a dubious look.

"I went home with a girl once who had one. I nearly rocketed through the ceiling when the damn thing hit me in the balls." I cast a sidelong look at him. "Mia talked you into getting this?"

He shook his head. "It's a surprise. She doesn't know I bought it for her."

"Well it'll definitely surprise her the first time she uses it."

"She saw some video on Twitter about how they're better for the environment and more hygienic, and how Americans are behind the rest of the world and missing out because we have a cultural anti-bidet bias, or something like that."

"A cultural anti-bidet bias?" I repeated with a raised-eyebrow grin.

The corner of his mouth twitched as he shrugged. "She's been talking about it ever since."

I nudged his arm with my shoulder. "She talked you into getting it."

"I thought she'd like it," he said with another shrug as he bent down for a closer look at the water jet. "I don't know how I'm gonna feel about it though."

"You'll have the cleanest pooper in town, that's for sure. And I can tell you from firsthand experience that it's really nice if you're about to engage in a little back door—"

"All right," he said, cutting me off with a grimace. "I don't need to hear the details of your sexual exploits."

"Let's just say we were both extremely satisfied customers and leave it at that."

He gave me an appraising look. "How satisfied was she after she never heard from you again?"

"Who says she wanted to?" I fired back defensively.

One of his eyebrows arched. "Did you even ask? Or did you hightail it out of there as soon as you'd finished enjoying her bidet?"

Josh took a dim view of my promiscuous habits. He'd expressed his opinion—that it was unhealthy for me and hurtful to the women I slept with—plenty of times before. As hard as I'd argued that there was nothing wrong with consenting adults having a good time, I knew deep down he was right. No matter how up front I tried to be about my lack of interest in commitment, I'd still hurt more than my share of feelings by not sticking around.

But Josh seemed to think I had a choice in the matter. As if I could just flip a switch inside my heart and decide to fall in love —or at least deep enough in like that I was interested in more than just sex. Apparently I was defective, because I didn't have that switch. It wasn't as if I hadn't tried. I'd learned through trial and error that relationships weren't for me. Trying to force the issue only resulted in more misery for everyone involved.

It wasn't a subject we were ever going to see eye to eye on, so I ignored his comment as I stooped to gather up my tools.

"You want a beer?" he asked gruffly, joining in to help. Josh wasn't what you'd call effusive, so I recognized it as his way of offering a mea culpa for the unwanted criticism of my life choices.

"Better not," I said, remembering I had band practice tonight. "But I wouldn't say no to some iced tea if you've got any."

I followed him downstairs and set my toolbox by the door while he poured two glasses of iced tea. We drank them at the round oak table in the kitchen of his parents' old house where I'd whiled away hours of my youth with Josh and sometimes Andie. The place hadn't changed much since those days. Same placemats on the same table, same cross-stitch staring at me from the wall—*The secret ingredient is always LOVE!*—same floral shades his mother had made hanging in the bay window. A faint smell of baking bread lingered in the air like an echo of the days when his mom would always have some fresh-baked treat waiting for us, but was probably just the scent of whatever Josh and Mia had made for breakfast this morning.

"Does it ever feel weird?" I asked him. "Living in your parents' house?" I'd never want to live in my dad's house, even if he decamped to Maine like the Lockharts had.

"Not really. It's never bothered me, but..." Josh paused and gazed around the kitchen. "I don't want Mia feeling like she's living in someone else's house. I've been thinking we should make some changes to the place so it'll feel more like it's hers."

"That's why you bought her the bidet," I said, understanding.

"Yeah." The corner of his mouth tilted. "Although I hear there are other benefits to it I might enjoy."

"All right," I said, grinning at him. "I don't need to hear the details of your sexual exploits." We both laughed, and I said, "It's a good gift. She's gonna love it. Hell, I might get myself one if I buy my own place."

"Why don't you?" Josh asked, reaching for his iced tea.

"Get a bidet?"

"Buy your own place." He eyed me as he set his glass back down. "Haven't you outgrown that shitty duplex you've been renting?"

"It's not so bad," I said with a shrug. "The rent's cheap."

"It's a college student apartment. You're thirty now," he reminded me unnecessarily. "We both are."

A disquieting sense of déjà vu prickled over the back of my neck, and I shifted in my chair. "Just because you've embraced settled domesticity doesn't mean it's what I want."

Josh lifted his hand in a placating gesture. "I just mean you deserve something nicer for yourself—a place you could install your own bidet, if that's what you want."

"Nice costs money."

"You're a good handyman and there's plenty of demand for the kind of work you do. If you took on more jobs and expanded your business, you could afford it. You could afford a lot of things."

"Yeah," I agreed reluctantly. He wasn't wrong. It was something I'd thought about before. A lot of times. But especially since the conversation with my dad yesterday.

"But?" he prompted when I didn't say anything else.

I looked down at the blue cotton placemat, tracing the ring

of moisture that had darkened the fabric around my glass. "But if I took on more work and expanded my business, then that would be who I am. My career. My life."

"Would that be bad?" His voice was carefully neutral. Trying not to sound judgmental. But I was more than capable of filling the judgment in for myself.

"I don't know." My hand clenched around my glass as I let out a gusty sigh of frustration. "But I'm not sure it's what I want. And it wouldn't leave much room for anything else."

"Anything else like...?"

I hesitated, almost too embarrassed to say it. "Like the band, I guess."

His forehead wrinkled in surprise. "The band?"

We'd started it together in high school. Me, Josh, and three other guys we knew who could play instruments. Josh had come up with our name—Shiny Heathens—and had been our lead singer until he left for college and I'd taken over lead vocals. It had just been Tyler, Matt, Corey, and me ever since. When Josh came back after college, he hadn't wanted to rejoin the band, so we'd kept it going without him.

I liked to think we were pretty decent, but it was only something we did in our spare time for fun. We'd always said we didn't have enough ambition to do more than play covers at local bars around town whenever they had a gap to fill in their schedules.

Only maybe I did have more ambition than that. Being a cover band limited us to third-rate gigs. If we had original material to play, there were a lot more venues that might take us on. So I'd been experimenting with writing songs on my own. I hadn't told anyone about it, because I wasn't convinced they were any good. But at this point I'd written enough to fill a whole set list.

It might be time to actually do something with them.

I keep waiting for you to show me a sign that you give a single god damn about anything at all.

I ran a restless hand through my hair, thinking about what my dad had said. Annoyed that he had gotten under my skin, which was exactly what he'd wanted.

Josh leaned back in his chair, hands clasped loosely over his stomach, and silently waited for me to say what was on my mind.

"I, uh..." I paused to clear my throat, dropping my eyes to the table. "I've been trying to write some songs, I guess."

"You have?" The excitement in his voice was unmistakable, but it only made me more embarrassed. He'd tried to talk me into writing songs when we first started the band, convinced for some reason I'd have a talent for it, but I'd stubbornly refused to even try.

"Yeah, a little," I mumbled, needing to minimize what I'd done to lower his expectations. High expectations were a trap I found it best to avoid whenever possible. "It's no big deal or anything."

"Sounds like a big deal to me. *I've* never written a song."

I forced out a laugh that sounded hollow. "I'm not sure I have either."

As soon as I said it, I remembered Josh's admonition about negative self-talk. I could tell he was thinking about it too, in the long look he gave me before he spoke, but he didn't repeat it.

"What does the rest of the band say?" he asked instead.

My chest felt tight when I tried to take a breath, and my confession came out sounding thready. "I haven't told them about it."

"But you're going to." Not a question. A statement. Telling me with just those four words that even though he knew I wanted to weasel out, he expected me not to. He wanted me to be better than that.

"Yeah," I agreed, because I'd always hated disappointing him. "I will."

"Soon?" This time it was a question, his eyebrows raised and his expression hopeful. "I wouldn't mind hearing what you've written sometime."

A lump formed in my throat, half gratitude and half fear. I could tell he was proud of me, but that just meant more high expectations—and a higher chance of failure.

To my relief, we were interrupted by the sound of the front door opening and Mia cheerfully calling out "Hello?"

"Hey," Josh called back, breaking into the kind of smile that used to be rare for him before she came into his life. "We're in the kitchen."

"Is Wyatt here?" Mia appeared in the kitchen doorway, a big smile on her face that I only got a glancing share of before her eyes locked onto Josh and lit up like he'd cured cancer.

He'd already gotten to his feet to greet her, his expression soft and shining in a way I still wasn't used to because it was so different than his usual guardedness. An unsettling ache bloomed in my chest as they kissed, and I averted my eyes while I carried my empty glass to the sink.

Mia detached herself from Josh and came over to kiss my cheek. "I thought that was your truck out front with the 'Eat the Rich' bumper sticker."

"Guilty as charged." Had I put it there just to piss off my dad and thumb my nose at the family fortune? Damn right I had.

"Your poor face," she said, frowning at my bruises. "Andie told me what happened."

"You talked to Andie?" I said.

"How'd Andie know about it?" Josh asked.

Mia looked from me to Josh and then back to me. "We had lunch today." Her eyes stayed on mine as she answered Josh's question. "She was at King's Palace Saturday night when Wyatt got into his fight."

When I'd showed up at the house today and Josh had seen my shiner, I'd told him about my little altercation, but I'd left out the part about Andie being the woman I'd stepped in to defend. I knew she wouldn't want me to tell Josh, because he'd only overreact, get all big brothery about it, and probably try to give her a lecture about her personal safety. He meant well, but he could be a little heavy-handed when he got worried about her.

Based on the way Mia was looking at me, I guessed Andie had told her a lot more than I'd told Josh. How much, exactly, I'd sure like to know. Had she told her about driving me home? Or what we'd talked about? My own memories were pretty hazy, so Mia might know even more than I did about what kind of shit I'd said in my inebriated state. I wanted to find out exactly what Andie had said, but I couldn't very well interrogate Mia in front of Josh.

"Are you staying for dinner?" she asked. "We're making meatloaf."

"Wish I could," I said honestly—especially if they were making Josh's mom's recipe. "But I've got band practice tonight."

Josh's gaze found mine and we shared a long, meaningful look. "Good luck."

"Thanks." I was going to need it.

———

I FROWNED at my notebook as I flipped through the pages looking for a song good enough to play for the other guys in my band. Josh was right. If I was serious about doing this, I needed to bring the rest of Shiny Heathens in on it and see what they thought. Get some honest feedback and maybe, if they were into it, some help with the arrangements.

Assuming they didn't think everything I'd written was crap.

There was a good chance it was all crap.

I had no objectivity. That was why I needed to show this stuff to someone else. But which song should I pick to start with? Trying to decide which one sucked the least was proving more difficult than I'd anticipated.

There'd been fleeting moments when I'd almost convinced myself some of these songs might be pretty good. Maybe even great. But in between those brief flashes of confidence lay vast gulfs of self-doubt when it felt like everything I'd written was as much of a failure as everything else I'd ever tried to do. Boy Scouts, FFA, baseball, football, college, the four jobs I'd been fired from, every relationship I'd tried to stay in. I'd flunked out —or been kicked out—so many times in my life, I couldn't even remember them all.

Why did I think I'd be any better at this? What did I know about writing songs anyway? Who was I kidding with this shit?

A glance at my phone told me I had twenty minutes left to decide if I was going to go through with this. Rubbing my temples, I flipped through a few more pages.

Jesus, reading these lyrics made me sick to my stomach. Some of this stuff was seriously personal. Almost half the songs were about Andie. A couple others were about my mom. One was about my dad. Another one about my brothers.

I couldn't just write about ordinary shit like my truck or the dog I'd had when I was a kid. No, I had to go and write about my *feelings*. Stuff I wasn't even comfortable saying out loud. And I was supposed to get up and sing about it to a crowd of people?

The thought of playing any of these songs for Tyler, Matt, and Corey scared the shit out of me. I'd never had problems with performance anxiety before, but then again, I'd never performed anything that was *mine*. Other people's songs were easy, because they didn't have anything to do with me. These songs were all about me. They unmasked my desires and heartaches, exposing all the feelings I'd tried to keep hidden underneath the surface. I'd laid myself bare on these pages. If people thought these songs were worthless garbage, it'd be the same as saying *I* was worthless garbage.

My phone rang beside me, and I blinked in surprise when I saw it was Andie calling. She almost never called me—if she wanted something, she usually texted. A spike of unease shot through me, and I nearly dropped the damn phone in my fumbling haste to answer it. "Hey you. What's up?"

"Are you busy?"

It was the first time I'd heard her voice since Saturday night, and my heart gave a squeeze of longing. But the fact that she hadn't replied with our usual greeting had me even more on alert.

"No." I leaned forward on the couch. "Why?"

"I need to talk to you about something."

That couldn't be good. Never once in the entire history of the universe had the phrase *I need to talk to you* preceded a pleasant conversation.

Squeezing my eyes shut, I pressed my fingers to my eyelids. "What?"

"It's kind of complicated. I don't suppose you could come over?"

"Right now?"

"Yeah, if you're free." Something about Andie's voice sounded off. It was too quiet. Too rough. Almost shaky.

I sat up even straighter. "Is everything okay?"

"Yeah." She paused. "Mostly. Sort of. Like I said, it's complicated. I'm not dying or anything though."

"Well, that's good. Jesus."

Her laugh lacked its usual warmth. "It's not an emergency, is what I meant. If you're busy—"

"I'm not." Band practice could wait. Whatever was going on with Andie was more important. "I can be there in ten minutes."

She blew out a breath, and it definitely sounded shaky. "Cool."

———

I MADE it to Andie's house in six minutes, which had to be a record. And that included texting the guys and telling them I wasn't going to make it to practice tonight.

My truck jerked to a stop in front of her house and I jumped out, my heart pounding as I ate up the distance to her front door. She answered my impatient knocking and stepped back to admit me.

"What happened to your face?" Worry stoked a flare of protective anger as I moved in close and tipped her chin up for a better look at the scratch across her cheek.

She batted me away, rolling her eyes. "I had a run-in with a tree at work. You want to pick a fight with it too?"

I blew out a breath and made myself calm down. Flying off the handle wasn't going to help her—and was exactly what Josh would do. Things couldn't be all that bad if she was still giving me shit.

"You want a beer?" she asked, heading for the kitchen.

"No." I closed the front door behind me. "I want to know what's going on."

She opened the fridge and got out a beer for herself. There were two empties sitting by the sink, and I wondered if they were all from tonight.

I waited, watching her as she took a long swig. Something was definitely up. Her face looked pale and was sporting that crease she always got between her eyebrows when she was worried.

She wiped her mouth and picked up an open letter on the kitchen table, holding it out to me. "I got this in the mail today."

I took it, my apprehension ramping up as soon as I saw it was from a law firm. My eyes widened as I skimmed the letter—then nearly bugged out of my head when I got to the dollar amount they wanted her to pay. "Holy *fuck*, Andie."

"This is the first communication I've ever had from anyone about owing any fees. I never received any notices or warnings about it before this."

I stared at her. "They hit you with this out of the blue? They can't do that."

Her mouth tightened. "And yet they did."

"This is crazy." I understood now why she'd sounded shaky on the phone. What I didn't understand was how she could be so calm. I felt like I was having a heart attack, and I wasn't the one on the hook for tens of thousands of dollars. "How are you not completely losing your shit right now?"

She huffed out a dark-sounding laugh. "I lost my shit plenty before I called you, believe me."

My heart lurched, and I moved toward her automatically, gathering her into my arms. I hated to think of her going through that alone. It was just like her not to call anyone until she'd pulled herself together again.

Her body sagged against me, and she let me hold her for a few precious seconds before she twisted out of my arms. Turning away, she took another long drink of beer like she was trying to steady herself. Because god forbid she let any hint of weakness show.

"There's a specific reason I called you," she said when she finally looked at me again. "A few months ago, I got a letter from someone who wanted to buy the house. I get scam junk mail like that all the time, so I just ignored it. But then this guy turned up at my door to make his offer in person. I wasn't interested in selling, so I turned him down. But he kept sending me letters every few weeks, promising a quick cash sale."

"Sounds shady." I'd crossed paths with a few house flippers who used a similar tactic to entice people into accepting a lowball offer. Fast cash, no agent fees, and usually half what the property was worth. But too tempting to refuse if you were someone in a financial pinch.

Andie nodded. "That's what I thought. I threw all the letters away, but I still had the card he gave me lying around." She picked a business card up off the table and handed it to me.

My jaw clenched as I read the company name on the card.

King Holdings, LLC

I stared at her, trying to keep my temper in check as my blood throbbed in my temples. "My dad tried to buy your house?"

"Not personally. But I presume it's one of his companies."

"Why didn't you tell me?"

"I didn't think much of it at the time." She leveled me with a pointed look. "And I didn't want you to get all worked up about it —like you're getting right now. I know how you are about your dad."

"With good reason."

"When I got that letter today, I went and looked up who all the HOA officers are. Half of them work for King's Creamery, including the president, a guy named Rodney Phelps who's been with the company nearly twenty years."

A lot of people in this town worked for my family, so that wasn't necessarily unusual, but it did make me suspicious. I knew Rodney a little. He worked in accounting and coached the company softball team.

I looked at the letter again and realized I recognized the name of the law firm that had sent the threat. It was the same one my dad used for his non-creamery business dealings.

"I guess what I'm asking," Andie said, "is if you think your dad might have gotten the HOA to do this in order to pressure me into selling?"

Nodding, I swallowed down the ball of anger in the back of my throat. "It's exactly the kind of shit he would pull."

Andie seemed to deflate before my eyes. "Well, fuck. In that case I really don't know what I'm gonna do." She sank onto one of the kitchen chairs and rested her elbows on the table as she rubbed her head.

"I'm going to fix this." My teeth gritted with resolve, even though I had no idea how to do it. But no way was I letting my old man hurt her like this. Andie loved this run-down old house, and my father wasn't going to bully her into giving it up.

She shot me a tremulous smile. "It's not your problem, Wyatt. It's mine. I'll figure something out."

"Hey." I sat down next to her and took her hand. "Have you forgotten this is what I do? Fixing houses is literally my specialty."

She let me twine my fingers with hers. "I appreciate that, but—"

"Listen to me. I've dealt with HOAs before. They like to swing their dicks around, but they'll back off if you agree to give them what they want. They're just trying to scare you with this shit."

"Well, it's working, because I'm scared. I don't have the money to pay for all these repairs they want, much less all the fines and late fees on top of that."

Hearing Andie admit to being scared made my stomach twist in knots. I didn't think I'd ever heard her say that before. It killed me to see her like this—especially knowing my own father was the one responsible for it.

"I can do all the repairs," I promised. "You won't have to pay for anything but materials, and I can get you a good deal on most of what you'll need. I know a lot of people who owe me favors. I can get this done without it costing you too much."

"Did you look at that list of everything they're asking for? There's no way you can do all of it yourself."

Lifting my chin, I sniffed in indignation. "I'm going to pretend I'm not hurt by your lack of faith in my abilities."

She shook her head, digging her fingernails into my hand to show me what she thought of my ploy for pity. My dick twitched in a spectacular display of poor timing, and I silently implored it to stand the fuck down.

"Wyatt, it's really sweet that you want to help me—"

"I can get it done." I steeled my expression, keeping my voice solemn. "I swear to you."

"Even if you can, I still won't have the money for the fines."

"Let me talk to them. Like I said, I've dealt with stuff like this plenty of times before. Nine times out of ten, if you agree to do all the requested maintenance, they'll waive most of the fees. I'll pay your HOA president a call and let him know you've engaged a contractor to take care of all the violations. With any luck, that will make him happy enough to back off."

I wasn't above exerting a little influence of my own. If my dad had used our family name to pressure the HOA into hassling Andie, maybe I could use it to pressure them into backing off. Let them know they'd made a mistake and picked the wrong person to go after by targeting a close personal family friend.

And if that failed, then I'd swallow my pride and go straight to the old man himself. Although I suspected I'd have a better chance of winning over Rodney Phelps than my dear old dad.

Andie's expression betrayed a glimmer of hope that shot straight through my heart. "You really think so?"

"I really do." I squeezed her hand. "We can fix this. I promise."

She blinked at me, and if I didn't know better, I'd swear she was trying not to cry. "Thank you. Seriously." As her teeth sank into her lower lip, my dick once again tried to make its inappropriate feelings known.

I pushed my chair back, grabbing the letter off the table as I stood up, and pulled Andie to her feet. "Let's walk through everything that needs to be done so I can start working up an estimate of what the materials are going to run you."

When I tried to slip my hand out of hers, her fingers tightened, and she hauled me back toward her. Her arms wound around my neck as she hugged me. "I don't know what I'd do without you."

I banded an arm around her, shoving my hips back to keep my inconvenient boner well away from her. My heart thumped wildly in my chest as she pressed her face into my neck, and I breathed in the sweet, outdoorsy smell of her hair.

One way or another, I was going to get her out of this mess. Even if I had to go to each and every one of my siblings and beg them to loan me the money to buy her way out of it.

There was no fucking way I'd let Andie down.

7

ANDIE

The day after I showed him the HOA letter, Wyatt texted me to ask if he could come over in the morning before I left for work. I told him sure, and that I'd be around until seven forty-five. But I didn't get my hopes up that I'd actually see him when morning came.

I loved the guy, but he wasn't exactly a shining pinnacle of punctuality and reliability. He also wasn't a morning person. I wasn't sure I'd ever seen him before ten a.m. unless he was still up from the night before.

Shattering my low expectations, Wyatt turned up on my doorstep at seven a.m. sharp. I'd just finished drying my hair and was still in my robe when I went to let him in.

This was the first time I'd ever asked him for help with the house. Up until now, I'd done as much of the work as I could myself and hired specialists for the plumbing, electrical, and HVAC issues that required more expertise than I could handle. Not that Wyatt wouldn't have been willing, but it had been a matter of pride for me to do it myself without leaning on anyone else for help. In particular, I'd avoided going to my brother or my brother's best friend, because I wasn't a kid anymore and didn't want to go running to them every time I got in a jam.

So much for that. But needs must when the devil drives.

I swallowed as Wyatt walked past me into the house carrying an enormous toolbox in one hand and a clipboard in the other. I hadn't seen much of him in full-on work mode like this, and it was quite a sight to behold.

He was dressed in work boots, jeans, and a tank top that showed off his muscular, tattooed arms and a considerable portion of his chest, with a leather tool belt slung low across his hips. I'd seen plenty of Wyatt's physique over the years, but something about this particular look on him really worked. Like *really* worked. I had to take a second to regroup before I followed him into the living room.

He'd set his toolbox down and was flipping through the papers on his clipboard by the time I caught up with him.

"This is for you." Licking his fingers, he pulled a few sheets off and held them out to me.

"What is it?" I shuffled closer and took them from him.

"That's your project plan. It includes a timeline for completing all requested exterior repairs and an itemized estimate of labor and materials required for each job."

I stared at it, overwhelmed into speechlessness by the professionalism of the document Wyatt had just handed me. It was four pages long, extremely thorough, well organized, and detailed. He'd clearly put a lot of work into it.

"'Course, you're getting all the labor for free," he went on as I read over it. "It's only on there to help me create the schedule, which, as you can see, has all the work completed by the deadline in just under four weeks. And if you look at the total cost estimate on the last page, you'll see we're well within the budget you gave me."

I gaped when I saw how low the total cost was. There was no

way he'd be able to get everything we needed for that amount. "Wyatt, this is nuts."

"What do you mean?" He was frowning when I looked up at him again.

"How are you going to get all this done for so little money? Just the paint alone should cost more than this total you've got here." I looked down at the numbers again to make sure I hadn't misread them.

"I told you, people owe me favors. I know a guy who's got a bunch of leftover trim paint he's giving me for free. I'm getting the rest of the exterior paint at cost from my buddy Doyle, whose dad owns a hardware store over in Smithville. Mary Alice at the nursery is giving me the soil and sod for the yard in exchange for building her a new greenhouse. Everything else I'm getting wholesale or with my contractor's discount."

"I don't know what to say." I was stunned. I had no idea Wyatt was this professional, or that he'd had so many favors to call in on my behalf. I shouldn't have been surprised though. He was one of the sweetest, most generous guys I knew, and he'd stuck his neck out for my family more times than I could count.

"How about something like, 'You're so amazing and impressive, Wyatt. I never should have doubted you.'" His mouth had tugged into a smirk like he was teasing, but I detected a whiff of bruised feelings underneath it.

My stomach churned with guilt for not giving him more credit, and I wrapped my arms around his waist and laid my head against his chest. "You're amazing and impressive, Wyatt. I never should have doubted you. Thank you for all of this."

He froze for a second, and I felt his breath catch in his chest before he recovered. "That's more like it," he said jokingly and twisted out of my arms.

We hadn't ever talked about the things he'd said last Saturday when he was drunk, or the stuff Mia had told me about my brother. This whole HOA situation had derailed all of that. But now it came crashing back, leaving me wondering anew if Wyatt kept pulling away from me because he *wanted* to pull away, or because he was scared not to.

"If you like the project plan, you're really going to like the next thing I have to tell you." His gaze dropped to my chest and the smile froze on his face before he jerked his eyes toward the ceiling.

Glancing down, I realized the front of my robe had gaped, and I'd just given him an eyeful of my boobs. *Great.*

"Sorry." I pulled it closed, trying to recover some of my dignity.

At least I knew it wasn't the first time he'd gotten a look at my chest. In addition to the vomit-shirt incident I'd just learned about, there'd been a few times in high school when we'd both been skinny-dipping at the Holler.

The clothing-optional swimming hole up at the state park had been a favorite hangout in our high school days. My brother had frequented it with his friends while hypocritically forbidding me from doing the same. Not that I'd actually wanted to go skinny-dipping with my brother—*yuck*. But you could bet I took advantage of his absence as soon as he went off to college.

The first time I ran into Wyatt there, he'd freaked the fuck out. I still remembered the look of panic in his eyes as he'd tried to cover himself. I got quite an eyeful before he managed to get his shorts on, and the image had made a permanent impression that still surfaced regularly in my dreams. He'd tried to make me leave, and we got into a fight when I refused. I'd ended the argument by stripping off my bikini top in front of him, and he'd averted his eyes exactly like he was doing now. He'd spent the whole rest of that night—and every other time he saw me there —hilariously trying to keep a watchful eye on me without actually looking at me, and somewhat less hilariously directing murderous glares at every guy who dared to glance in my direction. It had been both sweet and annoying as hell.

All of which was to say that Wyatt's eyes and my boobs weren't exactly strangers.

I cleared my throat. "What's the other thing you wanted to tell me?"

He glanced down cautiously, checking to make sure it was safe before he relaxed again. "I, uh..." He scratched the back of his head like he was trying to remember what we'd been talking about. "Right. So I talked to Rodney Phelps yesterday. We had a nice chat over a couple of beers, and he agreed to waive the fines and late fees if you get all the required repairs done by the deadline."

I clapped a hand over my mouth, too emotional for a moment to speak. "Are you serious? *All* the fines?"

Wyatt nodded, looking pleased with himself. "Everything except the attorney's fees. So you'll still have to pay like six hundred dollars."

"Oh my god!" Six hundred dollars had never sounded like such an inconsequential sum of money before. It was an amount I could actually afford to pay if Wyatt got the repairs done for what he'd estimated.

For the last thirty-six hours, I'd barely been keeping my shit together, functioning in a state of ongoing panic. The phrase "rearranging the deck chairs on the Titanic" had never felt so applicable before. That had been me, taking out the trash and making my bed while the threat of losing my house loomed over me like an enormous freaking iceberg it was too late to steer away from. But now that crushing weight had been lifted off my chest.

As much as I'd wanted to trust Wyatt and knew he had the best intentions, I hadn't been able to let myself believe he could actually get me out of this mess. He was the kind of friend who'd drop everything and rush to your side in an emergency, but levelheadedness and follow-through had never been his strong suits. Even if they had been, my pessimist's soul wouldn't let me trust that anyone could swoop in and fix everything.

But that was exactly what Wyatt was doing—literally. I wanted to throw my arms around him again and cover his whole face with kisses. I might even have done it, if he hadn't pulled away from me the last time I'd hugged him.

Enthusiastic hugs and sisterly cheek kisses had always been our norm. But lately I'd had the sense he wasn't as comfortable with our displays of friendly affection as he used to be. And I wasn't sure why. What had changed for him? Was it me? Or him? Either way, I didn't want to make him more uncomfortable than I already had—especially after I'd just accidentally flashed him my tits.

So instead of hugging him like I wanted to, I stood there awkwardly clutching my robe closed. Without an easy outlet for the deluge of emotions swamping me, I felt jittery and unsteady. My breath hitched as I tried to think of something to say, but nothing seemed adequate to express how touched and overcome I was by this incredible favor he was doing me.

"You okay?" He arched an eyebrow, cocking his head so his hair spilled into his face.

I nodded and cleared my throat, trying not to cry in front of him. I hated crying, but I really hated doing it in front of people. "I'm just trying to think of a way to say thank you."

He reached up to rake his hair back as he gave me a searching once-over. His concerned scrutiny made me more self-conscious than stripping off my bikini top ever had, and my eyes dropped to the floor as I fought the urge to hide under the coffee table.

Before I could embarrass myself by bear-crawling to the nearest piece of furniture, Wyatt set his clipboard down and folded me into a hug. I stiffened as his arms wrapped me up, but the familiar comfort of his body proved too strong to resist. I let myself relax into his embrace and slid my arms around his waist.

Instead of pulling away as I'd half feared he would, he held me even tighter, fitting my body against his. "You don't have to thank me." He spoke into my hair, one of his hands skating down my back as the other cupped the back of my head. "We're family."

The sweetness of the sentiment might have succeeded in moving me to the tears I was trying to suppress, if I hadn't been distracted by something else entirely.

The very *un*-familial erection that twitched against my stomach.

I stilled, my heart thudding into overdrive as we hovered there, our bodies pressed together, my face in his chest and his lips on my hair.

Slowly, Wyatt loosened his hold and untangled himself from me. Shuffling back a step, he rested his hands on my shoulders.

Don't look down, I commanded my eyes. *Do not attempt to look at the bulge in his jeans.*

Only by summoning every ounce of my willpower was I able to keep my attention focused on Wyatt's face. Which revealed absolutely nothing—no awareness or acknowledgement of what we both had just felt.

He has to know I felt that, right?

"It's going to be okay," he told me. "I told you I'd take care of this, and I will." It took me longer than it should have to realize he was talking about the house and not what was happening in his pants.

I nodded, not trusting myself to speak. Afraid that if I opened my mouth, I might just offer to take care of that pants situation for him.

But that would be bad. Now was not the time to go throwing

myself at him. Not when he'd just showed up to save my bacon —and by bacon I meant my house, which he was quite literally saving singlehandedly. He might think I was offering myself as some kind of thank-you or payment, which was definitely *not* the impression I wanted to give.

One boner didn't necessarily mean anything except that Wyatt was young and horny and his body parts had reacted involuntarily to my body parts. It wasn't proof he wanted *me*.

It was an interesting piece of evidence, however. One I definitely needed to think on some more before I decided what, if anything, to do about it.

8

WYATT

s it possible to die of blue balls? If so, I was in big trouble.

The last week and a half had been both the best and the most frustrating of my life. The best part was getting to see Andie every day, usually in the morning before she left for work and again in the evening when she came home. The frustrating part was seeing so much of her and getting hard pretty much whenever she was around. My nethers were in near-constant agony, and hiding the evidence of my urges was getting harder every day.

I'd learned my lesson, at least, and after that first day I made sure not to show up in the mornings until she was dressed and about to leave for work. Not that those practical park service khakis she wore didn't crank my engine—because they weirdly *really* did. But if I had to see her in that short little robe of hers again, I might actually lose my damn mind. The sight of her nipples peaking beneath the thin cotton and her smooth bare thighs was bad enough, but when that cursed thing had gaped open, exposing the swell of her soft, round breasts, I'd nearly had an aneurism from all the blood hightailing it to my dick.

She had to have felt my hard-on when I'd hugged her last

week. I should have kept my distance, but I hadn't been able to help myself. What was I supposed to do when she looked so much like she was about to cry? Withhold comfort from her because my willie didn't know its place? Screw that.

I was just grateful she hadn't said anything. As long as we both kept pretending my rock-hard cock hadn't poked her in the stomach, I might survive the next few weeks with my dignity intact.

Also, no more hugging. Hugging was definitely off-limits until I got these pants feelings under control.

Aside from the terminal case of ball ache, I'd loved spending this time with Andie. Knowing I'd get to see her had me looking forward to getting up in the mornings. Every day felt like I was seven years old again, waking up at the crack of dawn on Christmas, and Andie was the present waiting under my tree. For the first time in my lazy-ass life, I was rising with the sun, full of energy and eager to get moving so I could share a cup of coffee with her before she went off to work.

We'd talk about the things I planned to tackle on the house and what her work day had in store for her. I loved hearing about all the stuff she did to look after the wildlife up at the park. How complicated it was managing all those fragile, interdependent habitats and protecting the natural balance. She was so damn smart—she always had been—I wondered sometimes what she was even doing being friends with me.

After she headed out to save the forests and whatnot, I'd work at her place all day while she was gone, taking a special kind of pride in the fact that I was protecting something she loved so much. Building a better home for her and restoring a treasured piece of her family's heritage.

Maybe it wasn't as cool or important as the work Andie did at the state park. But it was important to *her*. And that made it important to me.

I had the run of the house during the day when she was at work. Just being in her space, surrounded by her belongings and her scent, made me feel closer to her. I made damn sure to be respectful. I wasn't about to betray the trust she'd placed in me by invading her privacy and poking through her stuff. I cleaned up after myself carefully when I used the downstairs bathroom or kitchen. But sometimes I'd linger inside for a few minutes longer than strictly necessary. Reading all the funny embroidery designs she'd made and hung up around the house for decoration. Looking at the family photos she had sitting out—a few of which even featured me. Smiling at the collection of magnets and ticket stubs stuck to her fridge, some of them mementos of places we'd been together. I never went so far as to enter her bedroom, although once, in a particularly weak moment, I'd stood in the doorway just to breathe the air where she slept.

But by far the best part of every day was the evening when Andie came home from work. As soon as I heard the sound of her Jeep Cherokee turning into the driveway, I perked up like a damn cocker spaniel. I'd watch her climb out of her car—looking sexy as hell in those damn khaki cargo pants that had no business hugging her hips and ass like that—and my junk would throb with every sub-bass pulse of my heart. I was one hundred percent Andie's bitch. Just like that, she'd become the center of my universe.

Most nights she picked up takeout for us on the way home. We'd crack open a couple of beers and sit at her kitchen table while we talked about our respective days like a damn married couple. It was the kind of comfortable domesticity I hadn't experienced much in my life, other than the time I'd spent with Andie's family growing up.

For reasons I didn't fully understand, it was something I'd always shied away from when other women had tried to offer it to me. I'd never wanted to stick around and do the things normal couples did. Unless I was doing them with Andie, apparently. I could have stayed all night doing nothing more than talking to her.

But I didn't. I always limited myself to one beer, then made myself go home as soon as we'd cleaned up dinner. Staying any longer would be too risky. I might be tempted to drink more, and then I might let my guard down, and then I might do something stupid and ruin this great thing we had going.

It was Friday today, and I was looking forward to the weekend. Not because I was taking it off, but because Andie would be working beside me. Last weekend we'd rebuilt the front steps together and replaced the rotted floorboards in the porch, and *damn*, if the sight of her working a nail gun wasn't one of the hottest things I'd ever seen.

Pure torture, mind you, but the sweetest kind of torture. The kind I couldn't wait to repeat tomorrow.

When I heard Andie's car pull up an hour earlier than usual, I dropped my paint scraper into my toolbox, wiped my hands off, and went around the house to greet her. I'd gotten her a surprise today, and I couldn't wait to show it to her.

Her face looked like a thundercloud as she slammed the door of the car, and as soon as I got close enough to get a whiff of her, I had a guess as to why.

"What the hell is that smell?" I scrunched up my nose as she shoved her messenger bag at me.

"Bark beetle pheromones." Instead of going in the front door, she headed around to the back of the house.

I followed her, hanging back a safe distance from the stink. "Why do you smell like beetle pheromones?"

"Because I spilled the damn solution when I was baiting traps." She sat on the back porch steps and started untying her shoes.

I tried and failed to suppress a grin. "So you smell like sexy beetle juice?"

She shot me a dark look. "Har har."

"Wait—so does this mean every beetle in the area is going to show up and try to have sex with you?"

"Yes, actually. Which is why I need to get these clothes in the wash before I end up ground zero in a beetle orgy." Before I had time to avert my eyes, she stood up and pulled her park service polo shirt over her head.

Andie had never been shy about her body. I'd learned that the hard way when she'd showed up at the Holler the first time and stripped right in front of me as I was trying to get her to leave. I'd nearly stroked out when she'd untied her bikini top, baring her breasts to me, god, and everyone else at the swimming hole that night. My eyes had been faster than my reflexes, so I'd gotten a knockout view before my nervous system had started functioning again and I'd managed to look away.

This time I tried to play it cooler. If Andie didn't consider it a big deal, then me clutching my pearls and acting the prude would only make things more awkward.

At least she was wearing a bra this time. A very practical black sports bra, even. Nothing more revealing than you'd see at the gym or a public pool. No reason to get worked up or excited. The sight of her bare stomach definitely shouldn't make my blood rush straight to my crotch, but then neither should those khaki pants she wore either.

Speaking of Andie's pants, she was already unfastening them, and before I knew it she'd shoved them off her hips and down to her ankles. I swallowed at the sight of her plain black panties and the exposed curve of her ass cheeks as she bent over to pick up her discarded clothes.

The Lord was truly testing me today. But I was up to the challenge. My dick was not the one in charge here—not where

Andie was concerned, anyway. The emergency override proto-
cols in my brain kicked in, and I leaped forward to offer gentle-
manly assistance.

"Here, I can put those in the wash for you." I held out my
hands to take her smelly clothes.

"Thanks." She folded them up into a ball before trading
them for her messenger bag. "Can you start them on the presoak
cycle with two cups of vinegar? It's in the cabinet next to the
machines."

I nodded and held the back door open for her, letting her
precede me into the house.

She dropped her bag on the kitchen table as I headed for the
laundry room. "And make sure you wash your hands after," she
called out. "I'm going to go shower for a year."

I started the washing machine while she went upstairs. Then
I used the Lava soap I'd left in the downstairs bathroom to scrub
my hands until they were raw and pink to make sure I wouldn't
attract any amorous beetles.

When I came out of the bathroom, I could hear the shower
running upstairs, and I tried not to think about the fact that
Andie was naked up there right now. Her skin slick with water,
her hands lathering soap over her body and combing through
her wet hair...

Fuck.

I went outside and put away all my tools to distract me from
thinking about Andie naked in the shower. By the time I came
back in ten minutes later, the water upstairs was off and I heard
the floorboards creaking overhead as she walked around her
bedroom. She came down a few minutes later, her hair wet and
hanging loose around her face, wearing an old T-shirt and a pair
of cutoff jeans shorts.

I met her at the door of the kitchen and handed her a beer.
"Feel better?" She certainly smelled much better—amazing,

actually. All traces of beetle love juice were gone, replaced by the honeysuckle scent of her shampoo, which always made me a little weak in the knees.

"Yes. And bless you for this." She tipped the bottle at me and took a long drink.

As she arched her back, my eyes drifted unwittingly to her chest where the peaks of her nipples showed through the thin cotton of her shirt. *Definitely not wearing a bra now.* Forcing my gaze elsewhere, I gulped down a mouthful of the beer I'd opened for myself.

"I didn't stop to get any dinner for us—for obvious reasons— but I figured we could order pizza." She padded over to the table and dug around in her bag for her phone. "Now that I've got that smell off me, I'm starving."

"You should take a peek in the freezer," I said, remembering the surprise I'd gotten her.

She glanced up at me, her eyebrows arching in inquiry, and I smiled as I inclined my head toward the fridge. Spinning on her bare feet, she yanked the freezer open and let out a squeal of delight when she saw the eight pints of King's Thar She Blows! bubblegum ice cream I'd stowed in there. "My favorite flavor!"

"I know." She really had the worst possible taste in ice cream, but I was willing to enable her disgusting cravings if it made her happy.

She rounded on me again, smiling for the first time since she'd come home reeking of bug pheromones. "You brought me ice cream? Even though you hate it?" Her eyes sparkled with a warmth that reached right into my chest and gave my heart a hard yank.

I shrugged like it was nothing. Like I hadn't done it hoping to make her smile exactly like she was smiling at me right now. "It was on my way."

It hadn't been. I'd made a special trip to the plant just for her and stopped into the warehouse to ask for a case of the revolting stuff to bring home.

She came toward me, and I knew she was going to kiss my cheek. It was something she did all the time, so I recognized the way she tilted her head up, her lips pursing as she drew nearer, and I knew she'd wrap her fingers around my forearm to lever herself up on her toes.

Every other time she'd done it, I'd turned my head away, presenting my cheek as I leaned down to make it easier for her to reach. It was instinctive by now. As natural as breathing.

I couldn't tell you why I didn't do it this time.

I had no idea what I was thinking, but instead of turning away from her mouth, I turned toward it.

Such a small, insignificant movement. Just a matter of a couple inches.

But it was the difference between a kiss on the cheek and a kiss on the lips.

Which was all the difference in the world.

9

WYATT

I caught Andie's mouth with mine, just like I'd always wanted to, and everything stopped. My heart, my breathing, my sense of time or place. My brain had already stopped working, clearly, or I wouldn't have done what I did.

My entire awareness tunneled to the plush sweetness of her lips pressing against mine as her momentum carried her into me. In that one fraction of a moment when we came together, every inch of me soared to life.

Until I heard her sharp, surprised intake of breath and reality came crashing down.

She jerked her head back and stared at me, wide-eyed, her lips slightly parted and her breathing heavy with shock.

I didn't know what to do. How to take it back. I would have given anything to undo the last second and erase it from both of our memories. All I could do was stare back at her, frozen in panic. My brain too nonfunctional to even form the words to apologize.

Andie's hand was still clamped on my arm, and I waited for her to let go and back away from me.

But she didn't.

Instead, I felt her grip tighten, her fingernails digging into my skin.

The sharp sting shot up my arm and straight to my spine, making my breath stutter loud enough that she must have heard it. Her eyes narrowed, studying me, as her tongue darted out to wet her lips.

Then she surged forward, hooking a hand around the back of my head to drag my mouth against hers. I froze for a split second before my body took over, responding to her on pure instinct.

My hands cradled her face as I angled my head to shape my mouth to hers. Her lips parted like silk sheets at the first tentative touch of my tongue, admitting me into her inviting warmth. I'd never tasted her before, and it was everything I'd ever dreamed of and more. Beneath the malty taste of the beer we'd both been drinking, Andie tasted like sunshine and sugar and strength. I delved deep, sinking into her sweetness, and gave myself over to the mindless pleasure of it.

Her hands dragged down the front of my shirt, then pushed up underneath it. When her fingers touched my bare skin, I made a low, feral sound in the back of my throat. I'd thought being around her was intoxicating, but this electricity between us was so much more intense and exhilarating than anything I'd ever experienced.

Liquid heat pumped through my veins with every racing beat of my pulse. My whole body sang as she explored under my shirt. Her nails scratched over my stomach, then her fingers dipped into the waistband of my jeans.

A sudden awareness of what she was doing—what *we* were doing—jolted me out of my stupor.

Guilt poured over me like an ice bath, and I tore myself away from Andie with an ungainly lurch. "Shit." I dragged my hand across my mouth, my chest heaving as I struggled for oxygen. "I'm sorry. I shouldn't have done that."

She licked her lips, which were swollen and pink from the pressure of my mouth and the scrape of my stubble. "Why?"

I blinked at her. "What?"

"Why shouldn't you have done it?"

"Because…" My fists clenched at my sides. "Because this can't happen with you and me."

Her eyes narrowed. "This isn't because of Josh, is it? Because you're scared of what he'd have to say about it?"

That was precisely what it was, but I knew what would happen if I said yes. Andie had a knee-jerk reflex against her brother's attempts to control her, and this would turn into another way for her to rebel against his protectiveness. She'd blow up at Josh and he'd blow up at me and everything would go to shit. It'd be skinny-dipping at the Holler all over again with me caught in the middle trying to keep them both happy.

I set my jaw. "No."

"Liar."

This wasn't an argument I could afford to lose, and I refused to back down. "It's because of me. Because I care about you, and I don't want to hurt you."

"Then don't hurt me."

She made it sound so simple. As if I was capable of avoiding it. Even though she, I, and her brother all knew damn well I wasn't.

I jerked my head back and forth as I shuffled backward another step. "I don't want to do this with you." The words tasted sour and corrosive as they came out of my mouth, but I made myself keep going. "We're friends, Andie. That's all."

She only betrayed the barest hint of a flinch, but it was like a knife stabbing right into my chest. "You said we were family."

"We are." My voice shook a little, and I dug my fingernails

into my palms. "That's why I can't do this. I'm not going to use you for casual sex. And I don't want anything more than that—from anyone." I forced all the conviction I could muster into the last sentence, hoping she'd believe the whopping fucking lie I'd just told her.

She didn't say anything. Although she was trying not to show it, I could tell I'd hurt her feelings. She had every right to be pissed at me. I'd initiated the kiss, and not only welcomed her response, but done my own share of escalating.

And now I was rejecting her after leading her on like a complete asshole. The only thing working in my favor was my own reputation. She already knew what a shitheel I was when it came to women, so she shouldn't be all that surprised.

I just had to hope I hadn't ruined everything. That she'd be able to forgive me so we could move past this and get back to the way things were before I'd stuck my damn tongue in her mouth.

I made a show of glancing at the clock on the microwave and cleared my throat. "Speaking of...I've actually got to go."

That snapped her out of her frozen silence real quick. "Are you shitting me?"

"I've got plans."

"With a woman?" Her eyes blazed with white-hot anger, but beneath it I saw an unmistakable flicker of hurt.

An oily coil of shame crept up my spine, and I cast my eyes down at the floor. "Yeah."

"You're really going to kiss me like that and then walk out of here to meet up with another woman?"

Lifting my eyes to hers, I forced a steadiness I didn't feel into my voice. "I am, yeah. That's why you don't want to go there with me. Because this is who I am."

Before she could say anything else, I crossed to the door and pulled it open, pausing on the threshold without looking back at her. "For whatever it's worth, I really am sorry. I wish I could be something other than what I am, but we're both stuck with me as is."

I let the screen door slam behind me as I walked away from her house.

———

I DIDN'T HAVE a date tonight.

Obviously.

That had been a lie. A gross one that I regretted. But it had sent the message I needed Andie to receive.

Loud and clear.

There was no chance of her ever kissing me again. That was what I'd wanted. But goddamn, it hurt.

After I left Andie, I drove straight to Tanner's place. He took one look at me and pulled out his best bottle of whiskey. While he poured two glasses of WhistlePig, I unloaded the sorry tale of my enormous fuckup and the events that had led up to it. The only part I kept to myself was Dad's involvement in Andie's HOA troubles. My mood was bad enough already without turning this into another bitch session about our father.

"So let me make sure I'm getting this right," Tanner said when I'd finished. "You finally worked up the courage to kiss the girl you've been in love with since forever...and then immediately walked out on her after making up a lie about having a date with another woman?"

"That pretty much covers it, yeah." I knocked back another mouthful of his very fine whiskey and leaned forward to refill my glass.

Tanner rubbed his forehead. "Jesus, Wyatt. You've made a lot of bad decisions in your life, but this time you've reached breathtaking new heights of foolery."

I threw myself back against his couch and splayed my legs

out, resting my whiskey glass on my knee. "Worse than when I painted a dick on Principal Whitmeyer's car?" That particular stunt had gotten me suspended for two weeks and kicked off the baseball team, but it was only one of the many self-destructive choices I'd made over the years.

"Maybe, yeah."

I took another drink, relishing the pain as it burned its way down my throat. "What was I supposed to do?"

"I don't know, how about just tell Andie how you feel about her?"

I barked out a laugh. "Sure. And ruin my oldest friendship? Sounds like a great plan."

"At least tell her the truth instead of a lie. Don't you owe her that much?"

I did, but I was too much of a coward to do what was right when an easier path presented itself—one that would get the job done decisively and with a lot less arguing. If I'd told Andie the truth—that Josh was the reason I'd slammed on the brakes —she wouldn't have let it lie. She'd have tried to talk me out of my reservations.

And I would have let her.

I shook my head, staring into my glass. "It wouldn't have worked."

"Maybe together you could have figured out a way to make it work."

"There's no making it work. On this particular issue, neither Andie or Josh are prone to being reasonable." My mouth twisted into a dark smile. "You know how siblings can get about stuff."

"So what?" Tanner said. "Maybe it's messy and painful for a while. But Josh won't stay mad at you forever. He'll get over it once you show him you know how to treat Andie right."

That was half the problem right there. When had I ever treated a woman right in my life? I wanted to believe I'd treat

Andie better, but what if I didn't know how? I couldn't even blame Josh for not wanting me dating his sister. Not with my track record.

I swallowed around the knot in my throat and made a face. "It smells like cat piss in here."

"Radagast has another kidney infection."

I glanced around, but didn't see Tanner's big old brown tabby anywhere. Usually he'd be trying to climb into my lap by now. "Where is he?"

"Probably asleep on my bed. The antibiotics make him nauseous."

"Is he okay?" I asked, but what I was really asking was if Tanner was okay. He'd had that cat for ten years. Our dad was allergic to cats, so we'd never been able to have one growing up. The first thing Tanner did when he got his own place, even before he bought himself a couch or a bed, was go to the local shelter and pick out a cat to bring home.

"He's a sixteen-year-old cat in renal failure, so no, not really." Tanner took a drink of his whiskey and shrugged. "But he's still got a few more good years left, hopefully."

"I'm sorry," I said, knowing it was going to tear him up when Radagast finally gave up the ghost.

He shook his head at me. "Don't change the subject. We were talking about you and Andie. You love her, don't you?"

I didn't have an easy answer to that. My feelings for Andie were too deep and tangled. I loved her as a friend, absolutely. And I fantasized about loving her as more than a friend. But I couldn't separate the two enough to know if I was *in* love with her. I'd never fallen in love before, so I had no idea what it was supposed to feel like.

"That doesn't mean I can actually pull off a relationship," I said, dodging his question. I scrubbed at my face and downed another mouthful of whiskey. "My track record with commitment doesn't speak in my favor."

"That's because you've never been in a relationship with a woman you actually cared about. It'll be different with Andie."

"You can't know that. I sure as hell don't."

"Love doesn't come with guarantees, Wyatt. You have to take a risk to reap the rewards."

"I can't." There was too much at stake. My knuckles whitened as I squeezed my fingers around the glass. "I can't lose her. And I can't lose Josh."

"You won't." Tanner leaned forward to grab the whiskey bottle off the table and refilled both our glasses. Neither of us would say it, but we both knew why I was so afraid of losing the people I cared about. He didn't need to point out that I hadn't let anyone new get close to me since we'd lost our mom.

She was diagnosed with breast cancer when I was nine and Tanner was eleven. She fought it for more than a year, but in the end all the surgeries and treatments hadn't been enough to save her. Six months before she died, our oldest half-brother, Chance —Brady's twin—was killed in a car accident. A few months after that, Brady left town and I never heard from him again—except for what I read in *Rolling Stone* after he got famous.

To call it the worst year of my life would be an understatement. I'd lost a lot of people who mattered to me in a short span of time. Our mom had been the glue that made our family a family, and without her it all felt flimsy and impermanent. Dad had pursued his own method of dealing with his grief—he married Heather just six months after my mom died, and Cody was born eight months later—leaving me and Tanner to cope mostly on our own. Thank god for Ryan, who'd done his best to hold the three of us together as stubbornly as our mom had before she got sick.

But ever since, I'd avoided close relationships. Friends, girlfriends, didn't matter. I kept them all at a safe distance. I became good-time Wyatt, because everyone liked having that guy around. Fun, irresponsible, charming, unreliable Wyatt. The guy who worked hard to get people to like him, then ghosted before anyone could like him too much. Because if I let anyone get close enough to see the real me, they might decide it wasn't worth sticking around. Always leave them wanting, that was my strategy. Better to leave than be left.

The only people who knew the real me were the ones who'd been there when my world fell apart. Tanner, Ryan, Josh, Andie —they'd all been grandfathered in.

I couldn't afford to lose any of them. I wouldn't let that happen. Not if I could help it.

"You need to have a little faith in people," Tanner said. "I think you should be straight with Andie about everything. She's a smart woman. Let her make her own decision."

"Tell me again how it went when you told Lucy you loved her?" The alcohol was making me sulky and mean, or I wouldn't have thrown his ex in his face. The one he still hadn't gotten over.

"Low blow," he shot back, frowning at me. "And totally different. You've been friends with Andie for most of your life. I'd only known Lucy for a little while."

And yet, he'd known her well enough to think he was in love with her, which showed just how different the two of us were. I kept everyone at arm's length, but Tanner fell in love fast and hard—way too fast and way too hard—which meant he'd had his heart broken a lot.

You had to hand it to the guy though, at least he practiced what he preached. He didn't hold back or bottle his feelings up. No, he'd courageously dropped the L bomb on Lucy after just a few weeks.

She'd run screaming for the hills, of course, leaving Tanner brokenhearted. Not that I could blame her. I'd have done the same thing in her shoes.

But at least Tanner wasn't a coward like me.

I leaned forward to set my drink down and propped my elbows on my knees, raking my fingers through my hair. "Fuck. I really screwed up tonight."

"All life is just a progression toward, and then a recession from, one phrase – 'I love you.'" When I swiveled my head toward him, he shrugged. "F. Scott Fitzgerald wrote that."

I ignored the aptness of the quote. "What if Andie's so pissed she can't move past this?"

"She's put up with your ass for this long."

I rubbed my eyes with the heels of my hands as I thought about tomorrow, and how I was going to have to go back there and face her. I didn't have a choice. Not if I wanted to save our friendship. I'd already screwed up enough by running out on her tonight. I wasn't going to bail on my commitment to help her on top of that.

Tomorrow I'd go back and try to fix what I'd broken between us while I finished the repairs to her house. At least I had that going for me. She needed me right now, so she probably wouldn't throw me off her property.

Andie was almost as good at holding a grudge as her brother, but I could wait her out. I'd just keep showing up and acting like nothing had changed until I'd worn her down.

What other choice did I have?

Take Tanner's advice? Tell her I love her, ruin my oldest friendship, then probably screw everything up with Andie anyway?

Pass.

I poured more whiskey into my glass and knocked the whole thing back. Tomorrow I'd face the music. Tonight I just wanted to be numb.

10

ANDIE

How fucking dare he kiss me like that and then head straight into the arms of another woman?

I couldn't decide if I was more pissed off or embarrassed. But really what I was, most of all, was hurt.

Wyatt had looked me right in the eyes and said he didn't want me. I'd let myself be vulnerable for one miserable moment —let myself believe that kiss might actually mean something— and I'd gotten kicked right in the teeth.

The annoying thing was, I couldn't even pretend to be shocked. It wasn't like I didn't know exactly who Wyatt King had always been. What had I expected? That he'd change his fickle, womanizing ways just for me? That I was special?

I was almost as mad at myself as I was at him. I'd let hope creep in, when I should have known better. I'd fallen prey to my own baser instincts as much as I'd let myself be fooled by his. Because I'd wanted to feel Wyatt's lips on mine, I'd thrown sense out the window.

If anything, it was worse now that I knew exactly what I was missing out on. Before last night, I could only imagine what kind of kisser Wyatt was. But now I knew precisely, because he'd given me the best kiss of my life.

Nothing else I'd ever experienced had come close to feeling like that. When he'd grabbed me and slanted his mouth over mine, it had hit me like a chemical reaction. Instant combustion. Friction and heat igniting the oxygen between us, generating more energy than one simple kiss had been able to contain.

My nerves were still vibrating with it this morning. That one damn kiss had left me weak and desperate for more, with an ache of incompleteness I hadn't been able to shake since he'd walked away.

How was I supposed to come back from that? How was I going to face him again without launching myself at him to finish what he'd started?

I'd have to figure it out, because that was one thing I would absolutely not be doing. No matter how badly I wanted to. Wyatt King was not getting a second chance to play me for a sucker. Fool me once, fuck you forever. That had always been my philosophy.

Only...I couldn't exactly cut Wyatt out of my life. There were too many ties binding us together. My brother, my aunt Birdie, my parents. A lifetime of friendship and shared memories. Even as mad as I was, I knew I wouldn't be able to stop caring about him. He'd been right about one thing. We were family.

I could limit my exposure though. Put up some defensive walls that were frankly long overdue. Stop torturing myself over someone who would never want me.

Unfortunately, I still needed his help with the house. There was no getting around that. I hated being dependent on anyone, ever, but I especially hated that I needed Wyatt so much right now, when I'd be better off enforcing more distance between us.

Speaking of which, I was starting to worry he might ghost on me completely after last night. It was almost eight thirty and there was still no sign of him. If he decided to leave me in the lurch, I was completely screwed.

Well, not completely. He'd done some of the work already. What was left was too much for me to finish on my own, especially when I didn't have enough vacation saved up to take time off work. But I could work on it myself this weekend. If Wyatt didn't come back by Monday, then I could try to get a home equity loan and hire someone to finish the rest. Not by the deadline probably, but I could talk to the HOA and ask for more time. Hopefully they'd give it to me, because I sure wouldn't be able to get a loan with a lien on the house.

I gave up waiting on Wyatt and went outside to attack the thicket of weeds growing along the back fence. It was pretty therapeutic, actually, snipping off the thick stalks and hacking at the roots, taking out my violent impulses on the vegetation and imagining it was Wyatt's face.

I'd been at it about twenty minutes when I finally heard his truck pull into the driveway. Instead of going to greet him like I normally would, I kept on working.

Yes, I was sulking. But I was also protecting myself. And honoring his wishes. He'd made it clear that we'd crossed a line last night that he wasn't comfortable crossing with me. The best way to keep it from happening again was to keep my distance. If he had anything else to say, he could come and find me.

Apparently he didn't have anything to say, because he still hadn't sought me out thirty minutes later when I finished clearing out the weeds. Fine. Two could play that game. It didn't bother me.

Except here I was, totally fucking bothered.

Angrily, I gathered up all the weeds to tie them into a bundle. The sky had clouded over while I'd been working, which had cooled things off a little. But the humidity was so thick it made it hard to breathe. I felt like my lungs weren't getting enough oxygen.

I was so intent on the work, I didn't notice Wyatt had approached until I turned around and nearly walked right into him. "Shit," I muttered, jumping back.

"Sorry." He held up his hands in a conciliatory gesture.

As we eyed each other I took some petty pleasure in the fact that he looked like crap. Unhappy lines creased his face as he shuffled his feet in front of me. He had the strained look of someone fighting a hangover and the bleary, hollowed eyes of sleeplessness.

Although, for all I knew it was because he'd had such a great time last night and partied too hard with whatever woman he'd chosen over me. A fresh pulse of anger rose in my blood, and I dodged around him to walk away.

"Andie, wait." His hand caught me by the arm, setting off sparks of longing everywhere his fingers touched my skin. "We should probably talk about last night."

I didn't look at him, but I didn't pull out of his grasp either. I couldn't make myself do it. I craved his touch too much. "What's to talk about? You made your position perfectly clear."

He dropped his hand, leaving a prickly impression behind on my arm. "You're mad."

"No shit." A drop of rain hit my face, and I looked up at the sky. The clouds overhead were dark and threatening, matching my mood.

"I meant it when I said I cared about you."

"Great." It shouldn't feel like a consolation prize, but it did.

"I'm really sorry about what happened."

I rounded on him, and my stomach churned when he shrank back from me. "Which part? The part where you kissed me, the part where you tried to take it back, or the part where you walked out right afterward to spend the night with another woman?"

"All of it. I didn't mean to hurt you."

"You don't have to mean it to do it." Another raindrop hit my arm, sending a cold shiver over the back of my neck, and I reached down to wipe it away.

"I don't want to lose you over this." The catch in his voice made me look up at him.

His expression was so anguished it drained most of the anger out of me. Fighting with him wouldn't change anything. It couldn't make him want me the way I wanted him. I was hurt and sad and tired of feeling that way, but I didn't want to lose his friendship either.

"I'm not going anywhere," I told him. "Are you?"

"No."

Even though I was still smarting from his rejection, I believed him. I believed that he cared about me and wanted to stay friends. That was all he'd ever be able to offer me, but it wasn't nothing. It was more than most people ever got of Wyatt King.

"Fine," I said. "All the same, it's probably best if we give each other a little extra space for a while."

His hangdog look got a little more hangdog, but he didn't argue. "I can keep working on the house though, right?"

The raindrops were falling with more urgency now, peppering my arms and face as I nodded. "I hope so. I can't do it without you."

"You don't have to. I promised I'd take care of it and I will." He wiped the rain off his face and glanced up at the sky.

My eyes followed his, and I frowned at the storm cloud overhead.

Wyatt looked back down at me and opened his mouth to speak, but before he could say anything the skies opened up and unleashed a deluge on our heads.

A ndie and I made a run for the back porch when the skies opened up. Once we were under cover, I turned and looked out at the yard, wiping the water off my face. The rain was pouring down in buckets, pockmarking the ground and collecting in the low spots already, forming muddy pools.

"So much for getting any work done this morning."

"Maybe it won't last long." She didn't sound hopeful.

"Maybe." I wasn't optimistic either. The dark clouds stretched as far as I could see in every direction.

A gust of wind blew the rain sideways onto the porch, driving us inside the house for shelter. Once we had the door closed, Andie grabbed a couple of dish towels and tossed me one to dry myself off with.

I wasn't thrilled about her request for space, but I could understand her need for it. Reluctantly, I might even be willing to admit it was the best thing for both of us right now. I couldn't risk a repeat of last night, and the closer I was to Andie, the greater chance there was that I'd slip up and act on my feelings for her again.

As I dried the rain off my arms, my eyes slid over to her and I caught her staring at me. Not in the angry way she'd been glaring at me a few minutes ago, but with a raw, pained expression that made my mouth go dry as she jerked her gaze away from me.

"Do you have any nine-volt batteries?" I asked, desperate for something to do to keep me busy.

Frowning in confusion, she swiveled her head back toward me. "Why?"

"Since I'm here, I thought I might as well check all your smoke detectors and change the batteries."

Andie yanked open a kitchen drawer and grabbed a package of batteries. "Knock yourself out." She slapped them into my hand and stalked out of the kitchen. "I've got laundry to fold."

Still pretty pissed at me, then. Cool.

After fetching Andie's stepladder out of the laundry room, I got to work on the smoke detectors. She walked past me carrying a laundry basket while I was fiddling with the one in the living room and neither of us said a word. Once I'd finished all the downstairs rooms, I carried the ladder up to the second floor. While I was unscrewing the smoke detector in the hallway, Andie edged around me and went back into her room without a word. I finished up and went into the guest room next, figuring I'd stay out of her hair as long as possible by saving her bedroom for last.

This guest room didn't see much use. Andie had converted the other spare bedroom into a sort of workshop for her craft projects, but this one was mostly just storage. I shoved a few boxes out of the way to make room for the stepladder and climbed up to reach the smoke detector. While I was up there I noticed the ladder was a little wobbly, as if the floor underneath was uneven. So when I finished putting in a new battery, I squatted down to examine the floorboards.

One of them was definitely loose. I pulled a screwdriver out of my tool belt and gently prodded at the edges of the board. It popped right out of place with barely any pressure, and I realized all the nails must have come out.

Or been removed on purpose.

There was something down there, in the space underneath the floor. Shoved off to one side, nearly out of sight, were some kind of papers. I reached my hand in the narrow gap between the floorboards and drew out a bundle of old letters tied up with a faded pink ribbon.

Sitting back on my haunches, I blew the debris off them and tried to make out the faded cursive writing. They were all addressed to a Miss Lillian Autry, which I remembered was the maiden name of Andie's grandmother who'd left her this house. I flipped through a few of them as I got to my feet, but they were all addressed the same, in the same handwriting, with no return address on the envelopes.

"Hey, Andie?" I called out as I wandered out of the guest room.

"In here," she said from her bedroom.

When I reached the doorway of her room, the familiar scent hit me square in the gut—a mix of her honeysuckle shampoo and the sweet, clean smell of her skin that took me right back to last night when I'd tasted her on my tongue.

"What is it?" She was sitting on the bed with stacks of folded laundry around her.

I held out the letters as I came toward her. "I found these under the floor in the guest room."

She took them from me and frowned at the handwriting. "That's my grandmother's name." She flipped through them, then slipped the top envelope out of the bundle. Being careful of the old, fragile paper, she slid the letter out and unfolded it.

I watched, curious, as her eyes skimmed over it and the corners of her lips curved. "It's a love letter."

"To your grandmother?"

"Listen to this: *My dearest Lillian, What can I say after the precious gift you gave me last night? I am shamelessly in your thrall. From this day forward, I exist only to give you pleasure and draw forth more of those little moans and quivers that gave me so much joy.*"

"Whoa." I grinned as I sank down on the corner of the mattress. "That's kind of racy."

"I know, right?" She grinned back at me before looking down at the letter again. *"Your body is my home, my harbor, my sanctuary, and I intend to lavish every inch of it with the care and attention it deserves when next we are able to come together."*

I blew out a breath. "Wow."

Andie's eyes were bright and amused. "I'm both impressed and grossed out."

"Respect to your grandad. Dude clearly had some serious game."

"I guess this helps explain how my grandparents stayed together for sixty years. They were high school sweethearts, only sixteen when they started going steady. My grandfather said it was love at first sight. He always used to tell me that the first time he laid eyes on my grandmother he knew she was the girl he wanted to marry. Can you imagine?"

"Not really." I swallowed a lump in my throat, thinking of the wish I'd made at almost the same age. The night Andie had fallen asleep next to me under the stars, and I'd wished I could marry her one day. And how I'd never felt that way about anyone else. Not once, in all the years since.

She flipped the letter over and kept reading. *"I want to be with you, now and always. My heart burns for you. My body aches for you. My soul belongs to you."* Andie laughed as she looked up from the letter. "I never realized my pawpaw had such a flair for melodrama."

"I think it's sweet." I'd never sent anyone a letter like that in my life. There was only one woman who'd ever inspired anything approaching that sort of devotion in me, and she was sitting right next to me, pissed because I hadn't been able to tell her honestly how I felt.

The closest I'd ever come was the songs I'd written, and I wasn't sure I'd ever find the courage to play them for anyone.

Andie arched an eyebrow at me. "I thought you were allergic to romance."

My throat grew tight, and I dropped my eyes to my lap. "Just because it's not for me doesn't mean I can't be happy for other people."

"Hmm."

When I glanced up again, Andie was frowning at the letter. "What?"

"Can you read those initials in the signature?" She thrust the letter at me.

I squinted at the old-fashioned writing. The letter had been signed only with a pair of initials. "HB? Yeah, that's an H. It's HB."

"Well, that's disconcerting."

"Why?" I handed the letter back to her.

She stared at it again, frowning. "Because my grandfather's name was Joe Fishbaugh." Her eyes lifted to mine. "He didn't write this letter."

12

ANDIE

I couldn't stop reading those damn letters Wyatt had found. The rain had long since stopped and he'd gone back to work outside, but I was still right where he'd left me.

I'd been sitting on the floor of my bedroom for the last two hours poring over every one of the love letters my grandmother's secret suitor had written her. Something about them had me captivated. Maybe it was the outpouring of emotion and stark longing scrawled across the pages, or the apparently illicit nature of their relationship. Or maybe it was just the mystery of it all.

Who had written these letters to my grandmother while she was supposedly dating the man she would go on to spend the rest of her life with? What had happened to him? What had happened to *them*?

It was clear from the multiple references to their trysts that it hadn't been a one-sided infatuation. My unmarried eighteen-year-old grandmother had met up with this mystery man repeatedly to engage in behavior that would have been seriously scandalous at the time. Based on the dates, their affair took place in the year before she married my grandfather—two years after they allegedly met and fell in love. And yet there was no mention of him at all.

All those stories my grandfather told me about their love at first sight had begun to feel like lies. But had he been lying to me or had my grandmother lied to him?

On some level I knew it didn't matter. They were all long gone. For better or worse, the story of their lives had reached its conclusion before I'd ever laid eyes on these letters. Whatever choices they'd made or twists of fate had intervened to determine their future were the reason I was alive today. The words on these pages didn't have the power to change anything about the past.

But I couldn't put them down. The more I read, the more invested I became in this man who'd obviously loved my grandmother. He wasn't just some fly-by-night lay. I only had his side of their correspondence, but based on his references to her letters and their conversations when they were together, she'd had some pretty serious feelings for him too.

My fingers shook with eagerness as I opened the very last letter in the bundle. I hoped it would explain what had happened between them and why two people so obviously in love hadn't ended up together. If the answer wasn't in this letter, I'd probably never know.

My dearest, sweetest, most precious Lillian,

You've made your wishes clear, and I will not stand in opposition to your happiness. My soul is shattered by the prospect of a life without you, the only woman I have ever loved, but I know I must give you up.

How can I say goodbye to a joy such as the one we've shared? The answer is that I cannot, and will not. Though I bid farewell to you and vow never to burden you with my company in the future, I will carry my devotion to the very end of my days.

The moments we shared will live forever in my heart. The memory of your soft sighs, tender kisses, and eager caresses will sing me to sleep every night that I draw breath. No other woman will ever be able to match you or replace you in my affections. You will always be the first, the best, the only girl for me. Though you may forget me and offer your heart to another, know that you will remain my dearest, truest love.

My life. My world. My Lillian.

Wretchedly and forever yours,
  HB

My chest hitched as I reached the end of the letter. The writing blurred, and I rubbed away the inexplicable tears that had filled my eyes.

I hadn't learned anything except that my grandmother had abruptly ended the relationship for reasons I'd never find out. After everything I'd read, all the emotions spilled out across these brittle, yellowing pages, I wanted more closure than this.

I wasn't usually a crier, but I couldn't seem to hold myself in check. Whoever the man was who'd written these agonized, impassioned words, he'd reached out of the past and touched some kind of nerve. I couldn't stop thinking about him, and how miserable he'd sounded, and how sad it all was. I couldn't stop hurting for him and my grandmother and the life they never got to have.

What the hell was the matter with me?

I never cried like this. And where was my allegiance to my grandfather, who I'd known and loved, and who had loved my grandmother for most of his life? I felt like I was losing my mind, bawling over sixty-year-old letters from a total stranger.

It was more than just the letters though. They'd been the catalyst, but now that the floodgates were open, the emotions I'd been tamping down for the last few weeks were bubbling up and erupting all over me. The stress over the house situation, the injustice of it, and my own impotence and inability to solve the problem on my own. My frustration with Wyatt. My unavoidable dependence on him after his rejection of me. The unrequited feelings I was afraid I'd never be able to shake.

Feelings that weren't so different than the author of these letters had described at the loss of his first and only love.

It was all just too much. Long-overdue sobs tore their way out of my throat. Apparently I was being punished for trying to hold my shit together, because I couldn't stop crying now that I'd started. Tears streaked down my face unchecked, and my whole body shook with every painful breath I heaved into my lungs.

"Andie?"

I looked up and saw Wyatt standing in the doorway, his expression bewildered and alarmed.

A fresh sob tore out of me at the sight of him. I didn't want him to see me like this. I didn't want my weakness on display in front of the man who'd already left a giant crack in my defenses. I shook my head and buried my head against my knees.

I knew I couldn't make him go away, but I couldn't stand to face him.

13

WYATT

I'd never seen Andie cry before. Not once in all the years I'd known her. Not even when she was a little kid.

She'd always been tough as nails. Seemingly immune to pain. Even that time she'd fallen out of the big tree on the farm and cracked her head open, she hadn't shed a single tear. I'd been scared shitless because there was so much blood, and she'd just sat there making jokes while Josh tried to hold her scalp together with his bare hands.

I had no clue what had made her cry like this, but it scared me even more than when she fell out of that tree. Instinct took over and I propelled myself at her, kneeling on the floor to pull her against my chest. I didn't know what else to do, so I held her, rocking her and stroking her hair as her body shook in my arms.

Eventually her heaving breaths eased, and her sobs quieted down to sniffles. She pushed out of my arms and turned her face away. "That was embarrassing," she muttered as she wiped away her tears.

"What happened?" My throat was so tight I sounded like the one who'd been sobbing instead of Andie.

"Nothing." She pulled her legs up underneath her. "Nothing at all."

Worry made me impatient, causing my words to come out sharper than I intended. "*Something* happened to make you cry."

She shook her head. "It's stupid. I was just reading those letters."

"Was there something upsetting in them?"

I didn't understand how a bunch of old love letters could have made her this upset. So what if her grandmother had once had a boyfriend on the side? Did it matter anymore?

"No, not really." She sniffled and rubbed her eyes. "Just more of the same stuff I read out loud to you."

"Andie." I reached for her face and turned it toward me.

Her eyelashes lowered as she ducked her head. "Don't look at me. I'm all gross and snotty."

"You always look beautiful." The words slipped out of me before I could think about what I was saying.

Surprise flashed across her expression as she lifted her eyes to mine.

I hadn't meant to say that out loud, but now that I had, I didn't want to take it back. How could I? She was the most beautiful person I'd ever known. My thumb stroked over her cheek, wiping away some of the wetness. "It's gonna take a lot more than bodily fluids to gross me out."

Her lips curved as she let out a soft huff of amusement.

I was so relieved to see her smiling that I bent my head and kissed away a tear inching its way toward her jaw. She stiffened, sucking in a sharp breath as my lips touched her cheek, but she didn't pull away.

Neither did I. Instead, I let my lips linger there for a moment before I found another tear to kiss away below her eye. Her eyelashes fluttered against my lips, and I moved higher, kissing her forehead before gazing into her eyes.

"Tell me why you were crying."

She swallowed and looked away. I let her go, dropping my hand from her face as she swiveled it away from me.

"It was the last letter." She picked up a page lying on the floor and passed it to me.

I skimmed it, then went back and read it again more carefully. After I'd finished my second read, my gut clenching at all the parts that hit way too close to home for me, I turned to her with a frown.

"Why did this make you cry?"

It was desperately sad, there was no denying that, but it shouldn't have been enough to get this kind of reaction out of Andie. She hadn't even cried at *Toy Story 3*, for Christ's sake.

"Because they obviously loved each other and they didn't end up together. It's such a fucking waste." She waved her hand at the stack of letters on the floor. "There's like twenty letters here describing in vivid detail exactly how devoted they were to each other, and it all came to nothing. It's not fair."

She blinked like she might start crying again, and I wrapped my arm around her shoulders, pulling her against my chest.

"I have a feeling this is about more than just that letter."

"I guess." Her fingers curled into the front of my shirt, which was soaked with her tears. "It's everything else too. The stuff with the house and..."

"And?" I prompted quietly when she didn't finish.

"And you, I guess." Her voice sounded heartbreakingly small for someone I'd always considered impossibly strong.

Hating myself for hurting her, I squeezed her shoulder and pressed my face into her honeysuckle-scented hair. Neither of us moved or spoke. We just sat there like that, leaning against each other. Holding on to each other.

I got the sense she was waiting for me to say something. Or do something.

So I did.

"I lied before," I admitted.

I felt her go rigid in my arms. "About what?"

"About having a date last night." I winced as shame twisted inside me. "After I left here I went to Tanner's and drank most of a bottle of whiskey."

She lifted her head to look at me. "Why did you lie?"

I swallowed, quailing under the weight of her regard. But now that I'd started this I felt obliged to finish it. Tanner was right. I owed Andie the truth. "Because I was afraid."

"Of what?"

My tongue shot out to lick my lips, tasting salt from her tears. It gave me the push I needed to force the words out. "Of the way I feel about you, and what'll happen if I let myself act on it."

"What will happen?" Her eyes bored into mine, dark and challenging.

"Your brother will never forgive me."

The way Andie's lips pressed together, I could tell she was pissed. But even worse than that: she was disappointed in me.

I leaned back against the bed and raked a hand through my hair. "Do you have any idea how fucking hard it's been? How much willpower it's taken to keep my hands off you, when all I want to do is touch you?"

"Yes."

With that one word, spoken on a shaky exhalation, my world tilted off its axis.

It shocked me into seeing the truth I'd blinded myself to, even though it had been right in front of my face all this time. I hadn't let myself acknowledge it, because if I ever did, there'd be no turning back.

Andie wanted me as much as I wanted her.

In case the point needed further confirmation, she swung her leg over my thighs and climbed into my lap.

My vision whited out as her soft curves settled against my growing hard-on. "Andie," I bit out in a strained voice, screwing my eyes shut.

"What?"

I'd meant to warn her to knock it off, but I couldn't make myself say the words. I didn't want her to knock it off. I wanted her to do it some more.

Her fingers ghosted over my face, exploring the stubble on my jaw and sending tingles shooting down my spine. The whisper of her breath warmed my lips, and I knew her mouth was dangerously close to mine.

I was afraid to open my eyes and look at her. Every nerve ending in my body was standing at attention, every muscle tensed in a state of hypervigilance. My hands ached to touch her, to reach up and explore the curves balanced in my lap, but I balled them into fists, refusing to let them have their way.

"Do you want me?" she asked, and a shudder rippled through me.

When I didn't answer fast enough, she squirmed in my lap, driving me to hiss out a tortured "Yesss."

"Then say it." Her voice was pitched so low I felt it all the way down in my balls. "Say you want me."

I opened my eyes finally and looked into her dark, steady gaze. Her face was flushed and her luscious lips parted. Begging to be kissed.

Who was I to disappoint her?

I reached up and touched her face, smiling at the way it made her lashes flutter. A surge of warmth swept through me, softer and sweeter than the sharp heat rising in my blood.

"I want you," I told her, letting the words set me free. "I've always wanted you."

14

ANDIE

A supernova of relief tore through my chest when Wyatt said the words I'd been longing to hear.

I want you. I've always wanted you.

The hunger in his eyes should have been enough to tell me the truth, but I'd needed to actually hear him say the words with his whole chest.

Even now that he'd admitted it, I hesitated. He'd been the one holding back all this time. Denying himself. Denying both of us. I didn't want to drag him into this. I wanted him to make the choice himself.

Finally. For once. I needed him to choose *me*.

With my gaze locked on his, I said, "Prove it."

The corner of his mouth twitched as his eyes went dusky. He dragged his thumb across my lower lip, and dear god, it took every ounce of my restraint not to throw myself at him.

Slowly, his hand slid around the nape of my neck, sending goose bumps shimmering down my arms. His fingers tightened and he pulled me closer. Close enough for our lips to touch, but just barely. A featherlight graze and nothing more.

My lungs burned with breathless anticipation as we hovered

on the precipice of a kiss for what felt like forever. Seconds, minutes, hours, eternity. When he squeezed the back of my neck, I let out a needy, impatient whimper.

His mouth pulled into a smile as he finally pressed it against mine.

A real kiss, at last. But a chaste one. Achingly careful. His lips doted on me like I was something cherished and special. A pleasure too precious to hurry.

But god, how I wanted him to hurry. I needed him, and I'd waited so long already. Liquid heat pooled between my legs, and I whimpered again.

He pulled back just enough to look at me, his eyes warm and crinkling. "You have to say it too." His breath teased my lips, which itched for another kiss. "Tell me you want me. I want to hear you say it too." The rough edge in his voice shivered through me, sending all the breath rushing out of my lungs.

I squirmed, feeling myself blush, and his jaw tightened as his erection twitched beneath me. I laid my palms on his chest and felt his muscles grow taut with anticipation. Felt the heat rising off his skin through his T-shirt. Felt his heart racing. For *me*.

"I want you. You have no idea how bad."

His lips crashed against mine in a bruising kiss, all chasteness and restraint forgotten. I melted against him as his tongue pushed inside my mouth, urging me to open wider as he delved deeper. The intensity of it startled a moan out of me, which inspired him to kiss me harder.

As our mouths slanted together, I pressed my breasts against his chest, craving more closeness. I couldn't get enough of him, of having him like this, open to me and welcoming. Our bodies locked together, his hands pulling me against him, the hardness in his jeans touching me exactly where I'd always ached to feel him.

My brain was still trying to catch up to the current reality and adjust to this new thing blooming between us. This was *Wyatt*—flirty, unattainable, beautiful Wyatt. The boy I'd wanted to kiss my whole life. But it was also my friend Wyatt—teasing, competitive, protective, and loyal. It was difficult to reconcile the two sides of him I knew with the way he was kissing me right now.

I was the one who pulled back first, and he made a noise of protest when we broke apart, a small, frustrated grunt that I took as a positive sign. Still, I braced myself, half expecting him to push me away again. Change his mind and withdraw from me the way he'd done before.

But no.

He did the opposite.

His hands squeezed my waist possessively, as if he were afraid I'd try to scoot away, and he looked at me, his blue eyes a soothing turquoise as they searched my face. My lips curved involuntarily, and Wyatt's answering smile, so bright and joyful, filled me with giddiness.

He touched a callused fingertip to my lips. "You," he said, like he couldn't believe it either, like he was checking to see if I was real, and we both smiled even wider as relief gusted out of us in twin sighs of happiness. His finger traced my lower lip, then gently nudged my chin to the side. "I just want to..." He bent his head and pressed his lips to my throat below my ear. "Taste you," he murmured, his breath a warm caress. "Right here."

I shivered when his tongue touched my skin, and I heard his breath catch as my hips rocked against him. His hand curled around the back of my neck as he moved up to my ear, nuzzling it gently before exploring the hollow beneath my jaw. Dragging his lips over the sensitive skin, his stubble leaving a trail of delicious prickles.

"I have a question," I said and felt his teeth graze my throat.

"Of course you do."

"Define always."

He pulled his head back, blinking in half-lidded bemusement. "What?"

"You said you've always wanted me. For how long exactly?"

His fingers tightened on the back of my neck, and he pulled me toward him, pressing a kiss to my cheekbone before resting his forehead against my temple. "I'm embarrassed to tell you."

"Why?"

"Because."

When he didn't follow that up with an actual explanation, I pulled back to look at him. "Wyatt?"

His arms tightened around me, and he buried his face in my neck. "Since I was seventeen."

The words came out muffled, and I blinked, trying to figure out if I'd heard him right.

He lifted his head when I didn't respond, his brow creasing with uncertainty. "Say something."

"Are you serious? Since high school?"

"Remember that night we watched the meteor shower?"

I nodded, caught by a sense of déjà vu.

"You dozed off and snuggled up to me in your sleep."

"I remember." Boy, did I ever.

"That was when I first realized...when we were lying there under the stars and you had your head on my chest, I felt—I don't know—content, I guess? Peaceful." His head dipped in embarrassment. "It probably sounds dumb, but it was the happiest night of my life up to that point."

My heart squeezed, and I threaded an affectionate hand through his hair. It was the sweetest thing anyone had ever said to me. But it was also a little hard to believe.

"Wyatt, that was forever ago." I realized now why he'd

brought up that night when he was drunk. It wasn't just a random memory. It meant something to him.

"I know," he said in a voice strained by the weight of every one of those years.

"You're saying all this time..." I couldn't even finish the sentence.

"Yes."

I pressed my hand to his face, and his eyes fell closed as he leaned into my touch. So trusting, so sweet, and so dear to me. He looked different like this. More exposed and closer to the surface. A new sense of possessiveness overtook me as I ran my fingers over his chin and traced the hollows below his lips where the stubble was sparser. I bent my head and whispered his name against his lips. They parted for me, his mouth hot as it strained toward mine, his tongue sweeping into my mouth.

I lost myself in kissing him. In being kissed by him. We kissed for a long time, relishing it like teenagers who'd just discovered how much fun kissing could be. Messy. Enthusiastic. Unrestrained. Experimenting with different pressures, different angles. It was so good, kissing him, I didn't ever want it to stop.

But the longer we kissed, the more the ache inside me grew. My fingers had tangled in his gorgeous, thick hair, and I tugged on it, wanting to feel more of him. In response, he dropped his hands to my ass and jerked me hard against him, the hard ridge of his erection pressing into me as his tongue plunged even deeper into my mouth.

Dropping my hands to his chest, I clawed at his shirt, frantic to touch his bare skin and feel it against mine. "Take this off."

He yanked his shirt over his head, exposing his beautiful golden torso. I stared, ogling him in a way I'd always been afraid to let myself do before, enjoying the way his breathing changed under the weight of my undisguised admiration.

"Touch me." His voice simmered with heat, stoking the growing fever inside me. "I want to feel your hands on me."

I didn't need to be asked twice. Wyatt's eyelids fluttered as I laid my palms on his chest again. Smoothing my hands over his skin, I explored the ridges and grooves of his pecs, ran my fingers through his chest hair, and traced the outline of his tattoos. Touching him exactly the way I'd dreamed of touching him.

When my thumbnail grazed his nipple, a tremor shuddered through him like an electric shock, and his hips bucked against me. He surged forward to kiss me again, but I pushed him back against the bed and pulled my own T-shirt off.

His eyes went wide as he drank in the sight of me, even though it was nothing he hadn't seen last night when I'd stripped on the back porch. I was wearing the same style of plain black sports bra, even. But this time he let himself look at me instead of forcing his gaze away.

I loved the feel of his eyes on me. For so long they'd slid right past me, never lingering or paying too much attention. It had taken me years to grow numb to the sting of his casual dismissal. Knowing now that it had been against his will, that he'd had to fight for self-control around me, didn't erase the memory of that rejection.

His attention was laser-focused on me now, and he was seeing every pore, bump, and freckle. I'd never been prone to self-consciousness, but the potency of his regard, so long denied, made me quake a little. As his hands reached out to cradle my rib cage, the rough drag of his calluses sparked on my skin like static electricity. He cupped my breasts through my spandex sports bra, and my breath caught as he grazed my stiff, sensitive nipples.

His eyes jumped to mine. "Can I take this off?"

"Let me." Sports bras were notoriously unsexy to remove,

and I'd learned the hard way not to let a man try to do it for me, unless I wanted to end up twisted like a pretzel with my shoulders bound up and the stupid thing stuck on my head. Hooking my fingers under the elastic band, I pulled it up and shimmied my arms out of the constricting garment, untangling it from my ponytail before tossing it aside.

"God damn," Wyatt breathed when I'd completed my contortions.

He reached for me again, and my eyes fell closed, my head lolling back as he palmed my bare breasts. I bit my lip when he dragged his thumbs across my nipples and trembled when he pinched them experimentally.

"Do you like that?" He increased the pressure, and a moan slipped through my lips. "I'll take that as a yes." His breath seared my chest when he spoke, close but not close enough.

I strained toward him, and his mouth found one of my breasts, his tongue circling my nipple like he was sampling a lollipop. My hips rocked against him of their own accord, making us both groan. I squirmed when he bit me gently, then a little harder, pulses of sharp pleasure shooting through me as he lavished my breasts with attention. Every nip, lick, and squeeze tightening the coil inside me, until it became too much—but also not enough.

Pushing him back against the bed once more, I claimed his mouth with mine, needing to taste him on my tongue again. My hands raked through his hair then dropped down to his chest. My nails dug into his flesh, and he made a low, feral sound in the back of his throat.

"Fuck," he hissed, shuddering when I experimentally dug my nails in even harder.

I pressed my mouth to his ear, gave his earlobe a nip, and said, "Okay."

"Not yet." His fingers tangled in my ponytail, pulling my

head back so he could look me in the eyes. A smile like sin played on his lips, and his voice took on a raw edge. "First, I want to see how many times I can make you come."

A stomach-clenching thrill shot through me, and I nearly bit down on my tongue.

Wyatt grabbed me by the hips, twisting as he tumped me off his lap and sprang to his feet. I stared up at him in surprise and he hauled me to my feet. "These need to come off," he said as he worked open the button of my pants.

I helped him shimmy them down my legs, along with my underwear, but when I tried to reach for his jeans he gave me a warning growl and shoved me backward onto the bed.

I landed on the laundry I'd spent an hour folding that morning, and he smiled as I squirmed to pull a stack of towels out from under my ass. Bending over me, he swept his arm across the bed, sending all the clean laundry tumbling onto the floor.

His St. Christopher medal dangled from his neck, and it brushed against my throat when his mouth covered mine. I closed my eyes, curling my hands in his hair, feeling a moment of tremulous awe as Wyatt's stubble scraped over my skin, his lips and tongue searing a path along my jaw, down my throat, and between my breasts.

But that was nothing compared to the way I felt when he dropped to his knees between my legs.

His arms wrapped around my thighs, and my stomach tightened in nervous anticipation as he yanked me to the edge of the mattress. Gazing at me with the look of a hungry animal, he licked his lips and slowly ran his hands up the inside of my thighs. I tried to hold still as he leaned in, consuming me with his eyes as his fingers inched higher. Slowly spreading me wider. Tearing down the last shreds of my defenses.

"*Wyatt.*" My hands twisted in the quilt as his name shuddered out of me. I'd never been shy about sex or my body, but I wasn't good at letting myself be vulnerable, and there was nothing more vulnerable than my current position. Helpless and gasping, exposed to him completely. Trembling with need.

His gaze met mine, and the strong, familiar connection between us melted away my apprehension. He lifted my legs over his shoulders, and our eyes stayed locked as he slid his fingers through my slick, swollen folds.

My back arched off the bed, but he pinned me in place with a hand on my hip. When he brushed a fingertip against my aching clit, my whole body convulsed. He did it again, his touch cruelly light, and I writhed in sweet misery.

"God, Wyatt, will you just..." I trailed off into a keening moan as he circled my clit, giving me the pressure I craved.

"Does it feel good?" His eyes found mine again. "Do you like it when I touch you?"

"Yes," I gasped, desperate for more pressure, more friction, more of his touch.

"Do you want to feel me inside you?"

"Oh god." I'd never wanted anything more, and I strained against the hand holding me down. "I need it. Please."

"I don't think I've ever heard you beg before. I fucking love seeing you like this."

The way he said it, his voice rough and unexpectedly tender, set off a whirlwind of flutters in my chest, but then he slipped a finger inside me, and my head slammed back against the mattress. "God, yes. Just like that. Don't you dare stop."

"I'm not going to stop," he murmured, rubbing his thumb over my clit as his fingers stroked me inside and out. "I love how wet you are for me. So gorgeous."

My whole body pulsed with white-hot pleasure. I was out of my mind, aching for release as he stroked me faster and harder, the friction almost more than I could stand.

"I love watching you fall apart on my fingers." His voice was breathy and eager. "I want to feel you come on them."

I whimpered as the tension coiled inside me, brutally close to the breaking point. Needing more but too far gone to speak.

"I love the feel of your beautiful pussy." When he spoke, I felt his breath between my legs, hot and teasing. "I can't wait to taste it."

Stars exploded across my vision as Wyatt's tongue stroked through my throbbing folds. The second his stubble scraped over my clit, the dam shattered and swept me away. My back bowed and I cried out as ecstasy pulsed through me in waves, turning my insides to quivering jelly while my walls contracted around Wyatt's fingers.

"One," he said, grinning as he stroked me through the aftershocks, relentlessly drawing out every last ripple of pleasure.

"Shit," I mumbled when my lungs remembered how to work again.

Honest to god, what kind of witchcraft? The man had me coming after one little stroke of his tongue. He'd barely even had to work for it.

His fingers slipped out of me, but his hand clenched hard on my hip when I tried to sit up. "I'm not done," he said and pushed his face between my thighs.

My hips jerked, everything still raw and throbbing in the aftermath of my orgasm. "Wyatt," I groaned as he licked my oversensitive clit.

He pressed harder with his tongue, mercilessly circling the tender knot of nerves. My core was still pulsating, my skin still tingling, and my awareness so heightened that I recognized the edge of another orgasm building almost immediately.

Fresh tendrils of tension wrapped around my spine as he spread me wide with his face, his tongue caressing me and his stubble burning in the perfect combination of pleasure and pain.

His eyes met mine, watching my reactions as he ate me out, experimenting with different angles and pressures. Quick and rough. Slow and decadent. Learning my body and what drove me to twist my hands in his hair and grind my hips against his face. What turned my whimpers into mindless cries.

Our eyes stayed locked the whole time, the connection between us scorching and unbroken as he drove me closer and closer to the edge. For so long I'd wanted his eyes on me, wanted all of his attention. And now I had it, and it was unlike anything I'd ever experienced before. I was being worshipped. Coveted. Revered.

"Yes," I gasped helplessly when he sucked on my clit. "Oh god. Right there." Pleasure spiraled through me as he hummed, the vibrations pushing me farther, building and building...

He sucked harder, and his teeth scraped over the sensitive tissue. I came with his name on my lips, jerking wildly against his face as ecstasy exploded inside me again.

Once more, Wyatt caressed every ounce of pleasure out of me until my limbs had stopped twitching and my hitching breaths had slowed. He stood, wiping his mouth, and the sight of it made my stomach flip over.

"Wow," I murmured, a ruined mess beneath him. God, that tongue of his. He should have it cast in bronze as a testament to its agility and magical orgasm-inducing powers.

His lips curved in a self-satisfied smirk. "That's two."

It was the sort of bantering and game-playing we'd always done, constantly challenging and pushing each other. Needing to win. As much as I usually enjoyed our competitive dynamic, it wasn't what I wanted right now. This didn't feel like a game to me, and I didn't want him to treat it like one. The problem with games was that they always ended with someone walking away a loser.

"Andie." He bent over me, frowning, and touched my cheek. "Hey."

I should have known he'd be paying attention. Noticing my every response to him. Sensing any shift in my mood. I reached for him, pulling him closer, and squeezed my eyes shut as his warm weight settled on top of me. "I just want..." I turned my head, seeking his mouth, and tasted myself on his lips when he kissed me.

"What do you want?" he murmured. "Tell me."

I wanted him to lose control. To let down his guard and let me in. I wanted him to need me as much as I needed him. But I didn't know how to ask for that. Or maybe I did, but I was afraid of what it said about me. That it would make me seem too clingy, too emotional, too soft.

Instead, what I said was: "You. I just want you."

"I'm right here." He pressed his forehead against mine and rubbed our noses together. "Can you feel me?"

"Yes." There wasn't anywhere we weren't touching. I could feel every inch of his body, the pulse in his throat jumping under my thumb, his chest expanding and contracting against mine, his breath warming my lips, and the hardness in his pants that throbbed with every beat of his heart.

When I eased my hand between us, I felt his shoulders shake and his stomach muscles flex. And when I stroked him through his jeans, I felt his breath catch as his head dropped to my shoulder. I felt every shallow exhalation and every tremor that traveled through him at my touch. It was exactly what I'd wanted, but I was greedy and I wanted even more.

Stilling my hand, I moved my lips to his ear. "These pants need to come off."

He let out a shaky breath, regathering his composure before

he pushed himself upright and stripped off his socks, then his pants, then his underwear. Until he stood gorgeously naked before me, his honey-colored hair and strong body burnished by the sunlight leaking in through the gauzy curtains, his swollen cock nestled in a bed of springy golden curls.

Surging forward, I wrapped my fingers around him, and his head fell back as his hips twitched. I loved the feel of him. How hard he was for me. How hot and sensitive the velvety skin was. When I stroked him, his stomach muscles rippled with tension. And when I ran my thumb over his glistening slit, he bit out a moan, thrusting in my hand as his eyes squeezed shut.

I dropped down to my knees and licked my way up the length of his shaft before taking the head in my mouth and swirling my tongue around it.

"Oh...*shit*." His fingers dug into my hair as his legs trembled. With a whimper, he grabbed my ponytail and dragged my head back. "No more. I can't fucking take it."

Lifting me off the floor, he dragged me in for a kiss. His fingers kneaded my ass as he ground his wet, hard cock against my stomach.

Breaking the kiss with a groan, he gazed at me with hungry, hooded eyes.

"Please, for the love of God, tell me you have condoms, because I do not want to go out to my truck like this."

15

WYATT

My eyes nearly bugged out of my head when Andie reached over and yanked open her bedside drawer. She grabbed the box of condoms inside, but my attention was captivated by all the toys she had in there next to her bed. I squeezed my throbbing dick as my mind conjured a vision of her naked between the sheets, using her collection of accessories to get herself off.

I leaned in for a closer look, and she slammed the drawer shut. "Focus, Wyatt."

"I am. I'm focused on what's in that drawer and what I want to do to you with all of it." That little bullet vibrator, for one thing...

"Later." She dug into the box of condoms and tore one off the strip. "Right now I want your dick inside me."

Her words shot through my veins like liquid fire. I wanted her in every way possible. Under me, on top of me, bent over in front of me. I couldn't wait to feel her all around me and hear her gasp my name again as she came on my dick.

I grabbed the condom from her and rolled it on as I gritted

my teeth. I couldn't risk letting her do it herself. The way her hands had felt around me, I might shoot my load before I ever got inside her.

A look I'd never seen before came into her eyes as she watched me do it. The only thing that had come close was the fiery blaze she got sometimes when she was angry with me. Her expression now was a different kind of fire, and it made my blood churn and my head spin.

I reached for her, pulling her down with me as I lay back on the bed. "I want to watch you as you ride me."

It was my best chance of stretching this out long enough to coax another orgasm or two from her. I wanted to take my time and make this good for her. I'd waited this long already; I'd happily wait as long as it took to give her all the pleasure she deserved.

Maybe on some level I was delaying because I didn't want this moment between us to end. Things were good as long as we were here, alone, enjoying each other. I'd always been great at this part—it was the stuff that came after I usually screwed up. I didn't know what would happen with Andie and me after this, and I was a little afraid to find out.

She'd scared me there for a second, when I'd sensed her tense up, her mind going somewhere I couldn't follow, her expression like a cold drip of water down my spine. Maybe she was already having second thoughts about me. If so, the longer I could stretch this out, the better, in case it was all she ever let me have of her.

Andie straddled my legs, and I reached up to cup one of her breasts while my other hand curled around her luscious hip. She was so fucking gorgeous. I wanted to bury myself in her and never come back out. The way she'd looked laid out on the bed a minute ago had nearly killed me. Open and vulnerable in a way I'd never expected to see. Welcoming me.

Trusting me. Completely bared to me and falling apart at my touch.

No way I was ever going to recover from that.

Her wet warmth brushed against me, and my hips jolted helplessly beneath her. I ground my teeth together as she squeezed her hand around me, taking her goddamn time about taking my dick.

Impatiently, I reached down and spread her silky folds with my fingers. When my thumb grazed her clit, she shivered and guided me inside her, sinking down on me all at once. She was so slick and hot and ready for me. Her eyes rolled back as I filled her up, a whimper slipping out of her on the final, shuddering inch.

I tried to hold myself still, even as I gasped at the sensation of her tight walls squeezing my aching dick—fuck, *fuck*—until all her weight had settled on my thighs. Then her eyes opened and met mine with a look that unexpectedly spoke of affection as much as lust.

It fucking *crushed* me.

If I could have, I would have frozen time and stayed right there in that moment forever, surrounded by her while her eyes seared into me, telling me how much she wanted me.

I'm yours, that look said. *And you're mine.*

I'd always had an easy time keeping sex purely physical. The armor I'd constructed to avoid catching feelings had been shored up by years of practice. But Andie had burned it all away, exposing something raw and incomplete inside me.

I reached up and tangled my hands in her hair, knowing I needed to hold on to her somehow. Whatever it took, I needed more of this feeling in my life. When I dragged her mouth down to mine, the change in angle sent a surge of pleasure rippling through my limbs, and I moaned into her mouth.

She started to rock, and my moan turned into a whimper.

Her hands pressed against my chest as she pushed herself upright, rolling her hips. The blissful look on her face as she moved on top of me was everything I'd dreamed of and more.

Leaning back, her gaze locked on mine, she braced herself on my thighs and lifted herself up. The sweet slide of her pussy as she sank back down made me gasp like a man drowning. Her beautiful tits bounced as she impaled herself on me, taking me deep and fucking me so hard I nearly lost it.

My thumb found her clit, and her rhythm faltered as a moan shuddered out of her. I rubbed harder, and her eyes squeezed shut, her head falling back. She moved back and forth, seeking more friction, grinding herself against my thumb, greedily using me for her own pleasure. I drove up into her, and she let out a cry as her walls spasmed around me. Gritting my teeth, I bucked my hips in sharp thrusts.

"Yes," she gasped, grinding down on my dick as I plunged into her. "Just like that, don't stop, I need more, please, I need..."

I fucked her harder, my fingers digging into her hip, holding her in place as she took my dick, my thumb moving faster on her clit, stroking her inside and out. Her cries grew more frenzied and desperate, then she clenched around me, sobbing my name as her orgasm pulsed through her.

"You're so perfect," I murmured, stroking my hands down her back after she slumped forward on my chest. "So fucking perfect."

She lifted her head to gaze at me, her eyes glassy and soft, and a burst of dizzying tenderness punched through my chest as I kissed her. Humming against my mouth, she shifted her hips, drawing a groan out of me before she moved her lips to my ear. "I want you on top of me. I want to feel you pressing down on me."

Her words shuddered through every part of me. Banding my

arm around her hips to keep her locked against me, I flipped us over on the bed.

A breath gusted out of her as I crushed her into the mattress, letting my full weight fall on her for a second before I braced a hand underneath me. Her shock dissolved into a laugh, and my tongue sought the spot below her ear that I used to stare at, longing to taste it. "That was three, by the way, in case you lost count."

"We're done with that. It's your turn now."

I shook my head, sucking on her tender skin until she squirmed. "I'm going to get you to four first."

"Not if I get you there first," she purred, dark and sweet as cane syrup.

A tidal wave of lust broke over me even as my competitive instincts kicked in. The two conflicting urges warred for dominance as I thrust deep inside her, wanting to break her again as badly as I wanted to let her shatter me into a thousand pieces.

Pushing myself up on my elbow, I grabbed one of her knees and lifted her leg as I slammed into her, driving deep enough to make her cry out. Her eyes rolled back in her head, and I grabbed her hand, pressing her fingers against her clit as I jack-hammered into her.

She moaned my name, sinking her teeth into her bottom lip as she stroked herself, the pressure of her fingers caressing my dick with every thrust. I thrust harder, feeling my control start to fracture, knowing I didn't have much time left in me to get her there. Her hand slipped down to squeeze my balls, and I just about lost it right then.

Grabbing her wrist, I wrenched her hand away and pinned it to the mattress as I let my weight bear down on her, trapping her beneath me. "You're mine," I growled, and she moaned, digging her feet into the backs of my legs as she arched against me.

My grunts mixed in with her cries as my hips pounded

against her, the needy pulse in my veins overpowering everything else. Her hands gripped my ass cheeks, clutching me to her as she ground into me. Pinpricks of pain streaked over my skin when she dug her fingernails in, and I choked out a cry.

Mercilessly, she dug deeper into my flesh. Just like when we danced, she knew exactly what I wanted from her. My body jerked as the sensation sliced through me, mingling with the pleasure, heightening it, driving me to the edge until it was too much to take.

Something cracked inside me and I gave up the fight, surrendering to the surge. Letting myself drown in it, drown in Andie. A lifetime of pent-up emotions, years of devotion and longing and frustration. It tore a ragged shout out of me as it seared up my spine and exploded behind my eyes in a spectrum of blinding color.

I slumped across her, just enough strength and consciousness left in me to keep from crushing her under my weight. As my chest heaved for oxygen, her fingers skimmed up my back and threaded through my hair in gentling strokes.

"I win," she said softly.

I nuzzled into her neck. "Pretty sure *I* just won."

"Let's call it a draw. I think it's fair to say we both came out on top." She swiveled her head, and her eyes gleamed in the filtered light as they met mine.

Laying my palm against her cheek, I kissed her tenderly before I pulled back with a smile. "We both *came* on top, anyway."

She laughed and pinched my nipple.

"Hey!" I hoisted myself up, arching an eyebrow at her. "Watch it, missy. Unless you're ready for a rematch already." The condom was starting to feel unbearable, and I winced as I reluctantly pulled out of her.

Freed from my weight, she stretched her arms overhead.

"That would be impressive. But I'm definitely going to need a halftime break."

I kissed her again, savoring the sweet taste of her mouth one more time before I went to clean myself up. "Halftime, my ass. That was just the first quarter."

16

ANDIE

W yatt was a cuddler. Who would have guessed? Certainly not me.

After I took my turn in the bathroom he dragged me back onto the bed and curled himself around me like an affectionate puppy. Both of us still naked, our legs intertwined, he nestled his face against my chest while I played with his hair.

I was loving this new side of him. I'd seen him be tactile and affectionate, of course, when he was trying to sweet-talk a woman into bed, but that was different than the snuggly, doting tenderness he'd revealed to me today.

The closest he'd ever come was a few times when he'd been drunk or sick or injured. Like when he'd fallen asleep in my lap a couple of weeks ago. It rocked me a little to think back on it—and on a few other memories like it—with the knowledge that he'd been struggling to hold himself back all this time. Only in a weakened state had he ever dropped his mask enough to let me glimpse this side of him.

I trailed my fingertip around the outer rim of his ear, and he let out a contented rumble, cupping one of my boobs as he snuggled closer.

Imprudently, I wondered if Wyatt was this post-coitally snuggly with all the women he slept with. It didn't particularly strike me as one-night stand behavior. Did that mean I was special? Different than the others? I wanted to think so, but I also knew better than to make assumptions.

As long as I'd known Wyatt, and as much as I liked to think he was an open book to me, the truth was I didn't have any idea what he was like in his intimate moments.

Hadn't had any idea, anyway, before today. I'd just collected a lot of new data, and it was going to take some time to process all of it. In the meantime, I was content just to lie here and enjoy the feel of his body on mine, the musky scent of his skin all around me, the happy little murmurs he made when I scratched my fingernails over his scalp.

The light filtering in through the curtains was slanted and golden-tinged. It was late afternoon, and we'd lost almost a whole day of working on the house. I should probably care about that. And yet right now I couldn't seem to. Not at all.

Wyatt kissed the top of my breast—the one he'd been holding in his hand—and repositioned himself on the pillow next to me. "Can I ask you something?"

"Sure." I looked over at him and smiled, loving the sight of him in my bed, how relaxed he looked, and how right it felt to be here with him like this.

He reached for my hand and twined our fingers together. "Earlier, you made it sound like today isn't the first time you've ever thought about me like this."

"Definitely not." I stared at our hands as he stroked his thumb over my knuckles.

"How long?"

I felt a moment's trepidation. Embarrassment at just how

long I'd been carrying this torch for Wyatt. He squeezed my hand when he sensed my hesitation, and I remembered that it hadn't been easy for him to fess up to his secret crush before. But he'd done it.

Now it was my turn to dig deep and do the same.

I rolled onto my side so I could look at him as I made my confession. "As long as I can remember." His hand stilled as furrows sprouted across his brow. I swallowed, my throat dry as cotton, and kept going. "I don't know exactly when it started because I can hardly remember a time in my life when I didn't have a crush on you. Even before I knew what a crush was, you were always in the front of my mind. I always wanted to be the center of your attention."

Wyatt opened his mouth, but no sound came out.

There was a chance I'd just freaked him out enough to send him running for the exit. Just because he'd gotten a stiffy for me at seventeen didn't mean he was ready to hear me confess to a lifelong, potentially disturbing obsession with him that extended all the way back to my prepubescent years.

I started to turn away, but his hand slid into my hair, pulling me back toward him. Our noses brushed, and my eyes squeezed shut as I blew out a long, shaky breath.

He pressed our foreheads together. "Andie." His lips touched mine in a tender caress. *"Andie."* He kissed me harder, the insistent pressure of his mouth coaxing me to open for him.

I melted against him as he cradled my face in both hands. His kiss telling me in no uncertain terms that he wasn't freaked out and he wasn't running for the exit.

Not yet, anyway.

I pushed the unwanted thought away, focusing instead on Wyatt's mouth and tongue and hands. The way they touched me. The way they claimed me. Eager. Seductive. Cherishing.

My god, all the years we'd missed. The lost time when we

could have been together. All those nights I'd spent alone, thinking about him. All the nights I'd spent with someone else, still thinking of Wyatt. All those times I'd watched him take home another girl and wished it was me.

It *could* have been me.

He dragged his mouth away from mine and wrapped me up in his arms, crushing me against his chest. "There's no fucking way I'm letting you go now."

My heart stuttered to a stop. "Were you planning on letting me go before?"

Loosening his arms, he took my face in his hands again and looked straight into my eyes. "No." He frowned when I let out a long exhalation. "Were you worried about that?"

Before I could think of a way to answer, he shook his head.

"This isn't just a casual fuck to me, if that's what you were thinking." He hesitated, doubt flashing across his expression. "I hope that's not what you wanted."

"No." I touched my fingertips to his lips. "I don't want to be someone you sleep with and then leave."

"You could never be that. You matter to me too much."

Something bright flared in my chest. Wyatt was the wish I'd been carrying around in my heart, and now he was telling me he was mine.

I burrowed against him, sliding my hands around his waist. Our bodies fit together like they'd been designed as a matching set, uniquely meant for each other. He enfolded me in his arms, surrounding me with comfort and safety.

Mine, my mind whispered as his heartbeat thumped in my ear.

But there was something else we needed to talk about still. I didn't want to ruin this fragile, burgeoning thing between us, but before it went any further, we needed to deal with the stupid, stubborn elephant in the room. The thing that had kept Wyatt away from me for so long.

My brother.

"Wyatt?"

His hand smoothed up my back, leaving a warm trail in its wake. "Hmmm?"

"What about..." I hesitated, loath to bring up the subject and spoil the mood.

He gave my ponytail a gentle tug. "What about what?"

"Josh." My mouth twisted with resentment as I spoke my brother's name. If it hadn't been for him and his misguided determination to butt into my life, so much might have turned out differently.

Wyatt went disturbingly still for a moment. Long enough for a sense of dread to settle in my stomach. Untangling himself, he rolled onto his back away from me and stared up at the ceiling. I felt a chill at the loss of his body heat as I watched a muscle twitch in his jaw.

He let out a long breath and raked his hands through his hair. "We can't tell him."

When I didn't respond, he turned his head to look at me. The worry lines had returned to his brow. "You know that, right?"

I didn't know any such thing. As far as I was concerned, Josh had way overstepped by interfering in my love life. I wasn't feeling inclined to coddle his chauvinistic attitudes. But I also wasn't the one in danger of losing his friendship. It was easy for me to stand up to Josh. I was his sister, so he was stuck with me no matter what I did.

"Please, Andie." Wyatt's face contorted, and he reached for my hand.

I frowned as I let him entwine our fingers. "Why? Why does he get any say at all about you and me?"

"Because I made him a promise."

It was a dumb reason to deny ourselves happiness, and it made me angry. "A promise he didn't have any right to ask for in the first place. A promise you never should have made."

Wyatt flinched at my tone and rolled onto his back again, scrubbing a hand over his face.

"Is this what you were trying to tell me that night you got in the fight?" I asked.

His head swiveled toward me. "I don't remember. Did I?"

"You said Josh made you promise to look out for me back in tenth grade. But that wasn't all he made you promise, was it?"

"No."

"Let me guess: he made you promise to keep your hands off me."

Wyatt turned his head back to the ceiling and nodded.

"That was high school," I said. "We're all grown-ups now. The statute of limitations on stupid high school stuff ended years ago."

"It doesn't work that way." His jaw set stubbornly. "A promise is a promise."

Under different circumstances, I would have found his fidelity admirable. Sweet, even. But since it was *my* choice that had been taken away by this ridiculous oath, and *my* wishes that had been thwarted without my knowledge, I merely found it frustrating and ludicrous.

"Oh come on," I snapped, getting angry now. "People say and do all kinds of shit when they're teenagers that no one takes seriously or expects to stick forever. That's literally why the courts seal juvenile records. Because what you do as a teenager shouldn't dictate the whole rest of your life."

"Josh takes this seriously. Trust me." Wyatt's eyes met mine. "You think I haven't ever tried to test the waters over the years? Believe me, I have. Grown-up or not, his opinion hasn't changed.

Not about this." He squeezed my hand in what felt like an apology and a plea for understanding all at once. "I wasn't being dramatic when I said he'd never forgive me."

Wyatt knew my brother as well as anyone—even better than me—and if he really thought Josh would end their friendship over this, then I guess I believed him. Hadn't Mia said pretty much the exact same thing? And that had been coming straight from my brother's mouth.

Wyatt knows Josh would kill him. That was what Mia had said. Those were the words Josh had used, and while he might have been exaggerating, he hadn't been kidding.

My brother had a temper he worked hard to keep in check, and he held grudges even better than I did. I tended to blow up at people, letting my anger burn hot, which meant it burned out faster. Whereas Josh kept his anger inside, allowing it to fester and grow. I'd seen him cut people out of his life before, turning his back on friends after one mistake or perceived slight.

I could understand why Wyatt didn't want to test him, even as disappointment burned in the back of my throat. I wanted Wyatt to fight for me. To care enough to stand up to Josh and tell him to shove his interfering nonsense straight up his ass.

The *one time* I actually wanted Wyatt to barrel-roll in to defend my honor, he didn't want to do it. Why did he have to be cautious about this one thing when he was so casually reckless about everything else?

I knew why, of course. Because my brother wasn't just some random stranger in a bar. Josh mattered to him.

Did I really want to force Wyatt into choosing between me and my brother? Was it a fair thing to ask or expect when he stood to lose a lot more than I did?

Would he even choose me if it came down to it?

Almost definitely not.

Josh was more than just Wyatt's best friend. In a way, he'd been his savior.

Wyatt hadn't had an easy time of it after his mother died. His father and closest brothers had been bound up in their own grief—first losing Chance, then Brady leaving, then finally Wyatt's mother. Tanner had always been a little withdrawn, and he'd withdrawn even further that year. Ryan had done what he could under the circumstances, but he hadn't been at home anymore to keep much of an eye on Wyatt. And Wyatt's dad—well. George King had never been warm and fuzzy, but he'd seemed to grow colder and even more distant just when his sons had needed him most. Maybe it had simply been grief—I couldn't imagine losing two sons and a wife like that—or maybe it had been selfishness, but his relationship with Wyatt had never recovered.

In a way, Josh had been all Wyatt had. They'd spent so much time together in the months after his mother's death, when Wyatt had desperately needed someone and felt like everyone else had abandoned him. Our house had been his retreat from all the unhappiness waiting for him at home, and my brother had been his primary support system.

It scared me to wonder what might have happened to Wyatt without Josh's levelheaded influence to keep him from spiraling out of control. Wyatt had always been impulsive—we were a lot alike that way—but I'd had a stable, loving family to keep an eye on me and keep me in line. Who knew what Wyatt might have turned to if he hadn't turned to Josh? It didn't seem like a stretch to think my brother had saved his life.

Josh's friendship was more important to Wyatt than I was. That was the way it had been for as long as we'd known each other.

If I tried to force the issue, I knew exactly what would happen. I'd lose.

"So what are we supposed to do?" I asked helplessly.

Wyatt rolled onto his side, his expression pained as he wrapped both his hands around mine. "We have to keep this —*us*—a secret."

"You mean sneak around?"

"Would that be so bad?"

Would it?

If I got to have Wyatt, but no one could know, I'd still have Wyatt, wouldn't I? Wasn't that better than not having him at all?

Still cradling my hand, he brought it to his lips and kissed it. "It's not like we'd never be able to see each other. We can keep hanging out like normal, as friends." His mouth dragged a trail across my knuckles. "We'll just have to be careful when we're around other people so no one catches on. Pretend nothing's changed."

"What about other women?"

His brow compressed. "I won't sleep with other women." He looked a little hurt I'd had to ask. "Obviously."

"Will you quit flirting too?"

"I..." He hesitated, frowning. "People will probably notice something's up if I stop showing interest in women altogether."

Regrettably, I had to admit it was a valid point. "So you're proposing what? That you continue to flirt with other women in public?"

Gathering me in his arms, he rolled onto his back so I was lying on top of him. "Can you live with that? If I swear to you that it's all for show and I won't let it go anywhere?"

"I don't know," I answered honestly as I traced a finger over the dragon tattoo under his collarbone. "What counts as flirting, exactly? How far are you allowed to go?"

If we were going to do this, I needed to know exactly where the boundaries were.

His thumb dragged across my lower lip possessively. "No kissing, definitely."

That was a relief. I was trying to be easygoing about this, but the thought of Wyatt kissing anyone but me made my blood boil.

I sucked the tip of his thumb into my mouth and bit down on it, causing his eyes to flare with heat. "No putting your mouth on anyone, anywhere."

"Agreed." The fingers of his other hand trailed up my side, caressing the curve of my breast. "And no touching in any bathing suit areas."

"That sounds reasonable." I lowered my lips to his chest, and his hand slid into my hair as I mouthed a wet trail across his skin.

"All the same rules apply to you. No sleeping with other men." The hand that had been on my breast stroked down over my backside and between my thighs. "You're mine."

I lifted my gaze to his, arching an eyebrow. "But I can flirt with other men?"

He looked conflicted, but he nodded. "You can flirt, just like me. But you have to abide by the same restrictions."

"No kissing and no groping."

He slid a finger inside me and I shuddered with pleasure. "Not with anyone but me."

"Deal." Lifting my hips, I spread my legs to give him better access as I took him in my hand.

Our little arrangement didn't sound so bad, really. Not as long as I could have him like this when it was just the two of us.

Hadn't I watched Wyatt flirt with other women for years and survived it? At least now I had a promise he'd be mine at the end of the night. However it might feel to see him pay attention to someone else in public, I had no doubt he'd be able to make it up to me in private.

Starting right now.

———

I WOKE the next morning to the glare of sunlight behind my eyelids and the scent of Wyatt all around me. On my pillow, on my sheets, on my skin.

Slowly, I opened my eyes, and Wyatt's handsome face filled my field of vision.

"Good morning." He had his head propped up on his hand beside me, and the sound of his sleep-roughened voice was sweet enough to bring a smile to my lips.

"Have you just been lying there staring at me while I slept?"

"Maybe." His mouth curved in a smile to match mine. "Guess I don't need to ask if you slept well."

It had been a long time since I'd let a man sleep over in my bed. I didn't usually sleep well with someone else next to me, but as with so many other things, Wyatt proved to be the exception.

I ran my fingertips over the stubble on his jaw, marveling at how unfairly attractive he looked for first thing in the morning. His bedhead was tousled to sexy perfection and the relaxed, tender look in his eyes set off a fluttery feeling in my stomach. "Did you sleep okay?"

"I did." He captured my fingers and pressed them to his lips. "You wore me the hell out."

"Not too much, I hope."

He leaned forward to brush a closed-mouth kiss across my lips that was really more of a nuzzle than a kiss. "No such thing as too much. Not when it comes to you."

Something soft and warm flooded my chest. I sank my fingers into his sexy bedhead and pulled him closer, my mouth seeking his greedily.

It still shocked me a little, that I could kiss him like this and he'd welcome it. I'd spent so long believing he didn't want me and telling myself that would never change. I was still getting used to this new reality in which I could kiss him as much as I wanted, and he'd gladly kiss me back.

His arms wrapped around me, pulling me to him as he lay back on the bed. When I fitted myself against him and rested my head on his chest, he let out a long, contented sigh. "Too bad we can't stay in bed all day."

My fingertips wandered aimlessly over his stomach. "Can't we?" I'd been awake less than a minute and I was already imagining all the ways we could entertain ourselves without ever leaving the bedroom.

He laughed. "Well, we could, but then who would finish prepping the siding for the painting I'm supposed to start tomorrow?"

"Right. The house." Reality deflated my blissful bubble. "I guess we can't just ignore it for the day."

"No, probably not. Especially since we already took half of yesterday off." His hand stroked down my back in a soothing caress. "But we don't have to jump up and get to work right away. We can stay here awhile longer and enjoy the moment."

"Good."

My stomach growled, and he laughed. "Or we could see about rustling you up some breakfast."

Reluctantly, I agreed to get up, despite the small, irrational voice in my head whispering that leaving the bed might break the spell and cause Wyatt to realize he didn't want to stick around after all. But my hunger won out, and I shrugged on my robe while Wyatt pulled on his boxer briefs.

I followed him downstairs and started a pot of coffee while he examined the contents of my fridge. He offered to cook up some breakfast sausage and eggs, and I volunteered to make grits to go along with it.

"With cheese?" Wyatt asked, his eyes lighting up. My mom's cheesy grits had been his favorite when we were kids. She'd taught me to make grits the old-fashioned way: low and slow with plenty of dairy fat. Good grits required patience and a cavalier attitude about your cholesterol levels.

"Of course," I said, and he smacked a kiss on my lips as he carried the sausage and eggs to the counter by the stove.

I still had my grandmother's O'Keefe and Merritt gas stove from the fifties, the kind with a built-in griddle and stovetop clock with matching Bakelite salt and pepper shakers. That big old stove was one of my favorite things about the house, and I'd paid a pretty penny to have it restored by a guy in Austin. Little had I imagined that one day Wyatt would be standing at it in his underwear making me breakfast.

Once I had the grits simmering on the stove, I poured two cups of coffee and set one next to Wyatt as he laid the sausage patties in my cast iron pan. It had also belonged to my meemaw and was probably as old as the stove, if not even older.

He seemed to know what he was doing, so I stood back and appreciated the view as I sipped my coffee. My eyes wandered over the familiar tattoos on his arms and the slightly less familiar ones on his torso. Only last night had I learned that the words inked around his rib cage were from his mother's favorite Fleetwood Mac song. They weren't the only song lyrics he'd had etched onto his skin. Lyrics from some of his favorite bands were woven through the tattoo sleeves on both his arms.

Looking at them now reminded me of the notebook I'd seen in his apartment. The one full of original songs he'd written.

"Hey, Wyatt?" I cradled my coffee mug with both hands, hoping I wasn't overstepping.

"Yeah?" He turned and leaned back against the Formica countertop, folding his arms across his bare chest.

"Remember the night I drove you home from King's Palace?"

"Only parts of it." He frowned as he scratched the side of his head. "Why? Did I say something embarrassing?"

I shook my head, because this wasn't about the things he'd said. "When you were puking in the bathroom I cleaned up your apartment."

"I noticed." He ducked his head guiltily. "Sorry, I should have thanked you for that and for looking after me that night."

"When I was in your bedroom, I saw a notebook sitting open on the bed."

Something a lot like fear came into his eyes. "Did you look at it?"

"I only saw a little of what was written on the top page—I didn't mean to pry. As soon as I realized what it was, I backed away."

He turned away from me and picked up the spatula. I could see the tension radiating through him as he pretended to check on the sausage so he wouldn't have to look at me, but I couldn't tell if he was angry, or just embarrassed to have his secret found out.

"I didn't know you'd been writing your own songs."

One of his shoulders twitched in a slight shrug. "I haven't showed them to anyone yet."

"Not even the other guys in the band?"

"No."

I set my coffee down and crossed the room to wrap my arms around his waist. "Why not?"

He didn't move, but he didn't shake me off either. "I don't know."

"Yes, you do." I wasn't letting him off the hook that easily. This was a big deal. There was passion on the pages of that notebook. Too much to keep hidden away. I already knew he was a talented singer and pretty damn good at playing guitar. What else could he achieve if he let himself make the attempt?

"They're too personal to share with anyone."

I pressed my cheek against his back. "Even me?"

He laid one of his hands over mine on his stomach. "Most of them are *about* you."

My heart jumped as I remembered the lines I'd read. *I think she was the one. Maybe she could have saved me if I'd let her.*

I'd assumed he was referring to some woman from his past. Not me. It had never even entered my head that those words had been about me.

I tightened my arms around him, squeezing hard enough to make him cough before I dragged him around to face me. His eyes tried to avoid mine, but I took his face in my hands and made him look me in the eye. "You've been writing songs about me?"

His throat bobbed as he swallowed. "Maybe." He was so bashful about it I couldn't stand it.

"Wyatt..." This fresh glimpse inside his head made my breath catch. I didn't have words adequate to the emotions tumbling around inside me, so I kissed him instead, pouring my whole heart into it and hoping he'd be able to feel what I meant.

He relaxed into me, the tension gradually bleeding out of him as I pressed kisses along his jaw and down his throat. His arms tightened around me, and he dropped his forehead heavily against mine.

I felt the weight of his vulnerability in the way he leaned into me and the fierceness of his grip. His desperate, aching need to be accepted and loved despite a lifetime of pretending the opposite. My lungs constricted with the responsibility of it. The need to protect him and support him. To give him what he'd been afraid to ask for.

"Will you play them for me?" I felt him stiffen again, but I held him tight so he'd know I wasn't going anywhere. Telling him without words that he could trust me with this.

He heaved a breath and nodded. "Sure. Sometime."

"I'd love that." I kissed his temple, then his cheek, then his lips. "Whenever you're ready."

His fingers tightened in my hair as his mouth covered mine in a tender, grateful kiss. Just as I started to give myself up to it, he pulled back and let go of me. "I've gotta flip the sausage."

Right. There was food cooking on the stove. I couldn't just jump his bones this second. *Damn.* While Wyatt tended the sausage patties, I went to give the grits a stir.

"The next time I go back to my place..." He paused to toss a glance at me, and the corner of his mouth tilted upward. "Maybe I'll get my guitar and bring it over here."

My heart somersaulted in my chest like I'd just won the lottery. "Yeah?"

He shrugged like it was no big deal, even though we both knew it was the exact opposite. "Maybe."

17

WYATT

I didn't end up making it back over to my place until Monday morning after Andie left for work.

The two of us spent most of the day Sunday prepping the exterior siding for painting. Andie did the power washing while I finished scraping and sanding the last of the peeling paint away. We made a good team, and with her help the work went quickly. By the time evening came around, we'd finished all the spackling and final sanding, and had everything ready for me to start applying the primer today.

I'd spent the night with Andie again last night, which meant I'd been wearing the same work clothes for two days now. Fortunately, neither of us had been doing a whole lot of clothes wearing when we weren't outside working. Still, by Monday morning, I was in desperate need of clean clothes, so I stopped off at my apartment on the way back from picking up the paint for the siding. While I was there, I threw some toiletries and a few extra changes of clothes into a bag.

If things kept going as well as they had been, I figured I might be spending a lot more nights at Andie's. At least I sure hoped so.

On my way out the door, I grabbed my guitar as promised.

In all the time I'd been trying to work up the courage to play my music for someone else, I'd never imagined the first time would be for the woman I'd written most of the songs about.

But now she knew.

She'd seen the damn notebook weeks ago. I remembered exactly what song I'd been working on that day too. What page had been lying open. What lyrics she'd read.

Fuck.

When I got back to Andie's house, I took my guitar case inside and set it on the kitchen table. Then I headed back outside and got started on that primer coat.

By the end of the day, I was tired and sweaty, but I had two sides of the house fully primed. Andie got home right as I was putting away the last of my tools. She parked in the garage next to my truck, and I stole a kiss before following her into the house.

Her eyes focused on my guitar as soon as she stepped into the kitchen. "Are you going to play for me tonight?"

"Later, maybe. I'm starving." I took the takeout bag out of her hand, peeking inside as I carried it to the counter. She'd stopped at Rita's for tacos on her way home. *Hell yeah.*

While I washed my hands, she grabbed us two beers out of the fridge and started unpacking the tacos. "Two pastor for me, and four barbacoa for you."

"Queso?" I asked hopefully.

"Of course." She plopped a paper bag of fresh tortilla chips on the counter, along with a Styrofoam cup full of melted cheese mixed with diced tomatoes, onions, and jalapeños.

I beamed adoring eyes at her as I pried the lid off. "You always did know the way to my heart."

She arched a teasing eyebrow. "Hot cheese?"

"Exactly." I dunked a chip in the chili con queso and shoved it in my mouth with an exaggerated sigh of happiness.

We ate our dinner standing at the counter as we caught each other up on our respective days. Mostly I listened to her talk as I wolfed down my four tacos in the time it took her to eat two. I loved listening to her talk. I'd happily listen to her read one of those software terms of service agreements just to hear the sound of her voice. But I especially liked the funny stories she told about her students and the wildlife up at the park.

Today there'd been a sighting of something called a tarantula hawk, which was not, as I'd first thought, a hawk that ate tarantulas.

"It's a wasp that hunts tarantulas," Andie said, her eyes shining with excitement. "They can get up to three inches long, and their sting is considered one of the most painful in the world!"

I held up my fingers three inches apart, trying to imagine encountering a wasp that big. "And you're...excited that you might run into one of these nightmare creatures up at the park?"

"Hell yes." She grinned and took a drink of her beer. "They say the pain from their sting is so instantaneously excruciating and debilitating that the best advice is to lie down on the ground and scream."

I'd just drenched a tortilla chip in queso, and I paused with it halfway to my mouth to blink at her. "That's the *official* advice? Like for wildlife experts and whatnot?"

Nodding, she stole the chip out of my hand and shoved it in her mouth. I shook my head at her, smiling as I got myself another chip.

"Lying down keeps you from running off and hurting yourself," she explained. "The pain is so bad that it causes loss of physical coordination, which makes it more likely you'll run into a tree or fall off a cliff or something. And the screaming allegedly helps take your mind off the pain. But the sting doesn't cause any lasting tissue damage, so the pain is only temporary. The best thing you can do is try not to hurt yourself while you wait it out."

"Huh," I said, not liking the image of Andie up there in the woods alone, lying on the ground screaming in pain. I knew she wanted to see one of those wasps for herself, but I dearly hoped she never did.

"I've always been curious how I'd do up against that kind of pain," she added, not making me feel the least bit better.

I frowned at her, thinking about her daredevil streak and how often it had gotten her hurt when we were kids. "Andie—"

"Not that I *want* to get stung," she clarified off my look. "Don't worry, I'm not going to take any stupid risks in the field. I just wonder about it is all. I'll bet I could take it." She grinned at me as she dipped another chip in the queso. On the way to her mouth, a little bit of cheese landed on the button band of her polo, right next to the V of skin showing below her collarbone.

"You've got a little something—" I pointed at her chest, feeling a stir of desire as my gaze flitted over the swell of her breasts. "Right there."

Hunger and fatigue meant I'd mostly been keeping my hands to myself since she got home. But now that my energy had been restored by the magical healing powers of barbacoa tacos and queso, I was feeling more like myself again.

AKA horny as fuck.

Frowning at her chest, Andie lifted a hand to wipe the errant queso away, but I stepped forward and caught her wrist to stop her. Bending my head, I slipped my fingers inside her collar and licked the cheese off her shirt.

Her momentary surprise shifted into an amused exhale. "Really, Wyatt?"

Still holding her wrist captive, I tugged another button open and nuzzled my face inside her shirt to kiss her exposed breast-bone. When I sucked at the delicate skin hard enough to give her a hickey, she twisted out of my grasp, laughing as she shoved me away.

"I'm going to take a shower," she announced, tossing a saucy look over her shoulder on her way out of the kitchen. "You can stay here with the hot cheese if you two want to be alone."

Yeah, no.

No way in hell was I letting Andie take that shower without me.

I followed her upstairs and we dragged each other's clothes off. As soon as we stepped into the shower, I pushed her up against the tile and lowered my mouth to hers. She squirmed when she hit the cold wall, and I pressed my weight into her so I could feel her body writhing against mine.

After a whole day spent apart, the need to touch her burned in me like a fever. I grabbed a handful of soap and lathered it over her gorgeous body, exploring every curve and inch of slick skin. She returned the favor with equal care and attention, then I got her off with my fingers while I whispered filthy things in her ear. I made her come a second time with the massage setting on her handheld showerhead, her head falling back on my shoulder as my fingers spread her apart to let the water jets drive her over the edge. After that, she paid me back by forcing me up against the cold tile wall and pulling me off until I broke apart, groaning her name.

When we were both spent and satisfied, we got out and toweled each other off. I stepped into a pair of clean shorts while Andie pulled on a tank top and a matching pair of cotton pajama shorts that exposed the bottom curve of her ass and had my dick already twitching back to life.

"I need a drink after all that." Shooting me a sly smile, she took me by the arm and led me back down to the kitchen.

Once we each had a fresh beer in our hands, Andie directed a pointed look at my guitar case. "It's time." Her voice was gentle but firm. "I want you to play me one of the songs you wrote."

My stomach tightened with nerves, but I knew it was no use putting it off anymore. There was never going to be a better time to do it than now.

I took a long drink of beer before I hoisted my guitar case off the table. Andie followed me as I carried it into the living room and settled on the couch. She sat in the armchair across from me while I tuned my guitar. When I'd finished, I glanced up at her, and she gave me an encouraging smile.

I wasn't as anxious about this as I'd expected to be. Maybe because I'd already done something much scarier. I'd exposed my biggest secret when I told Andie how I felt about her. And instead of something bad happening, something wonderful had.

I strummed a chord idly as I debated which song to play first. The most obvious answer was the one she'd already gotten a peek at. I might not have chosen it otherwise—I'd written a lot of pain and longing into that song—but since she'd already seen the lyrics, it wasn't like it would come as a surprise.

My fingers plucked at the strings as I cleared my throat. "I wrote this one a few weeks ago. It's called 'Bright as the Sun.'"

I didn't look at Andie as I started playing. The only way I could get through this was by hiding myself inside the music and shutting out everything else. My eyes fell closed as I sang the first verse. The words came out a little strained at first, but got smoother the farther into the song I got and the more I was able to lose myself in it. By the end, I'd almost fallen into a sort of trance. I had to shake myself out of it as I sang the last words.

My awareness snapped back to where I was with a daunting jolt, and the silence that fell in the aftermath of the final chord sucked all the courage out of me. I stared down at my fingers where they hovered over the guitar strings, afraid to look at Andie and read her reaction.

Over the nervous thumping of my heart, I heard her draw in a shaky breath. Curiosity won out over fear, and I lifted my eyes.

The awed look on her face knocked me back. She wasn't just pleased or impressed—although she sure seemed to be both those things. She was *teary*. Affected enough that she had to reach up and wipe her eyes.

The woman who almost never cried had been moved to tears.

By a song *I'd* written.

Holy hell.

When she blinked at me, I saw every emotion I'd poured into that song reflected in her eyes. It was as if she understood exactly what I'd been feeling when I wrote it. As if she'd felt it along with me as I performed the song.

Wordlessly, she got to her feet and came over to sit on the couch next to me. She laid one hand on my shoulder and pressed the other against my cheek.

As she gazed into my eyes, something sliced through me. A beam of pure, bright energy that burned away the last of my doubt and apprehension. I knew in that moment that Andie was seeing me—*all* of me—in a way I'd never felt seen before.

The real wonder of it was that she liked what she saw.

She tilted her head and pressed a trembling kiss to my mouth. "That was incredible." Her voice cracked a little, and she cleared her throat as she drew back.

A smile tugged at my lips. "So you didn't hate it?" I might be a glutton for punishment, but I was even more of a glutton for praise. It made me want to lie on my back and roll around like a dog begging for belly rubs.

"Are you kidding?" Her cheeks turned pink as excitement animated her features. "I'm so mad at you right now!"

I stared at her in confusion. "Why?"

"Because you've been hiding all that talent from everyone!" I grinned as she punched me in the shoulder. "What are you doing playing other people's music when you can write a song like that?"

"Oh. Well." I shrugged, tongue-tied with giddiness.

"Will you play me another one?"

I licked my lips at the prospect of earning more compliments. "Um, sure."

Andie scooted to the end of the couch, pulling her legs underneath her as she leaned against the armrest. Enthusiasm radiated off her in energizing waves.

Raking my hair out of my face, I sat up a little, repositioning my guitar across my lap. I played another song that was more up-tempo than the last, even though it was about my family. This time I stole a few glances at Andie while I was singing. The rapt expression on her face bolstered my confidence, and after that song I volunteered to sing another. And another. The more I played, the more I relaxed, and the more natural it felt to be sharing this part of me with someone.

When I'd sung six songs in total, I finally put my guitar back in its case. "That's enough for tonight. You've probably got the gist by now."

As soon as the guitar was safely out of my hands, Andie launched herself at me, pushing me back on the couch as she covered my face with kisses. My hands sank into her hair, but I couldn't stop smiling enough to kiss her properly. This loose feeling in my chest made me feel so light I could have floated off the couch if Andie hadn't been lying on top of me.

Propping her head on her hand, she pressed the tip of her index finger to the St. Christopher medal around my neck. "How long have you been writing songs?"

I tucked her hair behind her ear. "A year or two, maybe? I don't remember exactly."

"Why have you been keeping it a secret?" She poked my chest in disapproval.

My gaze skated away from hers. "I don't know."

"You can do better than that." She touched my jaw, drawing my eyes to her again. "Tell me."

Her soft, searching look acted like a tractor beam, pulling the truth out of me against my will. "I suppose I was afraid I wasn't any good at it."

"That doesn't sound like you. I've never known you to be afraid of failure or embarrassment."

I shrugged, unable to offer an easy explanation. That was what I'd wanted everyone to think, but it wasn't who I was. I'd only been pretending not to care all this time. You fail at enough things, and failure starts to feel like a part of who you are. It was easier not to put yourself out there and invite more failure. You learned not to try for anything that mattered, because then you couldn't prove once again to everyone what a useless fuckup you were.

"You've always said you didn't have any interest in writing or performing your own music, and I believed you." A crease sprouted across her brow. "I used to think I knew everything there was to know about you, but it feels like I didn't really know you at all."

"You know me *now*." My hand squeezed hers. "Better than anyone else ever has."

"When I saw that notebook in your apartment and realized what it was..." She hesitated, and my fingers twined with hers. "My first reaction after surprise was hurt—that you'd lied to me all this time, that you'd want to keep something like that from me."

"I'm sorry." Guilt twisted in my belly. "I couldn't tell you.

Writing those songs was the only outlet I had for my feelings about you."

"I get that now." The corner of her mouth twitched. "I was a little jealous too—of the girl you were writing about."

I laughed and tugged on a lock of her hair. "That was you, dummy."

"I didn't have any way of knowing that, did I?" The happy sparkle in her eyes caused a lump of gratitude to form in my throat.

"You really liked the songs?" I knew the answer, but I wanted to hear her say it again. I'd probably need to hear her say it about a million more times before I got used to it.

"I *loved* them. They're all so good. You shouldn't keep that kind of talent hidden away. You won't, will you?"

I didn't answer right away. I hadn't thought much beyond this moment. Now that Andie knew, there really wasn't anything stopping me from telling other people.

So why did I still feel so reluctant to do it?

"Wyatt?"

"We'll see," I hedged.

"You know what you could do? You could play a solo show at Zelda's to debut your new songs. You should talk to her about it."

Zelda's was a local bar near campus that featured live music every Saturday. Shiny Heathens had played there a couple of times when there was a spot in her schedule that needed filling, but Zelda preferred original songwriters when she could get them. Her place was more intimate and a lot less rowdy than the Rusty Spoke, the outdoor beer joint where we usually played. Andie was right. Zelda's would be perfect for a solo acoustic set.

But I wasn't ready to commit to something like that just yet.

"You need to tell the other guys in the band," Andie said, her voice bright with enthusiasm. "I'm sure they'd be willing to play your songs. And at-home recording equipment's gotten a lot more affordable. Y'all could produce your own EP and put it up on the internet for sale. You might even be able to get a spot at the Crowder Folk Festival this year."

My uncle Randy ran the folk festival and booked all the talent personally. But I'd never bothered to ask him about booking Shiny Heathens, just like I'd never asked him if we could play King's Palace. Like the dance hall, the festival was for showcasing serious musicians and up-and-coming songwriting talent.

"Once you've got a whole set list worth of original songs worked out, there's like a million venues around Austin where you could play. Shiny Heathens could be a real band."

"We're already a real band." An uncomfortable tightness wrapped itself around my chest. This was all too much to think about right now. I wasn't ready to do the things she was talking about, because I wasn't sure I wanted everything else that would come along with it.

"You know what I mean," she said. "You could be so much more than a cover band."

I moved her off me and swung my legs to the floor so I could push myself upright. My skin felt hot and itchy all over, and I scratched at my chest. "What if I don't want more than that?"

"Why wouldn't you?"

I dipped my head into my hands and rubbed my forehead. I didn't have an answer. Not one I could put into words, anyway. All I knew was that whenever I thought about seriously trying to make a go of it as a musician, I got a sick, sour feeling in my stomach.

Andie laid a soothing hand on my arm. "Wyatt, talk to me. I just want to understand."

"I don't know why." I looked at her helplessly. "I can't explain it."

She was quiet for a moment. When she spoke again her voice was gentle. "Is this about Brady?"

"No." I spat out the denial reflexively. But as I swallowed the flood of bitterness in the back of my throat, I knew she was right. My eyes fell closed as I shook my head. "Maybe."

It wasn't something I'd ever admitted before. Not even to myself, because I'd spent so long trying not to think about my oldest brother at all.

Andie hugged my arm and rested her head on my shoulder. She knew Brady was a sore spot, and that I'd mostly refused to talk about him since he left.

I opened my eyes and stared at the framed needlepoint on the wall across from me. *Get Your Shit Together*, it told me in colorful letters, surrounded by dainty embroidered flowers.

"I guess..." I exhaled a long breath, grimacing. "It makes me seem pathetic. Like I'm trying to follow in his footsteps or—or get his attention." I swallowed, and Andie squeezed my arm. "I don't want to be known as the famous rock star's little brother. Everyone will think I'm trying to ride his coattails and steal some of his spotlight for myself."

"It's not like that. Your music doesn't have anything to do with Brady or his career. You're talented in your own right." She gave my arm a tug, like she was trying to physically drag me away from my own negative thoughts.

I turned and kissed her head. "It doesn't matter. Doors will open for me because of Brady, and I'll never know if I deserve any of the chances I get."

"Who the fuck cares? That's not a good enough reason to deny yourself the chance to do something you love. You *are* talented and you deserve your own shot." Her voice was sharp and furious, but I knew her anger wasn't directed at me. Andie's mama bear instincts had been engaged. She'd kill me for saying it, but she could be just as overprotective as Josh when it came to the people she cared about. Those Lockharts were a fierce and loyal bunch.

I leaned back on the couch, and she loosened her vise grip on my arm so I could pull her against my chest. "No matter what I do or how I try to distinguish myself, I'll always get compared to him. I'll be trapped in his shadow."

That was the part that really bothered me. Knowing anything I tried to accomplish for myself would automatically and forever be connected to someone I resented so much. I'd never be able to detach myself from his legacy.

"He's not all that, you know. Just because he was lucky enough to join a band that got famous doesn't make him that good."

"He's that good," I said honestly. I'd followed his career closely enough to know just how much of Ghost Ships' success was due to Brady's songwriting.

"So are you," Andie insisted. "Look, families produce famous siblings all the time. Jaden and Willow Smith. Miley and Noah Cyrus. All the Olsen kids. Maybe you won't ever get to be more famous than Brady, but would it really be so bad if you were the Solange to his Beyoncé?"

"Beyoncé didn't cut Solange out of her life and ignore her existence for twenty years."

"So you'll be more like Liam and Noel Gallagher, then."

I shook my head. "I don't even want to be famous. I just want to play music."

"Then do that. Don't let Brady be what stops you. Live your own life the way you want. Fuck Brady."

I smiled despite myself, grateful to have Andie in my corner, spitting mad and ready to fight on my behalf. I pressed my face into her hair. "You know he's the one who taught me to play guitar?"

"I know." She took my hand and squeezed it. "And I know

how much it hurt you when he left. And how much it still hurts that he never once reached out after."

A caustic lump clogged in my throat. "He could have fucking called or at least sent a goddamn postcard."

"He should have. You deserved that much and more." Andie lifted her head to look at me and pressed her palm against my cheek. "He was in a bad place after Chance died. Whatever he was going through and whatever he felt like he needed to do to survive, you know it didn't have anything to do with you, right? You were just a kid."

"Yeah, a kid whose mom was dying." My face twisted as I spat the words. "And he walked away without even saying goodbye."

I'd worshipped Brady too. That was what hurt so bad. He was the only one of Trish's offspring who'd shown much interest in me as a kid. When my mom got sick, Brady had given me my first guitar and taught me how to play. He used to come over every day after I got home from school to give me lessons. Ryan had his hands full taking care of Mom at that point, and Tanner had retreated inside his books as usual. Brady gave me a way to distract myself from the scary shit that was happening. He'd helped me get through those horrible months of watching my mom get weaker and sicker.

And then right before the end, when I'd needed him most of all, he'd up and left without a word. No warning, no goodbyes, no forwarding address. He'd packed a bag but left his phone behind. No one knew where he'd gone or how to get in touch with him.

I knew he'd been fucked up by what had happened to Chance. Not only had he lost his twin, but Brady had been driving the car. It hadn't been his fault—they'd been T-boned by some drunk who'd gotten off with a slap on the wrist—but it couldn't have been an easy thing for him to live with. Brady had started pulling away after the accident, but I'd been too young to fully understand what was going on or know what to do about it.

I hadn't expected Brady to pull away for good. I hadn't been prepared to lose two brothers to that accident.

When my mom died a few weeks after Brady disappeared, I kept waiting to hear something from him. Thinking surely he'd call and check in to see how I was holding up. When he didn't call, I told myself he'd come back for the funeral. And when he didn't do that, I started to think maybe he was dead too.

I spent four years not knowing if Brady was alive. Until Ghost Ships started to take off and get some press. Then suddenly he was all over the music news sites and on the radio and playing at SXSW just an hour up the highway. By then I was too resentful to reach out to him myself. I just kept waiting for him to get in touch, but I never heard a damn word from him. Not when they had their first hit single, or when they headlined ACL Fest, or in any of the fifteen years since.

So yeah, fuck Brady. Fuck him for cutting me out of his life and making me think I'd done something to deserve it.

Andie's hand hooked around the back of my neck, her expression fierce and tender at the same time. "He wasn't there for you the way you needed, and that sucks. I know your dad wasn't either, and that sucks too. But you've got a lot of people still around who care about you, Wyatt."

I sank my fingers into her hair gratefully and pressed my forehead against hers. "Like you, you mean?"

"Of course me—and my whole family. But you've got your family too. Maybe you don't get along with all of them, but you've got more good ones than most people do."

She was right. I complained about my family a lot, but aside from Dad and Nate, they weren't so bad. A few of them were pretty great. And I had Andie. And Josh. I was actually pretty damn lucky.

I managed a half-hearted smile. "So you're saying I'm being a big old whiny baby?"

"No, I'm saying you're important to people, and you should try to remember that. Sometimes I worry that you forget it."

I did forget it. I'd spent a lot of years feeling alone even when I was surrounded by family and friends. I'd done some of it to myself on purpose, and I'd been doing it for so long that it had become a habit.

Andie reached up and tapped me on the nose. "You're a good songwriter. Do you hear me? You're *good*. If you want to do this, then you should do it. Don't make up reasons why you can't."

Don't make up reasons why you can't.

How long had I spent telling myself I couldn't have Andie? Denying myself a chance at happiness because I was scared to take a risk. If she hadn't needed my help with this house situation, I might have gone on that way for the rest of my life, numbing my feelings and pretending I was fine with feeling empty and alone.

Wasn't that exactly what I'd been doing with my music? Trying to pretend I didn't want to pursue it because I was scared it wouldn't work out like I hoped.

Maybe it was time to stop pretending and take a risk.

I pulled Andie closer and hugged her tight as I kissed her temple. "Thank you."

She nestled into my chest, holding me just as tight. "For what?"

"For knowing me."

18

WYATT

This week had been the best of my life. Hands down. No contest. I'd been floating around in a moony-eyed daze since last weekend, so happy I didn't know what to do with myself.

I'd stayed over at Andie's place every night, and hadn't been back to my apartment since Monday. The sex wasn't even the best part—although it was seriously, mind-blowingly excellent. The parts I loved most were the quiet, comfortable moments we were together. Having coffee in the mornings before we started our days, playing my guitar for her after dinner while she worked on those funny needlepoints she did, or cuddling in bed after we'd screwed each other's brains out.

We'd stayed up way too late most nights, our bodies tangled together in the dark, talking about everything and nothing while I ran my hands over her bare skin—or she'd run her hands over mine—getting to know each other inside and out until we finally drifted off to sleep in each other's arms.

Before Andie, the post-coital cuddle had always been my cue to leave. It wasn't that I didn't like cuddling—I fucking loved it— it was just that it tended to give women the wrong impression. If you stuck around too long, they started to get ideas. It set expectations I hadn't been able to meet. I'd tried sticking it out a few times with a few different women, but I'd never had the staying power for a relationship. I always got bored and restless and started looking for an exit pretty quick.

This thing with Andie was something wholly different and new.

I couldn't imagine ever getting tired of spending time with her. When we weren't together, I thought about her constantly, and when we were, I could barely tear my eyes away from her.

I'd never had these kinds of feelings when I was with a woman before. Mushy, gushy, sappy feelings. I didn't just want to jump Andie's bones—although I absolutely wanted to do that as much as possible. I also wanted to hold her hand and fall asleep spooning with her and just generally gaze at her adoringly all the time.

Like I was doing right now.

Fuck.

I had to remind myself we were supposed to be keeping our relationship a secret. Staring at Andie with hearts in my eyes while I was up onstage at the Rusty Spoke singing The Cars' "Just What I Needed" was pretty much a surefire way to blow our cover.

We were playing our regular gig out on the back patio for the bar's Friday night patrons. At practice earlier this week, I'd finally told the rest of the band about the songs I'd been writing. I'd played a few for them, and they'd seemed excited at the prospect of having original songs to perform at our gigs. Our drummer, Matt, who'd been taking piano lessons since he was five and was the best musician in the band, had volunteered to help me flesh out what I had, adding bass, percussion, rhythm guitar, and maybe even some synth to a few.

That was going to take some time though, so for now we were still just a cover band playing at our favorite local icehouse.

It felt good to be talking about my songwriting with people, finally. To share what I'd been working on and tentatively start making some plans for the future. And it had been Andie who'd given me the encouragement I needed to do it.

Shit, I was staring at her again. If I didn't cut it out, people were going to notice.

I dragged my gaze away from her and caught our bass player, Tyler, giving me a funny look. I needed to get my head in the game before I fucked something up. We were only halfway through our set, and it'd be nice if I could keep it together and not make us sound like amateurs.

The guitar solo provided a brief distraction to occupy my attention, but it was over too quickly and after that the rest of the song was pretty repetitive. Before I knew it, my eyes were drifting to Andie again, sitting at a picnic table with some of her friends.

We'd come to the Rusty Spoke separately tonight. She'd gotten here before me with her friend Rain, and when I walked in they'd been talking to a couple of guys they'd gone to high school with.

My blood had gone hot at the sight of Andie with another man—even if it was that doofus Evan Thayer, who I knew for a fact she'd never been the least bit interested in.

I hadn't gone over to talk to her, although I'd seen her glance my way a few times. I didn't trust myself to play it cool, so I'd kept my distance.

Now that I was onstage, Andie was right in my eyeline. Watching me. Staring at me at much as I was staring at her.

Evan was sitting next to her, and he leaned in close to say something in her ear after the song ended. My gaze went hard at the sight of him breathing on her and sticking his nose in her hair. As soon as he leaned away, Andie's gaze met mine again, and she arched an eyebrow as her mouth curved in a smirk.

Goddammit. She knew it was driving me nuts, and she was *enjoying* it.

While Matt and Tyler started us on the opening bars of "Are You Gonna Be My Girl," I scanned the patio for familiar faces. Most of the people who frequented the Rusty Spoke were close to my own age, so I knew a lot of them by face if not by name.

There was a younger group sitting at a table close to the stage who had the look of college students, and I guessed they probably went to Bowman. One of the girls had her eyes glued to me as she tapped her fingers along with the bass line. I winked at her and watched her cheeks turn pink.

When my guitar part came in, I glanced Andie's way and saw her eyes blazing and her mouth set in a hard line. I offered her a smirk of my own, enjoying the turnabout.

Once I started singing, I let my gaze fall on the college girl again. I was supposed to be acting normal, after all, and paying attention to the nearest pretty girl was my normal. It wasn't my fault the lyrics to the song sounded like a proposition. Or that she was mouthing them along with me and blatantly undressing me with her eyes while she coyly twirled a lock of her hair.

Well, maybe it was a little my fault. I had winked at her.

I felt Andie's glare on me the whole song, and it took everything I had not to look her way. When I finally did slide my gaze past her in the middle of the next song, she lifted her eyebrows in an expression that said *I'm going to make you pay for that, asshole.* Then she pointedly turned her whole body toward goddamn Evan Thayer, who was only too happy to have her attention.

Fuck.

It went on like that for the whole rest of the set. The two of us competing to see who was better at driving the other to distraction. I was pretty sure she was winning, based on the state of my blood pressure by the time we finally closed with a singalong rendition of "Don't Look Back in Anger."

After we'd packed up our gear and cleared the stage, I waded into the crowd on the patio, which had swelled and grown rowdier as the night wore on. Someone thrust a beer into my hand as I greeted a few people I knew. I let myself be pulled into a conversation with a couple of Matt's friends, but my eyes kept going back to Andie, who was still sitting next to Evan fucking Thayer.

Eventually some of the college students came over to talk to us, including the girl who'd been flirting with me. Her name was Hannah and she was way too young for me, but that didn't stop her from draping herself all over me—to the obvious chagrin of one of the dudes in her friend group.

I knew Andie was watching us and probably going out of her fucking mind, but this was what we'd agreed to. Although I made damn sure not to give Hannah any encouragement or let her attentions go too far—rules were rules, and I wasn't about to violate Andie's trust—I needed to maintain the charade of being single in order to avoid raising suspicion.

After a few minutes, I took pity on Hannah's poor moping guy friend and extricated myself from her company. As my gaze wandered in search of my next destination, I saw Rain get up from her table, leaving an empty seat on the end right next to Andie.

I still hadn't greeted her yet, and since I'd always made a point of saying hi to her in the past, I headed that way. After a whole night of keeping my distance, I needed to be close to her and talk to her, even if it was just so I'd have an excuse to stare at her for a few minutes.

Sliding into the empty spot on the bench next to Andie, I draped my arm around her shoulders. "Hey you." After our self-imposed time apart, that simple, casual touch both soothed me and set my heart racing. I'd missed her so much it felt like one of my own limbs had been removed.

She'd been talking to Evan and doing her best to ignore me, but now she turned and let me pull her in for a casual hug. "Hey you." Her voice was low and subdued, with an edge to it like she was straining to keep it even. I could feel her reluctance to cut our hug short as sharply as I felt my own.

"Hey, Wyatt." Evan leaned around Andie to give me a half-hearted nod. The guy had been chasing her forever and was clearly not thrilled to have me here competing for her attention. I might have mustered some sympathy for him if he hadn't just spent the last hour cozying up to my girlfriend.

I released Andie and returned Evan's greeting before my gaze found its way back to her again. Her expression was hard to read, and my brow furrowed as I studied her. "Everything okay?"

Her leg shifted subtly to press against mine as she offered a restrained smile. "Great. How about you? Having a good time tonight?"

"I've had better." I shrugged as I pressed my leg back against hers. "I'm hoping it'll improve later." My plans for later involved fucking Andie senseless, preferably after tying her up and lavishing attention on every beautiful inch of her body—but no one other than the two of us needed to know that.

Before Andie could say anything else, her friends Megan and Kaylee started talking to me, and I was forced to direct my attention across the table to them. I offered them a slightly more subdued greeting than usual as I kept my leg pressed up against Andie's.

I was so distracted by thoughts of what I wanted to do to her later that when her hand squeezed my thigh, I nearly jumped out of my seat. Recovering, I schooled my expression as Andie's fingers curled around my leg to touch the inseam of my jeans.

Heat erupted in the pit of my stomach as her hand slid higher, and I leaned forward to rest my crossed arms on the table and hide what was going on in my lap. As Andie casually chatted with her friends, her hand steadily inched up my leg, out of sight.

My whole body clenched in anticipation as she neared the painful hard-on in my pants. Wanting it—*needing* it—despite the risk of getting caught. The sense of danger heating my blood and making me want it even more.

Just before she got all the way there, her hand came to a stop. Simultaneously relieved and disappointed, I let out a long, shaky breath.

As soon as I let my guard down, Andie squeezed my thigh again, her fingers digging in hard enough to make me see stars as her hand grazed my dick.

My spine went rigid and I dropped a hand in my lap to cover hers, seizing it mid-stroke and holding it still. Andie didn't move, or look at me, or in any way acknowledge what we were doing. She kept right on talking to her friends while my hand held her hand on top of my dick.

My heart hammered as my better angels warred with the devil inside me. I couldn't have told you what Andie's friends were talking about if my life depended on it. I just kept nodding vaguely and hoped to hell no one asked me anything.

Andie's fingers pressed down, and the devil kicked those angels to the curb. Swallowing a rush of saliva, I let go of her hand.

Glutton for punishment? Hell yeah, that's me.

Her gaze drifted my way, and she smiled slightly—mischief glinting in her eyes—before turning back to her friends. Slowly, so no one would see her arm moving, she stroked her fingers over me.

A bead of sweat formed at my hairline, and I reached up to

wipe it away. She rubbed harder, and I gritted my teeth, forcing out a long breath through my nose.

"You okay?" she asked mercilessly, turning her gaze on me again. "You look a little flushed."

"I'm great." My voice was so rough it was almost a growl.

"Here, have my water," Kaylee said sweetly. "You're probably dehydrated from all that sweating you did onstage."

"Thanks." My fingers clenched around the plastic bottle she pushed toward me, nearly crushing it before I managed to check myself. Carefully, trying not to let my hands visibly shake, I unscrewed the lid and took a drink.

I nearly choked to death when Andie curled her fingers and dragged her knuckles over my cock. Coughing, I reached up to wipe my mouth as every eye at the table glanced my way.

"Pardon me," I rasped into my hand, my face reddening as Andie ruthlessly continued to rub me. Heat streaked up my spine, crackling like electricity as the pressure built inside me, and I shifted my leg, unable to keep still.

Andie watched me as she pressed even harder, and I had to bite down on my tongue to keep from groaning.

Fortunately, somebody chose that moment to climb up on one of the nearby tables and dance along with the song playing over the sound system. Everyone at our table turned to watch and egg him on.

Thank the sweet baby Jesus, because I couldn't hide my full-body shudder as Andie's hand moved faster, her lips parting and her eyes darkening as they stared into mine. I was about to go out of my mind from the tension scraping through my veins like ground glass.

Before I lost it and jizzed in my pants at the table, I hauled myself out of my seat, muttering an excuse about needing to take a leak as I tried to hide the raging bulge in my pants.

Stumbling inside the bar's cramped interior, I made my way

down the dingy back hall that led to the restrooms. Instead of going into the men's room, I pushed out the back door and into the loading zone beside the dumpster.

I sagged against the wall, trying to calm my breathing as I conjured a series of unsexy images to alleviate my current physical predicament. People chewing with their mouths open. My stepmother's spandex yoga outfits. The vomit and urine stains painting the side of the dumpster next to me. That one nearly did the trick until the door swung open, and Andie stepped outside.

I tossed her a glare as she let the heavy metal door slam behind her. "Are you trying to kill me?"

Her mouth quirked. "Maybe."

She took a step toward me, and I held up my hand. "Don't you dare."

Ignoring me, she slipped her arms around my waist and pressed her lips to the base of my throat. "I hated that fucking song," she growled into my neck.

"Which one?"

Her teeth bit into my skin hard enough to make me twitch. "You know which one."

I had a guess. "'Are You Gonna Be My Girl?'"

The song I'd sung while looking at that college kid, Hannah. The one with the lyrics that sounded like I was hitting on her, even though it had been Andie's face in my mind the whole time, Andie's long brown hair I'd been thinking about, and Andie's hand the only one I'd wanted to take.

I slid my fingers into her hair and tilted her head back so I could look at her. Channeling all my hunger and longing, I adored her with my eyes as I dragged my thumb slowly across her cheek. "You know you're the only girl I want, right?"

"I better be." Her voice was low and rough, with a betraying hint of rawness beneath the challenging tone.

"You are." I kissed her, and warmth spread across my chest as her mouth softened against mine. "No one else comes close to you. You're all I can think about." I moved my mouth to her ear, and she shivered against me. "You're mine."

"And you're mine." She curled a fist in my shirt and claimed me with her mouth, her lips lush and demanding as her tongue delved deep, marking her territory with a possessiveness that sent a thrill sizzling through me. "You better not fucking forget it."

Just when I was starting to consider the idea of fucking her right here up against the wall next to the dumpster, she broke off the kiss and pulled back. "I guess I'm gonna have to punish you for singing that song to another woman."

Heat licked up my spine and I nodded, grinning like a fool. "God, yes. I definitely need to be punished."

My god, how I adored this woman. It boggled my mind how she always knew exactly what buttons to push to turn me into a quivering mass of jelly. How did I ever get so damned lucky?

She trailed her fingers down my chest, smoothing the front of my T-shirt. "I'm going back inside to say good night to my friends. I expect you to be at my place by the time I get there."

"Yes, ma'am."

An unfamiliar giddiness fluttered through my stomach as I watched her walk away. It wasn't just desire, although she'd definitely gotten my motor revving. This feeling that filled me up, making me want to float off the ground, was something softer and a lot more powerful than simple attraction.

It should have scared the shit out of me, but I didn't feel any of my usual instinct to run away. Quite the opposite. I wanted to run toward Andie and everything the future held for us. Full speed ahead. All systems go.

Christ, would you listen to me? I was turning into Tanner.

Next thing you knew, I'd be telling Andie I loved her.

19

ANDIE

As I sipped my beer, watching the couples circle the floor at King's Palace, a single question kept bobbing to the surface of my mind.

What the hell am I doing?

This was the second night in a row that Wyatt and I had gone out separately together, willingly putting ourselves in this weird-ass situation. Playing this twisted game of pretending not to care about each other.

I shouldn't like it.

But I fucking loved it.

There was no reason we had to be here tonight. We'd chosen this. Freely and of our own volition.

Last night had been different. Shiny Heathens had had a gig, and there was no way I was letting Wyatt go to the Rusty Spoke alone. Not when I knew what he looked like up on that stage. Confident, swaggering, exuding raw magnetism. His voice as smooth as a lover's caress. His tattooed arms flexing as his deft fingers strummed the guitar strings. His hips swaying in those tight jeans and his golden skin shining with sweat. That dreamy *come fuck me* look he got on his face when he was crooning his heart out.

It was enough to drive a nun to lustful thoughts, much less the single women of Crowder.

I hadn't gone only to keep Wyatt in line, although jealousy had definitely been a factor. Along with maybe a hint of distrust, if I was being completely honest. I'd watched the man sleep his way through the population of this town far too long to simply accept that he'd suddenly given up his freewheeling ways. I *wanted* to believe it, but I wasn't good at taking things on faith. I needed to collect more empirical evidence to support the hypothesis before I'd be ready to accept it as truth.

So yeah, I'd been keeping an eye on him and on any women who might decide to shoot their shot with Wyatt King. But I'd also been keeping my eye on him because I'd always loved looking at him when he was singing on that stage.

How many times had I watched him up there and fantasized that he was singing to me? And last night he'd done exactly that. My fantasies had become reality, and it had been a powerful high. Seeing him up there looking like a sex god and knowing he was *my* sex god went a long way to making up for all those years I'd spent pining for him.

During the show last night, his eyes had singled me out in the audience with an intensity that had become familiar over the last week. I'd heard tones in his singing voice that echoed the sweet murmurs and dark growls he'd uttered in my bed. I'd watched his fingers move over those guitar strings with the memory of how they'd felt touching me.

It should have been enough to tide me over for a lifetime. Especially after we'd gone back to my place and had what was far and away the best sex of my life, all that pent-up jealousy and frustration driving us both to heights that made our prior efforts seem laid-back and tame.

There was absolutely no reason we'd needed to come to King's Palace tonight. We could have stayed home and enjoyed each other's company like two normal people.

But no.

Tonight was totally on me. I'd been the one to suggest coming here. Because I'd wanted another taste of that thrill I'd experienced last night.

It was weirdly addictive. The excitement of having a secret and flaunting it in front of people. Seeing how far we could push it without getting caught. Toying with each other. Making each other jealous. Getting off on it.

How fucked-up was that?

Based on how quickly Wyatt had agreed to my suggestion tonight, it was safe to say I wasn't the only one getting off on it. We were both on board this twisted train. *Choo choo.*

We'd been here an hour, and Wyatt had already asked four different women to dance, none of whom had been me.

I could tell he was messing with me. He kept making the rounds of the room, stopping to chat—or flirt—with everyone he knew along the way. Pretending not to see me. Acting like he was about to head my way, then breaking off to ask someone else to dance. After which he'd start the whole routine over again. Circling me like a raptor. Doing his best to torment me.

That was okay. I knew he'd find his way over to me eventually. He was having a good time delaying the moment we were both itching for, but he wouldn't be able to resist forever. He wasn't going to pass up a chance to dance with me tonight.

I'd been doing my best to ignore him and the rising fever in my blood. Sometimes, when I noticed him looking my way, I'd turned my back on him and go talk to someone else.

Flirting had never been one of my finer skills. My sarcasm and bluntness tended to get the better of me. I preferred teasing and bantering with men over being nice to them, but tonight I gave it my best shot.

I'd danced with three different men—including Wyatt's brother Tanner—and felt a reckless satisfaction the whole time, knowing Wyatt was watching me and grinding his teeth.

He wasn't the only one enjoying this game.

"It's weird that Wyatt hasn't come over to say hi yet." Megan frowned as she watched him talk to someone over by the bar, then turned her frown on me. "Don't you think it's weird?"

I shrugged. "I think it's just Wyatt being Wyatt."

"He was acting weird last night too," Kaylee said.

"Was he?" I asked, playing dumb.

Megan ignored me and pointed at Kaylee. "You know what? You're right. He seemed all distracted when he was sitting with us. And then he just up and disappeared without a word."

I sipped my beer to hide my smile, remembering why he'd been so distracted. The way he'd trembled at my touch under the table. Helpless to resist. Completely at my mercy. I loved seeing him lose control of himself because of me, and I loved knowing I had a special claim on him—even if no one else did.

Had I done it in part because I wanted to get caught? Had I been hoping to force the issue so we'd have to take our relationship public?

Not consciously, but I couldn't say I'd be that upset if we blew our cover.

Wyatt would though. I'd seen how freaked out he'd been by the prospect of my brother finding out about us. I was trying to be understanding, because I knew how much Josh meant to him. But maybe Wyatt had put my brother too high up on a pedestal. I knew Wyatt listened to Josh more than he listened to me or anyone else, and I knew he was afraid of disappointing him. Maybe he looked up to Josh a little too much—so much that he could be blind to my brother's faults. Sometimes it felt like Wyatt underestimated his own worth—his strength, his loyalty, his kindness; all the qualities I admired about him—because he'd convinced himself he could never measure up to the best friend he'd canonized.

Maybe all this was my way of rebelling against the stricture Wyatt had imposed on our relationship. It had been reckless, what I'd done. But god help me, it had felt good.

It was hard, not being able to touch Wyatt. Even though his eyes had kept seeking me out last night to show me how much he missed me, I'd needed to physically feel the connection between us. To remind myself it was *real*.

Rain cast a quizzical look at me. "Y'all didn't have a fight or something, did you?"

I shook my head. "He probably just left to hook up with someone. You know Wyatt."

I felt guilty about deceiving them. If it had been up to me, I would have happily come clean to my friends and everyone else about our relationship. There was nothing I would have loved more than to tell the whole world about me and Wyatt. To finally fess up to the feelings I'd been hiding for most of my life.

"Oh!" Kaylee perked up. "I think he might be coming over here, finally."

Once again, I watched my friends primp as they prepared for Wyatt's approach. And once again, I did nothing. I didn't need to primp in order to get his attention.

I caught a whiff of Wyatt's cologne just before his hand covertly squeezed my ass as he eased past me. He didn't acknowledge me though. Instead, he greeted Kaylee with a hug. Then Megan. Then Rain. Saving me for last.

As I watched him interact with my friends, I was relieved to see him toning down the flirting a few notches. It was one thing to keep our relationship private, but I didn't want him leading them on and compounding their disappointment.

I had to admit he'd been doing a good job of abiding by the conditions of our agreement. Whenever he hugged a woman, he made sure his hands never ventured lower than her shoulder blades. I'd seen him give a lot of one-armed hugs tonight and squeeze a lot of arms and shoulders, but he hadn't kissed a single cheek—or any other body parts for that matter. Good thing. I'd meant it when I said his lips were for me and me alone.

He didn't murmur into any of my friends' ears tonight, or play with their hair, or use any of his other signature moves on them. Although I'd seen him doing it with a few other women— including Brianna goddamn Thorne—intentionally trying to get a rise out of me. It had worked too. Every time I caught sight of him cozying up to another woman, my fingernails had bitten into the palms of my hands.

Wisely, Wyatt was being more circumspect with my friends, giving them the same brotherly treatment he used to reserve for me. The disappointment showed on their faces—except for Rain, who'd had a fling with Wyatt back in high school that had pretty well gotten him out of her system—but I was pleased to see he wasn't toying with people I cared about.

When he'd finished making his way around the table, he finally turned his attention on me. "Hey you." His gaze dragged slowly up my body, his blue eyes nearly feral by the time they locked onto mine.

"Hey you." I fought to keep my voice light as I resisted the urge to ogle him back.

He pulled me in for a hug that was anything but brotherly. One of his thighs pushed between my legs as he fitted his hips against me, letting me feel exactly how happy he was to see me. His nose nestled into my hair, and I felt his hot breath as his lips grazed my ear. "You look so fucking beautiful tonight, I'm about to spontaneously combust."

Heat pooled between my thighs, and I couldn't help pressing against him to try and ease some of the ache.

Before things got too obvious, Wyatt let go of me and turned to Kaylee. "Would you like to dance?"

While he led her away, I swallowed a mouthful of beer to cool myself down. My gaze followed them as they made circuits around the floor. Kaylee smiled and beamed at him the whole time, never noticing the way Wyatt's gaze kept returning to me. After one song, he escorted her back to the table and asked Megan to dance next.

He tossed me a smirk as he took her hand, and I rolled my eyes.

"Are you sure you and Wyatt aren't in a fight?" Rain asked me as we watched him spin Megan on the dance floor. "You're the one he usually asks to dance."

I tore my gaze away from him and offered her a shrug. "Maybe he's just in the mood to mix things up."

When Wyatt came back with Megan, he set his sights on Rain next, but she turned him down with a good-natured shake of her head. "Thanks, but I'll pass."

He clutched his heart and made a show of being wounded, but Rain only laughed and shoved him away. "Dance with Andie. Everyone's waiting to see you two show off some of your fancy moves."

Wyatt swiveled on his heel, eyebrows arching as his gaze locked on mine. "Shall we?"

I responded with a nonchalant nod, as if I couldn't care less either way.

Instead of taking my hand, he gestured for me to precede him. As he followed, he pressed his palm into the small of my back. "You're wearing a dress," he murmured into my ear.

"I am."

We reached the dance floor, and I turned to face him. My

hand tried to shake a little as I held it out to him. A fizzing sensation bubbled in my stomach when his fingers closed around mine, squeezing briefly before he loosened his grip.

"You don't wear dresses very often." He placed his other hand below my shoulder blade and guided me into the circle of dancers, where we fell into step together as easily as breathing.

"That's true, I don't."

He spun me a couple of times before pulling me back to him. "I like it."

"Do you? I couldn't tell by the way you're practically drooling."

"You always make me drool. But you in a dress makes me drool even more."

We did a move called a cuddle duck out, our hips bumping as he pulled me up against him before I ducked under his arms. As we moved back-to-back his ass rubbed against mine, and my body tightened in response.

"What happens if we do a flip when you're wearing a dress?" he asked when I was facing him again. As if he didn't know.

"Everybody in the room gets to see what color underwear I'm wearing." I'd briefly considered forgoing undergarments completely, but it was too risky a proposition with dancing on the agenda. I didn't want to get banned by Uncle Randy for flashing my naughty bits at all his customers.

A grin spread over Wyatt's face. "What color underwear are you wearing?"

I arched an eyebrow. "Wouldn't you like to know?"

"That's why I asked."

"I guess you'll have to find out with everyone else."

"Like hell," he growled, his expression darkening. "No one gets to see your underwear but me."

My lips twitched into a smile. "Then we probably shouldn't do any flips."

He spun me twice, then his arm wrapped around my neck for a moving dip as he bent me back over his leg, lowering me almost to the floor.

I responded intuitively to his every cue as he pulled me upright and led me through a complex series of spins and maneuvers. My awareness of him had always been strong, but it was even stronger now that we'd been intimate. I didn't even have to think about what I was doing. I understood his body, and he understood mine.

I was already feeling a little dizzy—both from the spinning and from the powerful connection between us—when Wyatt's arm curled around my neck, and he lowered me into a kissing dip.

His hair fell around my face as his eyes gazed into mine. My lips parted in anticipation, hungering for contact as his face moved closer and closer.

Our lips touched in a barely there kiss that only lasted for the length of a blink before he hauled me back to my feet and spun me away from him. His hand clenched mine in a painful grip as our eyes met again before he pulled me back into frame.

"You're trying to torture me, aren't you?" His voice came out in a rough growl, and his chest heaved from more than just the exertion of dancing.

My own breathing was as labored as his. "Is it working?"

"Yes." His blue eyes blazed bright as a gas-powered flame.

I tried to look stern even as my insides melted into a puddle of molten desire. "Like you weren't trying to torture me by dancing with every woman here before me."

"I was saving the best for last." His mouth curled in a playful smile, and he yanked me away from the dance floor so suddenly I stumbled into him. His arm wrapped around my shoulders as he guided me toward the bar. "I'm thirsty. Are you thirsty? Let's get something to drink."

"Okay." My head was spinning too fast to do anything but follow him. I felt drunk, but it certainly wasn't from the single beer I'd nursed over the last hour.

We got in line for the bar behind a group of chattering middle-aged ladies, one of whom I recognized from my aunt Birdie's Bunco group. Wyatt's arm stayed draped around my shoulders, and the heat radiating off him licked at my skin, making my whole body vibrate.

I glanced up and caught him staring at me with a greedy, dark look in his eyes. My stomach tightened, and I licked my lips.

His free hand clenched my arm, and he steered me out of the line and into the hallway that led to his uncle's office.

"The bar's back that way," I said as my feet shuffled to keep pace with him.

"Is it?" He hurried us past his uncle's closed office door. "Oops."

An exit sign glowed above the junction at the end of the hall, pointing out the delivery entrance off to the left. As soon as we rounded the corner, he pushed me up against the wall and his warm, wet mouth covered mine. I moaned against his lips as his hands roamed over my body.

"Wyatt," I growled when I felt him hike up my skirt.

"Andie," he growled back, daring me to stop him. His fingers crept up my thigh, pushing my skirt up, and I shuddered, knowing we shouldn't, but wanting it too bad to put a stop to it.

He shoved his hand under my skirt, and I whimpered as it traveled higher, closer to where I needed to feel him. As he watched me writhe, his lips tilted in a smile of satisfaction. When his finger brushed against my underwear, my head slammed back against the wall.

He cradled a hand around my skull as his fingers teased at

the damp fabric between my legs. "I like you in dresses." His voice was all smoke and gravel. "Easy access."

I glared at him as pleasure mingled with frustration, my whole body rigid and my muscles trembling.

"You should wear dresses more often." His fingers pushed my underwear aside, and we groaned in harmony as they slid inside me.

My hips jerked, desperate for more pressure and more friction. The fever burning in me threatened to short-circuit my brain, but a single lick of common sense remained to remind me of where we were and the dangerousness of what we were about to do.

I grabbed his wrist. "We can't do this here."

He blinked at me, glassy-eyed, before he seemed to register what I'd said. "Fine." He removed his hand from my skirt. "Then we need to leave and go somewhere we can do it. Right now." Wincing, he adjusted the inseam of his jeans.

I let out a breath as I smoothed my rumpled dress. "You left first last night. I should leave first tonight."

He nodded. "Okay."

"Make sure you hang around for at least ten minutes after I go, so people know we didn't leave together."

"All right." His head continued to nod in frenetic jerks. "Go. Hurry."

"Don't follow me out of here in case anyone's watching. Wait until I'm clear."

"Oh my god!" He huffed impatiently, running a hand through his hair. "You'd think we were spies or something."

"Hey, if you don't care about getting caught, then we can walk out of here hand in hand and announce to the world we're together."

My irritation over our situation must have bled into my tone, because his eyebrows drew together, and he hooked a hand around the back of my neck. "You know I want to do that, don't you? I'd do it in a heartbeat if I could."

"Likely story," I muttered, only half joking.

"Andie, shit." He pressed his forehead against mine. "Tell me you believe that."

I couldn't just hear the agony and desperation in his voice, I could feel it vibrating through him. This was hard for him too. It reminded me how lucky I was. He was wonderful in almost every way. Caring and thoughtful and devoted to me. So gorgeous he took my breath away.

So what if we had to hide our relationship for a while? We knew what we meant to each other. He'd shown me over and over again, hadn't he?

"I believe you." I brushed my lips against his, softly, warmly —but chastely, afraid of heating things up again, lest we throw caution to the wind.

His fingers tightened in my hair, and I felt some of the tension drain out of him.

"I'm going now." I kissed his forehead and unwound his hands from me, backing away. "I'll see you at my place in twenty minutes, okay?"

His rough reply followed me around the corner. "If I can wait that long."

20

WYATT

I stared at the wall in front of me, picturing Andie's face as I dragged the paint roller across it. I'd left Andie grading exams at the kitchen table this morning and come over to my brother Manny's to get his nursery ready for the newest addition to the family. Behind me, Tanner and Ryan were chattering about the creamery's upcoming Centennial Festival—a subject I had less than zero interest in—so I tuned them out, thinking instead about the new song I'd started writing.

It was about Andie, of course. But this one was different than the others I'd written about her. It wasn't wistful or forlorn or bittersweet, because it wasn't about unfulfilled desires. This new song was hopeful and upbeat. About taking a risk and finding joy.

I got so lost in my own thoughts, I didn't realize I'd been painting the same spot on the wall over and over again until Ryan's big hand landed on my shoulder.

"You might want to share some of that paint with the rest of the wall," he said. "I think you've got that one patch pretty well covered."

"Shit," I muttered, snapping back to the work I was supposed to be doing. The longer it took us to finish painting this nursery, the longer it'd be until I could get back to Andie.

"If I didn't know better, I'd think he had a girl on the brain." Tanner stood on a ladder by the window doing the brushwork around the wood trim. Of the three of us, he had the best eye for detail and the steadiest hand, so he got stuck with all the edge work.

Ryan grinned as he rolled mint green paint within a few inches of the ceiling. At six foot five, he was tall enough to reach without a stool. "Wyatt's always got a girl on the brain."

Tanner snorted as he dabbed his brush around the corner of the window casing. "No, he's always got his own dick on his brain. That's not the same thing at all."

I knew he was trying to bait me, and I scowled as I bent down to run my roller through the paint tray. "Y'all know I can hear you talking about me, right?"

"Oh, so you were listening." Ryan scratched his thick red beard. "Seemed like your mind was elsewhere."

Out of pettiness, I chose not to inform him that he'd just smeared green paint in his beard hairs. "I was tuning you out on purpose because you were boring me."

"I guess that answers my question about whether you're participating in the Centennial Festival."

I made a sour face. "Fat chance."

It was the hundred-year anniversary of the founding of the creamery, and they were kicking off the celebration with some kind of weekend-long festival at King Town Park, the ice-cream-themed amusement park next to the plant. I didn't know what it entailed, exactly, just that I didn't want any part of it.

Tanner shot me a disapproving look. "Josie said she's been trying to get in touch with you."

I was aware. I'd been ignoring my sister's texts, because I didn't want her guilting me into whatever she was trying to wrangle me into. Most likely she wanted the whole family present for some photo op or ribbon cutting or some other damn thing, so we could all stand around Dad and pretend to be one big, happy family with nothing but the town's best interests at heart.

After what my father had done to Andie, I wasn't in the mood to play along with it, even to make Josie happy. I didn't trust myself to be within restraining-order distance of my old man. Far better for everyone else if I just stayed away. At least then I couldn't cause a scene that would force Josie to do damage control.

"I've been busy," I said vaguely.

Ryan shot me a curious look over his shoulder. "Busy doing what?"

"Fixing up Andie Lockhart's house," Tanner answered before I could.

Ryan lowered his paint roller and turned around to look at me, his eyebrows lifting in surprise. "Andie hired you to work on her house?"

"She ran into some trouble with her HOA and needs a bunch of repairs done fast." I shrugged like it was no big deal. "I'm doing her a favor."

"I'll bet you are." Ryan smirked at me.

"It's not like that," I replied, bristling. I didn't give a crap about my own reputation, but I didn't want anyone gossiping about Andie.

I debated telling my brothers that it was Dad who'd been behind Andie's HOA problems in the first place, and how his lawyers had threatened her, hoping she'd sell the house so he could make a profit off her inheritance. But I decided not to drag them into it. Tanner already had enough tension with Dad because of work, and Ryan had always had a weirdly good relationship with my old man. Somehow he'd managed to be a better stepfather to Ryan than a father to his own flesh and blood. *Go figure.*

"How's it going?" Tanner asked. "You guys work things out?"

I knew he was asking about more than just the repairs to Andie's house, but this wasn't the time or place to talk about it. "Yeah, we're good. Everything's fine."

"Work what out?" Ryan asked.

"Nothing." I shot Tanner a warning look. Ryan didn't know how I felt about Andie, and I preferred to keep it that way. "Andie's HOA was being a pain in the ass, but I talked them around."

Ryan gave me a gruff nod of approval. "Let me know if you need any extra hands."

Tanner shook his head at me, clearly disappointed I hadn't followed his advice and confessed my feelings to Andie. Little did he know, I'd done exactly that. I just couldn't tell him about it.

As he refreshed the paint on his roller, Ryan cast a thoughtful look at me. "You should ask that girl out."

I frowned at him. "What?"

"I know you're into her. What are you waiting for? Stop playing around and make your move."

I turned an accusing look on Tanner. "What'd you tell him?"

Tanner held up his hands. "I didn't tell him anything, I swear."

Ryan snorted and turned back to the wall he was painting. "Like I need Tanner to tell me anything. It's only been obvious since forever that you're in love with Andie Lockhart. I keep waiting for you to come to your senses, but I'm starting to wonder if you've got any in that head of yours."

I had no idea I'd been that transparent, but it probably shouldn't have surprised me that Ryan had sussed it out. He'd always had an uncanny sixth sense when it came to me, always able to suss out when I was up to something. I had to be extra careful around him, or he'd be able to read me like an open book.

For a moment, I was tempted to tell them both the truth. That Andie and I were together and I'd never been happier. It would have felt good to share the news and tell them they'd both been right.

But I was the one who'd begged Andie to keep our relationship a secret. She hadn't wanted to do it and had only agreed for my sake. It'd be unfair of me to spill the beans to my brothers when I was making her lie to hers about us.

"That's ridiculous. I'm not in love with Andie." As I said it, the words left a sick, unpleasant feeling in my gut.

Because they were a lie. I *was* in love with Andie. And not just in a pining, teenage crush kind of way. But in an honest to god, head over heels, spend the rest of my life with her, till death do us part kind of way.

Holy shit.

Ryan shook his head as he pulled his paint roller down the wall. "I honestly can't tell if you're lying to us or to yourself at this point. But if you drag your feet too much longer, someone else is going to come along and snap her up."

"Let them." I kept my eyes on my own wall so I wouldn't have to look at Ryan while I lied to him. "Andie's great, but we're just friends. I'm not interested in snapping her or anyone up. I like my freedom too much to tie myself down to any one girl."

"Still not ready to grow up yet, huh?"

I managed to toss a cocky grin over my shoulder. "Never."

Ryan propped his paint roller in the tray. "Don't you ever look at Manny and Adriana and how happy they are, and wish you could have what they have?"

Yes. Wasn't that what I'd wished for at seventeen? To marry Andie one day so I could wake up next to her every morning.

Exactly like I'd woken up next to her every day this week. Now that I'd had a taste of what it could be like, I wanted it more than ever.

"Do *you*?" I shot back to shift the conversation off of me. "You're almost forty, and I don't see you settling down with anyone."

He flipped open the cooler to grab a bottle of water. "Only because I haven't met the right woman yet. When I find her, you can bet I'll happily trade the freedom of being single for a chance to make a life with someone I love."

I wondered if that was really true. Ryan seemed pretty set in his bachelor ways. He'd been living alone in the same house for fifteen years, and when he wasn't working shifts at the firehouse, most of his free time was spent training or traveling to the Scottish Highland Games he competed in around the state. I wasn't convinced he was as open to sharing his life as he claimed.

"When's the last time you even went on a date?" I asked him.

I remembered a time when Ryan had been...not a ladies' man, per se, but certainly popular with the ladies. I expected he was still just as popular with the ladies, but I hadn't noticed him returning their interest in a while. A long while, in fact. He'd had a few serious girlfriends and more than a few not-so-serious girlfriends in the past, but lately he hadn't had any girlfriends at all.

He glared at me as he wiped his mouth with the back of his hand. "None of your business."

"What, my love life's fair game and yours isn't?"

"Exactly."

"Pretty sure it's been a couple of years," Tanner chimed in. "By my recollection."

I tried to recall the last time I'd seen Ryan with a steady girlfriend. It had to have been a couple of years, at least. Had he gotten tired of dating as he grew older and more set in his ways?

Or had something happened to sour him on it? I couldn't recall any of his breakups being acrimonious, but then Ryan was unlikely to have told me if they were.

He'd always played his cards close to his chest, especially when it came to things like his love life. Maybe because he was so much older and considered himself more of a father figure to us than a brother. Or maybe that was just how he was with everyone. Not the type of guy to kiss and tell.

"We're not talking about me," Ryan growled, dropping into the dad voice he used whenever one of us was in trouble. "We're talking about Wyatt and what's got him so distracted."

Tanner and I traded an eye roll, both of us knowing it was useless to try and pry anything else out of Ryan.

Regardless, there *was* something I could tell my brothers, even if I couldn't tell them about Andie yet. Another secret it was past time I shared.

"I guess I might as well come clean," I said as I stooped to get myself a water. "Before you hear about it from someone else."

"Hear about what?" Tanner asked, stepping down from the ladder.

I grabbed another water from the cooler and tossed it to him. "I've been trying my hand at songwriting."

My brothers exchanged a silent glance before looking back at me.

"Since when?" Tanner asked, keeping his expression neutral.

I took a long drink of water, wiping my mouth before I answered. "A couple of years, I guess."

Tanner looked surprised. He probably thought I told him everything because he was the only person I'd told about my feelings for Andie.

"I didn't tell anyone about it until recently," I said, trying to make him feel better. "I was waiting until I was sure they were good enough to play for people."

"How many songs have you written?" Ryan asked.

"A couple dozen so far."

"That's impressive." Ryan gave me an approving nod. "I'm proud of you." He wasn't the sort to dole out compliments lightly. I hadn't given him that many reasons to be proud of me, and hearing him say the words now left me disoriented.

I ducked my head and scratched the back of my neck. "I talked to the band about it this week, and Matt's going to work with me to flesh out the music so we can build a set list of original stuff for the four of us to play together. And then, I guess, start trying to get some more gigs out of it."

"Wow," Tanner said. "Good for you."

"It'll be a while before we're ready to perform any of the new songs together." I dared a look at my brothers as I told the next part. "But I was thinking I might see if I could do a solo acoustic gig at Zelda's."

Ryan's eyes crinkled at the corners. "You should definitely do that."

"Yeah, that's a great idea," Tanner said. "We'd love to come hear you perform your songs."

I nodded and blew out a relieved breath. "Maybe I'll go talk to Zelda about it this week."

Ryan's face split into a grin. "You know what you should do? You should write Andie a love song, invite her to Zelda's, and dedicate it to her to declare your intentions."

I rolled my eyes. "Ryan."

"What? Women love that shit."

"It's true," Tanner said. "They do."

"I'm not declaring my intentions for anyone onstage at Zelda's or anywhere else."

I didn't need to, because I'd already told Andie how I felt and sung her all the songs I'd written about her. When I eventually performed them in front of an audience, she'd know exactly who they were for without me having to announce it to the whole world.

Ryan shook his head at me. "She's smitten with you too, you know. It's obvious to anyone with eyes. I don't know what you two idiots are waiting for."

"Her brother wouldn't approve," Tanner volunteered, earning a scowl from me.

"That's beside the point." I was going to kill him for bringing this up in front of Ryan.

"I don't know, I think it's square in the middle of the point," Tanner replied, apparently eager to hasten his imminent demise.

"Josh?" Ryan frowned. "What's he got to do with it?"

"I promised him I'd keep my hands off his sister, and it's a promise I mean to keep."

Ryan's eyes narrowed at me as he scratched his beard.

I braced myself for whatever well-meaning advice he was about to impart but was saved by Isabella, who hurtled into the room wearing butterfly wings and a green tutu.

"Whoa there, Tinkerbella." I scooped her up before she could run through the paint tray and hoisted her onto my hip.

"Isabella!" Manny appeared in the doorway, looking red-faced and exasperated. "I told you to stay out of here."

She shoved a soggy, half-eaten Nilla Wafer in my face. "Do you want some of my cookie?"

Manny tried to hide a smile as I dodged his daughter's attempt to put her spit-soaked cookie in my mouth, and I heard Ryan and Tanner snort in amusement.

"No thank you, but I'll bet Tanner does." I dropped her into his arms, and when he opened his mouth to protest she crammed that gross cookie right in his piehole.

That's my girl.

"Mmmm, delicious." Tanner shot me a murderous look over Isabella's head. "Thank you."

"It's looking great in here." Manny peered around the room at the progress we'd made. "The color's okay, right?"

My phone vibrated in my pocket, and I pulled it out while my brothers confabbed about the color Manny and Adriana had chosen for the nursery.

I had a new text notification from Andie, and I turned around to hide my smile as I swiped to read it.

Birdie invited me to dinner tonight.

My smile faded. I'd been looking forward to getting back to her as soon as we were done here. Especially after my bombshell realization that I was in love with her. I wasn't necessarily ready to tell her that I loved her yet, but I sure as hell wanted to see her. If she was having dinner at her aunt's house, that meant we'd be apart for even longer.

I swallowed my disappointment as I typed my reply.

OK guess I'll see you later then?

Apparently this was what being in love did to me. A few extra hours away from my girlfriend, and I was moping like the world had ended.

"Wyatt."

I turned around at the sound of Ryan's voice and found all three of my brothers looking at me expectantly. "Sorry, what?"

Ryan was holding Isabella now and trying not to wince as she tugged on his bushy beard. "Tell Manny your news."

My thoughts were so full of Andie, it took me a second to remember what news he was talking about.

"He's been writing songs on the sly," Ryan said for me when I didn't answer fast enough. "After years of pretending not to have any musical aspirations, our talented little brother's finally betrayed some ambition."

"Are you going to get the band to start playing your songs?" Manny asked.

"Hopefully." I told him how Matt was going to work on the arrangements with me and about my plan to approach Zelda about doing a solo set in the meantime.

"Be sure you let me know when," Manny said. "We'll try to make it to your show if we can. Depending on the baby situation, obviously."

"What do you say?" Ryan asked, peering down at Isabella. "Do you want to go to a concert and see Uncle Wyatt sing?"

She nodded, her expression solemn as she continued to pet Ryan's beard. "Yes, I do want to do that."

"Zelda's is twenty-one and up," I pointed out.

Ryan bent his head to address Isabella again. "Then Uncle Wyatt will just have to find someplace kid-friendly to play."

"You know what he should do?" Manny was pointing at me, but he was looking at Ryan and Tanner. "He should talk to Randy."

"Yes!" Tanner's head bobbed in agreement. "That's a great idea."

"Does he ever book anything at the dance hall but country-western?" Ryan glanced over at me. "Are your songs rock songs or country songs?"

"Either way," Tanner said before I could answer, "Randy has all kinds of contacts. I'll bet he could help him get bookings at other venues."

I didn't want Uncle Randy using his leverage to get me gigs —even if he'd be willing to do it, which was by no means certain —and I was about to say as much when my phone buzzed in my hand.

It was a text from Andie's aunt Birdie.

If you're free tonight, come to dinner. The usual time.

My stomach went into free fall. On the bright side, it meant

I'd get to see Andie sooner rather than later. The part that made my lunch curdle in my gut was that Josh was almost guaranteed to be there too.

I hadn't laid eyes on him since I'd started seeing Andie. I'd been avoiding him. Dreading coming face-to-face with my best friend after breaking my promise to him.

What were the odds he'd notice something had changed? Pretty fucking good. Even if he didn't, Birdie sure might. Or Josh's girlfriend, Mia. She'd asked me some pretty pointed questions awhile back that made me think she might have suspicions about my feelings for Andie.

Shit. What do I do?

I chewed on my thumbnail as my brothers continued to make plans for my musical career without bothering to solicit my input.

I could say no. Make up an excuse to beg off.

But that would just delay the inevitable. I couldn't avoid my best friend forever. The whole point of the charade was to preserve the friendship. At least at Birdie's we'd have plenty of buffers and distractions. Hopefully he wouldn't pay too much attention to me and Andie. Hopefully she'd be on her good behavior. Hopefully we could pull this off without arousing any suspicion.

I inhaled a deep breath and accepted Birdie's invitation.

God almighty, I hoped we were ready for this.

———

21

WYATT

I was the last to arrive at Birdie's house. Josh's truck and Andie's Jeep were both already parked out front when I got there.

My feet dragged on the walk from my truck to the house like I was wearing antigravity boots.

As I stepped onto Birdie's porch, I ran a nervous hand through my hair. Taking a deep breath, I summoned an attitude of cool nonchalance before I jabbed the doorbell.

Mia let me in. While I was giving her a hug, I heard Josh and Andie's voices inside, and my stomach gave a nervous lurch.

Mia pulled back and frowned at me. "Are you okay?"

So much for cool nonchalance.

"Long day," I told her. "But the sight of your pretty face has boosted my spirits."

Mia rolled her eyes—she was long since used to my bullshit—and I followed her into the house. Josh and Andie were in the kitchen helping Birdie with dinner. Andie looked up from cutting vegetables as I walked in. Her mouth didn't move, but when her eyes met mine, they gleamed like someone had turned up a dimmer switch. My insides turned to goo, and a feeling of peace overtook me at the sight of her. For a stupidly long moment we both stood there beaming at each other like a couple of knuckleheads.

Until Josh looked up from the onion he was slicing, and I jerked my eyes away from Andie in a hurry.

For fuck's sake. This was no way to maintain our cover.

"Hey, man." Josh nodded a greeting at me and went right back to his chopping. Apparently he hadn't noticed me and Andie making moony eyes at each other.

Whew.

I went into the kitchen, clapping a friendly hand on Josh's shoulder as I moved past him to greet Birdie. She stood at the stove in a long floral muumuu making fried chicken—my favorite—and she let me kiss her cheek before shooing me away from the sputtering pan of hot oil.

"You know where the drinks are," she said as she reached up to brush her short graying hair back from her forehead. "See if anyone needs a refill."

Birdie had been in my life even longer than Josh—longer even than I could remember. She'd not only been my preschool teacher, but also one of my mom's best friends, so she'd known me pretty much since the day I was born.

When my mom died, it was Birdie who'd sat with me and Tanner during the viewing before the funeral while Ryan and our dad stood next to the casket accepting condolences. I didn't remember much about that day, but I remembered holding on to Birdie's hand and trying not to cry, because our dad had told us we needed to be brave. And I remembered Birdie telling us it was okay to cry if we felt like it, so we'd stopped trying to be brave and the three of us had sat there and cried for my mom together.

I'd do basically anything for Birdie. Step in front of a bullet, donate a kidney, whatever she needed. I'd done all the renovations on her garage apartment at cost so she could earn some extra money by renting it out. Of course, then she'd turned right around and let Andie live there rent-free for a couple of years, because that was the kind of person Birdie was. She'd never been married or had kids of her own, so Josh and Andie were the closest family she had. Especially after their parents—Birdie's sister and her husband—had moved up to Maine a few years ago.

I picked up Josh's beer to test it for fullness before wandering over to where Andie was slicing cabbage. "You good?"

"I'll take another." She raised her beer bottle to her lips, and my mouth went dry as I watched her chug the last of it. "Por favor y gracias." When she handed me the empty, she let her fingers brush against mine.

I forced myself to turn away from her. "Mia? You need anything?"

Mia lifted her glass of bourbon as she finished setting the table. "I'm set."

"Andie was just telling us about all the work you've been doing on her house." Josh's gaze stayed on the onion he was slicing, but he sounded noticeably sour.

"Yeah, I've been working over there almost every day for the last couple of weeks." As I pulled open the fridge, I shot Andie a questioning look.

She rolled her eyes. "Josh is sulking because I didn't immediately go running to him for help when I had a problem."

"I'm not sulking," he replied in a tone that was definitely sulky. "I'm just wondering why you didn't even tell me about it." I could tell he was hurt, and I couldn't say I blamed him.

"You didn't tell him about the HOA letter?" I said as I set Andie's Shiner Bock next to her. I'd assumed she had, but that was what I got for assuming.

"I didn't tell anyone about it." She shrugged as she scraped sliced cabbage into a big ceramic bowl. "I didn't even tell Birdie until today when she called."

"You told Wyatt." Josh shot me a glance I couldn't read. "I guess that explains why I haven't heard from you lately."

Well, shit. I didn't like where this was going. Josh sounded like he might be getting suspicious already, and once he and Andie started sniping at each other, there was no telling what she might let slip in order to get a rise out of him.

"Did she tell you it's my dad that's behind the whole thing?" I said, hoping to distract them.

"No." Josh quit sulking and stared at me in surprise. "Are you serious?"

Birdie looked over from the stove with a frown. "Is that true?"

She'd always tried to keep her feelings to herself when it came to the subject of my dad, but I'd inferred a long time ago that she wasn't his biggest fan.

I dropped my gaze and nodded at my beer. "That's why Andie called me. Because the whole thing was my dad's doing."

"Why would he do something like that?" Mia asked.

She'd only moved here last year, so she wasn't familiar with my dad or what he was like. I assumed she'd probably been told some stuff by Josh or Andie by now, but she hadn't seen George King in action firsthand.

I shrugged and took a swig of beer. "He's involved in some new real estate venture that's buying up properties on the cheap in order to build condos."

"They've bought a bunch of properties in my neighborhood," Andie said. "It's not like he was targeting me specifically."

I couldn't believe she was trying to defend my dad after what he'd done to her, and I shot her a frown. "No, he's just indiscriminately bullying people into giving up their houses for less than market value so he can profit off their misfortune."

"Lucky for me, I had Wyatt on my side." Andie gave my arm a squeeze. "He's taking care of everything."

"That is lucky." Birdie flashed me a grateful look as she turned back to the stove.

"Are you sure it's all handled?" Josh glanced up from his cutting board and his eyes narrowed when he saw Andie's hand on me.

I shifted away from her. "Yeah, I've got it covered. Don't worry." I walked to the other side of the kitchen and pretended an interest in Birdie's chicken-frying to put more distance between me and Andie.

"Do you need help with any of the work on the house?" Josh asked.

"I'm good with a hammer," Mia volunteered. "I'm happy to come hammer things if that would help."

Andie threw her a smile. "I appreciate the offer, but Wyatt's got it under control. You should see the project plan he made for me."

I struggled to hide my flush of pride at Andie's compliment. "We're actually pretty close to done. I promised the HOA guy that all the requested maintenance would be completed by the end of the month, and we're on track to make that with a couple of days to spare."

"Wyatt talked him into waiving all the fines if we got the work done in thirty days," Andie added, beaming at me.

Josh's gaze met mine with a solemn nod. "Thanks for looking out for Andie, man. Seriously."

"Always," I replied earnestly, despite the guilt twisting in my gut. I might be a low-down dirty dog who was defiling his little sister behind his back, but I could at least keep my promise to protect her from everyone other than me. Looking for a distraction, I bent down to peer into the oven. "Are those rolls I smell?"

"They are, and you can go on and get them out for me,

honey." Birdie stepped aside to let me open the oven door. "This chicken is just about ready."

"Hot damn," I said. "I'm so hungry my belly thinks my throat's been cut."

Andie tossed the coleslaw while I carried the rolls to the table and Birdie dished up the last of the fried chicken. Mia handed Birdie a glass of bourbon as we all sat down. Birdie took her traditional place at the head of the table with Josh next to her. Instead of sitting across from her brother like she usually did, Andie sat next to him, leaving me and Mia to sit across from them.

I dared a glance across the table at Andie, and she gave me a quick smile that made my heart leap into my throat. Goddamn, she really had me bewitched. If Josh didn't notice, it would be a miracle.

As the food got passed around and the conversation turned to more mundane topics that didn't involve me, I relaxed and tried to have a good time. While I was biting into my second piece of chicken, I felt something nudge my foot under the table. Glancing up, I saw Andie smirking at me. She ran her bare foot across my ankle and then up my shin.

I reached for my beer, steeling my expression as her foot traveled higher, up my inner thigh and into my lap.

"You told me you'd had a long day," Mia said, addressing me. "What made it long?"

Every eye at the table turned on me just as Andie's toes settled against my dick.

I wiped my mouth before dropping my napkin into my lap, covering up Andie's groping foot. "I was over at Manny's house all day painting the nursery with Tanner and Ryan." I tried to keep the strain out of my voice as Andie's foot twitched in my lap. "I swear it took three times as long with their help as it would have if I'd done it by myself."

"When's the new baby due?" Birdie asked, smearing butter on one of her homemade dinner rolls.

Andie's toes nudged my dick again, and I clamped my hand down on her foot. "In a little over a month." I shot a glare across the table.

She smiled sweetly. "I'll bet Isabella's excited to be a big sister."

I summoned a sweet smile of my own. "Hey, did you ask Birdie about those old letters we found at the house?"

Birdie reached for her bourbon. "What letters?"

As soon as everyone's attention was focused on Andie, I pushed her foot out of my lap and adjusted myself so I could cross my legs, cutting off her access.

"Wyatt found a bundle of old letters underneath the floorboards in the front bedroom," Andie said. "They were all addressed to Meemaw."

"Imagine that." Birdie shook her head as she sipped her drink. "That was her bedroom when she was a girl. She could have hidden them there and forgotten all about them."

"What kind of letters?" Mia asked.

Andie's eyes met mine, and I remembered how I'd found her crying over them—and what that had led to next. I could only assume she was thinking of the same thing.

"Love letters," she said, blushing a little. "Pretty spicy ones, actually."

"Whoa." Josh shuddered as he scooped coleslaw onto his fork. "I don't think I'd want to read something like that about Meemaw."

Birdie smiled as she helped herself to another drumstick. "From your grandfather, I assume?"

Andie bit her lip. "No, actually."

Birdie glanced up in surprise. "Really?"

"There was no name or return address on the envelopes."

Andie paused with an uneasy glance at Birdie. "But the letters were all signed with the initials 'HB.'"

"Were they dated?" Birdie asked, frowning.

Andie nodded. "Meemaw would have been nineteen."

Josh's head swung toward Andie. "I thought she and Pawpaw started dating when they were both sixteen?"

"That's what I thought too," Andie said. "But there's no mention of him at all. Whoever this HB person was, she seemed to be having some kind of secret affair with him the year before she and Pawpaw got married."

"Well, isn't that something? Who'd have guessed?" Birdie gave an amused shake of her head as she bit into her drumstick.

I watched Andie and Josh exchange a look.

"You're not upset?" Josh asked Birdie.

She dabbed at her mouth with her napkin. "Heavens, no. It's got nothing to do with me. It's nice to know Mom got to sow a few wild oats before she settled down."

"So you don't have any idea who HB could be?" Andie asked her.

"No earthly idea. What a fun mystery! I'd love to see the letters. Maybe we can find a clue in them."

"I'll bring them with me next time I come over," Andie promised.

"There's no rush. They've kept all this time. They can certainly keep awhile longer." Birdie smiled. "Now, who wants another roll?"

After we'd eaten as much as we could stuff in our faces, we all pitched in to clear the table and do the dishes for Birdie.

"Anyone up for a game of Trivial Pursuit?" she asked as she presided over the cleanup from the comfort of her recliner.

"Me!" Andie and Mia shouted in unison.

"I'll get it." Leaving Josh and Mia to finish the last of the dishes, I headed for the spare room closet where Birdie kept the board games.

"I've got to pee," Andie announced and followed me into the back of the house.

As soon as we were out of sight, she grabbed me by the arm and dragged me into Birdie's spare room. Laying her palms on my chest, Andie pushed me up against the wall.

The heat from her hands spiked straight through me, and her eyes seemed to throw off sparks in the dim light. She tilted her head up, her lips teasing against mine as she pressed her pelvis into me.

I stifled a groan as my cock swelled in response to her.

"I missed you today," she murmured in a low voice that shivered in my belly.

My hips rocked into her of their own volition. Panicked alarm bells rang in my head, warning me that we could be caught at any second, but I was too aroused to heed them. Not when Andie's succulent lips were mere millimeters from mine.

I couldn't stop myself from kissing her. I might die by her brother's hand tonight, but at least I'd die happy.

Andie's mouth was hot and demanding, her tongue greedy as it tangled with mine. My hands slid over her hips and around to her ass, pulling her harder against me. She clawed at me, her fingers fumbling at my waist and scrabbling at the elastic band of my boxer briefs.

Sanity finally punctured my aroused stupor, and I grabbed both her wrists, yanking them away from my pants. "Jesus, Andie."

Her lips pursed in a pout, her expression a mix of longing and frustration.

"We can't do this," I said with more pleading in my voice than conviction.

"Fine." She stepped back, and the loss of her body heat left me unbalanced.

As I reached down to adjust myself, her gaze followed the movement hungrily. Her tongue darted out to wet her bottom lip.

"Stop looking at me like that."

Her eyes jumped to mine, widening with pretend innocence. "Like what?"

"Like you want to eat me alive."

She laughed softly and started toward me again.

I tensed like I was about to be attacked, my hand shooting out to ward her off. "Behave."

Her palm pressed against mine and moved it easily aside. I was too weak to resist her, and she damn well knew it.

Resigned to my fate, I let my eyes fall closed as she leaned toward me. Her lips grazed my cheek in a chaste, light kiss. I felt her withdraw and heard her soft step moving toward the door. By the time I opened my eyes, she was gone.

I took a moment to calm my beating heart and will my dick to settle the fuck down. Then I took a second moment. And a third. Only then did I retrieve the Trivial Pursuit game from the closet.

Andie was still in the bathroom when I rejoined the others. Josh and Mia were too busy making heart eyes at each other to pay me any mind as I sat on the couch and started setting up the board.

Birdie set her drink down and leaned forward in her recliner to help. "How shall we divide up the teams?"

"Boys against girls," Andie suggested, coming back into the room. She grinned at me as she dropped onto the opposite couch and reached for a box of cards.

"No way." Josh shook his head as he wandered in from the kitchen.

Birdie's copy of the game was the original edition that came out in the eighties, so her age gave her an advantage over the rest of us. Mia was basically a genius who had more knowledge of science, history, and literature in her pinky toe than I'd ever learned in my whole life. And Andie was some kind of freakish trivia savant whose mind was packed with so many random facts that any team with her on it was almost guaranteed to win.

Mia sat down next to Andie, looking smug. "Boys against girls sounds good to me."

Josh and I exchanged a look of resignation, knowing we were about to get crushed.

22

ANDIE

Wyatt lay sprawled on my bed, naked and breathtakingly beautiful with his skin glowing in the soft light of my bedside lamp. Expectant but relaxed. Waiting to see what I'd do.

Kneeling between his legs, I dragged my gaze over his body. I could tell he was aching for me to touch him, but I knew he liked the feel of my eyes on him too. He was enjoying the anticipation, and I was enjoying it along with him.

I splayed my fingers over his thighs and watched his chest hitch. As I ran my hands over his skin, I considered what I wanted to do to him.

I'd figured out pretty fast that he liked pain with his pleasure. Inflicting pain wasn't my kink, but I didn't mind indulging him a little. There was only so far I was willing to take it, no matter how much he might get off on it. Finding creative ways to scratch his itch without veering out of my own comfort zone had proven to be an entertaining challenge.

"Stay here," I told him as I climbed off the bed. "Close your eyes."

His eyebrows lifted in excited curiosity. "Why?"

"Because I told you to. Don't make me get the blindfold."

His answering grin was flirty and eager, game for anything. "What if I want you to get the blindfold?"

When we were alone like this, just the two of us, everything was perfect. The lie we'd been telling everyone didn't bother me, because this private part of us, the way we were together, was only ours. This Wyatt—open, trusting, as tender as he was seductive—was the secret Wyatt that was mine and mine alone. And the person I could be when I was with him—unguarded, adventurous, unafraid to seek affection and let my needy side show—that secret version of me was his. She wouldn't even exist if it wasn't for him.

Not bothering to hide my smile, I pulled open my bedside drawer and tossed a satin sleep mask onto his chest. "You better be wearing that when I get back." I tried to sound bossy, because I knew he liked it that way when we played, but I couldn't help the affection that leaked through, softening my tone.

I grabbed my robe and fastened it as I ran downstairs. It was Monday night, and we'd just gotten out of the shower after washing the dirt of the workday off each other. The leftovers we'd brought back from Birdie's last night waited for us in the fridge, but they could wait a little longer until we'd finished upstairs. I grabbed a pint of ice cream out of the freezer and snagged a spoon on my way out of the kitchen.

When I got back to the bedroom, Wyatt was blindfolded and waiting as instructed. His head lifted off the pillow at the sound of my return, and his brow furrowed as I set the ice cream lid on the nightstand.

He stayed still as I crawled back onto the bed, even though his body was vibrating with barely suppressed excitement. I nudged his legs apart so I could position myself between them again. Then I dug out some ice cream and touched the back of the spoon to his inner thigh.

His body jerked in surprise at the cold contact. "What is that?"

Instead of answering, I raised the spoon and dropped some ice cream onto his stomach.

"What the fuck?" he yelped as the freezing cold custard slid over his skin. "Is that *ice cream*?"

Laughing, I bent over him and licked it off his stomach. He shuddered helplessly as my tongue swept over his skin from his hip bone to his navel.

When I'd finished and sat back again, he reached up to yank off his blindfold. "You've got to be kidding me," he said when he saw the container in my hand.

I licked the spoon clean in the most pornographic way possible, laughing again as his eyes rolled back.

He shook his head when I dug the spoon into the ice cream. "Don't."

I lifted my eyebrows and let my gaze fall pointedly on his erection.

His eyes widened. "Don't you dare!"

"What?" I asked innocently as I carved out another spoonful of ice cream.

"Do not put that ice cream on my dick!"

My eyes met his. "You know the safe word."

I'd insisted we have one, for my own comfort as well as his. I needed to know he could always put the brakes on, so I'd never accidentally push him too far.

Conflicting emotions warred in his expression as I held the spoon aloft. I lowered it slowly, giving him plenty of time to make up his mind.

He squirmed as it came closer, his hands fisting in the comforter, but he didn't say the magic word to stop me.

Okay, then. Guess we were doing this.

Just before I tipped the ice cream onto him, my doorbell rang.

I let out a disappointed sigh and set the ice cream on the nightstand. "To be continued."

Wyatt pushed himself upright. "Want me to get it?"

"You're naked."

He got up and scooped his jeans off the floor. "You're only barely more dressed than I am."

I tied my robe sash tighter. "It's probably just someone selling something."

He pushed the curtain aside to peer out the window and froze. "Fuck."

"What?"

"Fuck. Fuck. Fuck." He tried to cram his legs into his jeans and nearly fell over. "It's your brother. *Fuck*."

"Okay." I tried to channel calm to counteract Wyatt's panic. "It's okay. I'll just go see what he wants. You stay out of sight."

"Andie, he's gonna know I'm here. My truck's still parked out front." He'd been moving it into my garage every night in case of exactly this eventuality, but he hadn't gotten around to moving it yet today.

"Don't worry," I told him. "I'll handle it." I had no idea how I planned to do that, but I'd figure something out.

The doorbell rang again, and I hurried downstairs. On my way through the living room, I spied Wyatt's guitar case and hastily shoved it into the coat closet.

Josh was raising his fist to knock when I finally pulled the door open. "Hi." I only opened it a few inches.

"Uh..." He hesitated as he took in my state of undress. "Hi."

"I just got out of the shower," I said, holding the neck of my robe closed.

His expression darkened in disapproval. "You make a habit of answering your door to strangers half naked?"

"I saw your truck out front. I knew it was you." I could tell he was gearing up to lecture me on my personal safety, as if I wasn't an adult who'd been living on my own for years. "What's up?" I asked, cutting him off before he could get started.

"I was out running errands, and I thought I'd stop by and check out all the work Wyatt's been doing."

"Don't you trust him?" I asked.

"Of course I trust him." Josh frowned. "He does great work. I just wanted to see it for myself." He turned and surveyed the front porch with an approving nod. "This sure looks a lot better than it did."

All the rotten wood had been replaced and the peeling paint scraped off and sanded. It just needed painting. "He's starting on the trim paint tomorrow," I said. "He just finished up the last coat on the siding today."

"Where is he, anyway?"

I played dumb. "I dunno. Around somewhere, I expect."

Josh walked over to the porch railing and leaned out, craning his neck as he looked from side to side. "I don't see him anywhere."

"Maybe he left?" I tried.

"His truck's still here."

"Huh," I said. "That's weird."

Josh gave me a squinty look. "You don't know where he is?"

I shrugged. "I was in the shower. He was here when I got home, but I'm not his keeper. He's probably around back." I shrugged again and cursed myself for it. Too much shrugging was an obvious tell. "Or maybe he's in the garage."

"Door's open." Josh hooked a thumb over his shoulder. "No one in there. But it's nice that he's got the door working again finally."

"I don't know what to tell you. Maybe look around back. You

should check out the yard while you're back there. He finished the grading last week and put in brand-new sod."

"Hey!" Wyatt appeared from around the side of the house, startling the pee out of me.

I had to bite my cheek to stop myself from yelping in surprise at his sudden materialization outside, fully dressed, when I'd just left him naked in my bedroom on the second floor a minute ago. There was no way he could've sneaked down the staircase directly behind me undetected, so I could only assume he'd jumped out the window.

When my brother turned to greet him, I shot Wyatt a concerned frown.

"You did a really nice job on this porch," Josh said. "I don't have to worry about putting my foot through it anymore."

Wyatt ignored me as he stomped his work boot on the steps. "Yeah, it's a lot sturdier now, right?"

"Your boots are untied," I told him.

Wyatt shot me an annoyed look as he squatted down to tie them. "If you want, I can walk you around," he said to Josh. "Show you what all I've done so far."

"That's why I came by," Josh told him. "I'm dying to see all the work."

"Awesome," I said. "Y'all have fun. I'm going to go put some clothes on."

I closed the front door, leaving Josh and Wyatt to wander around the house on their own, and ran upstairs. Sure enough, the bedroom window was wide-open. I peered out to make sure they hadn't come around that side of the house yet—eyeballing the sheer fifteen-foot drop Wyatt had made—before I pulled the sash down and yanked the curtains shut.

By the time I'd gotten dressed, put the bedroom back to rights, and returned the half-melted ice cream to the freezer, the boys were just finishing up their inspection. "You want a beer?" I heard Wyatt offer Josh as they came in the back door.

I shot Wyatt a disbelieving look for encouraging my brother to stick around.

"Nah, I'd better get home," Josh said, to my relief. "Mia will be waiting for me to start dinner." His gaze landed on me. "The place looks great. Wyatt's really done a lot in a short time."

"Don't I know it," I replied, darting a look at Wyatt before addressing my brother again. "Be sure to tell Mia we said hi." I moved toward the door, not so subtly trying to herd him that way.

"Are you done for the day?" Josh asked Wyatt. "It looked like you were all packed up."

He nodded. "Yeah, pretty much."

"I'll walk out with you."

"Great." Wyatt turned to me with a dismissive wave. "I'll see you tomorrow morning."

"Okey dokey." I summoned a smile as I followed them to the door. "Bye, now!" As I watched them walk toward the driveway, I noticed Wyatt was limping a little.

Fuming, I sat down at the kitchen table next and pulled an exam off the stack of grading I still had to finish. I could hear their voices outside, which meant they were standing around gabbing. Knowing them, they could be out there half the night.

It wasn't quite that long, but I'd graded two exams before I finally heard Wyatt's truck start up. I went to the front window and watched him back out of the driveway. Josh had just gotten into his truck out on the street, and he waved as Wyatt drove away. I stood at the window until my brother had pulled away too, then I went into the kitchen and started heating the leftovers we'd brought home from Birdie's last night.

I was just getting the chicken out of the microwave when I

heard Wyatt turn back into the driveway, pull into the garage, and lower the door.

When he let himself in the back door, I was waiting for him. He looked white as my meemaw's divinity candy, and I went straight to him and fitted myself into his arms. "Are you okay? Did you hurt yourself?"

His arms wrapped around me, and he exhaled a long breath as he pressed his face into my hair. "I just landed on my ankle funny. It'll be fine."

I pulled back and punched him in the chest. Hard.

"Ow!" He rubbed his chest, looking at me like I'd mortally wounded him.

"What were you thinking? You could have seriously hurt yourself pulling a stunt like that."

"It was a one-story drop onto soft ground."

"You could have broken a leg or something! How would we have explained that to Josh, hmm? If he'd found you bleeding on the ground below my open bedroom window?"

"I didn't break my leg, did I?"

"Not this time. But is it really worth taking a chance like that?"

"Hell yes," he replied, absolutely serious.

I pushed away from him and folded my arms across my chest. "I hate this."

The novelty of having a secret was fading fast. I'd had some fun with it at first, when it had felt like a game, but I didn't like deceiving people I cared about. Not about something this important to me.

Wyatt was more than just a casual lay. It'd be one thing if I were hiding someone I didn't care about. But I had real feelings for Wyatt—serious, squishy, possibly even love kinds of feelings that I'd never had for anyone before. It felt wrong to hide something that big from the people closest to me.

Maybe that was why I kept fucking with Wyatt in public and taking reckless chances like at Birdie's last night. I wanted to get caught so we could finally stop lying.

It made me wonder, if it was so easy for Wyatt to keep up the charade, did I really mean that much to him?

His brow furrowed like he had no idea what I could possibly be talking about. "You hate what?"

"All this secrecy and lying. It's not going to make it easier when Josh eventually does find out."

The corners of Wyatt's mouth pulled downward as he blinked at me. His bewildered expression implied he hadn't considered the possibility of Josh finding out.

Ever.

Like we'd just go on sneaking around...*indefinitely, I guess*?

I drew myself upright and narrowed my eyes at him. "We are going to tell him one day, right? Or were you thinking we'd just keep on hiding forever?"

I'd told myself Wyatt would get over his fear of Josh finding out. Eventually he'd find the courage to stand up to my brother. After we'd been together for a while, once we were on solid ground and more secure in this thing between us. Then he'd decide I mattered enough to be worth coming clean to Josh.

Maybe I'd been assuming too much. Maybe Wyatt hadn't planned on things ever getting that far.

He'd said I mattered to him, that he wouldn't leave me like he'd left everyone else before me. He'd told me he wasn't letting me go. But how often did men say things they didn't mean when they were coming down off an orgasm high? How often did they make promises they had no intention of keeping? All the time, right?

Wyatt might even have meant the things he'd said—just not as much as I'd taken them to mean. He could have meant he'd keep me around for a few weeks before tiring of me and moving on. Instead of just another one-night stand, I'd be one of the rare few granted a short-term repeat engagement. *Lucky me.*

The deer-in-the-headlights look on his face didn't instill confidence in me, and I wondered if this was it. The end of our experiment. The moment when he admitted I'd never be important enough to claim publicly.

I watched him, my heart pounding out an anxious beat in my chest as I waited for him to say something. One second turned into two, and two turned into three.

He released a long breath and closed the space between us. My arms were still crossed, and he unfolded them so he could take both of my hands. "No, of course not," he said. "We'll tell him at some point."

I searched his eyes, trying to discern if he meant it. "When?"

"I don't know. I haven't figured that part out yet."

"But you will?"

He nodded and pulled me to him, enfolding me in his arms. "I promise."

I leaned into him, letting the warmth and solidity of his embrace melt away some of the chill I'd felt a moment ago. I thought about the songs he'd written about me, and told myself they had to mean something. My brain still had its doubts, but my body and my heart wanted to trust him.

So I made a choice to let myself believe him.

For now.

23

WYATT

I stood back and surveyed the window trim I'd just finished painting. After further study, I added a few more brush strokes. Then another few.

I stood back again and made myself set the paint can down.

It was done.

I was just spinning my wheels at this point. The job was finished. There was some cleaning up left to do, but as of this moment all the work on Andie's house had been completed.

For some reason I didn't feel as happy about that as I should have. Maybe because I wouldn't have an excuse to spend every waking minute here anymore. I'd been dragging my feet all day because I didn't want this job to be over.

I liked being here—even when she wasn't with me—and working on her house. But more than that, I liked that she needed me. I liked being able to help her.

It wasn't that I thought she'd cast me aside as soon as I'd outlived my usefulness. Except...I guess maybe part of me was a little worried about that.

But I knew better. I did. Andie wouldn't do that. She liked having me around as much as I liked being here. Still, the demons liked to whisper their poison into my ear. Planting seeds of discontent where they could. Looking for cracks in my confidence that would allow their doubts to take root.

It didn't help that things had been weird between us since Josh's unexpected visit on Monday. At least, I felt like they had. Every time I asked Andie about it, she insisted everything was fine. But I couldn't shake this niggling itch in the back of my mind that kept telling me she wasn't being entirely truthful.

The sex was still as amazing as ever. When we weren't having sex we still cuddled and talked as much as before. But something felt different. Andie seemed more guarded somehow. Like she was holding back when she was with me. What exactly she was holding back, I couldn't put my finger on. But there was a subtle distance between us I hadn't felt before.

Maybe it was normal. I hadn't been in many actual relationships before, and none had lasted even this long. For all I knew, this was a natural evolution. We'd left the high of the honeymoon phase and touched down on the solid ground of reality— a place I'd never made it before. Strange and uncharted territory.

But what if it was more than that? I was terrified of screwing this up. Half convinced it was just a matter of time before I blew it—or before Andie realized I wasn't good enough for her.

It didn't help matters that the question Andie had asked on Monday kept haunting me.

When would I be ready to tell Josh about us?

I honestly had no idea. All I knew for sure was that I wasn't ready yet. I knew Andie was right, that the longer we snuck around behind his back and lied about it, the worse it would be when it finally came out. But it was going to be pretty fucking bad no matter when it happened, so it was a matter of minor degrees.

I couldn't envision Josh forgiving me and offering me his

blessing to continue dating Andie, which meant I didn't see any way to salvage our friendship. But it wasn't just Josh I was worried about. What if he somehow brought Andie around to his way of thinking and convinced her we weren't well-suited? Maybe I was just being paranoid, but I couldn't shake the fear.

Things had been going too well so far. I felt like I'd won the lottery and used up all my good luck—it was just a matter of time before the universe righted itself and I got struck by lightning.

For the time being, my plan was to avoid thunderstorms— aka telling Josh the truth—for as long as I could manage.

Not forever, obviously. I wanted to marry Andie one day if she'd have me. I couldn't very well do that without telling her brother.

We just needed to wait a while. Until we'd been together long enough for me to prove my intentions were serious and honorable. Long enough that Josh wouldn't be able to think the worst of me, and he'd have to believe I wasn't using her badly.

I knew he thought I was a dog when it came to women, and I couldn't blame him for being protective of Andie. In his shoes, I'd feel the exact same way. I wouldn't want someone like me dating either of my sisters either.

If I was going to win Josh over to giving me a chance, it would take time and patience. It wasn't something that could be rushed. At the very least, once I'd put a ring on Andie's finger, Josh would have to give me the benefit of the doubt. He'd know I wasn't planning to pull my usual cut and run.

But I couldn't pop the question tomorrow. That was the kind of misguided stunt Tanner would pull. The last thing I wanted was to freak Andie out by moving too fast, too soon.

I hadn't even told her I loved her yet. I was working my way up to it, but with things feeling weird this week, it hadn't seemed like the right time.

But maybe tonight should be the night. Andie would be thrilled when I told her the house was done. That'd be sure to put her in a good mood.

My phone rang, interrupting my thoughts. I was surprised to see it was a call from Zelda Blanc, the owner of Zelda's Bar & Lounge. I'd gone to talk to her on Tuesday about doing a solo set of my original songs there. She'd had me play a few for her and given me the okay, but she already had acts booked for the next seven weeks. My debut would have to wait a while.

That was fine by me. I wasn't in any big hurry. It was enough that I'd taken the first step. I could use the time to practice and work out some kinks. Finalize my set list. And I guess maybe tell some more people about it.

"You've got Wyatt," I said into the phone as I carried my paint can and brush to the garage.

"Wyatt, it's Zelda. What are you doing tomorrow night?"

I stopped in my tracks. "Tomorrow? Why?"

"Because the guy I booked tripped over his cat and broke his arm."

"He tripped over his *cat*?" I repeated to make sure I'd heard her right.

"He's just lucky it wasn't anything worse. Cats are sociopaths who'd just as soon kill you as look at you. I wouldn't have one of those furry little murderers in my house."

"Okay." I'd never realized Zelda had such passionate views on cats. "Good to know."

"Anyway, now I need to find a new act for tomorrow night. You want it?"

Nerves fizzed in my stomach like Mentos dropped into a Diet Coke. "Tomorrow?"

"That's what I said. Yes or no?"

It was too soon. I wasn't ready. I needed more time to prepare and get my shit together.

But then I remembered what Andie had said.

Don't make up reasons why you can't.

There'd always be reasons to say no. Fear would always be ready to supply them. The same fear I'd been hiding behind and using as an excuse. The fear that had been ruling me for far too long.

Fuck that. It was time to stop living in fear.

"Yes," I told her, feeling queasy. "I'll do it."

———

I RAN my hand through my hair, then cursed myself for messing it up after I'd gone to the trouble of styling it. I was wearing my best jeans, my best boots, and my best shirt. We were at T minus two hours until I took the stage at Zelda's, and I was so nervous I didn't know whether to scratch my watch or check my ass.

"Come here." Andie pulled me into her arms. "You're going to be great. Your songs are great, and everyone's going to love them."

The last twenty-four hours had passed in a blur of anxiety. I'd gone into hyperdrive prepping for my debut as a singer-song-writer. Agonizing over the set list. Practicing until my fingers hurt, then panicking that I'd injured myself practicing too much. Shuffling the song order around, then realizing I'd had it right the first time and shuffling it back. Your standard-issue freak-out, basically.

Andie had been amazing through it all. She'd talked me out of second-guessing myself a million times already and made sure I knew she believed in me. I don't think I would have gotten through this without her.

I let my head drop onto her shoulder, exhaling a deep sigh as she rubbed her hands over my back. "What if I forget the words?"

"You won't forget the words. I've heard you sing all those songs dozens of times. You know every word by heart."

"What if I mess up the fingering?"

"That's what he said."

I snorted. "You're never going to get tired of that, are you?"

"Fingering jokes? Definitely not." Her voice grew husky as she moved her lips to my ear. "I can assure you that your fingering skills are top-notch, so I wouldn't worry about it."

"I'm serious."

"So am I. Even if you do mess up a little, no one will know because they've never heard the song before."

"They'll just think the song sucks."

"Look at me." I lifted my head and she took my face in her hands. "You're Wyatt King. You don't get stage fright."

"Tell that to my stomach."

She bent down and cupped her hands around her mouth as she pressed them against my stomach. "Wyatt King doesn't get stage fright, so you better settle down in there. Don't make me get the Pepto."

It did the trick, because it got me laughing too hard to feel my nervousness.

"That's better." She pressed her palm to my cheek and brushed her thumb over the corner of my mouth. "That's the smile I want to see tonight."

Her hands warmed me everywhere she touched me. A tingly sort of energy seemed to flow from her to me, easing my restlessness. Giving me confidence and comfort.

I curled a lock of her brown hair around my finger. She was wearing it down, and it fell in silky waves around her shoulders. She'd changed into a dress, and I knew she'd worn it just for me.

"You look pretty." Once this ordeal was over, I was going to enjoy getting under that dress. I pressed my face into her neck and inhaled a long breath through my nose. "You smell nice too."

She laughed. "Clearly I need to dress up for you more often."

I lifted my head and grinned at her. "I like you when you're dirty too."

"I've noticed."

I kissed her lips lightly, brushing my nose against hers. "Make sure you sit right up front where I can see you. Every time I start to freak out, I'm going to look at your beautiful face, and it'll remind me I don't have anything to be scared of."

"You *don't* have anything to be scared of."

I pressed my forehead against hers, letting my eyes fall closed. "I had a nightmare about it last night." I couldn't even remember the last time I'd had a stress dream about anything, much less being up onstage.

"I know. You kicked me."

"Shit, I'm sorry."

She kissed the tip of my nose. "You're forgiven."

"I dreamed that no one came to see me perform. I walked out onstage and the place was deserted and deadly silent. It was just me and an empty room."

"It's not going to be empty. Lots of people are coming to see you, and that's on top of the usual Saturday night crowd at Zelda's."

Andie had been the one to call around and tell people about the show tonight. Not everyone—just a select few friends and family. I let her use her own judgment about it, because her judgment was better than mine. My instinct had been to tell no one—at least before my stress dream last night—but she wouldn't let me get away with that. She'd wanted to make sure that when I looked out at that room tonight, it'd be filled with friendly faces.

But the only face that mattered to me was the one right in

front of me. I didn't care who else came tonight as long as Andie was there.

That had been the most terrifying part of my dream. I'd stepped out on the stage, expecting to see her, and she hadn't been there. In the dream, I'd known somehow that she was gone for good. The bone-deep certainty that I'd never see her again had chilled me to my core. There'd only been one other time in my life when I'd felt that lost and alone, and it wasn't a feeling I enjoyed revisiting.

I banded my arms around her and held as tight as I could without hurting her.

The thought of losing Andie terrified me. I needed her like I needed air to breathe. I didn't know what I'd do if she ever left me.

24

ANDIE

I got to Zelda's Bar & Lounge early to secure myself a good table. Close to the front at the center of the stage, just like Wyatt had asked.

It wasn't a big place. The vibe was cozy and cluttered, with a divey art bar aesthetic. Groupings of mismatched tables and chairs filled the center of the brick-walled space, and an eclectic mix of retro booths and couches lined the two side walls. Everywhere you looked there was some kind of kitschy lamp or oddball decoration. Mannequins, hula girls, creepy-ass dolls, and weird taxidermy animals peered at you from every corner of the joint.

Proximity to the university, cheap pitchers of Lone Star, and the campy-cool vibe made Zelda's popular with Bowman students. Looking around me, I saw mostly younger faces, one or two of whom looked familiar from campus. It was about two-thirds full already. Once the rest of Wyatt's friends and family got here, it'd be a full house.

The stage at the back of the room was small, just barely big enough to fit a four-piece band with a drum kit, and framed by red velvet curtains Zelda had salvaged from the old movie theater downtown. Tonight the stage was set with just a single wooden stool and mic stand for Wyatt.

I checked the time on my phone and saw I had a new text from him.

The green room smells like armpits.

He was here already, then. Good.

Could be worse, I texted back.

How???

It could smell like asparagus pee, I replied. *Or cheese farts. Or Gwyneth Paltrow's vagina.*

He texted me back a bunch of vomiting emojis.

I hated that we'd had to come separately tonight. I wished I could have driven him. I should be back there in the armpit-smelling green room holding his hand. Bolstering his spirits. Making sure he didn't drink too much or smoke too much weed.

I knew he was perfectly capable of looking after himself before a show, but I'd never seen him this nervous about anything before. It'd thrown me a little, to see him so anxious. I'd always thought Wyatt was immune to self-consciousness. The king of not giving a fuck. Fearless and confident. At ease in any situation.

Only recently had I begun to understand just how much of that had been an act. It felt hugely important that he'd let me see behind his facade and trusted me with his deepest insecurities and desires. And because he'd done that, he was here taking this big step tonight. Sharing something he was passionate about with everyone.

But instead of being together for this big moment in his life, we were forced apart in order to maintain our secret. Separated by yet another pretense Wyatt had constructed. It didn't sit well with me.

"You got a good table."

I looked up at the sound of my brother's voice and smiled. "You made it."

"Of course we did. You think we'd miss this?" He edged around the table and held out a chair for Mia.

She sat down with a martini and gazed around curiously, her eyebrows lifting at a particularly deranged-looking taxidermy squirrel nearby wearing a top hat with a tiny cigarette hanging out of his mouth. "I like this place. It's got a lot of character."

"That's one word for it." Josh took a sip of his beer before setting it on the table. "Birdie's here too. She's at a table in the back corner."

"Is she alone?" I craned my neck, looking for her.

"No, she's with some of her Bunco ladies. I think they might have pre-partied, because they seemed really drunk." He gave an embarrassed shudder. "Donna McNutt tried to pinch my ass."

"It is a really cute ass. I don't blame her for finding it irresistible." Mia grinned as she reached a hand behind him.

"Hey, now." Josh's lips tugged into a smile as he grabbed her hand before it could reach his backside. "Let's not engage in victim blaming."

Mia leaned over to kiss his cheek before turning her gaze on me. "So this whole thing is kind of a surprise, isn't it? I gather Wyatt's been holding out on everyone."

"I'll say." I glanced at my brother. "Did you have any clue he'd been writing music?" If there was anyone Wyatt might have confided in before me, I figured it was Josh. Or at least he might have given him some hint about it.

Josh gave me one of his enigmatic smiles—the kind that meant he wasn't going to tell me what Wyatt might or might not have confided in him. "I always thought he'd be good at it. We did this poetry unit back in high school, and he really seemed to take to it. Mrs. Cantrell even hung one of his poems up on the board at the front of the classroom. I tried to talk him into writing some songs for the band, but he said he wasn't interested."

Mia stirred the olives around in her martini. "When I first met him, he told me music was just something he did for fun, and he didn't have enough discipline to take it seriously." Her astute gaze settled on me again. "I wonder what changed."

I looked down at my beer, pretty sure Mia had already guessed what had changed. I just had to hope she'd keep it to herself and not share her suspicions with my brother.

Josh nudged my arm. "When did you find out about it?"

"I told you, he was at my house yesterday working when he got the call from Zelda." That was the story I'd given everyone. My explanation for being the one to spread the word about Wyatt's show tonight. It was the truth, even if it wasn't all of the truth.

"You didn't know before?"

I didn't like lying to my brother, but when Wyatt first told me about his songwriting he'd done it in confidence. That wasn't a trust I'd betray even if we weren't hiding a relationship. But there was something I could tell Josh to avoid lying outright.

"Remember when he got into that fight at King's Palace about a month ago?"

Josh frowned. "Yes."

"I drove him home afterward, and while he was puking his guts out in the bathroom, I may have seen a notebook he'd left sitting out that was full of what looked like lyrics."

"You didn't tell me that part," Mia said.

I shrugged. "It seemed private. I felt bad for looking at it as soon as I realized what it was."

Josh seemed to accept this. "I guess he wanted to keep it to himself until he was ready to go public."

I pushed my chair back and grabbed my empty beer glass. "I'm going for another drink. Anybody want anything else?"

They both shook their heads, and I started for the bar before I got cornered into telling any more lies. All this prevaricating and truth-dodging was exhausting, and also it had made me need to pee. Depositing my glass in the tray of dirties, I headed to the bathroom.

The green room was probably back here somewhere, but I didn't know where and it didn't seem wise to go stumbling around looking for it. I checked my phone as I waited for a stall to open up in the ladies' room, but there'd been nothing from Wyatt since the vomit emojis. I dearly hoped he was holding up okay.

A girl with a pink streak in her hair vacated one of the stalls, and I slipped inside. Once I'd taken care of my business, I turned my stall over to the next person in line and went to the sink to wash my hands.

I smiled when I recognized the woman refreshing her lipstick in the mirror next to me. "Hey, Lucy."

She smiled back at me in the mirror. "Andie! Hi!"

Lucy Dillard had been two years ahead of me in high school, and we'd been in choir together. She was also the older sister of Wyatt's bandmate, Matt.

"Did you come to see Wyatt?" I asked as I dried my hands.

"Yeah, I drove Matt. His car's in the shop again." She held the door for me while I tossed my paper towels into the trash. "He says the songs Wyatt's been writing are really good. It sounds like the guys are all excited to start playing them with him. Have you heard any of them yet?"

I shook my head as I gestured toward the bar, dodging her question. "I was gonna get a drink."

"Oh yeah, me too."

We got in line and chatted while we waited our turn. Lucy worked in the marketing department at King's Creamery. They were busy getting ready for the big Centennial Festival that was coming up at the amusement park, and she was in the middle of telling me about all the stuff they had planned when I felt someone touch my arm.

"Andie."

I turned and found myself eye level with a barrel-sized chest topped off by a bushy red beard. Tilting my head back, I smiled into the friendly face of Wyatt's half-brother, Ryan McCafferty. "Hey! You made it."

Not only was Ryan a fireman, he also competed in Scottish Highland Games, which were basically feats of strength where giants in kilts tossed around tree trunks and boulders for fun. He was exceptionally large and strong, was my point. Which might have been intimidating if he hadn't also been a total sweetheart.

He wrapped me in a big hug and pressed a quick kiss to the top of my head. "Thanks for activating the phone tree."

"No problem."

Ryan's gaze drifted to Lucy behind me, and his smile slipped a little. He recovered quickly, fixing it back in place as he greeted her with a nod. "Lucy. Nice to see you."

"Hi, Ryan." Lucy's voice sounded strained. When I turned to look at her, I saw she wasn't looking at Ryan, but at Tanner, who was standing just behind him.

I remembered hearing that Lucy and Tanner had dated awhile back. Based on the stone-faced stares they were giving each other now, I guessed their parting hadn't been amicable.

Ryan stepped to the side and used his massive triceps to shove Tanner forward. "Say hi to the ladies, Tanner."

Physically, Tanner was the spitting image of Wyatt, though their personalities couldn't have been more different since Tanner was studious, levelheaded, and introverted. Despite his natural reserve, I'd always found him friendly, though you'd never know it from the way he was looking at Lucy now. His blue eyes were like icicles, his expression as cheerless as his voice as he greeted her. "Lucy."

"Tanner." Lucy's voice had gone from strained to downright squeaky.

Not knowing any of the particulars of their breakup or who'd been the injured party, I felt bad for both of them. Trying to distract from the awkwardness of the moment, I put myself between them and greeted Tanner with a hug.

He accepted my embrace more stiffly than usual, murmuring a subdued greeting before sidling backward behind Ryan again. The line moved up, and I took the opportunity to position myself at Lucy's side. She stayed quiet while I made small talk with Ryan, her eyes occasionally darting anxiously toward Tanner, who hung back in his behemoth brother's shadow, determinedly refusing to look at her.

Finally, after several awkward minutes, we reached the bartender, and Lucy and I placed our orders. Once we'd gotten our beers, I bid Wyatt's brothers goodbye. Ryan nudged Tanner again, who roused himself to offer me a parting smile before shooting another frosty glare at Lucy.

I took her by the arm and led her a safe distance away before stopping to study her. "You okay?"

She nodded as she tipped back her beer. "I probably shouldn't have come. I was hoping I'd be able to avoid him."

"You want to talk about it?"

Forcing brightness into her expression, she shook her head. "I'm fine. I just feel bad that seeing me probably ruined his night." She didn't look fine, despite her efforts to appear otherwise.

"Are you sitting with your brother?" I asked her.

"Yeah, over there." She nodded toward a booth that held Wyatt's three bandmates, who were currently chatting up some smitten college girls who'd clustered around them. From Lucy's expression, I surmised she wasn't in a big hurry to get back to them.

"I'm at a table up front with my brother and his girlfriend. Do you want to come sit with us?"

She gave me a grateful look. "I'd love that."

"Come on." I hooked my arm through hers and led her over to my table.

Josh knew Lucy from high school, and he got up to give her a hug before introducing her to Mia. While the three of them talked, I discreetly checked my phone again. Still nothing from Wyatt.

It was just a few minutes before he was due to go on, so I typed out a quick text.

It's a great crowd out here. Break a leg.

He replied a few seconds later with three heart emojis.

I laid my phone facedown on my lap and sipped my beer while I waited for Wyatt to come onstage. Ten minutes later, Zelda came out to introduce him.

No one knew exactly how old Zelda Blanc was or whether that was even her real name. She'd opened Zelda's in the nineties, but her life before she came to Crowder was shrouded in mystery and the subject of much debate. Some said she was an oil heiress or a widowed trophy wife. Others speculated that she'd been a "Dellionaire"—one of the hundreds of Dell employees who got rich off the company's initial public offering in the heyday of Austin's tech boom. Some of the more colorful rumors included tales of a criminal past, the witness protection program, and possibly some kind of entanglement with organized crime.

Witness protection seemed unlikely to me, given Zelda's tendency to stand out in any room she entered. I'd never seen her without a full face of makeup that included dramatic winged liner and brightly colored lipstick. She favored fifties-style dresses and wore a different wig every day, just like Moira Rose on *Schitt's Creek*. Tonight's wig was a bright green Bettie Page style that matched her green lipstick and the leaves on her flowered dress.

She kept the introduction short, welcoming everyone in her husky smoker's voice and mentioning the drink specials before announcing Wyatt as "a member of Crowder's most famous family" who'd be performing his own songs for the first time tonight.

I couldn't imagine he'd approved Zelda's mention of his family, but when he came out he betrayed no sign of annoyance —or any of the nervousness I'd seen earlier. He'd slipped into his laid-back stage persona and the Wyatt King charm machine was in full effect, all lady-killer smiles and smooth banter as he settled onto his stool and got ready to play.

My heart pounded like it was me up on the stage when he started the first song. It was one called "Bait and Switch" that he'd written about his dad, but he'd picked it for his opener because it was catchy and upbeat.

I could tell right away that he'd hooked the audience. The energy in the room changed as soon as he started singing. The murmur of conversation died down, and as I glanced around me I saw rapt expressions on every face. I caught my brother's eye and he grinned at me, proud and impressed.

When the song ended, the room erupted into applause. Josh leaped to his feet, hollering his approval. As shouts and whistles sounded off around the room, I finally saw Wyatt's mask slip a little. A look of bewilderment came into his expression as the ovation dragged on, like he couldn't quite believe all that cheering was for him.

His eyes found mine, and when I gave him a thumbs-up he broke into a heartbreaking smile.

"Wow." Josh's hand squeezed my shoulder as he leaned over to speak into my ear. "He's *good*."

"Yeah, he is." I kept my eyes fixed on the stage so my brother wouldn't see the emotion in my expression.

Wyatt got command of himself, flashing a crooked grin at the audience as he thanked them for their enthusiasm. "Y'all settle down now, because I've got a whole set to get through here before I can have a beer."

It earned him a round of laughter, and he grew even more relaxed, soaking in the attention. "This next song is called 'Bright as the Sun.' And it's one I wrote about regrets and the girl who got away." My heart clenched a little, but Wyatt was careful not to look my way.

It was slower and softer and a lot more melancholy than the opener. A hush fell over the crowd as he crooned the first verse in a voice aching with emotion. I held myself still, afraid to look at anyone as the words washed over me. Words he'd written about me. Full of longing and pain and bittersweet devotion.

No one knew that, of course, except me and Wyatt. My eyes burned as I blinked back the tears I couldn't afford to let myself shed. I kept waiting for him to look at me, but he never did. Not once. He probably couldn't. Not without giving himself away.

When the song ended there was a moment of reverent silence as the final notes hung in the air. Then, as if on some invisible cue, the audience exploded into applause.

I surreptitiously wiped beneath my eye as I clapped and cheered. When I glanced around, I caught Mia looking at me, her eyes narrowed and her expression thoughtful.

Well, damn. So much for maintaining my cool.

"Holy shit," Josh muttered, staring up at Wyatt in awe. "Ho-ly. Shit." He didn't seem to have noticed my reaction.

"Thank you," Wyatt said, bending down for the bottle of water sitting next to him. "I'm glad you like that one. I guess

we've all probably got someone in our past we still think about."
His grin turned sly. "Who knows? Maybe mine will hear that
song one day and come back to me."

This got him a few whistles and "ooohs" from the women in
the audience, and his eyebrows arched, eating it up.

It bothered me that he'd implied the song was about one of
his former hookups. He'd basically put out a cattle call to every
woman he'd ever slept with, each of whom would now be
wondering if she was the special someone he'd been singing
about. I understood why he'd chosen to make it seem that way—
I even recognized that it was good showmanship that would
probably help generate buzz and drive interest in his music. But
I deeply disliked the thought of his past lovers forming a line at
his doorstep in the hopes of rekindling some old flame.

I also didn't love that he still wouldn't look at me. Or that he
kept on not looking at me for the whole rest of his set. Despite
his request that I sit up front where he could see me, he didn't
seem to need my reassurance. I should have been glad he wasn't
freaking out, but as the night wore on and he sang song after
song exposing deeply personal feelings he'd never shared with
anyone but me, I felt more and more distance between us. Especially when he started doing his usual trick of picking out
various women in the audience to flirt with, making eye contact
with woman after woman—but never with me.

It didn't fill me with the same jealous hunger it had before. It
hurt. This didn't feel like a game. There was no thrill anymore.
No heated excitement. Watching him gaze at another woman
while soulfully mouthing words I'd thought were meant for me
made me feel hollow and cold. Like I didn't even exist.

By the time he finished playing his final song, I was struggling to hide the painful ache in my chest. I had to force a smile
as the crowd leaped to its feet to give him a standing ovation. I
was happy for Wyatt. I really was. He'd earned this. I was glad to

see his creative efforts rewarded with the praise and respect they deserved.

But I couldn't help feeling like I'd lost something.

Or maybe I hadn't lost it so much as realized it had never really belonged to me in the first place.

25

ANDIE

W yatt got mobbed as soon as he emerged from the shadowy recesses of Zelda's back hallway. I heard the commotion, and when I craned my neck I saw the crush forming as everyone tried to pay their compliments at once.

"His songs reminded me a lot of The National," Mia observed as her gaze followed mine to the back of the room.

"I was thinking Mat Kearney," Lucy said beside me.

Mia frowned at her. "I don't know who that is."

As a genius mathematician, Mia wasn't always up on current pop culture. I assumed because her brain had its hands full solving complex abstract math puzzles. I was kind of surprised she even knew about The National.

Josh shook his head. "More like Pete Yorn or Bob Schneider."

"I don't know who they are either," Mia said.

Josh smiled as he pulled her in for a kiss. "I know, sweetie."

Ryan McCafferty's thunderous baritone rose above the clamor at the back of the room, ordering everyone to back off and give his brother some space. The throng melted away, clearing a path as Ryan waded toward Wyatt.

"Let's go." Josh nudged my arm, pushing his chair back as he grabbed Mia's hand.

I looked at Lucy, but she shook her head. "I'm good here. Go on."

Leaving her at the table, I followed my brother and his girlfriend back to where Wyatt was currently being crushed in an enormous bear hug by his giant-sized brother. When Ryan finally set him down, Wyatt was red-faced and laughing so hard he doubled over at the waist.

"Someone get him a drink!" Ryan bellowed, and several arms shot out to proffer beverages. He grabbed a shot that looked like whiskey and shoved it in front of Wyatt. "Here, drink up. You've earned it."

Wyatt knocked back the shot before accepting a hug from a smiling Tanner. The two stayed clenched for a long moment, during which it looked like Tanner was speaking quiet words into his ear.

When they finally let go of each other, Wyatt turned his eyes toward us. They lingered on me for just a fraction of a second before Josh stepped forward and wrapped him up in a hug. I waited while my brother congratulated him, then while Mia hugged him, before Wyatt gave his attention to me.

The way he smiled at me went a long way to filling the hollow space in my chest. He threw open his arms, beckoning me forward, and when I went to hug him he lifted me up off the ground, squeezing me so hard all the air left my lungs. After my feet hit the floor again he loosened his grip enough for me to catch my breath, but he didn't let go.

"You did it," I said. "I'm so proud of you."

"You made it possible," he murmured, brushing his lips against my cheek. "I wouldn't be here without you."

Before I could react, he let me go and turned to greet the guys in his band. I stepped back to give them room and soon found myself standing on the outside of the group clustered around Wyatt. Manny was there, and Josie, and his youngest brother, Cody, and they all came forward to take their turn congratulating him.

I was so proud of him I felt like I might explode with all the feelings inside me, but I wasn't allowed to show it. I'd abdicated my girlfriend rights when I agreed to keep our relationship a secret. I didn't get to stand by his side all night, sharing his moment of triumph. That honor went to Wyatt's family and his best friend and his bandmates. I'd bumped myself out of the line of succession.

Mia appeared at my side, slipping her arm through mine to pull me closer. "You okay?" She was as tall as my brother and had to bend down to speak into my ear.

I nodded, watching Wyatt enjoy his moment in the sun. I knew he had to be feeling good, and I had no intention of bursting his bubble. This was his night. He deserved to enjoy it.

It wasn't long before one of Wyatt's bandmates proposed moving the party to the Rusty Spoke. After Wyatt had talked Tanner and Ryan into coming with them, he pointed at Josh. "You're coming too, right?"

Josh nodded and turned to me and Mia. "You two up for it?"

I shook my head. "I'll leave y'all to your fun."

I knew what would happen if I went along. I'd spend the whole night watching everyone else talk to Wyatt while I'd have to keep my distance and pretend he didn't mean the whole world to me. The thought of it made me want to break things, and I didn't want the thing I broke to be Wyatt.

Josh looked a little surprised, since he was used to me tagging along with them. But he accepted my answer easily enough. He probably assumed I was sick of Wyatt after having him around every day for the last few weeks, working on my house.

"I'm going to pass too," Mia told Josh before turning to me. "Would you mind giving me a ride home?"

"Sure, no problem." I could use the company, and I had a feeling Mia had guessed as much.

"Suit yourselves." Josh came forward to kiss Mia goodbye, and she let go of me to step into his arms.

I looked away as they embraced, envying their easy affection and the fact that they didn't have to hide how they felt about each other. Lucy caught my eye, standing over by the door looking like she was fixing to leave, and I went to say good night to her.

"Are you going with the guys?" I asked her.

"No, I told Matt to find himself another ride home."

I couldn't blame her for not wanting to be around Tanner after the way he'd acted toward her earlier. "You're gonna be all right?"

She nodded. "Thanks for letting me sit with you." Her gaze moved over my shoulder, and she smiled. "Hey, Wyatt. You were great up there."

"Lucy," I heard him say just behind me. "Thanks for coming tonight." His hand pressed against my lower back, and my heart fluttered at the contact.

Lucy bid us goodbye without lingering to chat. As we watched her make her way out the door, Wyatt leaned down to speak into my ear. "You're not coming?"

I could tell he was disappointed. But I also knew he'd have a better time without me than he would with me there feeling resentful and unhappy. I couldn't tell him that though. Not without infecting the rest of his night with my sour mood.

I didn't turn to look at him, because I was afraid of what my eyes would say. But I leaned back into his hand, letting him know I wasn't pulling away. "You'll have more fun without me getting in the way."

"You could never be in the way." He sounded hurt and worried, so I tried to reassure him.

"I'm so proud of you right now, I don't think I'd be able to keep my hands off you. I want you to be able to relax and enjoy yourself without having to worry about blowing our cover."

"I only want to be with you."

It helped to hear him say it, but it didn't change the reality of the situation.

I turned to face him, resting one hand on his shoulder as I leaned up to kiss his cheek. "We can't. Tonight you need to go celebrate with all the family and friends who came out to support you. We'll celebrate together tomorrow. Just the two of us."

His arms tightened around me in a fierce hug. "Promise?"

"Cross my heart." I saw Mia coming toward us and pulled out of his arms, forcing a grin. "Text me tomorrow when you recover from your hangover."

"Are we still going home?" Mia asked, glancing back and forth between me and Wyatt.

"Yep." I offered him one last smile as I backed toward the door. "Stay out of trouble."

———

"WYATT'S REALLY TALENTED." It was the first thing Mia had said since we'd gotten in my car a few minutes ago.

I nodded as I pulled onto the highway. The goat farm where she lived with my brother—the farm I'd grown up on—was on the far side of campus, a few exits past the university's main entrance.

"Some of those songs were pretty interesting."

I kept my eyes on the road. "Mmm hmm."

"He's sure written a lot of love songs for a guy who once told me he was allergic to commitment."

I couldn't think of anything to say, so I didn't say anything.

"I like Wyatt a lot," she continued after a moment. "I didn't think I would when I first met him."

"I remember." Wyatt's flirting hadn't worked on Mia. She'd been too smitten with my brother to succumb to Wyatt's charms.

"I remember you tried to warn me off him."

I cut a quick look at her. "I did no such thing. I just wanted to make sure you knew to guard your heart around him."

"Have you been guarding your heart, Andie?"

My hands tightened on the steering wheel as I prepared myself to lie yet again. "How many times do I have to tell you—"

"I think Wyatt's a good person," she interrupted. "I wanted you to know that, in case there was anything you wanted to talk about. I'm also really good at keeping secrets. Just putting that out there."

For a second, I was tempted to take her up on it. But I'd given Wyatt my word. Anyway, it was bad enough that Wyatt and I were lying to Josh. No way was I going to ask Mia to do it too. "I appreciate the offer, but I can't."

She gave me an understanding smile. "Wyatt has a lot of layers to him that he doesn't like to let people see. You two are a lot alike that way."

"I guess." I checked my rearview mirror as I pulled off the highway. The service road was deserted behind us. This side of town was mostly farm and ranch land. There weren't many people out and about this late on a Saturday night.

"Josh has a few blind spots when it comes to you. I'm the same way with my younger sister. Our overprotectiveness can be misguided sometimes, even if we think we're looking out for your best interests."

I glanced at her as I turned onto the farm road that led to my parents' old place, but I didn't say anything.

"Because Josh only sees you as his little sister, it means he doesn't always see you clearly. Tonight, for instance, I don't think he noticed that anything was wrong." She paused. "But I did."

I felt her eyes on me and shifted in my seat. "It's not that I don't want to talk about it..."

"I know," she said softly. "You can't."

Neither of us spoke for the last few minutes of the drive. I pulled off the blacktop, onto the gravel road to the farm, and the Jeep jolted as we drove over the cattle guard. I parked in front of my parents' old house next to Mia's Toyota hatchback and cut the engine before turning to look at her.

"I'm not saying this is about Wyatt, you understand? That is explicitly *not* what I'm saying."

She gave me a solemn nod. "You never said anything at all to me about Wyatt."

I leaned back and rubbed my forehead, trying to figure out how to talk about it without actually saying what it was I was talking about. "I sort of agreed to keep something secret in order to protect someone else, and now I'm starting to regret it. I don't like all the lying and sneaking around, but I don't know how to avoid it without the other person getting hurt."

Mia seemed to consider this. "I'm assuming this other person is someone you care about a lot?"

"Yes." I hesitated. "More than I've ever cared about anyone."

Her eyes widened as they leaped to mine. "And does this other person feel the same way about you?"

"He does." I spoke so softly it was almost a whisper.

Mia nodded, her lips curving in a brief smile before she grew serious again. "I can understand why you wouldn't want someone you care about to be hurt. But from where I sit, it seems like this arrangement is hurting you. And if this other person really cares about you, he wouldn't want you to be hurt any more than you want to see him hurt."

I chewed on my lower lip. "He might not know how unhappy I am about it."

"Because you haven't told him?"

"Maybe not in so many words."

Mia reached across the console to squeeze my arm. "One thing I've learned from being with your brother is how important compromise is. Sometimes you have to meet halfway, and sometimes you have to be willing to give things up for each other. That takes trust on both sides. You *both* have to make sacrifices so no one's carrying more than their share of the burden."

Her words made sense, but they didn't sit easy with me. "You're saying right now I'm carrying more than my share of the burden?"

She nodded. "In order to arrive at a compromise, you have to be honest with the other person about what you need." She gave me another one of her pointed looks. "If you pretend to be strong and fine all the time, he won't know how to help you. You have to ask for things when you need them."

My nose wrinkled at the suggestion. "I'm not good at asking for help."

Mia let out a light laugh. "I've noticed. Josh is still offended you didn't tell him about your house problems, you know. He would have helped."

"I didn't need his help."

"I know." Her eyes met mine. "But you asked *someone* for help, didn't you?"

———

WYATT DIDN'T TEXT me until noon the next day. I was frankly surprised to hear from him that early after what I imagined had probably been an epic night of drinking and bro bonding.

His first two texts confirmed my assumption.

Wyatt: I barfed
Wyatt: A lot

I laughed at the screen, feeling sorry for him and also amused as I typed my reply.

Andie: Are you feeling better now or are you texting from the toilet bowl?
Wyatt: Better
Wyatt: Mostly
Andie: Have you eaten anything?
Wyatt: I drank a Monster Energy
Andie: I meant food
Wyatt: No food at my place
Andie: Do you need me to bring you food?
Wyatt: No! Do NOT come over here
Andie: That bad? Should I call a hazmat team?
Wyatt: Maybe
Wyatt: Can I come see you?

I was dying to see him, but I didn't want him taking any unnecessary risks.

Andie: Can you drive?
Wyatt: I'm fine
Andie: Really?
Wyatt: Give me 30 min

My heart leaped at the prospect of seeing him again. Last night had been our first night apart since we'd started sleeping together, and I hadn't liked it one bit. Funny how fast you could get used to having someone around.

Andie: Do you want me to make you cheese grits?
Wyatt: Yesssssssssss
Wyatt: God
Wyatt: Please
Wyatt: I love you

I blinked at the screen to make sure I'd read that last text right.

But the words didn't change. They were right there in front of me.

Wyatt had typed the words *I love you.*

And now they were permanently archived on my phone. Impossible to take back.

But had he meant it? Like, *meant it* meant it? Or had he simply meant it in a jokey, friendly kind of way? Given that he was hungover and probably not thinking all that well this morning, the latter seemed likely.

Although...maybe the fact that he wasn't thinking well was what had caused him to let the truth slip out so offhandedly.

Either way, I didn't know what I was supposed to do about it. So I did nothing.

Well, not nothing.

I made cheese grits.

They were nearly ready by the time I heard Wyatt's truck pull into my garage. I was just turning off the heat when Wyatt let himself in the back door. I'd given him a key when he started doing the work on the house, and he still had it. He hadn't offered to give it back to me, and I had no intention of asking for it.

I heard his footsteps approach and smelled fresh soap and shampoo as he hugged me from behind.

He nestled his face into my hair. "I missed you." His voice was low and gravelly from all the singing he'd done last night, and it sounded like heaven to my ears.

"I missed you too." *So much.* My hands tangled with his as his mouth trailed down my neck, sending ripples of shivery warmth through my body.

"You smell amazing."

I smiled. "Pretty sure that's the grits you're smelling."

"No." He gave me a playful nip with his teeth before nuzzling the spot with his nose. "The grits smell good, but you smell *amazing.*"

"Are you hungry?"

"Yes."

He spun me in his arms, cradled my jaw in his hands, and kissed me like a starving man—with passion and a little desperation. I loved his mouth and the way he used it. Savoring me. Cherishing me. Worshiping me with his lips and tongue. Wyatt kissed like a man who loved kissing—not just as a means to an end, but as a pleasure in its own right.

When his lips finally left mine, I smiled up at him breathlessly and brushed his hair back from his forehead. "Hey you."

He dipped his chin and leaned his forehead against mine. "Hey you."

His hand smoothed down my neck as we stood there together, silent and still. Taking comfort in each other's company. Enjoying the quiet contact after last night's separation.

I only had so much stillness in me, however. The three-word phrase Wyatt had texted me was emblazoned in my mind, and I couldn't stay silent for long.

"Wyatt?"

"Hmm?" He didn't move except to squeeze the back of my neck.

"The last text you sent me—do you remember what it said?"

I held my breath as I waited for him to answer.

"You mean the one that said 'I love you'?"

My heart skittered nervously in my chest. "That's the one."

"You want to know if I meant it." He spoke in a quiet, measured voice.

We were too close for me to see his face, so I couldn't read his expression. I had no insight into what he was thinking or feeling. "Did you?"

Lifting his head from mine, he moved his mouth to my ear. "Yes."

The word shimmered through me with a shock of giddiness. I pulled back to look into his eyes, and what I saw in them reflected the truth of what he'd just said.

His hands tightened on my hips, his thumbs slipping under the hem of my shirt to rub circles on my bare skin. "I love you," he repeated.

"Wyatt," I breathed, the surge of happiness blossoming in my chest making it hard to speak.

He brushed his lips against my forehead, then his mouth moved over my face, pressing tender kisses to my eyes, my cheeks, the corner of my mouth, my jaw.

"I love you too," I whispered.

He went still at my words, frozen in the act of kissing my neck.

I'd never said those words to a man before. Yet saying them now felt as easy as saying my own name.

Wyatt lifted his head, and his wide, bright eyes ensnared me. A soft smile curved his lips, and I strained toward him, my hands gripping his arms as I captured his mouth with mine. Claiming him as my own.

When we finally broke apart, I wrapped my arms around his neck, needing to keep him close. He bent his head to the side and his stubble scraped over my cheek, sending shivers down my spine as his hot breath caressed the skin beneath my ear.

"Can I ask you something else?" I murmured.

He looked at me, raising both his eyebrows. "Anything."

"Did you mean to say it?"

His eyes danced in amusement. "Did I mean to tell you I love you for the first time over a text message when I was hungover? Hell no."

A laugh bubbled out of me, and he laughed along with me.

"But I'm not sorry I did." He cradled my hand in both of his and held my palm against his mouth. I felt his lips pull into a smile against my skin.

"I'm not sorry you did either." I slid my hand along his jaw, and he leaned into my touch like an attention-starved puppy. "You know, your grits are probably getting cold."

His head popped up, his eyes going wide. "Can't have that. It's a crime against grits."

I laughed and went to get two bowls.

———

WYATT and I spent the rest of Sunday holed up at my house together. But come Monday morning, I went back to work, and he headed home.

The last few weeks had been pretty intense. He'd all but moved into my place while he was working on the house. It had made practical sense at the time, but it meant we'd basically gone from zero to sixty on the relationship highway.

Now the work was done. He'd documented the repairs on

the house and sent it all off to the HOA with time to spare before the deadline. We could close that chapter of our lives and settle into a more normal routine.

Normal meant Wyatt coming over most evenings after we both got off work. He was busier than usual, because he had a backlog of repair jobs waiting on him that he'd had to put off while he was working on my house. Plus, he was spending a lot of time collaborating with Matt on the new songs and starting to rehearse some of them with the band.

I wasn't jealous of the time he spent away from me though. I loved seeing him energized by this new sense of purpose in his life. He seemed happier, and though I liked to think at least a little of it had to do with me, I knew I wasn't the only reason for the fresh light in his eyes and the perpetual smile he wore on his face.

Regardless, even when his evenings were taken over by work or extra rehearsals, he always came back to my house at the end of the night. If he was out late, he'd crawl into bed beside me after I'd fallen asleep and wake me with his lips and his loving caresses.

It had been two weeks since Wyatt's show at Zelda's, and I hadn't ever gotten around to taking Mia's advice and telling Wyatt how much I disliked keeping our relationship a secret. It didn't seem so pressing when we were alone together. Things between us were good. Perfect, even. I didn't want to upset the balance we'd struck. Not when it still felt so new and precious.

Yes, I wanted to tell the whole world that he was mine and I was his. But it could wait. For a little longer, at least.

So what if Wyatt had to hide his truck in my garage every night? It was easy enough to do now that he'd fixed the door.

So what if I never spent time at his apartment in case someone recognized my car parked out front? It wasn't like either of us were eager to spend more time at his gross bachelor pad.

So what if we couldn't go out in public together? He was so busy he didn't have free time for going out much anyway.

It was fine.

Except.

Shiny Heathens had a show at the Rusty Spoke next Saturday, and I was dreading it. They were going to play a couple of Wyatt's new songs during their set for the first time. I knew he was excited about it and wanted me there.

But I wasn't sure I could bring myself to go.

Not unless he was willing to acknowledge our relationship publicly. No more hiding. No more lying. No more sneaking around.

Which meant we needed to have a conversation.

Soon.

26

WYATT

"Think anyone will notice I'm wearing your deodorant tonight?" I sniffed my pits as I strutted out of Andie's bathroom, stark naked and freshly showered. I liked the smell of her deodorant on me. I liked that my wet hair smelled like her shampoo too. It was like carrying a little bit of her around with me.

She was sitting on the edge of the bed, and the frown on her face stopped me in my tracks.

"What's wrong?" I dropped my arm to my side. "I'll quit using your stuff if it bothers you."

She arched one eyebrow and patted the mattress next to her. "We need to talk about something."

Well, shit. I didn't like the sound of that.

"Is this the kind of conversation I should put my drawers on for?"

The smile she offered me wasn't encouraging. "Maybe."

I grabbed a pair of clean boxer briefs out of the laundry basket and dragged them up my legs. Pushing a hand through my damp hair, I sat down next to her.

She turned to face me, pulling her leg up underneath her. I

mirrored her position and reached for her hand. My thumb rubbed a circle in her palm as I waited for her to tell me what was up. Whatever it was that had her troubled, she didn't seem in a hurry to spit it out.

I squeezed her hand. "Talk to me, sweetheart."

Her eyes were uncertain when they lifted to mine. "How much longer do we need to wait before we can finally tell people we're together?"

The question took me off guard. She hadn't brought the subject up in a while. Based on our last conversation about it, I'd thought we'd agreed to wait. That she was okay with holding off for now. I didn't have an answer ready to give her, and when I didn't respond quick enough she followed up with another question.

"Are you ever going to be ready to go public?"

The resentment I heard in her tone blindsided me. I reached for her, needing to soothe her anger and lay her fears to rest. She let me pull her to my chest, and I folded her up in my arms.

"Of course. I told you we would, didn't I?" Guilt gnawed at me as I said it. Truthfully, I hadn't given it any further thought since the last time she'd asked the question. I'd been too happy enjoying her company to dwell on a problem I still had no idea how to solve.

"When?"

"I don't know."

"How about tonight?"

"Tonight?" The word choked out of me in an undignified-sounding yelp.

She pushed out of my arms and studied me, her lips flattening in displeasure. "Why not tonight? Give me one good reason."

"I—" My brain flailed helplessly, and I snapped my mouth

shut while I chose my words. "Because Josh's feelings on the subject haven't changed."

"They haven't changed in ten years. They're not going to change unless we do something to change them. If you're waiting for him to magically wake up and sing a different tune, you'll be waiting forever." She paused, her expression narrowing with distrust. "But maybe that's the point."

"What does that mean?"

"Maybe you're just using Josh as an excuse to avoid commitment."

I reared back. "Hey. No. Of course I'm not doing that. You don't really think that, do you?"

"You've always been the guy who can't be pinned down. Is it really so far-fetched?"

"You're damn right it is!" I was irritated, and my voice came out louder than I intended. But after everything we'd shared, it hurt to hear her flinging my past in my face. I clenched my teeth, because I didn't want to yell at her. This time when I spoke, I tried to keep my voice reasonable. "That's not who I am. Not with you." My eyes pleaded with her to believe me. "I thought you knew that."

"I thought I did too. But I have to tell you, Wyatt, I'm starting to wonder if I'm being played."

My mouth went dry. "Andie." I pushed a nervous hand through my hair. "Shit. No."

She turned her face away, and I saw a muscle tick in her jaw as she stared at a spot on the wall. "Are you sure this is really just about my brother? There's not something else that's holding you back?"

"Like what?"

She hesitated before answering. "Like you being afraid to let anyone love you too much."

My mouth opened, but I couldn't force any words out.

When I didn't answer, she turned to look at me. "Are you sure this whole secrecy thing isn't just a way of keeping me at a distance so things can't get too serious?"

The doubt I saw in her eyes hurt my heart. It scared me enough to compel me into action.

"That's not true." I reached for her hand. "This is serious to me. I'm a hundred percent in this."

"You're not though. As long as we're sneaking around and keeping it a secret, we're no better than two kids playing house. It's all just make-believe. This thing between us isn't real as long as you don't have to acknowledge it to anyone. You get to keep on acting like the same old carefree Wyatt and don't have to admit that you've let yourself have actual feelings for someone. We might as well not exist."

My heart pounded a painful beat in my chest. I was sweating and my limbs shook with the fear of losing her. I had to make her believe me. I had to fix this.

I tugged on her hand. "Andie, look at me." When she didn't move, I dropped to the floor and knelt in front of her, pushing between her knees so she couldn't avoid me. "I love you and I want to be with you."

Her lip trembled a little, and it just about broke me. "Then *be with* me."

"I am." My hands squeezed her thighs. "I'm right here."

"But you won't be with me tonight. As soon as we get there, you'll go off and do your thing, leaving me to sit on the sidelines and watch you pay attention to everyone else there but me. I hate it. I hate lying to our friends and our families. I hate having to pretend not to love you. I hate the way it feels when you pretend you don't love me."

Her words made me sick with guilt. "I didn't know it was that hard for you."

"It is. I don't want to do it anymore. I want you to choose me,

Wyatt, and I want everyone to know you did it. I want to be able to tell people you're mine and I'm yours."

"Okay." I gathered her to my chest, stroking her hair as I covered it with kisses. "Okay, we will. I promise."

"Tonight?"

At my hesitation, she went stiff in my arms, but I held her even tighter. "I need to tell Josh myself before we go public. I owe him that much. He needs to hear it from my mouth, not the Crowder gossip mill."

She huffed out a reluctant breath. "Fine. But you're going to tell him?"

"Yes."

"When?"

"The next time I see him."

Her mouth went hard. "That's not good enough. You could avoid him for weeks if you wanted to."

"I won't. I'll call him tomorrow and arrange a meetup."

Somewhere quiet enough to talk. Private. It'd probably be best to do it at the farm. Preferably when Mia was around to soften his disposition. I had a suspicion she'd be on my side, and he'd be less likely to blow up at me in front of her.

"You swear?"

"On my mother's soul," I answered solemnly.

This seemed to appease her, and she relaxed in my arms. "Okay."

I sagged in relief, clutching her to me before tipping her face up. My heart clenched as I stroked my thumb over her cheek. She was so incredible and caring and strong and basically perfect in every way. I didn't deserve her, but I couldn't live without her.

I brushed a soft kiss over her lips. "I love you. I don't ever want to give you a reason to doubt it."

"I love you too."

Some of the knots in my chest eased. I could do this for her. I could tell Josh and deal with the fallout. Whatever happened with me and him, at least I'd still have Andie on my side.

Speaking of which...

"Does this mean you don't want to come to the show tonight?" The indecision on her face prompted me to add, "I promise I won't flirt with anyone this time."

"Does it really matter to you if I'm there?"

"It means the world to me to have you there, but I understand if you don't want to do it."

She looked doubtful. "You really won't flirt?"

"I won't smile at a single woman the whole night."

"I'd like to see that," she scoffed.

"Just watch. You'll see." I meant it. No more playacting. Not if it caused Andie pain.

"Fine," she said. "I'll come tonight. But the next time we go out together, I want it to be as a real couple."

"I promise. This'll be the last time. No more secrecy after tonight."

———

I KEPT my word to Andie. When I got to the Rusty Spoke that night, I didn't smile at a single woman.

It wasn't easy. The manners that had been drilled into me from birth made smiling as instinctive as breathing. I was a natural-born pleaser. Friendly by default.

But I managed it. For Andie. Even though my behavior left a lot of people perplexed. I kept getting asked if something was wrong. A few people definitely walked away thinking I was mad at them.

Whatever. It was worth it. I glanced over at Andie, and she gave me a thumbs-up. She'd been watching me, and so far I hadn't let her down. She didn't exactly look happy to be here, but she didn't look actively unhappy either.

Ever since she'd arrived, she'd been sitting with Tanner's ex, Lucy. I hadn't realized the two of them were so friendly. Out of respect for my brother and his injured feelings, I usually tried to avoid Lucy as much as I could. I wasn't inclined to be friendly with a woman who'd stomped on Tanner's heart, but because she was Matt's sister, I couldn't really give her the cold shoulder either.

So I didn't go talk to Andie. Instead I stuck close to the other guys in the band and tried to keep my head and my mouth turned down.

"Wyatt!"

I winced at the sound of Brianna Thorne's voice, and just barely evaded the kiss she aimed at my cheek as she came in for a hug.

"Hey, Brianna." I tugged her wrist off my neck and ducked out of her embrace before she could get too friendly.

"You've been keeping secrets, you naughty thing!"

My heart stopped in alarm. "What?"

"I heard about your little show at Zelda's!" She gave me a playful shove, using it as a pretext to caress my chest. "How could you not tell me about your songwriting debut? I'm so mad at you."

As I sidled farther out of Brianna's reach, I darted a look at Andie and saw her frowning. I gave her an apologetic shrug, hoping it would allay some of her displeasure.

"Everyone's been raving about your music for the last two weeks," Brianna said. "I'm just dying to hear it. Maybe I could talk you into giving me a private concert some time."

I winced as she batted her eyelashes at me. "We're actually gonna play a couple of the new songs tonight, so you'll get to hear them with everyone else."

"Ooh! Exciting! I can't wait!"

While she doggedly chattered at me, unbothered by the disinterested signals I was attempting to give off, my gaze wandered over the faces around the patio, evaluating the size and mood of tonight's audience. The Rusty Spoke seemed a little more busy than usual, and I wondered if it was because of the buzz about our new music.

A familiar face in the crowd caught my attention, and my stomach twisted.

Josh was here. He was in line at the bar with Mia, and he lifted his hand in a wave when he caught me looking his way.

I hadn't expected him to be here tonight. He didn't often make it to our shows, and he hadn't said anything to me about coming.

Tyler caught my eye and motioned toward the stage, letting me know it was time to get the you-know-what on the road. I nodded and downed the last of my beer. Brianna wished me luck, and I managed to dodge a second hug by ducking behind Corey to toss my bottle into the recycling bin.

Once we took the stage, I relaxed a little. With a guitar in my hands and a good ten feet of distance between me and the audience, I didn't have to worry about fending off any amorous advances. I avoided making eye contact with any women in the audience and mostly sang to the back fence or concentrated on my guitar. Every once in a while I'd let my gaze drift past Andie, but with Josh here I didn't dare look at her too much.

We played covers for the first half hour until the crowd was good and warmed up. When I finally introduced the first new song, they answered with enthusiastic cheers and hollers. We'd been rehearsing it all week, and I was pretty proud of how it had turned out. But I wasn't prepared for the response it got.

When you were up onstage, you could tell when an audience was along for the ride and when you were barely holding their attention. You could see it in their faces and body language. But you could also feel it in the air like an electric charge.

As soon as we launched into "Bait and Switch," I could tell the crowd was into it. The atmosphere was crackling with energy. People were on their feet, nodding to the music. By the time we got to the repeat of the chorus, they were singing along and dancing.

To a song I'd written.

It blew me away. I'd never felt anything like this high.

When it was over, I stood there grinning like a fool as the roar of applause washed over me. I threw a look back at Matt and the other guys, and saw the same stunned smiles on their faces. The same elation. The same growing hope for what our future might hold.

The rest of the set passed in a euphoric blur. We played another one of my songs, one that was a little slower, but still a crowd-pleaser.

Throwing caution to the wind, I let my gaze settle on Andie while I sang it, because it was one of the ones I'd written about her. I wanted her to know I was thinking about her, and that I appreciated having her here.

The smile in her eyes banished most of my anxiety about our earlier conversation.

After the show, once we'd packed up our gear, I ventured back onto the patio. As I made my way through the crowd, accepting high fives and congratulations, my eyes searched for Andie.

I finally saw her standing off in a quiet corner of the patio by herself. Watching me. Like she'd been waiting for me.

I wove my way over to her. "Hey you."

"Hey there, Mr. Rock Star." She grinned at me, and I swept her up in a hug and spun her around. "That was awesome," she said when I finally put her down. "I'm glad I was here to see it."

"I'm glad too." I couldn't stop smiling. "I guess maybe they liked the songs."

"Maybe? Are you kidding? They loved them."

"It's kind of bananas."

"No it's not." She reached up and ruffled my hair. "It's exactly what I expected. How do you feel?"

"Dazed."

She handed me her beer. "Drink this." I tipped my head back and chugged what was left. "My brother's here."

My mood deflated a little at the reminder. "I saw."

"It's the perfect chance to tell him." She actually looked excited at the prospect.

I blinked at her. "What, tonight?"

"Yes tonight. He's in a good mood, you're in a good mood. What better time than now? It'll be fine."

I gentled my tone, trying to pacify her. "Sweetheart, no. Not here. Not like this."

"You said you'd tell him the next time you see him." She sounded annoyed by my reluctance.

"I told you I was going to call him tomorrow so I could arrange to meet him on my own terms. Someplace private and quiet where we can talk it out."

"He's right over there. All you have to do is walk up to him and say the words. I'll go with you and we can do it together. It'll be easier with the two of us presenting a united front."

There was a lot of sense in what she was saying. But I wasn't prepared to do it right this second. I'd reconciled myself to calling Josh tomorrow. I needed every minute between now and then to marshal my courage for the task.

Besides, I'd just had one of the best nights of my life, and I didn't want it to end in a fight with my best friend.

I shook my head. "It's not a conversation I want to have in a public place."

"Why not?" she shot back, bristling with anger. "How's that going to make a difference?"

"I don't want to cause a scene." I laid my hand on her arm, trying to calm her down. "Like we're fixing to do right now if you don't lower your voice."

She jerked out of my grasp. "Since when have you ever in your life cared about causing a scene? It sounds to me like you're just making excuses. Like you have no intention of doing what you promised."

"That's not true," I replied tightly. "I told you I'd do it and I will. But you've gotta let me pick my moment."

"There's never going to be a good time to do it. So you might as well nut up and get it over with."

"Sweetheart, listen—"

Her eyes blazed with fury. "Call me sweetheart one more time and I swear to god—"

"Is everything all right?" Josh appeared beside us, wearing a dark frown. He laid a hand on my shoulder, but it wasn't a friendly hand. It was a deeply concerned hand. An *I just saw something I don't like, care to explain yourself?* hand. His eyes narrowed as they traveled back and forth between me and Andie. "What's going on?"

This wasn't the way I wanted him to find out about us. He was already on edge, his big brother senses tingling after seeing us arguing. He'd probably seen her twist out of my grasp. It was pretty obvious from the way Andie was glaring at me that I'd done something to piss her off. Not exactly the best way to make my case as good boyfriend material.

My eyes pleaded with Andie, begging her not to reveal the truth. To cover my ass this one last time.

Her expression offered no sympathy whatsoever. "Well, Wyatt?" she said, her voice dangerously calm as her dark eyes seared into me. "Do you want to tell Josh what's going on?"

Both her tone and the look on her face told me in no uncertain terms what she expected me to do. *Now or never,* her eyes threatened. *What's it going to be?*

I swallowed.

The reckoning I'd been dreading for the entirety of my adult life was at hand. This was my put up or shut up moment. Time to shit or get off the pot.

So I did.

Or rather, I didn't.

I didn't tell Josh the truth.

I chickened out.

"It's nothing," I heard myself say.

I hadn't made any kind of decision to say it. The words just came out of my mouth, like someone else had temporarily taken the wheel. My mental faculties had switched to autopilot mode, and I'd lost control of my own decision-making apparatus.

The disappointment on Andie's face filled me with shame.

She'd asked me to do this one thing for her. Told me how much she needed it. And I'd fucking chickened out. Because I was a coward. A gutless, low-down, good-for-nothing worm.

"Andie?" Josh's eyebrows lifted, waiting for his sister's confirmation or denial.

"You heard him." Andie's voice was devoid of all emotion, but she couldn't hide the hurt in her eyes. "Apparently it's nothing." She watched me to make sure the import of her final remark landed before she turned and walked off. As she disappeared inside the bar, I saw Mia hurry after her.

"What the hell was that about?"

I dragged my attention back to Josh, my mind racing for an explanation that would satisfy him. "I've been having some girl trouble and she was trying to give me advice I didn't want to take."

The falsehood fell off my tongue as smoothly as expensive

whiskey, because I was better at lying on my feet than telling the truth. I always had been. It was my modus operandi. The way I'd always gotten out of uncomfortable situations and avoided difficult conversations. And it was a big part of the reason Josh didn't think I was good enough for Andie.

He was right. I was a dog.

He gave me a dubious look. "Why didn't she say that, then?"

"You know Andie." I shrugged as if that was all the explanation required.

Josh studied me with unnerving sharpness. "The thing is," he said slowly, "it looked like something more than that to me. She looked pretty upset. It seemed like you two were having a fight."

"I told you, she's pissed about the way I treated one of her friends." It was a plausible enough lie, since it had happened before. A couple of times, actually.

Josh didn't seem to be buying it though.

He moved a half step closer, leaning toward me to speak in a low voice. "You know, Mia thinks you've been carrying a torch for Andie, and I told her she was way off base. But now I have to ask: Is there something going on with you and my sister, Wyatt?"

There was no mistaking the implied threat in his tone. If I confirmed his suspicions, I'd be offered no forgiveness or understanding. Any hopes I might have had for a harmonious accord between us were long gone now.

Maybe once some time had passed, and he'd had a chance to cool off, maybe then we'd be able to try again. Andie and I could sit him down and talk to him together. Present that united front she'd been talking about.

After I'd smoothed things over with her, of course. Which would take some doing. We'd argued plenty in the past, but it had always been minor shit. Petty quarrels and friendly bickering. I'd never seen her this upset before. Not with me, anyway.

It made my heart hurt to think about the look on her face. To know she was probably inside with Mia right now cursing my name. I needed to make things right with her.

But first I needed to get Josh off my back. I could only deal with one problem at a time.

So I looked my best friend in the eyes, and I straight up lied to him.

"There's nothing going on between me and Andie. Not the way you're implying." I let some of my frustration leak into my voice. I even glared at him a little, jutting my chin out as if I resented the question.

He regarded me for a long moment. Then he gave me a nod, seemingly satisfied with my answer.

"Now if you're done interrogating me, I'm in need of a drink." I turned and headed for the bar.

My mind was reeling as I pushed my way through the patio, still trying to process everything that had happened in the last few minutes. How badly my good night had gone to shit.

I was so distracted, I didn't see Brianna until she was right in front of me.

"Oh my god, Wyatt!"

I stopped short as she stepped into my path. I'd only narrowly avoided bowling her over, and we were so close her breasts were nearly grazing my chest. I jerked back, but she grabbed both my arms, halting my retreat.

"Those new songs were incredible! I had no idea you were so talented. And so romantic too. You big softie! That second song was totally swoony. Tell the truth now, was it about me?"

My mouth opened to deny it, but before I could get the words out she grabbed my face with both hands and crushed her mouth against mine.

Shock froze me in place long enough for her to get her tongue inside my mouth. My gorge rose at the unwanted intrusion, and I grabbed her by the shoulders and removed her from my face.

"It wasn't about you, Brianna." I struggled to keep my voice steady and my revulsion in check. I didn't want to hurt her feelings. It wasn't as if I hadn't led her on in the past, giving her every reason to think I'd welcome her advances. "I'm sorry, but I'm not interested tonight."

I turned away so I wouldn't have to witness her disappointment.

And then I saw Andie.

Standing just outside the door of the Spoke.

Watching everything.

27

ANDIE

Mia had followed me to the bathroom when I walked away from Wyatt and my brother. I was so mad I wanted to scream and smash things. But I wasn't going to cry. Not in front of Mia. And especially not in this grimy bathroom with some drunk girl talking on her phone in one of the stalls. I just needed a minute to cool off and gather my dignity.

Then I'd walk out of here with my head held high, get into my car, and drive myself home. After that, there'd be plenty of time for crying.

"At least let me drive you," Mia said.

I shook my head as I bent to splash cold water on my face. I didn't want to talk about it. I just wanted to get away from here so I could be alone with my misery. "I'm fine."

"You're not."

"I'm not," I conceded as I grabbed a paper towel.

I was hurt and disheartened. Wyatt had let me down. He wasn't ever going to tell my brother the truth. When push came to shove, he wasn't willing to put himself out on a limb for me.

He'd let me think I mattered to him, but the truth was I wasn't that important after all.

I felt like I'd been played, and I couldn't see a way for us to move on from here.

The realization made me feel sick.

"Come on." Mia herded me out of the bathroom. "We don't have to talk if you don't want to, but I'm driving you home."

"Yeah, okay. Thanks." I pushed out the door to the patio and stopped dead.

Wyatt was sucking face with Brianna Thorne.

The air left my lungs with a pain so sharp it felt like I'd been punched in the diaphragm.

They were in a full-on lip-lock. Open-mouthed. With tongue, even.

My whole body felt cold.

Numb.

As I watched, Wyatt detached himself from Brianna. He said something to her, then turned around and saw me. His eyes went wide with panic—and guilt.

I ran for the parking lot.

I had to get away from there. Away from him and everyone else. I heard him call my name, but I didn't slow down. I just kept running, my feet crunching on the gravel as I wove my way through the cars. My vision blurred with tears. I was crying. There was no stopping it at this point.

I didn't know where I was headed. I couldn't remember where I'd parked and wasn't paying attention to what direction I was going. I was just trying to get as far away as I could.

"Andie!" Wyatt caught my arm, forcing me to an ungainly stop. He loomed in front of me, the familiar scent of his skin filling me with longing and misery. His hands clasped my shoulders so I couldn't turn away, but I closed my eyes, refusing to look at him.

"I didn't kiss Brianna, she kissed me!" He was breathing hard, his voice desperate and pleading. "I swear, I didn't do anything to encourage her. She threw herself at me with no warning."

I actually believed him. Maybe that made me a sucker, but I didn't think he'd set out to kiss Brianna. That wasn't why I was so upset.

It was because I knew she'd only kissed him because he'd let her think he was interested. If he hadn't been so afraid of people finding out we were together, she would have kept her tongue to herself. He'd toyed with her, just like he toyed with everyone.

"Andie, say something."

"I asked you to choose me and you didn't." The words choked out of me, my voice rough and shaking.

He pulled me to his chest, and god help me, I let him. I let his arms encircle me and let myself lean into him as he held me. I wanted his comfort more than I wanted my dignity. I needed him. I didn't want to give him up.

"I'm so sorry. I fucked up tonight. But I love you."

Something inside me snapped at those words. His sweet talk didn't mean anything if he wasn't willing to stick his neck out for me. It was just an empty gesture.

I wriggled out of his arms and shoved him away. He stumbled backward, and when he started to reach for me again, I flinched away from him. "Don't."

Pain streaked across his face. "Andie, please..."

I shook my head, unmoved by his suffering. "You're more afraid of making my brother mad than you are of hurting me."

"That's not true."

"It is!" I shouted at him as the tears streamed down my face. "You just proved it. I can't count on you when I need you. I never should have let myself love you."

He reeled back like I'd struck him. "Please don't say that."

"Andie?" Josh was running toward us with Mia trailing a short ways behind. He caught up to me and grasped me by the arms, his face creased with concern. "What's wrong?"

My chest hitched as I choked on a sob, and I sagged against him, burying my face in his chest.

"What happened? Why are you crying?" Josh's voice sounded frantic as he hugged me to him. I guess he had good reason, since he wasn't used to seeing me cry. He probably thought someone had died.

It wasn't that I never cried. I cried plenty. I just never did it in front of anyone. Not since I was a preschooler. I'd always loathed being seen as weak, so I'd learned to hold my tears back until I could do my crying in private.

Except it hadn't worked tonight. The sucker punch of seeing Wyatt with Brianna had cracked the brittle control I'd managed to retain over my emotions. And now I couldn't seem to stop sobbing into my brother's shirt.

"Let's just take her home," I heard Mia say.

"What the hell's going on?" Josh demanded, still holding on to me as he turned toward Wyatt. "Why is she crying?"

"Because of me," Wyatt answered in a flat, hollow voice.

I felt Josh go rigid. He detached my hands from his shirt and turned to face Wyatt.

"Josh, don't." I reached out to stop him.

His eyes burned with cold fury as he pulled out of my grasp and charged at Wyatt.

28

WYATT

I stared up at the water-stained ceiling in my apartment, trying to muster the will to get up and take a shower. I'd spent the better part of the last three days drunk. Not so much trying to forget as trying not to think at all. Seeking refuge in unconsciousness. Preferring oblivion to the company of my own thoughts.

I was sober at the moment, but I didn't expect it to last. It hurt too much to be sober. When I was sober I couldn't stop myself from thinking about Andie and the way the light had gone out of her eyes when she'd seen me with Brianna.

She hadn't even looked mad, just...empty. Hollowed out. That was the scariest part. I'd seen her mad plenty of times. I could've dealt with mad. We could have worked it out.

I didn't know what to do about that emptiness though.

I never should have let myself love you.

Her words haunted me. They kept tumbling around in my head, leaving painful cuts everywhere they touched. The truth of them etching themselves into my brain matter.

I reached out for the whiskey bottle on the coffee table and found it empty. With a groan, I pushed myself upright and swung my legs off the couch. The blood rushed to my throbbing head, and I pressed my fists against my eyes.

The bruising on my face had mostly faded. My nose was barely even tender anymore. All this pain I was feeling was of my own doing. I deserved this hangover as much as I deserved the bloody nose Josh had given me Saturday night.

I hadn't bothered to defend myself when he came at me. I'd broken Andie's heart, just like he'd always feared I would. He'd had every right to give me that beating.

It hadn't been much of a beating, truth be told. Just a single, well-placed punch.

Part of me had been disappointed. I deserved a lot worse than a bloody nose.

Once the worst wave of dizziness had passed, I dragged myself to my feet and wandered into the kitchen, looking for another drink. While I was staring into my empty liquor cabinet, there was a knock on my door.

I flinched at the sound and decided not to answer it. It was probably just some dude selling magazines anyway.

My caller knocked again and shouted at me through the door. "I can see your truck out front, Wyatt. If you don't answer the door, I'm calling 911."

Mia.

Her threat was a good one, because I sure as hell didn't want Ryan getting dispatched on a wellness check to my address.

"Hang on, I'm coming." I made my way to the door and yanked it open.

Mia silently took in my disheveled appearance as I cringed at the godforsaken sunlight behind her.

She was a tall woman—at least an inch taller than me—and the feeling of being looked down on by her was only compounded by my current state of affairs. Turning my face away from her wordless examination, I gestured for her to enter.

As she stepped into the living room she frowned at the mess around her. "Your apartment is disgusting."

"I know." I sank down on the couch and leaned forward, rubbing my hands over my head.

"You don't look so great either."

I let out a sour laugh. "Thanks."

Her nose wrinkled. "Or smell so great."

"Did you just come here to insult me? It's fine if you did, I'm just wondering."

"I didn't come here to insult you."

"Then why?"

"I wanted to make sure you were okay."

I leaned back on the couch and arched an inquisitive eyebrow at her. "I would have thought I was persona non grata to the Lockhart clan after Saturday night."

She didn't say anything, but I could tell from the way she was chewing on her lower lip that I was right. My ribs ached to think about it. I hadn't just blown up my relationship with Andie. I'd lost her whole family too.

Swallowing the noxious stew of guilt and shame in my gut, I said thickly, "I'm guessing your boyfriend wouldn't be too pleased about you being nice to me right now."

Mia gave me a long look. "You were nice to me after I broke your best friend's heart."

I shook my head and stared down at my lap. "That was a different situation."

She hadn't let Josh down the way I'd let Andie down. She hadn't broken any promises or told any lies. Their rough patch hadn't been her fault the way this mess was all mine.

"Maybe," she said, "but I'm still allowed to be concerned about you."

I rubbed at a spot on my T-shirt that might have been either puke or pizza sauce. "I'm fine."

"I'd be very surprised if that was true."

Her scrutiny made me uncomfortable, as did her concern. I didn't have any right to her compassion. I'd made this bed of thorns I was lying in, and I deserved every ounce of the misery I was feeling.

Pushing myself to my feet, I made for the door, hoping she'd take the hint and follow. "You don't need to worry about me, Mia. So unless there's anything else—"

"There is, actually."

My steps faltered, and I turned around with a weary sigh, readying myself for some kind of well-meaning lecture. "What?"

"It's about Andie."

"What about her?" I knew she had to be smarting, but she was strong. I figured she'd recover from my betrayal a lot faster than I would.

Mia hesitated, looking torn. "I'm only telling you this because I know you care about her, and because I thought there might be something you could do about it."

A spike of worry stabbed through my chest, and I suddenly got a lot more awake. "Something I could do about what?"

"She got a notice yesterday that her HOA had gone ahead and put the lien on her house."

"What? They can't do that."

"They did. The paperwork was very official-looking."

"For the full amount?"

Mia answered with an anxious nod.

"Jesus," I breathed. Andie must be going out of her mind. She'd never be able to raise that kind of money, which meant she'd lose the house.

"She didn't want me to tell you, but I just thought—"

"I'll take care of it."

"Can you?"

"I can and I will." I might not be the man Andie needed me

to be, but I could damn well protect her from getting screwed over by my father.

———

THE FIRST THING I did after Mia left was call Rodney Phelps, the president of Andie's HOA.

"What the hell, Rodney? We had an agreement."

There was a pause on his end before he said, "You're gonna have to explain to me what you're talking about."

"Andie Lockhart's house. You went ahead and put the lien on it even though she made all the repairs you wanted by the deadline."

"That wasn't my doing. The lawyers handle all that for us. Once the HOA hands a problem over to them, they go off and do what they do. I've got no part of it anymore."

"That's not what you told me before."

"It's not?" His transparent attempt to feign ignorance made my blood boil.

"You know it's not. You told me if she got the repairs done, you'd waive all the fines and late fees and everything would be square."

"I don't believe I did say that. I'm not sure where you got that idea from."

"I got it from your mouth when you sat across from me at Dooley's drinking the beer I'd bought you. You looked me right in the eye while you said it, as you know damn well."

"I'm sorry, Wyatt, there must have been some miscommunication. I never said that. And I know you don't have anything to that effect in writing, which means we never had any kind of agreement."

"You lying snake," I spat into the phone.

"I don't know what to tell you, son. Ms. Lockhart is responsible for the payment of all fines and fees levied by the HOA. If she feels she's been treated unfairly, she can take it up with our attorneys."

My teeth ground together. "Tell me something, Rodney. Just to satisfy my curiosity. Were you blowing smoke up my ass from the start, or did my father strong-arm you into going back on your word?"

"We're done with this conversation." The line went dead.

Son of a bitch.

So much for Rodney. That left me with only one avenue of appeal.

My dear old dad.

―――――

"WYATT! WHAT AN UNEXPECTED SURPRISE." My father's longtime assistant beamed a smile at me when I walked into his outer office suite at the creamery's corporate headquarters. "Is your daddy expecting you?"

"Yes," I lied as I strode purposefully toward the closed door to the CEO's office.

I'd known Connie since I was in grade school. I'd been in Cub Scouts with her son Jared, who'd sold me my first joint. She was a nice enough lady, but she was also the Cerberus who guarded the gates to my father's domain, and it was her job to get in my way.

"Well now, honey, hang on and let me tell him you're here." She jumped up to try and block my way, but I grasped her hand and slipped my other arm around her like we were about to waltz.

Giving her a grin, I spun her around and out of my way. "Don't trouble yourself, Connie. I'll just see myself in." I lunged for the door and threw it open before she could catch up to me.

My dad looked up from his desk, startled by the sudden incursion. A droning voice emanated from the conference call speaker in front of him, rambling about quarterly reports or some other mind-numbing corporate bullshit.

"We need to talk," I announced as I stalked into the room.

Connie fluttered nervously in my wake. "I'm so sorry, George."

My father held up a hand to quiet her and tapped a button on the speaker. "Folks, I'm gonna need to step out for a minute. Carry on without me."

He tapped the speaker again, disconnecting from the call, and offered Connie a tight smile. "It's all right, Connie. Can you please close the door on your way out?"

When she was gone and my dad and I were alone, he leaned back in his chair and crossed his arms, regarding me coolly. "Well? You've got my full attention. What would you like to talk about, son?"

I advanced on him, stopping at the edge of his desk. "I want you to leave Andie Lockhart alone."

He frowned, looking perplexed, but whether it was real or fake I couldn't tell. "I don't know what you're talking about. I'm not doing anything to Andie Lockhart."

"What about King Holdings, LLC?"

Comprehension came into his expression, hardening it. "What about it?"

"They've been trying to buy the house she inherited from her grandmother."

"They've made offers on a lot of houses. It's a real estate venture. Buying and selling property is their business."

"What about bribing her homeowners' association to hit her with a load of trumped-up fines and bogus late fees so they can put a lien on her house? Is that their business too? Intimidating people so you can steal their houses out from under them?"

"No one bribed anyone." He sounded defensive, which meant I'd hit close to the truth. "If she's in violation of her HOA's covenants, they're within their rights to assess fines and file a lien until any uncollected fees have been paid. It's all perfectly legal and has nothing to do with me."

"Bullshit!" I leaned forward, slamming my hands on the desk. "It's your lawyers sending the threats, and your old friend and loyal employee Rodney Phelps in charge of the HOA that's just now decided to assess three years' worth of late fees on fines they never informed her of in the first place. You've got her HOA in your pocket, just like you've got this whole town in your pocket."

He held up a hand. "Now listen—"

I cut him off, too steamed to let him get his say in yet. "You're twisting the law to your purposes and using your lawyers to scare anyone who dares to get in your way. You'll do anything to make a few extra bucks and you don't give a damn who gets hurt in the process!"

"Well." The stony glower he directed at me belied the mild tone of his voice. "It's nice to know you have such a high opinion of my integrity."

"Any opinion I have of you has been well-earned," I shot back. "Tell me, how many other people have you strong-armed with your little scheme before Andie? How many other HOAs have you bought to do your bidding?"

"What do you want from me, Wyatt? What exactly are you asking me to do here?"

"I want you to leave Andie and her house alone. Release the lien, clear all the outstanding fees, and make sure the lawyers, her HOA, and your little real estate venture all back off and stay that way. King Holdings doesn't get to have her property."

"Is that all?"

"No. I want everyone else you've been using these bullying

tactics on let off the hook too. No more liens, no more HOA threats. If someone doesn't want to sell, you accept it and move on."

His eyebrows twitched. "And if I don't?"

I straightened my spine and crossed my arms as I stared down at him. "Then I'll start telling anyone who'll listen everything I know about you. The way you do business behind closed doors, the kind of father you were..." I paused for effect before I unleashed my bombshell. "And I'll tell everyone about the affairs—including the one you had while my mother was dying."

I watched him digest what I'd just said. I'd never told him I knew about his infidelity. How he'd betrayed my mother, both before and after her cancer diagnosis. That he'd been sleeping with his current wife, Heather, the whole time my mom was going through chemo.

I'd seen them kissing once. At the hospital, of all damn places. My mom had been in surgery, and my dad had left us in the waiting room with Ryan while he went outside to take a call. I looked out the window, and there they were in the parking lot. Playing tonsil hockey while my mother was on the operating table.

After that I'd started watching my dad more closely. Keeping track of his comings and goings. Snooping through his stuff. Eavesdropping on phone conversations. I'd figured out a lot about his extracurricular activities and just how long they'd been going on.

Because my mother had died so young and my dad had seemed to grieve so much, everyone assumed their marriage had been perfect before it was tragically cut short. A myth had evolved about my mother, that she was the one true love of my dad's life, and they would have stayed together if she hadn't died, and wasn't it all so terribly sad, blah blah blah. The fact that he'd married Heather six months after my mom's death hadn't done anything to puncture the fairy tale. He'd been so inconsolable, everyone whispered sympathetically, it was a shame that in his weakened state he'd let himself be ensnared by the first gold digger who happened along.

Except *I* knew better. And I'd only ever told one person on earth about it: Brady. I'd never even told Tanner or Ryan, because Brady had told me not to. He'd said they had enough to carry without adding that to their burden. So I'd carried it by myself.

The cheating wasn't the only reason I had to resent my dad, but it was a big one. All this time I'd been holding it against him, and he'd had no idea I'd known about it.

Until now.

It must have shed new light on some aspects of our relationship for him. But if he was reassessing any of his assumptions about me, he didn't let it show. My dad had a first-rate poker face. It was one of the things that made him so good at business.

His expression remained neutral and his voice infuriatingly calm when he said, "Are you sure you're prepared for the fallout from something like that? It's not just me that kind of talk will hurt."

I was all too well aware of that. It was why I'd carried his secret for so long. The ugly truth might embarrass him, but it would also hurt some of my brothers and sisters. Tanner and Ryan, for a start. Not to mention Cody and Riley, my dad's kids with Heather.

And then there was what the scandal could mean for the business. My dad's reputation as a loving family man, benevolent business owner, and pillar of his community were fundamental to the company's image. He was the face of King's Creamery. The genial father figure at the bow of the ship.

Throwing dirt on that image would impact the company's

revenues. I didn't doubt that the business would survive it, but the financial consequences would ripple through my whole family—and a lot of the town.

Even so, I was prepared to do it. My father had crossed a line this time and I couldn't stand by and let him get away with it. I would do whatever it took to protect Andie. If people were hurt in the process, it'd be my father's chickens coming home to roost. His own mistakes and his alone to blame for it.

I met his gaze steadily and spoke with steel in my voice. "Try me."

He studied me for a long moment, undoubtedly evaluating the depth of my conviction. Deciding whether to call my bluff.

"Why now?" he asked, narrowing his eyes. "You've clearly waited years to play this card. Is it the girl?"

"Her name's Andie," I growled.

"You care about her that much?" He looked surprised. "Are you in love with her?"

"None of your goddamn business." I wasn't looking to have a heart-to-heart with my father about my romantic life. That wasn't a subject I ever wanted to discuss with this man.

"You are. You're in love with her." He shook his head, smiling. "My god. I never thought I'd see the day. Finally."

"Finally what?" I was confused by my father's sudden change of mood. His words sounded like he was taunting me, but the edge had gone out of his tone.

"You finally let yourself care about something enough to fight for it."

I opened my mouth to respond, but I didn't have a comeback ready. While I stood there blinking at him, my dad picked up his phone and found a number in his contacts. He put it on speaker and set it on his desk. A man picked up on the second ring.

"George, what can I do for you?"

"Bob, did you file paperwork to put a lien on Andrea Lockhart's house, by any chance?"

"I did. Last week."

My dad glanced up at me, arching an eyebrow. "I take it that was at Daniel's behest?"

"That's right. He's got me working with the HOAs."

"I'm gonna need you to get that lien released, Bob. Today."

"Okay." Bob sounded confused by the request, but not enough to argue with my father. "If that's what you want."

"Let's get Ms. Lockhart's debt wiped clean, all outstanding fees waived, and I don't want any of this showing up on her credit rating. Do you understand me? Make sure no one bothers this girl anymore."

"Gotcha."

"Thanks. And let's set up a meeting with Daniel sometime this week. I'll have Connie get in touch about the scheduling."

"Sure thing, George."

"Thanks, Bob. I appreciate it."

"Have a good one."

My father ended the call and looked up at me. "Satisfied?"

I nodded, trying to school my expression to cover my surprise. I hadn't expected him to roll over this easily. "What about the other people you've been hassling?"

"That's what the meeting with Daniel is about. I'll let him know I don't approve of his tactics. We'll make things right with everyone he's been targeting. You have my word on that."

I nodded again, feeling off-balance. Now that the focus of my wrath had been neutralized, the head of steam I'd worked up had nowhere to go. "Fine."

"I didn't know what Daniel was doing," my father said. "And I sure didn't know he'd targeted a friend of yours."

"You should have known. How many times have I heard you tell people the buck stops with you?" He might have kept his nose out of the specifics, but I didn't for a second believe he'd been surprised to hear what was being done to line his pockets. His ignorance had been an intentional choice in order to maintain deniability.

"You're right," he replied solemnly. "It's my responsibility. I'm sorry for any trouble it caused Andie. She's a good kid." His gaze sharpened as it met mine. "I've always liked her. I'm glad you do too."

I scowled, not interested in my father's approval. Not now, when I'd gone so long without it.

He leaned back in his chair, regarding me. If I didn't know better, I'd have thought he looked regretful. Maybe even a little sad. "You know, son, you didn't have to come in here leveling threats and making a scene to get my support. All you had to do was ask."

"I guess maybe it was a paperwork mix-up or something? The lawyer actually *apologized* to me. Can you believe that?" I was still in a state of shock as I filled Mia in on the surprising phone call I'd received today, releasing me from the nightmare that had consumed the last twenty-four hours of my life.

Yesterday, just two days after my blowup with Wyatt, I'd come home to a notice that a lien had been placed on my house. My emotional state had already taken a beating, so getting that news on top of everything else had sent me into a tailspin.

I'd spent most of today on the phone, trying to get someone to explain what had happened. I couldn't go to Wyatt because I wasn't currently speaking to him, so I'd tried to get in touch with the HOA, the bank, and the law firm who'd filed the lien, but I'd been stymied by voicemail, automated phone systems that stuck you on hold forever, and promises of callbacks that never happened.

I was just about to start calling attorneys, hoping to find one I could afford to hire, when I'd finally gotten a return call from the law firm. An attorney named Bob Hays told me the lien had been placed in error, that it would be removed posthaste and all record of the debt erased. As well, he assured me I was off the hook with the HOA and I'd be receiving confirmation to that effect in writing. Then he'd offered me his personal apology for the inconvenience.

"So it's all taken care of?" Mia asked, topping off my wineglass. I'd called her after I'd gotten off the phone with my new best friend Bob, and she'd come over after her last class to celebrate the good news.

"Apparently." I wouldn't truly be able to relax until I'd seen it in writing, but I wasn't in a state of pants-shitting panic anymore.

"What a relief."

"I know." I blew out a long breath and sank back against the couch. "I honestly didn't know what I was going to do."

"I'm glad you called me yesterday. You shouldn't have to deal with something like that alone."

I'd called Mia because I wasn't talking to Wyatt or my brother. They'd claimed the top two spots on my shit list after Saturday night—until I'd gotten the notice about the lien. But since that situation had apparently resolved itself, they were right back up there at the top of the list.

My brother probably wouldn't be in the doghouse for long. I expected we'd patch things up soon enough—once I'd cooled off enough that I could look at his face without wanting to punch it.

Wyatt was another matter. I didn't know if I'd be able to forgive him—or trust him. Part of me wanted to, but another part of me was afraid that'd be inviting him to hurt me again.

It was too painful to think about him. Especially because, layered over the pain and disappointment, I felt a constant ache of longing. He'd hurt me, but I still missed him. Then I'd get angry at myself for missing someone who'd hurt me, which only made me more angry at Wyatt. It was a pointless, self-perpetu-ating cycle of misery, and I was trying to break myself out of it by not thinking about him at all.

I smiled at Mia. "Thanks for holding my hand during my freak-out."

"Anytime." She held up her wineglass. "Here's to not losing your house."

We clinked them together and I took another sip. "An error. My god." I shook my head in amazement. "I mean, what even? The whole thing is so weird."

"Yeah." Mia hesitated, wincing a little. "I should probably tell you something."

"What?"

"I went to see Wyatt this morning, and I told him about the lien."

I stared at her. "I told you I didn't want to ask him for help."

"You didn't ask him for help. I did." She didn't look sorry. In fact, she looked proud of herself.

"You think he had something to do with this?"

She shrugged. "He said he'd take care of it. He seemed pretty determined."

I wasn't sure how that made me feel. Uncomfortable that I'd needed him to do it. Worried that it made me beholden to him. But also glad to know he cared enough to intervene on my behalf.

Even as I had the thought, I was gripped by a fresh wave of sorrow. He might care about me, but that didn't mean I could trust him with my heart.

He hadn't even tried to contact me since the dustup in the parking lot. I'd expected him to call or come by to try and patch things up, but apparently even that was too much to expect. It was nice that he cared about me enough to make a phone call on my behalf, but he didn't care enough to talk to me himself. It just served as further proof that he'd rather lose me than subject himself to a hard conversation.

"Did I do the wrong thing?" Mia asked. "I just knew he'd want to help if he could. He screwed up, but he cares about you."

I shook my head as I took another sip of wine. "He told me he loved me, you know."

"Do you love him?"

"I thought so. I guess I still do, and that's why it hurts so much."

I didn't want to be angry with him. I missed him and I wanted to be with him. But I didn't know if I could forgive him—or if I should.

"Andie, Wyatt loves you—and you love him. You two have been friends all your lives. That has to be worth something."

"Love isn't always enough."

"You're right, it isn't." She turned to face me, pulling one of her legs up underneath her on the couch. "Even though I loved Josh, I thought we'd never be able to make it work because our lives were headed in such different directions. Loving him didn't make any of those challenges go away. I had to make a choice to stay. To find a way to make it work despite the challenges. I had to choose love, and I had to fight to hold on to it. We both did."

"I tried. I was all in with both feet." My voice cracked and I gulped down more wine. "Wyatt was the one who gave up. He had plenty of chances to fight for us, and he wouldn't." I reached up to wipe away a traitorous tear. I'd been crying a lot the last few days. My control over my emotions was shot all to hell.

Mia's expression softened and she squeezed my arm. "People make mistakes, but they can also learn from them and do better. Your brother and I both made our share. But we gave each other another chance. We took a leap of faith that the rewards would outweigh the risk."

I huffed out a dark laugh. "I'm not real good at faith."

"I'm not either," Mia said. "But I'm pretty sure it's the kind of thing you get better at with practice." My doorbell rang, and Mia unfolded herself from the couch. "I'll get it."

She came back a moment later with my aunt Birdie, who was carrying a rectangular cake pan. "I made you a breakup cake," Birdie announced as she walked through the living room on the way to the kitchen. "Shall we dig in?"

Mia and I exchanged smiles as we grabbed our wine and followed Birdie into the kitchen. Her baked goods were always welcome, but her breakup cakes were legendary. It was just a plain old Texas sheet cake—or so she claimed—but it was the best chocolate sheet cake ever made. I was convinced there was a secret ingredient that made it so good, and one day I was going to pry it out of her.

Birdie set the cake down and greeted me with a tight hug. "I'm sorry about Wyatt, honey. But I'm so glad to hear your house troubles are all over. What a blessing."

Not so much a blessing as Wyatt's doing. My heart twisted anew at the reminder.

Mia handed Birdie a glass of wine and passed out forks while I uncovered the cake. I laughed at the words she'd piped onto the icing: *Fuck That Guy.*

"I felt a little bad using my traditional breakup message this time," Birdie said with a small frown.

"No, it's perfect. It's exactly what I needed." I grabbed a fork and dug in, sighing around a mouthful of chocolatey deliciousness.

I hadn't been able to drown my sorrows in ice cream, because ice cream reminded me too much of Wyatt. But cake was even better. There was something decadent and deeply comforting about jamming your fork right into a cake this big and shoveling it into your mouth. That was why Birdie's breakup cakes were sheet cakes. Because they were meant to be eaten straight from the pan.

"Oh my goddddddd," Mia moaned. "My mouth just died and went to heaven."

Birdie's eyes twinkled. "And that's why my friend Laura-Beth calls it 'orgasm cake.'"

Mia's cheeks reddened as she laughed along with us. "Well, she's not wrong."

I speared another forkful of cake. "Chocolate contains phenylethylamine, the same chemical that stimulates the brain's pleasure centers during orgasm."

"That's another reason it makes a good breakup cake." Birdie took a sip of her wine as she turned to me. "That reminds me. While I'm here, can I look at those old letters of my mother's you found?"

"Of course!" With everything else, I'd forgotten all about the letters. I set my fork down and pulled open the kitchen drawer where I'd stashed them, meaning to take them to Birdie's the next time I went over there. "Here." I handed them to her.

She slipped one of the letters out of its envelope and scanned it while Mia and I continued to devour the cake. "Oh my." She patted her chest and let out a little laugh.

"Is that one of the smutty ones?" I asked, glancing over at the page in Birdie's hand.

"Well, yes," she answered, "but that's not what I was chuckling about. I know who your grandmother's secret suitor was."

"You do?"

"Yes. It was your grandfather. He's the one who wrote these letters."

"What?" I stared at her. "But the initials in the signature don't match his name."

Birdie shrugged. "That's Daddy's handwriting. I'd recognize it anywhere." She flipped the letter over and squinted at the signature. "I don't know why he didn't sign his own name. Maybe it was some kind of game or secret code—" She broke into a sudden grin. "I know what it means. Honey Bunny! That's what she used to call him."

"Honey Bunny?" I echoed. "So they were already engaged when he was writing these letters?"

"Probably. They were at least going steady, even if he hadn't put the ring on her finger yet." She patted her chest again as she went back to reading. "My word. These are expressive."

"But they broke up," I said. "The last letter is a goodbye letter because she'd broken up with him."

"Clearly it didn't take. Thank goodness for that, or neither of us would be here right now."

"He was so devastated."

Birdie nodded, seemingly unfazed. "He would be, wouldn't he? I wonder what he did to make her break up with him that time."

I blinked at her. "That time?"

"Oh yes. They had their share of ups and downs. Daddy spent a month sleeping on his friend's couch when I was in grade school. And a few weeks living out of the Holiday Inn a few years later when Momma kicked him out again." Birdie smiled to herself. "Your pawpaw wasn't always an easy man to live with. And your meemaw wasn't always a forgiving woman."

"I thought their relationship was perfect."

Birdie gave me a pitying look. "Oh honey, no relationship is perfect. Do you know how many breakup cakes I've made over the years? And fully half of those people ended up getting right back together. Look at Josh and Mia. I made him a breakup cake last year, and now they're as happy as two toads in a puddle."

"Maybe it's the cake," Mia said, smiling around a mouthful of chocolate. "Maybe it's actually good luck. Or maybe the secret ingredient is some kind of love potion."

"Maybe." Birdie said with a cryptic smile. "But I like to think if two people are meant to be together, they'll always find a way back to each other."

This, from my proudly single aunt who'd once jilted a man at the altar and run off to follow the Lilith Fair tour around the country. The woman who triumphantly delivered a breakup cake to every newly broken heart in town. I'd never imagined she was such a romantic.

"Wait," Mia said, frowning at Birdie. "When you made Josh's breakup cake last year, what did it say on top?"

Birdie pressed her lips together and gave Mia's shoulders a squeeze. "It doesn't really matter, does it, honey? The cake worked its magic and everything turned out just fine."

30

ANDIE

"I'm still mad at you," I said, glaring at my brother.

Birdie had tricked me. She'd badgered me into coming with her to the King's Creamery Centennial Festival today. To "cheer me up" she'd claimed. We'd ride some rides, take in the entertainment, and eat our weight in ice cream.

Except it was obvious now the whole excursion had been a setup to effect a reconciliation between me and my brother. We hadn't been here more than half an hour before we'd "accidentally" bumped into him and Mia as we were exiting the bumper boats.

Josh ducked his head, hunching his shoulders forward as he frowned at his feet. "I figured you might be."

At least he had the decency to look shamefaced.

I turned my glare on my treacherous aunt, who'd engineered this involuntary sibling reunion under fraudulent pretenses. I'd been bamboozled. Hoodwinked. By my sneaky, slippery, shifty aunt Birdie. Who was currently answering my glare with an extremely self-satisfied smile. I should have pushed her bumper boat under the waterfall when I'd had the chance.

Mia jabbed Josh with her elbow. "What else do you have to say for yourself?"

I transferred my glare from my aunt to my supposed friend, who'd clearly been in on the conspiracy as well. I was surrounded by deceivers at every turn.

"I'm sorry," Josh said, looking up at me again.

I crossed my arms and met his sheepish gaze with a pitiless stare, determined not to make this easy for him. "For what, exactly?"

He darted a nervous glance at Mia before answering. "I never should have interfered in your dating life. It's none of my business who you want to go out with, and from now on I promise never to threaten or try to intimidate any of your potential suitors."

I scowled. "Your girlfriend told you to say all that."

"That's true," he admitted. "But I still mean every word. Mia made me see how I've been making your life harder by letting my overprotective instincts get the better of me. You're not a kid anymore. You're a grown adult capable of making your own choices and I should have respected that and trusted you to know your own mind."

"Thank you," I said grudgingly. "I appreciate that you're willing to admit when you're wrong, which you are most all of the time. It must get exhausting for you being wrong so much."

Josh's jaw clenched. "Next time I won't try to stop you from making the bad choice to date a compulsive womanizer who throws women away like used napkins," he said petulantly, earning another elbow jab from Mia. "Ow! Quit abusing me, woman."

I rolled my eyes at my brother's stubbornness, but I couldn't suppress the smile tugging at my lips. He might drive me up the wall, but I'd never been able to stay mad at him for long. He was the only brother I had, and I had too much affection for him—

just like I had too much affection for my meddlesome aunt and interfering friend to hold a grudge for the trickery that had forced my brother and I to the peace table.

When he caught sight of my smile, Josh stepped forward and folded me into a hug. "I really am sorry. But I hope you know it was all out of love."

I squirmed out of his embrace and gave him a playful shove. "I know that, you big dork."

"He's also sorry for punching Wyatt," Mia said.

"I'm not," Josh countered with a defiant jut of his chin. "That part I don't regret. I still reserve the right to punch any man who makes my little sister cry." He crossed his arms, leaning toward me as he added, "I'd be glad to punch him again if it will make you feel better. Just say the word."

Mia let out an exasperated huff. "There are better ways to resolve conflicts than with your fists, cowboy."

Josh's mouth twitched into a mischievous grin. "Undoubtedly, but sometimes you just need the satisfaction that comes with a good face-punching."

Birdie threaded her arm through mine, looking pleased with herself. "Now that we're all getting along again, I say we seal the deal with some ice cream." Her eyes twinkled as she smiled at my brother. "Josh's treat!"

The suggestion was met with unanimous enthusiasm, and we headed over to the nearest ice cream stand to place our orders. My chest hurt a little as I eyed the flavors in the case and saw the Thar She Blows! bubblegum ice cream with sour gummy candy bits. My favorite flavor would forever remind me of Wyatt now, and I wasn't sure I'd ever be able to enjoy it again.

Today marked a full week since our fight, and I still hadn't heard a word from him. I could have reached out to him myself, but my pride wouldn't let me. I wasn't the one who'd had someone else's tongue in my mouth. Wasn't I entitled to some groveling after that? The fact that he wasn't willing to put in the effort felt like a pretty clear sign that I'd been right all along. He'd never been all that invested in us being together in the first place.

The thought depressed me, so I decided I needed chocolate and lots of it. As if I hadn't gotten enough from Birdie's breakup cake. There might not be enough chocolate in the world to soothe my aching heart, but that didn't stop me from ordering myself two scoops of Double Double Fudge and Truffle.

As I was enjoying my towering cone of chocolate ice cream swirled with a fudge ripple and chocolate truffle candy pieces, Birdie suggested we venture over to the temporary stage that had been erected to host the live entertainment all day. It was mostly magicians and jugglers and other family-friendly fare, but I wasn't too old to appreciate a good magician or juggling act.

At least I knew I wouldn't have to worry about running into Wyatt as we wended our way through the amusement park. It was why I'd let Birdie talk me into coming here today. I knew he wouldn't be caught dead at King Town Park on any day, much less lending his presence to a special event like the Centennial Festival this weekend.

The whole rest of his family was here though. I'd caught sight of Josie a couple of times already, rushing to and fro looking harried. And I'd seen Manny at the petting zoo earlier with his daughter, Isabella. Currently, the whole clan was gathered up onstage—minus Wyatt, of course—wearing matching T-shirts and providing a smiling backdrop as George King gave a speech.

We found an empty spot on the grass, and sat down just as Wyatt's dad was wrapping up his speech. There was a smattering of polite applause, but most of the people hanging out on the grass didn't seem to be paying much attention. There were a lot of tired-looking parents supervising kids hyped up on ice cream, some groups of giggling teenagers, and a few young couples enjoying the sunshine and each other's company.

The Kings filed off the stage while Josie took over the mic to introduce a children's musical group called The Rainbow Sprinkles, who would be joined by special guest Sheriff Scoopy. A ripple of excitement spread through the younger members of the crowd. Sheriff Scoopy was the King's Ice Cream mascot, a favorite with the under-eight crowd.

As The Rainbow Sprinkles started to play a kid-friendly cover of "Old Town Road," some poor soul dressed up in a big plushie ice cream cone costume with a cowboy hat and sheriff's badge wandered out onto the grass below the stage and was immediately mobbed by a dozen squealing kids.

"Should we head out?" I asked, not really keen to sit around listening to saccharine covers of pop music.

Mia looked up from her phone and shook her head. "I don't want to walk around with my ice cream. Let's sit for a while longer."

I shrugged and stretched my legs out on the grass, leaning back on one arm as I finished off my double scoop. The King family were still milling around next to the stage, watching Sheriff Scoopy lead the kids in a line dance. Whoever was in the suit today had impressive moves, given how hard it must be to maneuver inside all that synthetic stuffing. Cody King had his phone up and was filming Sheriff Scoopy's dance, which probably meant it was one of his friends who'd been roped into the sorry job.

Some preteens had joined in the line dance to show off their moves, and Sheriff Scoopy peeled off to dance through the audience, trying to entice some of the shyer kids to get up and dance with him. When the song ended, the band shifted into "I'm a Believer," and even more kids got to their feet and started dancing to the popular tune. Sheriff Scoopy tried to coax a few of the moms into dancing with him, but without much success. Only one took the bait, and he whirled her around a couple of times before letting go of her and setting his sights on me.

I rolled my eyes as he danced toward me, gyrating his hips like an ice-cream-shaped Elvis. When he extended a large gloved hand, I shook my head firmly.

My brother snorted and gave my shoulder a shove. "Go on, Andie, I think he's sweet on you."

While I was glaring at Josh, Birdie snatched my ice cream cone out of my hand. "Here, honey, let me hold your ice cream for you while you dance."

Sheriff Scoopy took the opportunity to seize my hand and yank me to my feet. Wrapping a fuzzy-sleeved arm around my waist, he swept me into a clumsy waltz. I humored him for a minute, unable to resist laughing as I tried to avoid stepping on his big clown boots. When I tried to slip out of his grasp after I decided I'd been enough of a good sport, he gripped me tighter and spun me before lowering me into a dip.

I stared up at his giant ice cream head, wondering who was inside the costume and how annoyed I should be at the impertinence. When he pulled me back to my feet, I twisted away and tried to go sit back down.

The next thing I knew he'd grabbed me around the waist and thrown me over his padded ice cream shoulder, caveman-style.

I briefly considered kicking him in his frozen gonads to make him put me down, but decided I'd rather not get into a physical altercation with a beloved children's character in front of a whole audience of kids and their parents. Resentfully, I let him carry me up onto the stage, where he deposited me next to the band. I wasn't thrilled about being dragooned into whatever audience participation gag this was, but I stood there and pretended to go along with it for the sake of the little kids watching.

Gazing out at the crowd, I saw my brother laughing his ass off at my impending humiliation. A couple of Wyatt's brothers were laughing too, and Cody was still filming, the rat bastard. Whoever this Sheriff Scoopy was, I was going to hunt him down and exact my revenge in the most uncomfortable and embarrassing way possible.

While I was plotting my retribution, the song came to an end and the singer passed the mic to Sheriff Scoopy. He moseyed toward me and dropped down on one knee at my feet.

Oh, Jesus. I braced myself to play along with some vaudevillian fake proposal or whatever nonsense this was.

What I didn't expect was for Sheriff Scoopy to pull off his big ice cream head and unmask himself as Wyatt King.

31

WYATT

I t occurred to me, as I dropped to my knees up on that stage, that I might have made a major miscalculation here.

Andie's stunned expression was hard to read. She might be seriously pissed about all of this. It was hard to gauge from her frozen, wide-eyed stare.

The point had been to prove that I wasn't afraid to tell the world how I felt about her. I didn't think just saying it to her would be enough to make her believe I meant it—not after the way I'd let her down before. I figured I had to *show her* how much I meant it. By saying it publicly. Which required getting her out in public.

Doing it here at the festival had been Mia's idea. I'd begged her to help get me in the same place as Andie somewhere that I could make a public declaration. After Mia had enlisted Birdie to coax Andie out to the festival today, I'd called Josie and shocked the hell out of her by volunteering to play Sheriff Scoopy.

It had seemed like the perfect way to show Andie how serious I was and how far I was willing to go for her—even so far as debasing myself in front of my family and participating in this stupid festival they'd cooked up to promote the creamery.

No doubt Josie was currently regretting letting me don the Sheriff Scoopy costume. She hadn't known about the rest of my plan. I hadn't told her, because there were very strict rules in place to maintain Sheriff Scoopy's public image, including never, ever talking out loud or being seen out of character. Taking off the headpiece in front of a whole audience of kids to make a big romantic speech to my girlfriend? Definitely a major no-no. My sister was probably putting out a hit on me right now.

But that was a problem for later. At the moment, all I could think about was Andie and how to win my way back into her affections.

I had no idea if this was going to work. It might have been a mistake doing this in front of an audience. She might think I was trying to embarrass her. Or pressure her by putting her on the spot. She might not be in any frame of mind to hear me out. I could very well be setting myself up for a brutal public rejection.

There wasn't anything to do about that now. For good or ill, I'd committed myself to this course of action. The only way out was through.

Raking a hand through my sweaty hair, I lifted the microphone to my lips. "Andrea Camille Lockhart..."

Her eyes widened even more when I said her name, her mouth snapping shut as she drew back a half step. My stomach dropped in apprehension, but I bowled onward, hoping I could talk my way out of the mess I'd made.

"I'm on my knees begging you to give me another chance. I love you, I always have, and I want the whole world to know it. Every single love song I've ever written is about you. When I try to picture my future, all I can see is your face. If you'll let me, I promise to spend the rest of my life trying to make you happy."

Andie blinked, her lips parting in what I dearly hoped was the start of a smile.

I lurched unsteadily to my feet, fighting with the puffy goddamn cowboy boots I was wearing. When her lips curved in amusement at my struggle, I felt something shift in my chest.

Stepping closer, I took her hand in my comically large glove and said, "You're it for me, Andie. I want you to be my one and only girl. Please say you'll take me back and let me love you forever."

I was sweating bullets as I lowered the mic, and not just because it was hotter than Satan's asshole inside this godforsaken costume. The smile on Andie's face had faded when I started talking again. She seemed to be studying me now. Thinking hard, like she was trying to make up her mind.

I rated my chances of success somewhere south of fifty-fifty.

But then I saw the corner of her mouth twitch, and my heart gave a little leap. Because I knew that mouth twitch. I'd known it all my life. And I knew it meant Andie was about to smile.

Sure enough, her expression cleared. Her eyes seemed to dance, and her lips curved in the sweetest smile I'd ever seen. It sucked the breath right out of my chest, it was so beautiful.

"Yes," she whispered as she nodded her head.

Distantly, I was aware of people cheering. But in my stunned euphoria I only had room for one thought in my head. I needed to kiss this woman standing in front of me.

I lunged for her at the same moment she lunged for me, and we ended up colliding clumsily, the damn ice cream suit hitting her in the chest and trying to push her away. My arms wrapped around her, keeping her from falling back, and her hands grabbed onto my face as our mouths finally came together.

I kissed the hell out of her, not caring about all the little kids watching. I kissed her like my life depended on it, because I was pretty certain it did.

Relief flowed through me like warm water, washing away all my emptiness and fear. But I quickly got frustrated, because I couldn't touch her with anything but my lips. I needed my hands on her and I needed to feel her touching me, but she couldn't reach me inside this big dumb suit any better than I could reach her.

I broke off, growling in vexation, and grabbed her hand again. The band started playing "Be My Baby" as I led Andie offstage. People were still clapping, and I heard some of my brothers catcalling their approval, but I didn't pay them any attention as we stepped into the wings. I guided Andie down and around behind the stage before I let go of her and started wrestling my way out of the Sheriff Scoopy suit.

Or trying to, anyway. The cursed thing was the devil to get off, and I nearly tore a rotator cuff trying to wriggle myself to freedom.

I heard Andie snort and turned toward the sound, unable to see anything since I'd managed to get myself trapped with my head stuck inside the ice cream cone. "Don't just stand there laughing at me, woman. Help me out of this infernal contraption. It smells like vomit and BO in here."

Andie laughed even harder, but I felt her hands on me, guiding my arms out of the suit before pushing it down off my head. As soon as my hands were out I took over, shoving Sheriff Scoopy's puffy hell cocoon down far enough that I could step out of it. I freed my tennis shoes and kicked the thing away, shuddering with revulsion as I brushed the lint off my T-shirt and shorts.

Dragging my hands through my hair, I finally turned back to Andie. She was doubled over laughing, and the beautiful sound was like music to my ears. I'd put that fucking Sheriff Scoopy suit back on every day, for the rest of my life, if it meant I got to hear her laugh like that.

Smiling, I folded my arms while I waited for her to get control of herself. "I hope you appreciate how much I've humiliated myself today."

"Oh I do," she gasped, wiping tears of amusement from her eyes. "I definitely do."

She took a step toward me, and I closed the rest of the distance between us, gathering her in my arms and burying my face in the clean, fresh scent of her hair. Her hands pushed under my T-shirt, skimming over my back, and I breathed out a long, contented sigh.

"Dammit, Wyatt!" The sound of Josie's voice had us jumping apart. "Do you know how much of the Sheriff Scoopy code of conduct you've violated in just the last ten minutes?"

Putting my hands up in a gesture of peace, I turned to face my sister as she stalked toward us. When she was angry, she looked a lot like her mother, Trish, who was a formidable and terrifying woman. "Listen, Josie—"

"I should have known you were up to something when you volunteered to wear the Scoopy suit!"

Josie halted in front of me and propped her fists on her hips. Her furious glare shifted from me to Andie, and I prepared myself to leap to her defense.

Before I could get any words out, Josie's face lit up in an unexpected smile. "Good for you for making him grovel." After she'd delivered those words to Andie, she turned back to me, inexplicably still smiling. "And good for you for going after her. Finally. God."

"What?" I blinked at her.

"We've all been wondering if you'd ever wake up and realize how perfect you and Andie are for each other."

"Who's we?"

Josie rolled her eyes. "If you ever bothered to read the family group text, you'd know how much we all gossip about you."

Well, shit. I was definitely going to start reading it now.

Surprising me yet again, Josie stepped forward and hugged me. "You better treat her right or I will kick your ass myself. Do you hear me?"

"Does this mean you're not mad at me?"

My sister let go of me and stepped back, her gaze narrowing. "I should be, but I'm too happy for you right now." She raised a threatening finger. "But don't you ever dare pull any shit like this again."

"I won't." I tried to look contrite despite the grin on my face.

Josie turned to Andie and gave her a quick hug. "Good luck. You're going to need it with this one."

"Oh, I know." Andie shot me a smirk as Josie released her.

Shaking her head in displeasure, Josie bent to retrieve the Sheriff Scoopy suit from the ground where I'd discarded it. Her nose wrinkled as she gathered it up in her arms. "Ugh, this thing smells like vomit and BO. We should probably get it dry cleaned more than once every ten years."

I shuddered again as Josie walked off, holding the stinky suit as far away from her as her arms would allow.

Andie slipped her hands around my waist from behind and rested her chin on my shoulder. "Wyatt Earle King, what am I gonna do with you?"

I turned in her arms and cupped her face in my hands. "Love me for the rest of your life?" I answered hopefully.

"I guess I'll have to." Her tone was teasing, but her eyes were so soft and loving it stole the breath from my lungs. The way she was looking at me broke me apart and put me back together again. I couldn't believe I'd come so close to losing her.

"I'm going to treat you right from now on," I promised her. "I'm going to work every day to be worthy of you." I'd never be able to control everything that happened in my life. I couldn't control all that much of it, to be honest. The only things I had any real control over were my own actions. I could choose to be the kind of man Andie deserved. I could keep choosing it, over and over again, every minute of every day, until that was the kind of man I became.

"Wyatt." The worry crease bloomed between her eyebrows. "You've always been worthy. Don't you know that?"

"Jesus, Andie." I brushed a tender kiss across her lips and slid my nose along hers, taking comfort in the simple act of being close to her again. "I was so fucking scared up there. I was convinced you were going to reject me. That I'd blown my one and only chance with you."

"You didn't seem scared."

My hand slid into her hair and curled around the back of her neck. "I think I peed in the Sheriff Scoopy suit a little. Giving that speech was like painting a bull's-eye over my heart and handing you a freshly sharpened steak knife."

"But you did it anyway." She sounded proud of me, and it made my heart swell.

"I did. And you didn't stab me in the heart."

"I could never."

"Even if you did, I'd probably keep right on loving you. That's how far gone I am. But I'd rather we not test the theory, if it's all the same to you."

"No stabbing. Got it." She tilted her head up and pressed her lips to mine.

I let myself sink into the warmth of her mouth, savoring the sweet taste of her tongue. My fingers worked their way under her tank top, gliding over her bare skin and up the sides of her rib cage.

She pushed on my chest when my fingertips skimmed the bottom of her bra. "Mind yourself. This is a family establishment."

I growled my frustration as I lowered my hands to her waist.

I was going to need to get her out of here soon so I could take her home and show her properly how much I loved her.

As if she could read my mind, she grabbed my hand and started pulling me away from the stage. "You drove yourself here, right? Tell me you've got your truck."

"It's in the employee lot." I wrapped my arm around her shoulders, tucking her against my side. But as we rounded the back of the stage, my steps faltered at the sight of Josh striding toward us.

I steeled myself, ready to meet his displeasure head-on, but hoping to keep things civilized and nonviolent. He was still my best friend, and I wanted to make things right with him. But I needed him to understand that my feelings for Andie weren't negotiable. I wouldn't give her up for him or anyone else.

Josh came to a stop in front of us, his dark gaze narrowing as he took in the sight of my arm around Andie. She stiffened as her eyes flashed in challenge, daring him to object.

As much as I appreciated her rottweiler energy on my behalf, this was my rift to mend—and my battle to fight if it came to that. Although I hoped it wouldn't.

I turned my head and nuzzled her temple. "I need to talk to Josh. Can you give us a minute?"

Her eyes sought mine, communicating her reluctance. I nodded to let her know she could trust me with this. Finally, she relented, throwing her brother a warning look as she walked off.

I watched her go, waiting until she'd joined Mia a little ways away—far enough to be out of earshot—before I met Josh's steady gaze with one of my own. "Are you planning to punch me again?"

"Depends." His voice was deadly calm. "Are you going to break my sister's heart again?"

"No."

"Then I won't have to punch you."

I let out the breath I'd been holding, but his stony expression didn't change.

His chin lifted. "I'm not sorry I did it."

"I don't expect you to be sorry. I deserved it."

At that, he seemed to hesitate. "I've been informed it's none of my business who Andie chooses to go out with, and I'm not allowed to interfere in her personal life anymore."

I didn't say anything. It didn't surprise me that he'd gotten an earful from Andie, but whether he actually intended to abide by her wishes was another matter altogether.

A muscle clenched in his jaw. "You made her cry."

I dropped my eyes to the ground and nodded, my own jaw clenching in guilt. "I know."

"She never cries, and you made her cry."

"I know."

"You swore you'd never hurt her. You promised me."

I lifted my eyes to his, hoping my expression would convey how much shame I felt. "I know I did. I fucked up and let her down. I let you both down, and I'm sorry for it."

He studied me for a long moment. "When you were up onstage pleading your case just now, you said you loved her. Did you mean it?"

"Yes. I've been in love with her since high school."

It seemed to catch him by surprise, and the ice in his gaze cracked a little. "That long? Why didn't you ever say anything?"

"Why do you think?"

He frowned. "Hang on—I didn't want you messing around with her and treating her like one of your disposable playmates, but I never suspected you had actual feelings for her. If you'd told me—"

"What? You would have believed me? Given me your blessing?"

"Hell yes."

I let out a wry laugh. "Bullshit."

His expression shifted to dismay. "Maybe not at first, sure. It might have taken some convincing, but...shit, Wyatt, you're my best friend. Of course I would have."

I stared at him, unable to believe my ears. "Oh."

"So, you've been carrying this torch around for over ten years because you were afraid to tell me you were in love with my sister?"

"I thought I'd have to choose between her and you. And I didn't want to lose either of you."

"Well, shit," he said. "That's the stupidest fucking thing I've ever heard."

I blew out a breath, smiling despite myself. "I guess it is, yeah."

Maybe Andie had been onto something when she accused me of using Josh as an excuse. It was possible I'd been projecting my own doubts onto him, making his opposition into a bigger obstacle than it needed to be—when really the problem all along had been me.

Josh cleared his throat, casting his eye downward. "I'm sorry for making you think that. I guess I wasn't as good of a friend to you as I should have been."

Now he had me feeling guilty again. I shook my head, unwilling to let him shoulder all the blame for my choices. "I might not have given you enough credit."

Josh eyed me shrewdly. "Maybe you didn't give yourself enough credit. I told you all that negative self-talk was trouble."

I squinted at him. "Does this mean we're good? Do Andie and I have your blessing?"

The smile faded from his face as he winced. "It's not my place to hand out my blessing to anyone. As all the women in my life have made abundantly clear, Andie gets to make up her own mind about who's worthy of her." His eyes met mine, softening into sincerity. "But I'm happy for you that you found someone to love. And if it's my sister...then I guess I'm happy for both of you."

I blew out a breath. "Thanks." Breaking into a grin, I charged at him and gave him a hug. "I'm glad we're good."

"Me too." He choked off a laugh as I banded my arms around him like I was going to pick him up the way I used to when we were kids. "I'm still not sorry for punching you though."

I let go of him and gave him a friendly shove. "It was a weak-ass punch anyway."

"That's because I pulled it. The next time you make Andie cry I won't be so generous."

"You made up!" Mia bounded over and smacked an approving kiss on Josh's cheek before turning to give me a hug. "I'm so glad."

"Me too." I gave her an extra-hard squeeze to show how grateful I was for her intervention on my behalf.

"Anyway." Andie appeared at my side and latched onto my arm. "This has been fun, but we're gonna go now."

"Where'd Birdie get to?" Josh asked as Andie started hauling me in the direction of the park exit.

"She went off with Wyatt's uncle to ride the Ferris wheel," Mia answered. "She said he'd take her home."

Andie and I stopped in our tracks. Moving as a unit, we spun around to goggle at Mia.

"What?" she hesitated at our surprised expressions. "That's okay, right? He seemed nice."

"Which uncle?" I asked carefully.

"He had a mustache. Randy, I think?"

I blinked as this unexpected information sank in. My gaze snapped to the Ferris wheel in the distance as I turned the idea over in my head, trying to decide how I felt about it. Were they up there right now? The two of them squeezed into one of those two-seat passenger cars, giggling like schoolchildren. Or even holding hands like teenagers on a date. It was difficult to imagine, but I didn't necessarily find the idea disagreeable. My favorite uncle and my mom's best friend. There was a certain kind of harmony to it.

Andie turned to Josh with a frown. "Did you know about this?"

He shrugged and slipped his arm around Mia's waist. "I no longer have opinions about anyone's love life but mine."

Mia swiveled her head to look at him, her eyes widening. "Love life?" she repeated as if she hadn't considered the possibility before. "You mean Birdie and Wyatt's uncle...?" She looked at Andie, then at me. "Do you think—I mean, are they...?"

Andie shook her head. "I don't know. I can't think about it right now."

It was hard to make out if she was upset or not. I hoped not. I certainly had worse uncles Birdie could have chosen.

She looked at me. "Shall we get out of here?"

"We shall." I wrapped my arm around her shoulders and steered her away.

As she fell into step with me and tucked her body against mine, a sense of rightness shimmered through me. The two of us, together, moving through the world as one.

"How does it feel?" she asked as we navigated through the park on our way to the employee exit.

"What?" I asked, wondering if she could read my mind.

"Everyone knowing about us." She gestured at the people around us, some of whom were staring or shooting us knowing smiles. Word of my Sheriff Scoopy performance seemed to have spread.

I stopped and pulled Andie against me, clasping my hands behind her back. "It feels like finally getting everything I've ever wanted." My expression and tone were equally solemn so she'd know I meant it. "You're my wish come true."

The way she smiled made me feel like I could fly. But it was nothing compared to the way she kissed me. Like I belonged to her. And she belonged to me.

Someone let out a wolf whistle, and our lips broke apart, both of us hazy-eyed and laughing but still holding on to each other. Unwilling to let go.

She's going to be my wife.

My heart glowed as the thought drifted through my mind. For the first time in my life, it didn't feel like an unattainable fantasy. It felt like a future within my reach.

Our future.

"Put your underpants back on right this second! Do you hear me, young lady?"

Manny's shout carried across the town square as I picked my way through the maze of picnic blankets laid out on the green. I headed toward the familiar voice, which led me to the spot where Wyatt's family had camped out for the free concert.

Adriana was stretched out next to Josie, who was holding the new baby. On the other side of her, I was mildly surprised to see Nate sitting in a lawn chair next to Ryan and Cody. I spied Riley a few blankets away with a group of teenage girls. Tanner was here as well, chatting with my brother and Mia. On the blanket beyond them, Birdie was sitting with Randy King.

It still weirded me out a little that Wyatt's uncle was dating my aunt. But she seemed happy, which was all that mattered.

As I approached, a tiny naked human with a headful of black curls rocketed into me and hugged my legs. I stopped and smiled down at Wyatt's niece. "Well hey there, Isabella. I see we're having some naked time."

She jumped up and down, still holding on to my leg. "Where's Uncle Wyatt?"

As far as Isabella was concerned, I rated far below her favorite uncle as a person of interest. But she'd gotten used to the idea that wherever I was, Wyatt was almost always close by, which made me conditionally more interesting. Unfortunately for her, I was on my own today.

"He's getting ready for the concert," I told her. "We're all gonna get to watch him sing in a little bit."

She spun around, pressed her naked buttocks against my shins, and proceeded to shake it like a Polaroid picture. "I'm rubbing my butt on you!"

"You certainly are," I agreed, laughing.

"Isabella! Please don't do that to Andie." An aggravated-looking Manny trotted toward us with a small dress and underwear in his hand. "You need to put your clothes back on."

I looked up at him and smiled. "I believe this naked munchkin belongs to you.

Manny sighed. "Sorry about the butt rubbing. It's her new thing."

"It pairs nicely with the nudist streak."

"Yes, she's a true master of her craft," he muttered dryly as he wrangled his daughter back into her clothes.

When she was dressed again, I squatted down and offered Isabella my hand. "Can you take me to see your new baby brother?"

"Okay." She wrapped her chubby, sticky fingers around mine and dragged me over to the blanket where her mother was sitting with Josie.

I returned Ryan's wave as we walked past, then greeted Adriana and Josie.

"Mama!" Isabella let go of my hand to crawl into her mother's lap. "Andie wants to see the baby."

"Is he awake?" I asked, peering down at the bundle in Josie's arms.

"Let's see." She flipped back the blanket draped over her shoulder to shield him from the sun. "Yeah he is. Look at those pretty eyes."

Baby Jorge had been born a month ago, somewhat dramatically, after Adriana's water broke in the middle of the cookie aisle at the HEB. The panicked store manager had called 911, and Ryan had roared up in his fire truck before Manny could get there to drive his wife to the hospital. Which turned out to be a good thing, because Adriana was already fully dilated and that baby wasn't waiting around. Jorge had been delivered by his Uncle Ryan in the grocery store parking lot with Manny and the whole engine crew acting as Adriana's birthing coaches. It was the most exciting thing to happen in Crowder since...well, since Wyatt had declared his love for me onstage at the Centennial Festival while dressed as Sheriff Scoopy.

"Hey there, cutie pie." I crouched down to touch Jorge's soft little feet, which were the only part of babies I really liked. Mostly babies just reminded me of miniature-sized shriveled old men—incontinence, whining, and all.

"Hey Andie, we saved you a seat," Tanner called out, nudging Josh over to make more space on the blanket.

I stopped off to give my aunt Birdie a kiss before squeezing onto the blanket between Wyatt's brother and mine. Mia leaned around Josh to pass me a bottle of water from the cooler they'd brought. Summer had evicted spring with a vengeance, and with the midday sun overhead it was hot as a goat's butt in a pepper patch.

"How nervous is he?" Tanner asked me, peering over the top of his sunglasses.

I'd just come from backstage, where Wyatt and the other

members of Shiny Heathens were getting ready to perform their very first show featuring all new music. The mayor had decided to add live music to the First Saturday Farmers Market, which was taking place behind us at the other end of the town square.

Part of me couldn't help wondering if someone in Wyatt's family had nudged the mayor into it—like his uncle Randy, maybe—but I hadn't shared my suspicions with Wyatt. Given his stated feelings about his family exerting their influence on his behalf, I decided it would be better not to put that bug in his ear.

I *had* cornered Birdie to ask if Randy had been behind it, but she'd pled ignorance of the entire matter. Whether she was being truthful, I couldn't honestly say. That woman could be cagier than a zoo tiger when she had a mind to be.

"He's doing okay," I told Tanner. "Only a regular amount of nervous."

Wyatt had come a long way since he'd anxiously played his first song for me. Working on his songs with the band had done a lot to build his confidence in his own talent. All the positive buzz they'd been getting hadn't hurt either. They'd been drawing bigger and bigger crowds at the Rusty Spoke as they gradually added more original songs to their set list. Wyatt had always bloomed in the spotlight, but now that he was earning attention for his talent and hard work instead of his good looks and come-hither smile, he really seemed to be thriving. I didn't worry about him nearly as much these days. Not like I used to.

"That's good." Tanner glanced around us. "Looks like a lot of people came out today."

"It's a bigger crowd than we usually get for just the market," Josh observed. He had a booth at the farmers market where he sold the cheeses he made on the farm, so he was here every month. Today, however, he'd paid someone to run the booth so he could watch the show.

"Guess all those flyers worked," I said. We'd spent an after-noon putting them up all over town, wanting to make sure Wyatt had a good audience for his first big show.

"Oh god," Josh muttered beside me, covering his eyes as he ducked his head.

"What?"

"Nothing."

I jabbed him in the arm with my elbow. "Liar."

"I just accidentally saw Adriana's nipple is all."

I heard Tanner snort as I goggled at my brother's embarrass-ment. "You're a goat farmer. How can you be squeamish about nipples?"

Josh shot me a scowl. "I'm not squeamish."

"Prudish, then."

"I'm not that either."

"Women's breasts are no different than goats' teats," Mia interjected from Josh's other side.

He gave her a long look. "They're a *little* different."

I arched an eyebrow at him. "Please explain how."

"I'm not having this conversation with you."

Mia leaned around Josh to address me. "It's because he's not attracted to goats, but he is attracted to women, and therefore their breasts." She directed a smug look at him, clearly enjoying herself. "Right?"

"Can we just drop it?" he pleaded. "This subject is making me uncomfortable."

That was definitely not happening. It was way too much fun tormenting my brother. "Why do women's breasts make you uncomfortable?" I asked him. "You understand they don't exist for sexual pleasure, right? They're for feeding babies, which is pretty much the most wholesome thing in the world. That nipple you saw is simply performing the biological function it was designed to do. It's not its fault that men can't stop being horny for five seconds and let a nipple do its job without being attracted to it."

"I am not attracted to Adriana's nipples," Josh said, sounding horrified.

"What's wrong with my sister-in-law's nipples?" Tanner deadpanned. "Are you saying they're not attractive?"

"There's nothing wrong with them," Josh shot back irritably. "I'd just prefer not to know what they look like. Out of respect for her and Manny."

Mia rounded on Josh, and I actually saw him shrink back at the look on her face as he realized he'd really put his foot in it now. "What does Manny have to do with it?" she demanded. "They're not *his* nipples. Unless you think a woman's nipples are the property of her husband."

"I hate this conversation," Josh muttered, shaking his head.

"You know what?" I said, leaning around him to address Mia. "It's ridiculous that women are supposed to keep their functional, biologically necessary, baby-feeding nipples covered up while men get to walk around with their weird, useless, vestigial nips hanging out in public."

"I agree," she said with a nod.

"Like, why am I forced to look at men's nipples but women aren't allowed to let their nipples out in public? Maybe our nipples want fresh air and vitamin D too."

Mia waved her fist in the air. "Free the nipple!"

"Hear, hear," Tanner chimed in.

Josh dropped his head into his hands and rubbed his temples. "Can everyone just please stop saying the word nipple? I'm literally begging you."

"I have nipples!" Isabella announced, appearing in front of us. She pulled up her dress to show us as Tanner dissolved into muffled laughter beside me.

I grinned at her. "Yes you do, baby girl!"

She looked down at herself, frowning in concentration as she counted her nipples. "One, two." She held up two fingers proudly. "Two nipples!"

"Good job!" I leaned forward to give her a high five.

"They're coming out onstage," Mia said.

"Thank god," Josh mumbled.

"Look, here comes Uncle Wyatt," Tanner told his niece, directing her attention to the stage behind her.

She spun around and clapped her hands. "Uncle Wyatt!" she shouted, pointing as she bounced up and down.

Wyatt's eyes scanned the crowd as he stepped up to the mic to greet the audience. When he found us he broke into a grin and pointed back at Isabella, giving her a wave.

As soon as they launched into the first song, she started dancing. They always started their sets with the upbeat "Bait and Switch." They'd played it often enough at their Rusty Spoke shows that I heard a few people around us singing along with the chorus.

Isabella's energy finally started to flag halfway through it. Tanner pulled her into his lap and got her comfortably settled as we all clapped at the end of the song.

After the applause died down, Wyatt introduced the next song, which was "Bright as the Sun." He hadn't played it in public since his debut at Zelda's, and my chest ached a little at the memory of that night. But today he boldly sought me out in the crowd, his lips curving in a sweet smile when our gazes tangled. "Andie, this one's for you."

This time I didn't have to hide my emotions as Wyatt sang the words he'd written about me. Matt had amped it up a little, giving it a driving beat and bass line, but the words were just as bittersweet. Wyatt's gaze came back to me again and again, like he was singing directly to me, and I felt the connection between us like an invisible thread leading straight from his heart to mine.

"Thanks very much," he said after the song had ended and the applause had died down. His eyes sought me out again, crinkling with affection as he wrapped his hand around the mic. "That's a song I wrote about regrets, but really it's about fear and letting love slip your fingers because you're too scared to fight for it."

Josh nudged me with his shoulder when I reached up to wipe my eyes. I nudged him back, for once not minding if he or anyone else saw me get teary. I was too happy to care. Too full of love for Wyatt and strengthened by his love for me.

Isabella fell asleep in Tanner's lap not long after that. Mia was leaning back against Josh, who was tapping the beat out on her thigh. On the next blanket over, Randy leaned close to Birdie and murmured something in her ear that made her smile. I stretched my legs out to soak up the sun, and let my eyes fall closed as the music washed over me.

Halfway through the set, Wyatt brought Lucy out onstage to sing a few songs with him. I glanced at Tanner, and saw his jaw clench at the sight of her. His blue irises were dark and stormy as he stared at the stage, and his hands had balled into tense fists.

I nudged him gently. "You okay?"

He gave a jerky nod. "I didn't know Lucy was singing with them."

"Wyatt didn't tell you?"

"No."

They'd been rehearsing together for a few weeks. Wyatt had written a duet, and Matt had recruited his sister to sing it with them and provide harmony on a few of the other songs. I wondered why Wyatt hadn't told Tanner about it. Maybe he'd been afraid his brother wouldn't come to the show if he knew.

When Lucy started singing, I heard Tanner suck in a breath. I turned to study his face, which was so like Wyatt's and yet so different in almost every way. As he watched her sing, I could swear I saw something that looked like yearning come into his eyes.

"She's got a nice voice, doesn't she?" I'd been in choir with her in high school, so I was well acquainted with her amazing voice. Tanner seemed to have been taken off guard by it, however.

"She sounds like an angel," he replied quietly.

Yep, I decided, that was definitely yearning. He still had it bad for her.

"What happened with you and Lucy?" I asked him.

His gaze didn't move from the stage as he said, "It didn't work out."

"So...what? It was a mutual decision?"

His lips pressed together. "Something like that."

"It's just that you seem awfully hung up about it still for an amicable breakup. Did she do something unforgivable?"

Tanner dragged his gaze away from Lucy finally, his eyes narrowing slightly as he regarded me.

"I'm just wondering if I need to be mad at her," I added when he didn't answer.

"No." There was a sadness in his eyes as he shook his head. "She didn't do anything wrong."

"Did you?"

He huffed a bitter laugh. "Yeah, I fell in love with the wrong person. But it's not her fault she didn't love me back."

My lips pulled to the side as I tilted my head. "I feel like it's kind of her fault for not appreciating how awesome you are. How could any sensible woman resist falling in love with you?"

His mouth quirked. "You say that, and yet you didn't fall in love with me, did you?"

"Only because I was too busy being in love with Wyatt. Maybe if I'd met you first."

"Nah." He shook his head as he turned back to the stage. "You and Wyatt were always meant to be together. Like biscuits and gravy."

"If that's true, it means there's someone who's meant for you too. The biscuit to your gravy is out there somewhere waiting for you. You just haven't figured out who it is yet."

"Sure."

I poked my finger into his arm. "Or maybe you have, and you just haven't won her over yet."

He lifted his head and peered at me, frowning. "Why am I the gravy? Why can't I be the biscuit?"

"I don't know. Because biscuits are soft and pillowy?"

"Yes, but gravy's wet and creamy." His lips tugged to the side as his eyes sparkled with humor. "And you can put sausage in it."

I clapped my hand over my mouth to keep from laughing too loud as Tanner grinned at me. It was good to see him smiling again. He and Lucy were both so nice and both a little dorky in a way that made it seem like they ought to be perfectly suited. It sucked that things hadn't worked out between them.

"Fine," I said. "You can be the biscuit if you want to be the biscuit."

"Thank you." His attention caught on something behind me, and his smile faded. "Our dad's here."

"What?" I turned to look, following his gaze. It took me a second to spot him, but sure enough, there was George King standing at the far edge of the green in the shade of a live oak tree. "I didn't think he was coming."

Wyatt hadn't spoken to his father since he'd confronted him about the lien on my house. I assumed someone in the family had told him about the concert today, but it had never occurred to me he'd actually show up.

"Nor did I," Tanner said.

"Why is he over there by himself lurking in the shadows?"

Tanner shook his head and turned his attention back to the stage. "I can't claim to understand why that man does anything he does."

Thirty minutes later, Shiny Heathens played their last song, thanked the audience, and exited the stage to enthusiastic applause. Shortly thereafter, Birdie and Randy packed up their blanket and bid everyone goodbye. Nate left soon after that, but the rest of us stayed on the green, basking in the slight breeze stirring the air while we waited for Wyatt to come find us. Josh went to go check on his booth at the farmers market and came back with a box of fresh-baked cookies from one of the other stalls, which he passed around for everyone to share. He'd run into my friends, Kaylee and Megan, and they came over to chat for a few minutes before heading home. They hadn't been nearly as surprised to find out about me and Wyatt as I'd expected. None of my friends had. I guess we hadn't done as good a job of keeping our secret as we'd thought.

Finally, after what felt like forever, I spotted Wyatt strolling toward us from the stage, his gait cheerful and his posture relaxed. Ryan bellowed his name, and Wyatt broke into a grin as he lifted his hand to wave. Isabella, who was recovered from her nap and bursting with energy again, ran to meet him, and he caught her in his arms and perched her on his shoulders.

I watched, patiently waiting as he greeted his family and received their compliments on his show. Once he'd paid his courtesies to everyone else, he finally turned his attention to me. Saving the best for last.

His eyes locked onto me like a ravenous wolf, and he dropped to his knees in front of me with a breathtaking smile. "Hey you."

It used to hurt when he smiled like that, but it didn't cause me pain anymore. Now it made my blood hum with happiness and my heart beat with love.

"Hey you," I replied as I met his smile with one of my own.

Wyatt cupped my face in both hands as his lips touched mine in a soft, loving caress. But not too loving. Not with our families around us. We'd save the real kisses for later, when we were alone. For now, we kept it chaste. But also tender, refusing to be hurried no matter who was sitting next to us.

Until Isabella threw her arms around Wyatt's neck and tried to climb him like a jungle gym. He grabbed her with a playful roar, peeled her off him, and smothered her with kisses until she ran away shrieking about his beard poking her.

Smiling, he watched her run to Ryan for protection, only to be attacked by more kisses and a much thicker beard. Everyone laughed as Ryan lumbered after her, pretending to be a big kissy bear while Isabella ran circles around him, squealing with delight.

Wyatt's eyes were twinkling like sapphires, so bright and happy I felt like my heart would explode. Hugging his arm, I leaned in to kiss his cheek and felt his smile grow wider under my lips.

"Look around you," I whispered in his ear.

His gaze skated to either side of us as his brow wrinkled in confusion. "What am I supposed to be looking at exactly?" His voice was rough, the way it always was after a show, and it melted my insides like buttercream icing left out on a summer day.

"All these people." I lifted my fingers to his jaw, lightly scratching his beard with my nails. "All this love. Your family. Look at everything you have."

He blinked, his lips tilting as he pressed his forehead against mine. "And you." His hand wrapped around the back of my neck, holding me still. Holding us together. "I have you."

I let my eyes fall closed, soaking in this perfect moment. "I'm your family too."

"You're more than just my family," he said. "You're my home."

ACKNOWLEDGMENTS

This book would never have come into being without the amazing community of romance authors I've been lucky enough to meet both online and in person over the last several years. In all my several careers, I've never felt as supported, included, and appreciated as I have since becoming a part of Romancelandia. What a joy it is to have finally found my people.

In particular, I owe thanks to Julia Wolf, Brenda St. John Brown, and Serena Bell, not just for being lovely humans, good friends, and tremendous writers, but also for reading an early draft of this manuscript and helping me figure out what was missing from Wyatt and Andie's story. This book wouldn't be half as good without their insights and encouragement.

Finally, to my readers—thank you for coming along on the next step of this journey. I'm so excited to share this new world with you, and I hope you'll welcome all the residents of Crowder, Texas, into your hearts. It's a long way from STEM heroines in Los Angeles to small town Texas brothers, and I'm honored that you trust me to make the trip worth your while.

ABOUT THE AUTHOR

SUSANNAH NIX is a RITA® Award-winning and *USA Today* bestselling author who lives in Texas with her husband, two ornery cats, and a flatulent pit bull. When she's not writing romances, she enjoys reading, cooking, knitting, and obsessing over TV shows.

To learn more about Susannah Nix, visit:
susannahnix.com

Or follow her on social media:

f facebook.com/SusannahNix

🐦 twitter.com/Susannah_Nix

📷 instagram.com/susannahnixauthor

BB bookbub.com/profile/susannah-nix

g goodreads.com/susannah_nix

D1280800

TAKING THE CHRISTIAN VIEW

TAKING THE
CHRISTIAN VIEW

A. M. HUNTER

JOHN KNOX PRESS
ATLANTA, GEORGIA

Published in Great Britain
by The Saint Andrew Press, Edinburgh, 1974
and in the United States
by John Knox Press, Atlanta, Georgia 1974

Library of Congress Cataloging in Publication Data

Hunter, Archibald Macbride.
  Taking the Christian view. Atlanta, John Knox Press, 1974.

  84 p.
  1. Theology, Doctrinal--Popular works.
2. Christian life--1960-   I. Title
BT77.H85 1974   230   73-16919
ISBN 0-8042-0721-6

© A. M. Hunter 1974

Printed in the
United States of America

Contents

		PAGE
	Preface	vii
1.	The Bigger World	1
2.	Christ from the Bigger World	11
3.	Man in the Bigger World	23
4.	Living here and now in the Bigger World	36
5.	Life for ever in the Bigger World	50
6.	Christian Prayer	62
7.	Christian Life-style	71
	Epilogue: Call to Commitment	80

Preface

This little book tries to 'introduce' the Christian Faith in simple, untechnical terms. I had in my mind's eye more especially lay folk who were interested in Christian doctrine but might shy away from a large and learned book on the subject. A big book on Christianity, like a long creed, can easily scare off the humble seeker after Christian truth. On the other hand, the notes (plus suggestions for further reading) which I have appended to various chapters, e.g. on the arguments for God's existence, Christology and the Sacraments, are meant for those who might be minded to pursue the 'theology' of the various chapters in more depth. The ordinary reader, if he so wishes, may 'skip' them.

Let me gratefully acknowledge three debts: first, to T. E. Jessop, emeritus professor of philosophy at Hull University, whose notes for the use of padres (in the Second World War) suggested 'the Bigger World' approach of the first five chapters; second, to Dr William Lillie of Aberdeen University, whose published essay on 'Christian Style' influenced my brief treatment of Christian Ethics in Chapter 7; and, third, to my friend and neighbour in Ayr, the Reverend David G. Gray (formerly of St Peter's Church, Dundee) who read the typescript and enriched it with his comments.

A. M. HUNTER

1. The Bigger World

'When you are asked to give a reason for being a Christian, always be ready to give one, but do it modestly and with due deference.' So wrote St Peter, 1900 years ago, when Christianity first came under fire in the world (1 Pet. 3: 15). Today, when the Faith is again under attack from many quarters, the same readiness is being demanded of us. To help the ordinary Christian to do this is the aim of this book. Our first study will be 'the Bigger World' itself. Next, we shall discuss 'Christ from the Bigger World', before going on to describe 'Man in the Bigger World'. 'Living here and now in the Bigger World' will be our fourth theme, and the fifth 'Life for ever in the Bigger World'. We shall round off the series with a chapter on 'Christian Prayer', another on 'Christian Life-style', and a challenge to 'Christian Commitment.'

The best way to start is not with 'the Bigger World' but with —

THE OBVIOUS WORLD

An atheist in Hyde Park was once loudly telling his audience, 'Nobody with any sense believes what they can't see' when a heckler interrupted him, 'Then, mister, we don't believe you have any brains, because we can't see them.'

An apt rejoinder to a foolish remark! Yet lots of people today live as if the atheist were really right. The only world they really believe in is the Obvious World. They assume that the world is just what we see it is — an earth with trees, animals and men on it, with — somewhere up in the sky — a sun, a moon and myriads of stars. Reality is what they can touch and see, and there is no more to it.

But isn't there? There are colours we shall never see because man's vision lies between the violet and the red bands of the spectrum. So there are sounds we shall never hear because they are above or below the range of the human ear. In fact, there is a tremendous reality which lies for ever beyond the scope of our senses, so that our human consciousness, so far as it depends on our senses, resembles a tiny spot-light moving over a murky landscape.

Humbly to realize and admit this — that we 'know only in part' and are surrounded by

great mystery — is the best approach to what
we have called 'the Bigger World.'

THE BIGGER WORLD

If ours is a very earthly-minded generation, all
down the centuries there have been people who
firmly believed not in the Obvious World alone
but in a Bigger one as well. We pass over
Christ who lived habitually in that Bigger
World, because he is in a class by himself and
because we are going to talk about him later.
Out of innumerable witnesses to the reality of
this Bigger World let us choose three: a prophet,
a scientist and a poet.

Here, first, is a young man called Isaiah. It
is the year 740 BC and he is in the temple at
Jerusalem worshipping, as we so often do, in a
conventional way, when suddenly the veil
between the seen and the unseen vanishes, and
the Bigger World is laid bare before him. 'In
the year that King Uzziah died,' he says, 'I
saw the Lord sitting upon a throne, high and
lifted up; and his train filled the temple . . .
and one called to another and said, "Holy, holy,
holy is the Lord of hosts, the whole earth is full
of his glory." And the foundations of the
thresholds shook at the voice of him who called,
and the house was filled with smoke' (Isa. 6 : 1–5).

Isaiah has had a soul-shaking experience of

the reality of the Bigger World, and from that time on he becomes God's prophet.

The Bible is full of men like him. Think of Jacob at Bethel, of the man who wrote Psalm 139, of Stephen the first Christian martyr, of Paul of the Damascus Road, of John the seer whose visions are recorded in *Revelation*.

Now, leaving the Bible, let us come down many centuries to a man called Blaise Pascal. Called 'the glory of France,' he ranks among the greatest intuitive geniuses of all time. Pascal is a brillant scientist and mathematician, apparently quite absorbed in the things of time and space. But one night, suddenly and unforgettably, the Bigger World is revealed to him. He sets it down in writing, stitching the record into his doublet where it is found after his death. This is how it reads: 'The year of grace 1654, November the twenty-third, from about half past ten to half past twelve, Fire, fire, fire. The God of Abraham, Isaac and Jacob, not of the scientists and philosophers, the God of Jesus Christ, my God and thy God. Certitude. Joy.'

From that hour Pascal's life is changed. 'Thou wouldst not seek me hadst Thou not already found me,' he says, and becomes a great champion of the Christian Faith.

Come down, finally, to London, almost to our

own day, and a man named Francis Thompson, author of the famous *Hound of Heaven*. Here is another man of genius who, though all his life dogged by poverty and ill-health, is haunted by the nearness of the Bigger World, calling it —

'the traffic of Jacob's ladder
Pitched betwixt heaven and Charing Cross,'

and setting down his belief in such verses as these:

'O world invisible, we view thee,
O world intangible, we touch thee,
O world unknowable, we know thee,
Inapprehensible, we clutch thee!

The angels keep their ancient places,
Turn but a stone, and start a wing!
'Tis ye, 'tis your estrangèd faces
That miss the many-splendour'd thing!'

Isaiah, Pascal, Francis Thompson — and how many more! — all unshakeably convinced that there is a Bigger World, ever over and around us, beyond the curtain of our senses, and that —

'The drift of pinions, would we hearken,
Beats at our own clay-shuttered doors.'

Now this experience of a Bigger World is not something open only to spiritual high-brows. It is very old and universal. *Homo sapiens*, we

might say, is incurably religious. All men, at
one time or another, have a sense, however
faint and fleeting, of this Bigger World transcending and yet invading this world of space
and time. Many are the ways in which these
experiences come. They may come when we
see the sun setting in a splendour that is, as we
say, 'not of this world.' They may come when
our souls are ravished by great music, or we
marvel at a new-born babe, or we stand at the
death-bed of some good fine friend suddenly
taken from us. But, come when they will, they
have power to subdue us, to make us feel that
we are greater than we know, causing us to
cry out, 'God is in this place, and we knew it
not.'

Are all these experiences — these apparent
visitings from on high — just illusions? No, you
cannot dismiss as illusory what has been felt by
many men all over the world, white and black,
learned and unlearned, princes and peasants.

What then? Well, this sense of the Supernatural, this conviction of the real-ness of the
unseen world, this feeling of awe in the presence
of the Holy, is the raw material of religion.
Your religious man is the man who has faced
up to it seriously and has not funked it. Then,
having done so, he realizes that he has been
living with blinkers on, tears them off, finds

this workaday world a more wonderful place than he had conceived, and gets down on his knees because he cannot help it.

THE IMPORTANCE OF BELIEF

Now let us ask, Is it important to believe in this Bigger World?

A great Scottish theologian, P. T. Forsyth, has said, 'If life be a comedy to those who think, and a tragedy to those who feel, it is a victory to those who believe.'

Why should it be so?

First: because belief in a Bigger World makes human life a *bigger* thing. It enlarges our view of reality. What it adds is not another star or two — but God. The discovery of a new star might excite Patrick Moore and his fellow-astronomers, but it would make no real difference to most of us. The discovery of God makes all the difference. Not only does it introduce us to a more-than-human Power with whom we have to do, but, when faced with the challenge of the astronomers' immensities, may make bold to say, 'We believe that our God is Lord of all your worlds.'

Second: because it makes human life a more *meaningful* thing. We begin to see that we are not just 'poor windle straws' tossed about 'on the roaring pool of time'; that life has a

B

purpose, and that (as Silas Marner said) 'there's dealings with us, there's dealings.'

Finally: because it makes human life a more *hopeful* thing. For to believe in God, as Christians believe in him, is to believe that our small lives matter to him, that he 'will not leave us in the dust', that death is not the terminus of our journey, but simply a milestone on a road which is to end at a Father's house on high.

Note

We have argued the case for the Bigger World without recourse to the classical arguments for the existence of God.

Easiest to understand is the argument from *Design*. All round us and in us there seem to be evidences of deliberate design — of means adjusted to ends. The universe is not all 'spots and jumps': it appears to bear marks of purpose. The human eye, in itself a little miracle of design, can adapt itself to near or distant vision; the stars wheel in courses apparently appointed for them. Does not design on so vast a scale imply the existence of a great Designer?

Next, the argument from *Cause*. Every effect must have a cause. Show me a watch, and I infer the existence of a watchmaker. Again, if there is movement in the universe, as there is, it must have its origin in a 'First Mover'. Show me a world, and I must believe in a World-Maker.

A third argument is based on *Conscience* — on moral experience. In each of us is implanted a moral law, a sense of right and wrong (however blurred and faint it may seem to be in some men). Since we did not imagine it, this sense of moral obligation — this feeling of 'I ought' — must be part of the eternal nature of things. What kind of a world must it be in which we have this sense of moral obligation, and in which, when we follow its dictates, we feel we are acting reasonably? Must it not be one in which the moral ideal resides in the very heart of reality — in a Supreme Being who cares greatly about such things?

These arguments (and we have not exhausted them) do not prove beyond all peradventure the existence of God. Neither, by themselves, will they turn an unbeliever into a believer, an atheist into a theist. Yet, taken together, they provide strong rational support for believing in God.

The other thing to remember is that *there are various kinds of certainty* besides logical demonstration or, what is most esteemed today, scientific verification. For example, a philosophical sceptic may never be able to demonstrate satisfactorily his wife's existence either to his colleagues or himself. Yet in practice he is quite sure that she does exist. So, though a man may be unable to produce a water-tight demonstration of God's existence, he can be as practically sure that God exists and is worthy of his trust, as he is that his wife exists and loves him.

The classical arguments for God's existence do not however tell us much about the nature of God. Therefore for an answer to the question, 'What is God like?' we must turn from natural religion to revealed, to God as he has revealed himself in Christ.

2. Christ from the Bigger World

In the first chapter our theme was 'the Bigger World'. We said that the Obvious World — the world before our eyes and noses — was not the only one, that there was a bigger unseen one, over and around us — transcending the Obvious one and yet interpenetrating it — of which every one, at some time or another, had a fugitive sense. This sense of the Bigger World — to which we called some famous witnesses — was the raw material of religion. It produced in us feelings of awe, reverence and worship.

Now we pass from religion in general to *the* religion, to Christianity. We are going to think about 'Christ from the Bigger World.'

THE HISTORIC REVELATION

Here we are dwelling in the Obvious World, and yonder in that Bigger World is the Being we call God under whose mysterious providence we spend all our days. What is he like? Can we know anything about him?

Well, clearly if we are ever going to know anything about him, he must make himself known — must reveal himself — to us, here in this world. Has God ever done this? The Christian answer is that he has. We Christians do not deny that God has given clues to his nature in other religions or that he may reveal himself to men in a general way — in the beauty of his created world or in that amazing order of Nature which it has been the glory of modern science to have discovered. What we do claim is that *once in history* God specially revealed himself in a human being. This human being was Jesus of Nazareth, the son of Mary, who 'suffered under Pontius Pilate' and died outside the Jerusalem city-wall in the year AD 30 (the probable year of the Crucifixion).

A moment ago we used the phrase 'once in history'. Perhaps you may have heard of the lad who once pained his parent by announcing, 'To tell you the truth, Dad, I don't care one little bit what anybody ever did.'

We may guess that the history lesson in school that morning must have been uncommonly dull. But this attitude to history will not do. History does matter. When Henry Ford once opined, 'History is bunk', it was the inventor of the 'tin Lizzies' who was talking 'bunk'. Only human ostriches close their eyes to the past, to history, and the lessons that may be learned from it.

If you grant this, let us ask the question, What is the most important event in history? The Christian answer is, 'The Coming of God in Christ into this world.' This is why we divide all history into two halves: BC and AD — before Christ and after him.

(From this you will note how deeply Christianity is rooted in history. The Gospel is in fact the story of Divine redemption *from within history*, not by the propagation of doctrines but by the wrenching of one man's flesh and the spilling of his blood on one particular piece of ground, outside one particular city wall, during three particular hours of an April day in AD 30.[1])

God came from the Bigger World in Christ — this is the Christian claim. 'In Christ,' says St Paul, 'God was reconciling the world to himself' (2 Cor. 5: 19). Says St John: 'The Word (i.e. the saving purpose of God) 'became flesh' (John 1: 14). The claim is that God once broke openly into history, stood among us as a man to show us what he is like, and then died as a man on a Cross to deliver us from our sins and to bind us to himself for ever.

[1] G. Dix, *Jew and Greek*, p. 5.

A stupendous claim, you say? Yes, and the
New Testament writers found it stupendous
also. But they did not try to water it down to
make it easier to believe. Down the centuries
innumerable Christians have believed it. Nearly
a thousand millions believe it today. Why?
Why do they — why do we — believe that
Christ is God come to us from the Bigger
World?

THE REASONS

(1) *Because the Jesus of the Gospels cannot be
fitted into our picture of a mere man.*

A man he was of course — 'a real man
living upon victuals'; a man who not only ate
and drank and slept, but experienced hunger,
thirst, weariness, disappointment, sorrow,
death . . . Anyone can see he was a man — a
very good and great man. But you cannot
read the Gospels perceptively without also
realizing that to call him 'just a man' is not
enough. There is a plus — a something more —
in Jesus which we find in no other man.

Study the earliest Gospel, Mark, and you
will see how strongly Jesus' first hearers and
followers in Galilee felt this. They were quick
to perceive that there was something unearthly
and uncanny about him. Mystery not of this
world surrounded him, and the words the

evangelist uses to describe their reactions to what he did, bring this out: they were 'amazed', 'astounded', 'awe-struck'.

This plus, or something more, was present in his very *words*, in his frequent 'I came's', heavy with a sense of destiny,[1] as in his 'Amen I tell you's', charged with divine authority.[2] The Oxford don Walter Pater was once discussing Christianity with the novelist George Eliot who thought its number was up. 'I don't agree,' said Pater. 'You think the Christian religion is all plain. I don't. Take that saying of Jesus "Come unto me, all you that labour and are heavy laden, and I will give you rest." There is mystery in that.' Yes, there is mystery — and majesty — in what Jesus says. Who is this who claims that, though heaven and earth pass away, his words will not (Mark 13: 31)? Who is this who avows, 'No man knows the Father except the Son, and he to whom the Son wills to reveal him' (Matt. 11: 27)? Who is this who asserts that one day all nations will stand before him to be judged (Matt. 25: 31–46)? No mere man makes such statements, or we know him to be either deluded or mad.

Yet it is not only in his words that Jesus is

---

[1] E.g. Mark 2: 17, Matt. 5: 17, Luke 12: 49.
[2] See my *Exploring the New Testament*, pp. 9–12.

mysteriously and majestically different: it is in his *person* also. The Jesus of the Gospels shows no consciousness of sin; he is sheer goodness through and through, and none of us, God knows, is that. So also with his *deeds*. While steadfastly refusing to be a mere wonder-worker, none the less, relying on God's help, he can cure the mentally-deranged, make blind men see, deaf men hear, lame men walk and on occasion recall men from death or its *penumbra*. In short, the Jesus of the Gospels has about him the authentic aura of a higher world: in and through him the mighty Spirit of God is at work.

Here then is the problem: Jesus who is clearly a man, but just as clearly something more. Faced with this problem, you can do one of two things. You can dodge it by explaining away the extraordinary, the superhuman, things in Jesus. Or you can face up to it by expanding your thought to fit these facts. This is what we Christians do. We say that Jesus belongs not merely to our world but to God's. We say he is not only human but divine.

(2) The second reason why we set Jesus on that side of reality we call Divine is *because no man after his death has exerted the influence he has.* This was what John Drinkwater meant when he wrote:

'Shakespeare is dust and will not come
To question from his Avon tomb,
And Socrates and Shelley keep
An Attic and Italian sleep . . .

They see not. But, O Christians who
Throng Holburn and Fifth Avenue,
May you not meet, in spite of death,
A Traveller from Nazareth?'

How do dead men influence us? Through our remembering them as, for example, every 25th day of January, Scotsmen remember Robert Burns, the lad who was born in Kyle'. But the extraordinary thing about Jesus is that, since he died, he has been influencing men *directly*, *livingly*, by meeting them. They have found all down the centuries, as they still find, that Christ comes to them, unseen but not unknown, in work and worship, in prayer and sacrament, as a living Person.

'Lo, I am with you always, even unto the end of the world' (Matt. 28: 20), the risen Christ had promised. And it is the testimony of uncounted Christians down nineteen centuries that he has kept his promise. From Paul of Tarsus to Sadhu Sundar Singh, from Polycarp of Smyrna to Grenfell of Labrador, from John of Patmos to John White of Glasgow, however their words may differ, the testimony has been the same: 'Christ is alive, and he has had dealings with us, and we with him.'

Samuel Rutherford lies in his Aberdeen jail, and this is what he records in his diary, 'Jesus Christ came to me in my cell last night, and every stone glowed like a ruby.'

R. W. Dale of Birmingham paces his study on Easter eve when the reality of the living Christ 'comes on him like a burst of sudden glory'. 'Christ is alive!' he says, and ever after the Resurrection becomes the prime article in his creed. C. F. Andrews testifies to the Christ who has been his constant companion on 'the Indian Road'. 'I do not picture Jesus as I see him in the Gospel story,' he writes, 'for I have known the secret of his presence, here and now, as a daily reality.'

'My friend in Stoke was ill,' says Charles Raven about the turning-point in his life, 'and I visited him. He was not alone. Jesus was alive and present with my friend, as he had been alive and present with the eleven in the Upper Room. He was alive and present with me.' 'He comes to us,' wrote Albert Schweitzer, 'as of old he came to them by the Lakeside, and he speaks to us the same word, "Follow me!" ' It is the testimony of Christ's true followers in every time.

Of course the only way to test the truth of

this testimony is to come to him. You are not asked to swallow a creed but to meet a living Person. But when you do, you will want a creed to express your experience, and you will find it easy to sing the words of the *Te Deum*:

'Thou art the King of glory, O Christ,
Thou art the everlasting Son of the Father.'

THE SUM OF THE MATTER

Now let us see what follows from this conviction that Christ is God come to us from the Bigger World.

First: we know something definite and joyful and good about him who dwells in the Bigger World, about 'the humanity of God.' 'In Jesus we see the human life of God, and it is unlike anything we could have guessed. We could never have imagined that power would be hidden under gentleness and that God would walk on the earth as the poor man's Friend.'[1]

Second: we know that this holy and loving God has not left us men to 'stew in our own juice.' In Christ he has not only come into our world in blessing, but he has dealt with our sins and opened up a new way for sinners to return to God.

But this is to anticipate our next study. So

[1] Stephen Neill, *Who is Jesus Christ?*, p. 94.

let us close this one on a note of challenge. Do we really believe that God came from the Bigger World in Christ? Apparently we do. We divide all history into two parts — BC and AD. Then why don't we really believe our belief? Why don't we resolve to live as people who really believe it, by building our whole life — our family life, our civic life, our national life — on the only foundation which can endure (Matt. 5: 24–27) — the foundation which is summed up in the two words, Jesus Christ?

Concerning Christology: a Note

When we say that Jesus is both human and divine, we raise the problem of what theologians call 'Christology' — the mystery of Christ's person — how divinity and humanity can co-exist in him. All down the centuries learned men have wrestled with this mystery. Some have so over-stressed the divinity as to lose sight of the humanity. Others have so emphasised the humanity as to obscure the divinity. A true solution must do justice to both sides.

If the reader wishes to study the problem in depth, he should read P. T. Forsyth's *The Person and Place of Jesus Christ* (1909). Forsyth proposes a solution in terms (a) of God seeking man and (b) of man seeking God. In Jesus, he says, we find both these movements — the downward and the upward — perfectly united, i.e. perfect revelation and perfect religion. 'Jesus,' he declares, 'worked out the salvation he *was*, and moved by his history *to* that supernatural world *in* which he moved by his nature.'

Belief in the divinity of Christ is not necessarily tied up with acceptance of the Virgin Birth (Matt. 1: 18–26; Luke 1: 26–38). St Paul, for example, held Jesus to be divine without ever mentioning it; and good theologians have argued that, if there was to be a true Incarnation, Jesus must have been born into the world as other men are. On the other hand, the doctrine accords with Christian belief in the uniqueness of Christ and forms a fitting prelude to a life which was crowned by resurrection from the dead.

What St Matthew and St Luke are seeking to say in their references to Mary's virginal conception of Jesus through the action of the Holy Spirit is that *God sent Jesus*. 'The Virgin Birth is an affirmation of mystery and miracle. It affirms that here God is at work.'[1] If a man decides to regard it as primarily poetry, he must take care not to drain away the vigour of that

[1] J. K. S. Reid, in *A Theological Word Book of the Bible* (Ed. A. Richardson), p. 277.

affirmation. On the other hand, the man who takes the story literally — holds that Jesus had no earthly father — must preserve the New Testament conviction that Jesus was a real human being.

3. Man in the Bigger World

Our first study was 'the Bigger World' itself, our second 'Christ from the Bigger World.' Now we set the whole matter on our own doorstep: we are going to think about 'Man in the Bigger World,' to see ourselves as God sees us.

WHAT IS MAN?

Let us begin at the beginning with the question, What is Man? Ask a biologist, and he will reply, 'Man is an animal.' Physically speaking, this is perfectly true. You and I are animals — 'two-legged animals without feathers', as Carlyle said. So far as our bodies are concerned, we go through the same physical process — birth, life, death — as the animals. What is more, there survives in us a bit of the ape and the tiger, not to mention a bit of the donkey and the mule!

But to say that we are *only* animals is just not true. If we are only animals, we are mighty

c

queer ones. If we are only animals, our love of beauty, our longing for goodness, our desire for truth are simply inexplicable. Animals don't do these things — don't stand spell-bound before the glory of a setting sun or an unfolding rose, don't experience moral constraints (the still small voice of conscience and the feeling of guilt when we disobey it), don't dream dreams of universal brotherhood (like Robert Burns in his 'A man's a man for a' that') and justify them by spiritual and moral considerations. Let animals eat and hunt and mate and sleep, and they are perfectly content.

Plainly we have a double nature — a Jekyll and Hyde make-up — and are dwellers in two worlds. Somebody has put it this way: 'There are two selves in man, one pointing to the sty, the other to the sky.' That is, if we have one foot in the animal world, the other foot is out of it, and it is the one out of it that matters.

Now watch what follows from all this. On this view, our life takes on larger meaning. We begin to see that our true kinship is not with the beasts that perish, but with God. No accidents, we were made for something — to develop the non-animal side of our nature, to become as like God as men can be. 'There must be no limits to your goodness,' said Jesus pointing us to the divine ideal, 'as your heavenly

Father's goodness knows no bounds.' (Matt. 5: 48 NEB).

THE CHRISTIAN VIEW

Now we are coming to the Christian view of Man. It is that, if Man is an animal, he is one 'made in the image of God'. What does this mean?

It means that we have something of God's likeness in our make-up, conscience and reason being parts of it. It means that God is able personally to speak to us, and be answered by us. It means that God cares for us, and wishes us to live in a personal relationship with himself, as his children. Why? 'In order to be shaped to the likeness of his Son,' Paul says, 'that he might be eldest among a large family of brothers' (Rom. 8: 29 NEB).

'And if children,' Paul declares, 'then heirs, heirs of God and fellow-heirs with Christ.' (Rom. 8: 16f.). Heirs of what? Heirs of everlasting life. We are made to live not merely for three score years and ten but for ever.

Children of God and heirs of immortality — is there anything else we must add to the Christian view of Man? Yes, we are responsible beings, responsible and accountable to God. We are not just 'puppets on a string' — playthings of an Inscrutable Fate who dance as It determines. We are children of a heavenly Father to whom he has given free-will — liberty to choose the right and reject the wrong.

OUR HUMAN PREDICAMENT

So far, good. But now the trouble begins. For if this is our true status and destiny, we don't live up to it. Not a single man of us. Why? Because every man has a *bad streak* in him — is sick of a disease with the staccato name of sin.[1] Our forefathers called it 'original sin'; and, whether we like the phrase or not, it stands for something terribly real. In fact, as Richard

---

[1] At the root of sin lies *egoism*. Every man wills to make himself the centre of the world and to judge everything by his own self-interest. This egoism affects not only bad men but good ones, making humble men proud of their humility and righteous men self-righteous. It needed the coming of Christ — and especially his Cross — to show up sin in all its malignity, as the canker in man's soul, his defiant No to God. What we call 'sins' are separate acts springing from this basic rebellion against God.

The other thing to note is the *corporate* nature of sin, so strongly stressed in our day by Reinhold Niebuhr. It corrupts not individuals only but societies and cultures. For to be human is to be enmeshed in a net-work of evil which arises from that very freedom which man, alone in the creation, possesses. Only a total 'drop-out' from society could escape this corporate sin which tarnishes every human ideal and is the source of those destructive evils which cause man's greatest achievements to turn sour.

Crossman has said, there is a good deal more evidence in the world today for the Christian doctrine of 'original sin' than there is for the Marxist doctrine of 'the classless society.'

What it means is that our human nature is badly warped, has an ugly twist in it. The knowledge of this drives some people to despair, while it turns others into cynics. Both these reactions Christianity condemns, but it stresses the fact in two ways.

First, it says that our wrong deeds are more than offences against ourselves and our neighbours. They are offences against God, i.e. sins. For sin is any wrong-doing seen against the background of the Bigger World. Christianity says that the bricks you and I drop hurt a long way off — that they go up to heaven and hurt God. So when a man sins, he is putting himself at a distance from God. His first need is therefore to get back into right relations with God.

Second, Christianity says that this wrong-doing of ours is not a surface affair but goes deep down into our nature. Even the best of men, on occasion, give way to the downward pull of their lower natures. Here is a weakness which man, by himself, cannot cure. He may try will-power, or education, or psychology. They may help, but they cannot cure his malaise. What he really needs is help from higher places — what in fact the Bible calls 'the grace of God.'

GOD'S ANSWER—THE GOSPEL

How then are we to get back into right relations with our Maker and Father? Well, Christianity says not only that God can help us but that he has already done what is needed. This was what God sent his Son into the world to do (John 3: 17): to bring us back into right relations with himself and give us the power to lead new lives.

We have seen that Christ came into the world to show us what God is like. Yet he did more: his whole mission on earth culminated in his death on a Cross. Why did Christ choose to crown his ministry with the sacrifice of his own life, as the Gospels say he did? The earliest Christians answered, 'Christ died for (our) sins once for all, the righteous for the unrighteous, that he might bring us to God' (1 Pet. 3: 18; cf. 1 Cor. 15: 3). As our sins had separated us from God, so Christ, God's sinless Son, died by his Father's appointing, to remove them.

This is what the theologians call the Atonement; and many are the theories[1] they have

---

[1] One of the noblest is McLeod Campbell's *The Nature of the Atonement* (1856).

devised to explain it. None of them — not all of them put together — may claim to fathom all the mystery or make clear why the Cross is the place where God in Christ dealt decisively with our sins. If we ask why Christ died on that 'green hill far away', perhaps we cannot improve on the words of the hymn:

> 'He died that we might be forgiven,
>   He died to make us good,
> That we might go at last to heaven,
>   Saved by his precious blood.'

If this still leaves us asking questions, a homely parable may help us to understand better.

You and I are like the boy who has misbehaved and been sent into his room in disgrace. There he sits, sullen and resentful. Suddenly he becomes aware of his Elder Brother in the room, sharing his disgrace and punishment. 'Surely he hasn't done wrong?' he thinks. Then on his Elder Brother's face he sees a look he can't quite fathom. It almost looks as if his Elder Brother were glad to be there. Then the Elder Brother asks him to go back to his Father. The boy refuses. But his Elder Brother says, 'All is forgiven. Father will take you back *for my sake.* Come along with me.' So, shamefacedly, the boy goes. But when he comes into the Father's presence, he sees the same look on the Father's

face he had seen on his Elder Brother's. And
the Father takes him into his arms and forgives
him.

That is the Gospel, the story of how God
sent his Son — our Elder Brother — into the
world to do what was needed to bring us back
to himself, and to give us the power of the
Holy Spirit to help us lead new lives.

WHAT MUST I DO?

If God has done this for us, what must we do?

First, we must realize our own need, see
ourselves for what we really are, people in
need of something more than higher education
or psycho-analysis. What we need is 're-
modelling' or, in the drastic metaphor of the
Bible, 're-birth' (John 3: 3).

Then we must see God as he really is, as a
holy Father whom our sins have been hurting.
If we see God like this and our sins as offences
against him, and decide, like the boy in our
parable to go back to God in the company of
our Elder Brother — and this is what the New
Testament means by 'repentance' and 'faith' —
then we shall learn — and it is the only way we
can learn — that the Gospel is true and that
God can re-make us.

For a few (like Paul) the re-making may seem
to happen all at once; for most it will take time

and include setbacks. We will find that bits of 'the old man' (our old unregenerate nature) keep sticking to us like pieces of egg-shell to the young chick. But the decisive thing has happened. Like the boy, we are out of dis-grace into grace; and we are now called on, with God's help, to become what we potentially are, new men and women.

This then is the offer God makes us in the Gospel — new and fuller life here and now, through faith in Christ his Son, divine power to help us to achieve it, and, after death, the promise of all the blessed things God has prepared for his 'adopted' sons (Gal. 4 : 5 f.).

At this point it is 'Over to us!' The decision — and according to the New Testament it is a life or death one (John 3: 16) — is ours — ours to accept God's offer or reject it. As simple and as destiny-deciding as this.

Note : Concerning the Trinity and the Holy Spirit
When we spoke of 'God's help' to enable us to lead the Christian life, we meant the Holy Spirit.

According to St Paul (Eph. 2: 18), Christians have access to God the Father, through Christ, in the Holy Spirit. The early Christians felt that they could not express all that they meant by the word 'God' till they had said 'Father, Son and Holy Spirit.' They were *implicit* 'Trinitarians'. This does not mean that they believed in three Gods. Rather they believed (as we do) in a *triune* God — one God who exists and manifests himself in three different modes. Someone has summed up the doctrine thus: 'God everywhere, God there, God here,'[1] That is, God the 'Almightly Father of all things that be', God who became man in Christ, and God present here and now, and not merely in Palestine nineteen centuries ago. This last is God the Holy Spirit.

The Holy Spirit is not an emanation from God but God himself at work in human life. When Jesus said to Nicodemus, 'Listen to the wind' (John 3: 8), he was referring to the Spirit as the wind of God, to a power not of this world which, though invisible and mysterious, is undeniably real and effective.

(Both the Hebrew and the Greek words for 'spirit' — *ruach* and *pneuma* — meant originally 'wind.')

God as Spirit was at work in his world (e.g. in the prophets) before Christ came. But, according to the New Testament, the Spirit did not become the corporate possession of God's true people until after Christ had died

---

[1] Another way of putting it is: 'God for us', 'God with us', 'God in us'.

and risen and ascended. It was on the Day of Pentecost, seven weeks after the Crucifixion, that the little company of Christ's people became signally aware of a new vivifying power in their midst, making the truth of the Gospel real to them and inspiring them for their mission.

By studying the writings of Paul and John we may learn much about the nature and function of the Spirit, called (in the Nicene Creed) 'the Lord the Life-giver'. Given not so much to supply Christ's absence as to accomplish his presence, the Holy Spirit is the power which enables men to interpret 'the mind of Christ' and animates Christ's 'working Body', the Church, enabling its members (or 'limbs') to live according to God's will declared in Christ. The source of all spiritual gifts, the Spirit's finest fruit is love.

In short, the Holy Spirit is (to borrow Henry Scougal's phrase) 'the life of God in the soul of man.' Not so much God above men, or God alongside men, as God inside them. Whether we know it or not, the Spirit is the power which prompts every true prayer we make, the power which helps us to confess Christ as Lord, the power which inspires all true and lovely and heroic Christian living.

This 'holy help' from on high, we need ever

to remind ourselves, is not something — or rather Someone — who belongs only to the first century of our era. On the contrary: As the hymn says —

> 'The centuries go gliding,
> But still we have abiding
> With us that Spirit Holy
> To make us brave and lowly.'[1]

Yet the Holy Spirit's function is not simply to make Christians 'brave and lowly.' If the Church is the home of the Holy Spirit, and the obvious sphere of his working, the Spirit is not confined to the bounds of the institutional Church. Beyond its limits God's Spirit is operative in the wider world, moving in all sorts of unlikely men and places, creatively and renewingly. It is the recognition of this truth which should ever be stimulating the Church to fresh conquests for Christ in the great pagan world around us. Once, in a public lecture on the Holy Spirit the Comforter, Dr Ramsey,[2] the Archbishop of Canterbury, reminded his hearers of a scene in the famous Bayeux tapestry. In it William the Conqueror is marching behind his troops with a drawn sword in his hand, evidently prodding them onwards to deeds of valour. Beneath is the legend: 'King

---

[1] F. C. Burkitt, in *Songs of Praise*, 183.
[2] W. Neil, *The Truth about the Early Church*, p. 114.

William comforteth his soldiers.' Not 'comforting' in the modern sense of that word but 'prodding' — inciting, urging forward — is one of the Holy Spirit's main tasks, with us Christians, in the world today.

4. Living here and now in the Bigger World

The subject of our last chapter was 'Man in the Bigger World.' In this one we are going to think about living, here and now, in the Bigger World.

'Man shall not live by bread alone', says the Bible. If you and I were only animals, we might be content with 'bread alone.' But, whenever man becomes aware of the Bigger World, he realizes that a well-filled stomach is not enough and that he has 'an aching void this world can never fill.' This is because, as St Augustine said so beautifully long ago, God has made us for himself and our hearts will never rest till they rest in him.

How is man to satisfy this longing for something more than bread? The answer is, by keeping in touch, so far as he can, with the Bigger World.

Now, ideally, the Christian tries to do this always, and not merely when he is in his pew on Sundays. For Christianity is not a separate little slice of life — a holy interlude once a week — but the whole of life. It ought to be a life lived every day, in home or at work, against the background of the Bigger World.

Nevertheless, the pressures of this world being what they are, if the Bigger World is to become real to most of us, we have got to avail ourselves of certain well-tried avenues of approach to it — 'means of grace' is the old-fashioned phrase — in order to keep our lines of communication with the unseen world in good repair.

WORSHIP

To begin with, there is worship. Why do you and I go to church on Sundays? Not primarily to hear Mr So-and-so preach (however flattering this may be to Mr So-and-so's ego). We go to make our response to the Bigger World, i.e. to worship.

Worship is literally 'worth-ship' — the avowal of God's 'worth'. It is our due and grateful acknowledgement of God's grace and goodness. If you say that you feel no need to worship, this is really beside the point. The justification of worship is not so much that man needs it as that God deserves it. Robert Burns once wrote:

'The great Creator to revere
Must sure become the creature.'

But Christian worship is more than just 'revering the great Creator.' The God we worship is the God both of Nature and of Grace. He not only —

'made the earth,
The air, the sky, the sea',

he also —

'sent his Son
To die on Calvary'

yes, and 'raised him from the dead so that our faith and hope might be in him.' (Christian theism, it has been said, is 'resurrection theism.')

Now the pattern of our worship ought to make this clear. The hymns we sing praise not only the God 'who made all things' but the God who in Christ has stooped low to bless us, so you and I might lift up praying hands to him crying, 'Abba, Father' (Rom. 8: 15).

Again, the Old Testament lesson takes us back to the preparation for Christ's coming in the history of Israel, the People of God whom he chose to be the channel of his revelation to all men. (*Why* God chose Israel may be a profound mystery; but the great prophets of the Old Testament make it clear that Israel's election was not to exclusive privilege but to universal service and witness — to be 'a light to lighten the Gentiles.')

The New Testament lesson tells how God fulfilled and crowned that revelation of himself by sending his Son to save us. (See Jesus' parable of the Wicked Tenants in Mark 12: 1–9 and compare Heb. 1 : 1–4.)

And the sermon? Well, if it is a true sermon — and not just someone making himself a public nuisance with his private opinions — it will have the same purpose, the same theme: the Gospel of our salvation in all its incomparable majesty and comfort.

What does worship do for us? It 'edifies' us — builds up our life into Christian manhood and girds it with the strength and peace of God himself.

PRAYER

The next avenue to the Bigger World is Prayer.

What is Prayer? It is opening our hearts, in the way Jesus taught us, to the unseen Father who dwells in the Bigger World: adoring, confessing, pleading, submitting, or just waiting — in fact, doing everything a child does in his father's presence. Once you see it this way, you realize how mistaken it is to regard prayer

D

as merely 'asking God for things', as though prayer were only a crying up the chimney of the universe to a celestial Santa Claus. Of course we are bidden by Christ himself to 'ask' God, assured that he will answer, though the answer may not be what we expect; but true prayer is essentially an aligning of our wills with God's. And 'in his will is our peace' (Dante).

Perhaps the main point to be made here is that, if you wish the Bigger World to become real to you, there is no substitute for the discipline of the inner 'room' (Matt. 6: 6), for private prayer.[1] If you embark on a correspondence course, you are told at the outset that you must work at it every day, and not just when you feel in the mood. And is not this equally true of 'a correspondence fixed with heaven'? What Brother Lawrence called 'the practice of the presence of God' is the life's blood of religion.

BIBLE READING

The third avenue is Bible-reading.

Why should we read the Bible? To make our acquaintance with great literature and so improve our English? Of course the Authorised

[1] Here John Baillie, *A Diary of Private Prayer* is strongly recommended as an aid to devotion.

Version of the Bible (1611) is our greatest book of English prose. Yet it is not as literature, but as the record of revelation, that Christians prize it.

It is the record — or written account — of how God revealed himself, bit by bit, to his ancient people Israel through the prophets, and how, when 'the fulness of time came,' God perfectly revealed himself in the Man Christ Jesus who was, and is, his Son and image.

We read the Bible therefore to understand that revelation better; and as we read these old, yet ever new, stories of the men who lived in the Bigger World, from Abraham and Amos to Paul and John, we find that our grip on it becomes firmer. These men of the Bible — the great heroes of faith listed in the eleventh chapter of Hebrews plus the apostles and prophets of the New Testament — infect us, infuse us, inspire us with their own experience of God, as they point us to Christ who is the very image of the Almighty Father. Thus, our own knowledge of the Bigger World becomes deeper, wider, surer.

THE SACRAMENTS

Finally, there are the Sacraments: Baptism (which is the sacrament of initiation into God's

family, the Church), and the Lord's Supper
(or Eucharist) which is the sacrament of our
continuing fellowship in it — or, as it has
been called, 'the iron ration' of the Christian
soldier fortifying him afresh to do battle with the
world and all its evils (by pointing him back
to the Upper Room and the Cross, and forward
to the consummation of God's Kingdom in
heaven, but, here and now, conveying the saving
grace of an unseen but present Saviour).

In the sacraments the Gospel of our Redemption through Christ is visibly acted out, as it is
made effective by the power of the Holy Spirit,
the Lord the Life-giver. The grace, or divine
help, which they convey is no different from
that which comes from faithful acceptance of
true preaching of the Word. Only, in the sacraments, as Robert Bruce (not the king but
a famous Scottish divine) put it, 'we get a
better grip of Christ.' The sacraments have been
called 'Christ's love-tokens to his Body the
Church'; and it is our duty to keep them bright
by careful use.

These then are the normal ways of approach
to the Bigger World. But one point remains
that needs to be heavily underscored. While
the success of our life in the Bigger World will
greatly depend on what we do when we are
alone — when, in the inner room, we lift up

praying hands to the unseen Father — we cannot live the Christian life in isolation, like Robinson Crusoes. Membership of the Church is not an optional extra: we cannot be proper Christians without belonging to it. Study the New Testament, and you will find that to be a Christian is to be 'in Christ', and that this means being a member of the great Society of which Christ is the living Head — the Church. The New Testament knows nothing of un-attached Christians. Or consider the matter in a more mundane way. What should we think of a man who said that he wanted to be a soldier but that he could be a perfectly good one without joining the army? An unattached soldier is a nonsense: so is the notion of a solitary Christian. (Anybody who says he can be one is like the witness with the lisp who was asked by Sir Walter Scott, when sitting on the Bench, to which branch of Christ's Church he belonged. 'Sir,' he replied, 'I'm a thek [sect] by myself.')

In short, membership of the Church, so far from being a matter of personal choice, is a spiritual necessity. All true Christian ex-perience is 'ecclesiastical' experience, experience gained, enriched and matured in the company of our fellow-Christians.

The long and the short of it is that if you

want to be a true Christian, you must join God's
family. Not only so, but you must also 'forsake
not the assembling of yourselves together'
(Heb. 10: 25). By so doing your are keeping
your appointed tryst with your heavenly
Father, as with Christ his Son, and you have
the promise that where two or three are
gathered together in his name, there (by the
Spirit's power) he is in the midst of them.
And this is why you must —

> 'Walk together to the kirk
> And all together pray,
> While each to his great Father bends,
> Old men, and babes, and loving friends,
> And youths, and maidens gay.'

1. *Postscript on the Church*

Much good would be gained if we could re-
educate ordinary Christians into the true —
the Biblical — meaning of the Church, namely,
the People of God. It is so easy to equate the
Church with a building — our own particular
place of worship; or with a denomination, our
own one of course; or even with a clerical class
('Here comes the Church' we say when the
minister comes along.)

But the Church is not a building, or a
denomination, or a clerical class. It is the
Ecclēsia of which Paul writes so memorably in

Ephesians — the new and true People of God, set up by Christ's death and resurrection and the coming of the Holy Spirit, with a lineage that goes back to Abraham and a mission that embraces all men. If people could be taught to think thus 'bigly' about the Church, our sectarianism and our denominationalism would be seen for the sorry things they are, and our eyes would be opened for the vision splendid of the Coming Great Church, which is the aim of the whole ecumenical movement.

2. *Note on the Sacraments*

The New Testament knows only two sacraments — Baptism and the Lord's Supper.

Originally the Latin word *sacramentum* was the oath of allegiance which the Roman soldier took to his emperor. When the Christians took the word over, they thought of themselves as binding themselves in loyalty to Christ, the Captain of their salvation.

Sacraments are trysting-places where Christ by faithful appointment meets his people in blessing. They are the Gospel of God's grace in Christ acted out, made visible. They appeal to our souls through our senses and, by the work of the Holy Spirit, 'give us a better grip' of the Saviour.

BAPTISM

Baptism is a rite wherein water is sprinkled on a child in the name of the triune God (Father, Son and Holy Spirit). Why do we baptize? Because Christ himself submitted to baptism, because after his Resurrection he commanded his followers to baptize all converts (Matt. 28: 19), and because, from the beginning, the Church practised baptism (Acts 2: 41).

What does Baptism signify?

Baptism is a *Door*: the appointed door of entrance into the Church. Baptism represents our welcome into God's great family. By Baptism a child becomes a member of the Church *in petto* — in reserve.

Baptism is a *Sign*: a sign of the love that died to redeem us. It is the sign of God's forgiveness of sins which Christ effected on the Cross, which he called his 'baptism' (Mark 10: 38, Luke 12: 50). By it we share in the virtue of all he did for us in that 'baptism of blood' on Calvary in which all men, in principle, received Baptism long ago, without their co-operation or even their faith.[1]

(To take an illustration. Sometimes a child's grandmother presents him with a christening mug which he uses when he begins to sit at

[1] Cullmann, *Baptism in the New Testament*, pp. 9–22.

table. Then a day comes later when he begins to ask who gave him the mug. 'It was your Granny.' 'Where is she?' 'She is dead.' 'And she loved me before I could speak — as soon as I was born?' 'Yes.' So love comes home to the child as a mysteriously beautiful thing that has surrounded him from his very beginning.

The gift of the mug is Baptism, as the water is the Spirit of God in Baptism. And all signifies that gracious love of God which in Christ took the first step for his salvation.[1])

Baptism is a *Promise*: the promise by the parents that they will bring up their little ones in the Christian Way, so that, when they grow up, they may redeem and confirm that promise by becoming, of their own free will, full members of the Church.

THE LORD'S SUPPER

The second sacrament has been variously called 'the Lord's Supper', Eucharist (which means 'thanksgiving') and Holy Communion.

As 'the Warrant' for it (I Cor. 11: 23–25) reminds us, the Supper takes its origin from the Last Supper when Jesus, using broken bread and outpoured wine to symbolize his body and blood, invited his disciples, by partaking in

[1] P. T. Forsyth, *Church and Sacraments*, pp. 162f.

faith, to make their own all that he was doing by his death for men's salvation.

We celebrate the sacrament because Christ commanded us to do so: 'This do in remembrance of me.' And, as in Baptism, it is the work of the Holy Spirit to make its blessings real.

The Lord's Supper has been well described as 'retrospect and prophecy, with renewal of the Covenant face to face.'[1]

First, we look back and dynamically remember the death of Christ for our salvation.[2] If we remember aright, the Cross steps out of its frame in past history, and we re-enact the crisis of our redemption. We are there with the Twelve in the Upper Room on 'the night in which he was betrayed'. We are there at the empty tomb on the first Easter morning to hear again the tremendous tidings: 'He is risen; he is not here.' (Mark 16: 6).

But, second, we also look forward. 'You proclaim the Lord's death until he comes,' says St Paul. The Supper has a forward-look. It 'speaks to us softly of a hope.' It lifts our thoughts to Christ's coming in glory when God

[1] David S. Cairns, *An Autobiography*, p. 201.
[2] To 'remember' in the Bible is to make the past live again in the present. See article 'Memory' in *A Theological Word Book of the Bible* (Ed. A. Richardson), pp. 142f.

shall wind up the scroll of history, and all the blessedness of heaven.

Looking backward, looking forward, memory and hope — but there is a third element in this sacrament which binds memory and hope together and which alone entitles us to call it as we do — Communion. It is the real presence (through the Spirit) of the living Christ who comes, unseen but not unknown, to bless his people — himself at once both Host and Feast. The broken bread and the outpoured wine are 'his love-tokens to his Body the Church.' They are signs which really convey what they symbolize, because (as long experience shows) they deepen and enrich the relation between the Saviour and his people. So Christ renews the 'New Covenant' once sealed by his blood on Calvary.

Yet the 'renewing of the Covenant' is not his only. As we are his faithful followers we renew it also, engaging ourselves afresh to the high Captain of our salvation, pledging ourselves to be better and truer members of his Body the Church, and promising to fight ever more bravely under his banner to our life's end.

5. Life for ever in the Bigger World

Of all the questions in the book of Job none is more challenging than, 'If a man die, shall he live again?' (Job 14: 14). To put the issue in religious terms: does the Almighty put us into this world, and bless and discipline us for three score years and ten, merely in order to snuff us out at the last, like spent candles? Or is Browning right —

'What's time? Leave Now for dogs and apes.
Man has Forever'?

The Christian answer is: 'I believe . . . in the Life Everlasting.' According to our Faith, God's whole purpose in creating and in redeeming us is for fellowship in the eternal Kingdom of God — a society of redeemed persons living for ever in the presence of God. In other words, our present life on earth is a sort of education which God our Father puts us through that we may be fit persons to enjoy all those blessed things which God has prepared for those who love him.

IMMORTAL LONGINGS

Christians are not the only people to have 'immortal longings.' It is a significant fact that no nation or tribe known to us but has believed in an after-life of one kind or another. And we may well ask: If (as many believe) death is the Everlasting No, striking man finally down to the dust, why is there this Everlasting Yea in his heart?

Not only so, but down the centuries wise men from Plato onwards have piled argument upon high argument to show that death is not the end of our earthly pilgrimage. From the incompleteness of human life (and especially all young lives tragically cut short), from the crying injustices of this world (and especially the sufferings of the innocent), from the greatness as well as the misery of man, all have concluded, 'There must be another world in which all lives will come to fruition, all wrongs will be redressed, all mysteries will be made plain.'

Moreover, as we know, certain people called Spiritualists claim that, with the help of medium and seance, they have proof positive that the dead live on. (It is but fair to add that the trivialities which reach us from the darkness of the seance room will never satisfy the deepest questionings of Christians about eternity.)

Thus, with no mention of Christ and the Gospel, men have persuaded themselves that death is not the end. But the Faith has other and better testimonies than these.

THE CHRISTIAN CASE

The Christian Hope of life for ever in the Bigger World rests on two strong pillars:

(1) The first is *the character of God as he has revealed himself in Christ.* Put in its simplest terms, it is this: we believe in a God whose nature is holy love, and that when God loves once, he loves for ever.

So Jesus himself believed. Once, in controversy, the Sadducees tried to trap him with a trick question about the after-life in which they themselves did not believe, only to receive the profound reply, 'Have you not read in the book of Moses, how God said to him, I am the God of Abraham, of Isaac and of Jacob? God is not the God of the dead but of the living. You are greatly mistaken.' (Mark 12: 26f.)

What he was saying was something like this: 'Never think of God as the bereaved mourner of dead friends. If God could not save his friends from perishing, what a poor, shabby, impotent God he would be! Why, he wouldn't be worth calling God at all. And if God is the God of Abraham, of Isaac and of Jacob, as he is — if they are his men and he is their God, they just cannot be dead and done with. Of course, they have paid the last debt to nature, as we all must. But that cannot be the end of their story. The Lord hath need of them. Therefore: they are alive and in his holy keeping for ever.'

It is on the faithfulness — the leal love — of God and on the reality of the religious life that this argument rests. If God is such a Father as Christ declared him to be, loving us with an everlasting love and willing to give up his only Son to save us, then he cannot allow 'the last enemy', death, to break for ever the strong bands that bind us to himself. Are we to believe that the purposes of the infinitely good and wise Father Above will be defeated by a germ, by a fall of coal, by a surgeon's mistake? No, when God loves once, he loves for ever; and death, for the Christian, is not a passing to extinction but, as it was for Christ himself, a going to be with the Father. We are 'thirled' to a Love that will not let us go, even at the last frontier of human existence. The friends of God do not perish.

(2) The second strong pillar on which our

Christian Hope rests is *the Resurrection of Christ himself.*[1]

The Resurrection of Christ is not a legend or a fairy tale. It is a fact, nay, for the Christian, the supreme fact of history, a fact supported by the most cogent evidence. Without it, the New Testament would never have been written. Without it, the Christian Church would never have come into existence — or lasted for nearly two thousand years. Without it, Christians would not meet regularly on the first day of the week, the day on which Christ conquered death.

But an empty tomb and a resurrected Christ mean a Christ who 'dies no more, death no longer has dominion over him' (Rom. 6: 9). They mean a Christ who is living and reigning

---

[1] It is true to say that the climax of the Gospel story is the vindication, in his own case, of Jesus' reply to the Sadducees. The friends of God, Jesus had told them, do not perish. Now a sound argument is good, so far as it goes. But an argument put to the test (the *experimentum crucis*) and proved true, is yet more impressive. By the Resurrection Christ became the supreme instance of his own high argument.

When Christ was finally crucified, it must have seemed to his disciples as if the finest life they had ever known — could ever conceive — had gone out in utter darkness. But on the first Easter Day he had come back to them in all his risen glory. Death had not made an end of him. Somehow he had made an end of death, had shattered its grim dominion. He had become the crowning example of his own great argument. Death had been for him the gateway of life; and so it would be for all who were his, for all who were incorporate in him by faith.

now, a Christ who promised his followers, 'Because I live, you will live also' (John 14: 19). How vibrant with that promise are the mono-syllables of the modern hymn —

> 'They buried my body
> And they thought I'd gone,
> But I am the dance
> And I still go on.
>
> They cut me down,
> And I leapt up high;
> I am the life
> That'll never, never die;
> I'll live in you
> If you'll live in me —
> I am the lord of the Dance, said he.'

Eternal life is God's gift to us in Christ — the living Christ. *He* is our immortality, and in union with him we become 'nurslings of immortality'. 'I know that my Redeemer liveth,' says the Christian, 'and because I am his — one of the sinners for whom he died — I hope, by his grace, to be one day where he now is.'

THE LAST THINGS

We believe then in the Life Everlasting; but this is not all. With the authority of the New Testament, we believe that God will one day

E

consummate his Kingdom inaugurated in Christ, vanquish all evil, and judge and reward men according to the good or evil they have done. To be in heaven will mean life in God's presence for ever; to be in hell will mean permanent exclusion from it.

Who goes where? That there is such a thing as final exclusion from God's presence is the teaching of the New Testament; but it is not for us to say on whom this dread sentence may fall. What we may believe is that the God and Father of our Lord Jesus Christ will not suffer it to fall on any who do not freely and deliberately pronounce it on themselves. 'We are all predestined in love to life, sooner or later — *if we will*.'[1]

Reinhold Niebuhr[2] rightly warned Christians against claiming 'any knowledge of either the furniture of heaven or the temperature of hell.' Yet certain things we are entitled to say.

First, *we may foretaste the life of heaven here and now*. Eternity does not merely lie at the end of time but pervades it. The gift of the Holy Spirit is 'an earnest of our heavenly inheritance' (Eph. 1: 13f.). Every genuine Christian experience is a sample in advance — a first instalment — of the heavenly life.

[1] P. T. Forsyth, *This Life and the Next*, p. 16.
[2] Reinhold Niebuhr, *The Nature and Destiny of Man*, II p. 304.

Second, when we die in union with Christ, *we pass into no lone immortality.* The consummation of the Christian Hope is supremely social. The life hereafter is a family life, a society of redeemed persons living for ever in God's nearer presence.

Third, 'Flesh and blood cannot inherit the Kingdom of God' (1 Cor. 15: 20). That is, the nature of our resurrection is given us in Christ's, and it is not one of matter but of form. We believe not in 'a resurrection of relics' but (as Paul teaches in 1 Cor. 15) in 'a spiritual body' — a body suited to the conditions of the next world as our flesh-and-blood body is suited to those of this one.

Fourth, when we talk about heaven, *we must use the language of symbol.* In the nature of the case we are dealing with what 'eye hath not seen neither hath ear heard'. The garden of God (Luke 23: 43), 'Jerusalem the golden' (Rev. 21: 18), a Father's house with many rooms' (John 14: 2) — these are three New Testament symbols which suggest and signal at a blessedness beyond all human telling. Provided we do not take these symbols too literally — as our forefathers sometimes did — we have a right to use them, and by them to nourish our immortal hope while yet we abide in this house of our pilgrimage.

But there is a fifth and quite fundamental thing to be said. In what Conan Doyle might have called 'The Case of the Doctor's Dog', it is told of a dying man that he asked his godly doctor to tell him something of the place to which he was going. As the doctor fumbled for a reply, there came a scratching at the door, and his answer was given him. 'Do you hear that?' he asked his patient. 'It's my dog. I left him downstairs, but he has grown impatient, and has come up and hears my voice. He has no notion what is inside this door, but he knows that I am here. Isn't it the same with you? You do not know what lies beyond the Door, but you know that your Master is there.'

Our Master is there; and whatever else heaven may be, it is the land where Christ dwells, and also (we believe) all those leal and good souls whom 'we have loved long since and lost awhile' and who now serve God in the Church Triumphant.

This then is the Christian Hope. With such a Hope we are called to labour unwearyingly in the Lord, knowing that such labour is not in vain (1 Cor. 15: 58). Communist gibes about 'pie in the sky when you die' should not worry us. The Christian Hope is no 'opiate of the people', but a challenge to a more strenuous work for Christ and his cause on earth. It is a 'hope so great and so divine' as to give human life a meaning and a goal which the men of our day, groping about in darkness and despair, need more than anything else to assure them that life is worth living, that Christ is God's Clue to its meaning, and that 'the best is yet to be.'

Note: By Faith or by Love?

Here we handle a problem which perplexes many Christians. The New Testament seems to say two contradictory things: (*a*) that here and now God of his grace 'justifies' (i.e. acquits, or forgives) sinners on the score of their personal faith in Christ his Son, and (*b*) that at the Last Judgment God will judge us for the good or evil things we have done.

Let us clarify the issue and see if we can clear up the difficulty.

First: in the Gospels God's grace to sinners is declared in Christ's teaching (e.g. in the parables of the Pharisee and the Publican and the Prodigal Son) and actualized in that saving ministry of his which culminated in his giving of his life to ransom 'the many' from their sins. Similarly, after the Resurrection, Paul and the other missionaries of the Gospel declare that God of his grace justifies sinners on the score of their faith in Christ who died for their sins.

Second: Both Christ and his apostles insist that our final acceptance with God will depend on the good works and loving acts which, in our lives, we have done or failed to do. (In evidence we need only point, in Christ's case, to his parable of the Last Judgment in Matt. 25, and in the case of the apostles, to passages like Rom. 2:6, 2 Cor. 5:10 and 1 Pet. 1:17).

The problem is: Does our final acceptance with God depend on our faith or on our conduct?

The New Testament says that our 'justification' (our forgiveness) is all of God's gracious doing. As we respond by faith to his 'amazing grace' shown in Christ and the Cross, we are here and now forgiven and set on the road to salvation. On the other hand, both Christ and the apostles, looking away to 'the Great Day', insist on the need for us to do good deeds and show compassion to our fellow-men in their misery.

This can only mean that when, in answer to our faith, God forgives us sinners for Christ's sake and sets our life in another key than the natural and our feet on a new and upward track, he expects his forgiveness of us to issue in *our* forgiveness of others and in acts of love to our needy brethren. Otherwise, ours is not true, living faith; on the contrary, as St James said, it has about as much life in it as a corpse (Jas 2: 14–26)! Love is the work of faith, and where it does not appear, our 'justification' has failed of its divine purpose, and the Last Judgment will reveal it in its true colours.

Humanly speaking, therefore, are we saved by our faith or by our works? The Either–Or is wrong. The right answer is: by our 'faith working through love' (Gal. 5: 6). Paul sums up the matter in Eph. 2: 10: 'We are God's workmanship' he says, meaning that our present salvation is all due to God's gracious action on us; *but* we are 'created in Christ Jesus *for good works*,' and at the last reckoning (whatever form it takes) God will look for evidence of these happy fruits in our lives.

6. Christian Prayer

In his diary for 1 March 1939, Edwin Muir, the distinguished Scottish poet, described how he underwent a kind of 'conversion' by reciting the Lord's Prayer as he was taking off his waistcoat before going to bed. He was (he says) 'overcome with joyful surprises when he realized that everything in the Prayer, apart from the Being to whom it is addressed, refers to human life, seen realistically and not mystically, and that it is about the world and society, and not about the everlasting destiny of the soul.'

It might be a good thing for many of us Christians to undergo a conversion like Edwin Muir's. Every Sunday we repeat the Prayer together; but so familiar are its words that we seldom stop to think what they mean; and too often they become just a piece of holy patter. (Incidentally, that word 'patter' comes from the first word of the Lord's Prayer in Latin — *Pater Noster* — and to 'patter' is to repeat the Prayer, parrot-wise, like a bit of holy Mumbo Jumbo.)

'Pray then like this,' said Jesus (Matt. 6: 9). So let us try to understand what Jesus meant when, in response to his disciples' request (Luke 11: 1), he first gave them the Model Prayer.

Its Plan is simplicity itself. At the beginning an Invocation (or Address to God); at the end a Doxology (or ascription of praise); and, in between, six petitions: three are for the greater glory of God in the world, and three are for our human needs.

OUR FATHER WHO ART IN HEAVEN, or, simply, 'Our heavenly Father' — this is the Invocation. ('Who art in heaven' is not so much — if the irreverence may be pardoned — God's postal address as a reminder that if God is Father, he is a *holy* Father: the Father 'of an infinite majesty' — as the *Te Deum* says — who demands our reverence as well as our love.)

Here of course the key-word is 'Father.' For any religion the supreme question is, 'What is God like?' And for Christians there is only one right answer to it, Christ's: 'God is our heavenly Father.' Not a Principle, not a Force, but a Person; and not any kind of a Person but a Father. It was Christ's way (compare his parable of The Asking Son in Matt. 7: 9–11) to say to his disciples, 'Think of the very best

human father you can imagine. God is all that
— and incomparably more!' Great beyond all
our comprehending, holy beyond all our
conceiving, but a Father — a Father who cares
for his children, who is sad when they go astray
and glad when, like the prodigal in the story,
they come home; the Father to whom his own
life was one long, loving obedience, and to
whom, as he died, he committed his spirit
(Luke 23: 46); the Father who took him
out of the grave and gave him glory so that
our faith and hope might be in him (1 Pet. 1:
21).

This is the God we address as 'our Father'.
Mark that pronoun 'our'. When we say it, we
join ourselves with the whole family of God in
the wide earth. For this is 'the Prayer that
spans the world.'

The first petition reads: HALLOWED BE
THY NAME. 'What's in a name?' we say, as
if it were just a label devised for the postman's
convenience. But in the Bible the 'name' stands
for a person's 'nature' as he reveals it, so that
God's 'name' means God's 'nature' as he has
revealed it.

Now God has disclosed his nature in various
ways — in the beauty of his created world, in
his gracious acts in history, above all, as Abba,
Father in Christ his Son. So, when we pray

'Hallowed be thy name', we pray that God may cause his fatherly nature to be known and reverenced everywhere, and that men may come to honour him by doing what he would have his children do.

The second petition runs: THY KINGDOM COME.

What is 'the Kingdom of God'? If this question came up at an 'Any Questions' programme, the odds are that most people would answer it in terms of some Super Welfare State under Christian auspices. But their answer would be pretty wide of the mark. In the New Testament, the Kingdom of God is the kingly Rule, or Reign, of God, and it is nothing if not divine and dynamic. It is not some man-made Utopia, still less some Communist's earthly paradise. It is a 'break-through' from the Bigger World. It is God in his royal power invading history to deliver his people from their sins and woes. More than that, it is the very heart of the New Testament Gospel, or Good News, that God's Reign really and finally began when he sent his Son, and by his life and death and resurrection, reconciled a sinful world to himself.

This, however, was only a beginning, and from this small beginning (as Christ said in his parables of the Mustard Seed and the Leaven) was destined to come, one day, a great Ending. God's Reign, then, has been inaugurated; it has not yet been consummated. So, when we pray, 'Thy Kingdom come!' we are praying God to *complete* the great saving purpose he took in hand when he sent us Christ.

When that Kingdom fully comes, all evil will be done away, and all the promises of the Beatitudes will come fully true. Then the mourners will be comforted, the pure in heart will see God face to face, and his redeemed children will be for ever at home in their Father's house on high.

Now turn to the third petition: THY WILL BE DONE ON EARTH AS IT IS IN HEAVEN.

Only God can consummate his Reign. Does this mean that man is simply to sit back and wait for it with folded arms, as a parody of Merrill's hymn, 'Rise up, O men of God', puts it:

'Sit down, O men of God!
His Kingdom he will bring
Whenever it may please his will.
You cannot do a thing.'

No indeed! This petition reminds us that we have our part to play. But notice what we have too often done with it. We have turned 'Thy will be done' into a cry of pious resignation, when Jesus meant them as a summons to God's

servants to be up and doing: 'Thy will be done
— and done by me!'

What is God's will? Answer: what pleases
God. And what this is, Christ has told us in the
Sermon on the Mount and elsewhere. It is
health, not disease; loving, not hating; giving,
not grabbing; service, not selfishness; the
Golden Rule (Matt. 7: 12) and not the rule of
the jungle. In God's presence it is always so,
and here we pray that in this respect earth may
become like heaven.

So the first half of the Prayer ends. Having
asked for 'the heavenly things',[1] we are now
free to pray for the 'earthly' ones — for our
own basic human needs — in fact, for provision,
for pardon and for protection.

GIVE US THIS DAY OUR DAILY BREAD.
This, the fourth petition, teaches our dependence on God. Sometimes we say, 'So-and-So
has independent means'. But nobody really has.
We cannot command the harvest; and all the
tractors and combine harvesters in the world
would be so much useless metal if God did not
quicken life within the seed. No, our 'daily
bread' comes ultimately not from the farmer,

[1] A saying of Jesus preserved not in the New Testament but
in early Church fathers ran: 'Ask for the big things, and the
little shall be added to you. Ask for the heavenly things, and
the earthly shall be added unto you.'

not from the miller, not from the baker, but from God the Creator. And this our dependence on him we acknowledge whenever we say 'Grace before meat'.

Yet notice two things. First, Jesus authorizes us to ask God only for what we really need. This is a prayer for daily bread, and not for daily cake: for the staff of life, and not for caviare and champagne. Second, this petition is not an invitation to inertia. It does not rule out the human effort required to make God's gifts our own. As somebody has said, 'God feeds the sparrows, but he doesn't push the crumbs into their mouths.'

The fifth petition reads: AND FORGIVE US OUR DEBTS AS WE FORGIVE OUR DEBTORS.

From bread we now turn to sin. For there is another hunger, the soul's hunger for forgiveness of all the sins — whether of commission or of omission — which separate us from God; and, as we all sin every day, so every day we need to ask God's forgiveness.

Note that Jesus calls sins 'debts'. 'Debts' is a metaphor for sins, the wrongs we have done, the good we have left undone. The word stands for all that we should do towards God and our fellow men — all we should do and, alas, so often don't.

But mark well the words that follow: 'as we

forgive our debtors.' Where forgiveness is concerned, we are always dealing with a spiritual triangle: God, my neighbour, myself. Our sins have repercussions on other people, as theirs have on us. Any real forgiveness must therefore pierce the barbed-wire entanglement of human wrongs and estrangements. And if it is to do this, there must be wire-cutting on man's side as well as on God's. In plain terms, we need not expect God to forgive us unless we are really ready to forgive those who have wronged us.

The last petition reads: AND LEAD US NOT INTO TEMPTATION BUT DELIVER US FROM EVIL.

This is a cry for protection in time of spiritual danger. But watch that word 'temptation'. It does not mean enticement to do evil — God never so entices (Jas. 1 : 13). It means, as the New English Bible says, 'testing' or 'trial'. Now God does permit such 'testing', and without it we would never develop any moral muscle or backbone. Yet every such 'trial' involves the risk that we may succumb to the downward pull of evil. Therefore in this petition we ask: 'Lord, spare us moral adventures; but when they do come, help us to come victoriously through our ordeal.'

Then, as with a peal of trumpets, the Prayer ends with the Doxology: FOR THINE IS THE

KINGDOM AND THE POWER AND THE
GLORY FOR EVER. AMEN.[1]

This then is the Lord's Prayer, the Prayer
that long ago Jesus taught his disciples in
Galilee, the Prayer that teaches how to pray.
Nineteen centuries have gone by since Jesus
first gave it; yet not a word of it is out of date.
It is still the Prayer of every true Christian, the
Prayer he ought to pray (and not merely
'patter') every day — every day and with 'all
that in him is.'

[1] The Doxology is not found in our oldest New Testament
manuscripts, and is therefore not an original part of the Prayer.
But if it is a very early Christian addition, it is according to the
mind of Christ; for, as Professor Jeremias has shown in *The
Expository Times*, Feb. 1960, p. 142, Jesus meant his disciples
to end the Prayer with an ascription of glory, but left the actual
formulation of it to his followers. They did so worthily, for the
Doxology ends the Prayer as it began, in the thought of the
sovereignty and glory of God.

7. Christian Life-style

Sir Arthur Quiller-Couch (better known by his pen-name 'Q') tells how he once stood in a ballroom when there entered the most beautiful girl he had ever seen.[1] It was her first ball, and, by some freak, she wore black with a crescent of diamonds in her black hair. Here was absolute beauty. It startled. 'Alas,' 'Q' goes on, 'though we did not know it, she had not long to live. But just then I saw being presented to her, among others, the man who was to be, for a short time, her husband. When the men had moved away, I saw her eyes travel to an awkward young naval cadet who sat glowering on a far bench. Promptly the girl advanced, claimed him, and swept him off into the first waltz . . . When it was over,' says 'Q', 'I made some kind of banal remark to him — as that, for example, I was glad to see the Navy kept its old knack of cutting out. But he looked at me, almost in tears, and then

[1] Arthur Quiller-Couch, *The Art of Writing*, p. 209f. (abridged).

F

blurted out, "It isn't her beauty, sir. You saw it? It's — it's the style!" '

The New Testament has no precise word for 'style.' The nearest we come to it is when, in the book of Acts, we find the earliest Christians described as 'men and women who followed the Way' (with a capital W, e.g. Acts 9: 2). By this was meant the kind of life which found expression in their own fellowship and in their dealings with others — what we should nowadays call their 'life-style'. We still talk about men and women 'having a way with them.' No doubt outsiders felt thus about the first Christians. Robert Burns sang about his earliest sweet-heart, Nellie Kilpatrick —

'And then there's something in her gait
Gars ony dress look weel.'

So there was a something — a *Je ne sais quoi* — in the early Christians' 'gait' — their 'walk' — their life-style, which marked them out, like the beauty in the ballroom, and made their pagan neighbours wonder at the secret of it all.

What then is Christian life-style? What is there, or should be, in the Christian's behaviour that ought to 'give him away' as surely as Peter's 'north country accent' gave him away in the high-priest's courtyard (Matt. 26: 73)?

I

The Christian Design for Life is contained in
the Sermon on the Mount (Matt. 5–7), which
opens with the Beatitudes. 'How blest' (i.e.
divinely happy), says Jesus in the sixth
Beatitude, 'are the pure in heart!' Here we may
find the first element in Christian style. Who
are the pure-hearted ones Jesus has in mind?
They are the men and women whose basic
inner truth and honesty shine through their
every act and word, whose goodness is not
merely skin-deep but goes down to 'the red-ripe
of the heart' and cannot but appear in all they
say and do. One thinks of Nathanael in the
Gospels. 'Here,' said Jesus, 'is an Israelite
worthy of the name. There is nothing false in
him.' (John 1 : 47 NEB).

The first thing then in the Christian's life-
style is his transparency of character. In his
make-up there is nothing sham. Like a good
coin he should ring true. Like a piece of good
glass you should be able to 'see through him.'

This is not to say that the Christian should
be a starry-eyed simpleton or a gormless goose.
You have only to read Christ's parable of the
Unjust Steward (Luke 16: 1–18) — in Scotland
we should call him 'the Rascally Factor' — to

see how high he rated 'common savvy.' 'Ah,' he said in that story, 'if only my followers would show as much gumption in God's business as worldlings do in theirs!' Nor did Christ despise common prudence in a world where cheats and crooks and 'con men' abound. 'Be wise as serpents,' he told his disciples, 'and innocent as doves' (Matt. 10: 16). But, as the men he condemned for 'hypocrisy' (play-acting) were those who, under a mask of godliness, concealed ungodly lives, so the men after God's own heart, he said, were the transparent ones, whose character and motives were as translucent as April sun through an April shower.

II

Now take a second element. 'If you greet only your brothers' said Jesus in his Sermon, 'what is there extraordinary about that?' (Matt. 5: 47. NEB).

The second mark of Christian life-style is its extravagance, its going beyond the customary and the conventional. 'There must be no limits to your goodness' said Jesus, 'as your heavenly Father's goodness knows no bounds' (Matt. 5: 28 NEB).

'In the New Testament,' wrote Thomas

Erskine,[1] 'religion is grace and ethics is gratitude.' Christian goodness is therefore 'grace goodness' — that is to say, our response in Christian living to the grace of God we have received in Christ. 'Grace,' David S. Cairns said, 'is the extravagant goodness of God' to us undeserving men. This being so, Christian goodness ought to be the kind that has God's extravagance about it, ought to be (as the Scots say) 'byordinar' goodness.

This is the kind of goodness Christ calls for in his Sermon on the Mount. Take one example only — what he has to say there about retaliation. To the natural man, 'revenge is sweet.' He lives by the law of tit-for-tat. Let somebody wrong him, and he resolves at once that, whenever he gets the chance, he will repay the wrong-doer in his own evil coin. So he 'feeds fat his grudge' and revenge becomes, what Walter Scott called it, 'the sweetest morsel ever cooked in hell.'

But what does Christ say? 'If a man slaps you on the right cheek . . .' — a pause while each listening disciple thought furiously about what was to be done. But Christ's completion of his sentence must have taken all their

[1] Thomas Erskine (1788–1870), a Scottish layman of deep religious insight, friend of Carlyle, McLeod Campbell, and F. D. Maurice.

breaths away: 'Well, you have another one, haven't you?'

Christian goodness ought therefore to be extravagant — ought to be a kind of 'daft' goodness. And has not this 'daft' goodness ever been the mark of Christ's greatest servants down the centuries? Take only one instance, a modern one: think of Albert Schweitzer, in his thirties, on the way to greatness in three fields of human achievement — theology, music, philosophy — deliberately turning his back on Europe and all its 'glittering prizes', in order to become 'a poor negro doctor' in the swamps of equatorial Africa.

Of course in the world's eyes such conduct is clean crazy. Giving up (let us say) £10,000 a year and all that goes with it for a pittance and a life of hardship — the man must have been mad. Yes, but what divine craziness! And need we worry about the world's verdict when such conduct carries Christ's benediction: 'Anything you have done for one of my brothers, however humble, you have done for me'.

III

And now for the third element in Christian life-style. 'By this shall all men know that you are my disciples,' said Jesus to them, 'if you have love one to the other' (John 13: 35). The third mark of Christian life-style is *agapé*, that New Testament Greek word so inadequately translated by 'charity' (which has sadly come down in the world of words) or even by 'love', which nowadays can mean almost anything from Hollywood to Heaven.

A. C. Craig[1] has said: 'The word "love" always needs a dictionary, and for Christians the dictionary is Jesus Christ. He took this chameleon of a word and gave it a fast colour, so that ever since it has been lustred by his life and teaching, and dyed in the crimson of Calvary, and shot through with the sunlight of Easter morning.'

Agapé, Christian love, means 'caring' as Christ 'cared' for all the last, the least and the lost, while he walked this earth. For us it means caring practically and persistently for all who meet us on life's road — caring (and this is the hardest thing of all) even for the unlovely and the unlovable.

Such caring is the supreme mark of Christian style. No finer tribute was ever paid to General William Booth, founder of the Salvation Army, than when, at his funeral in 1912, an ex-prostitute sitting near Queen Mary, leaned over and said to her, 'He cared for the likes of us.'

[1] A. C. Craig, *The Sacramental Table*, p. 50.

Well did the great Roman Catholic layman, Baron von Hügel say to his niece on his death-bed: 'Christianity taught us to care. Caring is the greatest thing. Caring matters most.' (Is not this what Paul was saying in 1 Cor. 13?)

Transparency of character, extravagant goodness, and a great capacity for caring — these are the marks of the Christian's life-style. But perhaps to these three we should add a fourth — that word so very unpopular in many circles today — obedience.

Dr William Lillie tells of an Aberdeenshire farmer who, after a meeting at which it had been decided to unite two rival kirks in the village, declared, 'It's nae richt, and it's nae sense, but I suppose it's the will of God'. Are we not all aware that there arise situations where our limited moral reason gives us no clear guidance? It is then, like the honest farmer, we need, however reluctantly, to recognize the will of God and do it. This command to do God's will may come to us in various ways; but the Christian man or woman, hearing it will obey. Like Martin Luther, at a supreme hour of his life, he will say, 'Here I stand. I can do no other.'

There is one word more to be said. The radical sickness of our society today — of which all thoughtful people are only too sadly aware

— needs for its cure, above all else, a radical infusion of Christian style. But, if this be granted, let it also be insisted, against all those humanists who want morals without religion, that you cannot have the fruit without the root. In plain prose, you can get authentic Christian style only from committed Christians, from men and women prepared to stand up and be counted as confessors of Christ the Lord of all good life.

Epilogue: Call to Commitment

We began our studies with the sense of the profound mystery which surrounds us all and which is the precondition of religious belief. Then, having expounded the Christian revelation, we ended our chapter on Christian lifestyle with the need for commitment. In this epilogue[1] let us underscore these two points.

I

First, the sense of mystery. Nowadays some people seem to think that it is only a matter of time — and of bigger telescopes and better microscopes — till modern scientists will have banished mystery from the universe. But our greatest scientists (whatever those who write the 'potted science' of the popular press may say)

[1] I have here borrowed from a remarkable university sermon by Sir Thomas Taylor, late Principal of Aberdeen University. The reader will find the full text of his sermon in the volume *Where One Man Stands*, pp. 11–20.

are emphatically not of this mind. They are far from believing that their discoveries have negated the ancient conclusion that *omnia abeunt in mysterium* ('all things run off into mystery'). On the contrary, face to face with mystery, they are much readier than their predecessors of fifty years ago to avow their nescience. The result is, I believe, that the intellectual temper of our time is much more favourable to a religious view of the world than when Haeckel was writing his *Riddle of the Universe* (1901) and science seemed to be explaining everything.

Mysteries therefore will always remain — it is no part of the Christian claim that one day they will all be done away — at any rate, this side of eternity (cf. 1 Cor. 13: 9–13). But for the Christian — and here is the difference which 'Christ from the Bigger World' has made — who is humble enough to accept the Good News in Christ, they are now *mysteries of light*, and not of darkness.

On many questions the Christian may frankly acknowledge his ignorance. The problems of evil and undeserved suffering are two of them.[1] These are often said to be the

---

[1] The two best modern discussions known to me are: P. T. Forsyth, *The Justification of God* (1917) and John Hick, *Evil and the Love of God* (1965).

biggest obstacles to Christian belief. But they are not new ones: they were known to Job, and there is nothing in the arguments of modern unbelievers which had not occurred to Voltaire. To such problems the Christian has no slick or complete answers. But he at least has never held that it was part of God's purpose that a good time should be had by all here and now. How could he when the chief symbol of his faith was a Cross — a Cross appointed by the Father for his well-beloved Son?

From all this it follows that the Christian's creed need not be a long one. The man who wrote the book *De Paucitate Credendorum* ('On the fewness of things necessary for belief') had the right idea. Dr James Denney[1] once declared that all essential to Christian belief was covered by the confession, 'I believe in God through Jesus Christ, his only Son, our Lord and Saviour.' And, properly understood, this is true. What is wanted is a minimal creed and a maximal faith — that we really believe our beliefs.

II

But, this said, what is needed is complete commitment to this brief, basic creed. When

[1] James Denney, *Jesus and the Gospel*, p. 398.

we are young, untrammelled freedom and independence seems the height of felicity —

> 'I'm tickled to death I'm single.
> I'm tickled to death I'm free.
> I've got my independence.
> I've got the front-door key.'

But as we grow older and wiser, what seemed true at twenty no longer seems true at fifty. When we reach that stage in our earthly pilgrimage, more and more we begin to see the futility of a rootless existence, to realize that it is commitment to a certain view of life which gives men adult human stature, and that it is a matter not of logical proof but of personal decision.

What then are we mortals to do faced as we are with circumambient mystery? Long ago, Socrates asked the same question, and advised those who sought an answer in the following words: 'I would have him take the best and most irrefragable of human theories, and let this be the raft on which he sails through life — not without risk, I admit — *if he cannot find some word of God which will more surely and safely carry him.*'

'If he cannot find some word of God . . .' What remarkable and strangely prescient words! Four centuries later, in Ephesus, St John wrote:

'And the Word became flesh and dwelt among us, full of grace and truth; we have beheld his glory, glory as of the only Son from the Father ... No one has ever seen God; the only Son who is in the bosom of the Father, he has made him known' (John 1: 14 ff.). He also said, 'This is the victory that overcomes the world, our faith.' (1 John 5: 4). We Christians do not deny the ultimate mystery which surrounds our human existence, but we believe that in Christ we have God's master-clue to its meaning, and in that faith we travel —

'Till travelling days are done.'

DATE DUE

F			
OC 21 '77			
DE 20 '77			
DE 2 '80			
DE F5 '80			
F			
GAYLORD			PRINTED IN U.S.A